SATPREM

A sailor and Breton, although he was born in Paris in 1923, Satprem was arrested by the Gestapo when he was twenty years old and spent one and a half years in concentration camps. Devastated, he traveled to Upper Egypt, then to India, where he served in the French government of Pondicherry. There he discovered Sri Aurobindo and Mother. Deeply struck by their Message—"Man is a transitional being"—he resigned his post in the French Colonies and left for Guiana, where he spent a year in the middle of the jungle, then went on to Brazil and Africa.

In 1953, at age thirty, he returned to India to be near Mother, who sought the secret of the passage to the "next species," becoming her confidant and the witness of her experiences for almost twenty years. His first nonfiction work was dedicated to *Sri Aurobindo or The Adventure of Consciousness*. At the age of fifty, he brought out the fabulous logbook of Mother's own journey, *The Agenda*, in 13 volumes, then wrote a trilogy—*The Divine Materialism, The New Species, The Mutation of Death*—followed by an essay, *The Mind of the Cells*.

At fifty-nine, he withdrew completely from public view to attempt the last Adventure: the search for the "great passage" leading to man's evolutionary future. A last interview, in 1984, gave rise to *Life without Death*, in which he described the beginning of his experience in his body.

D0880097

BY THE BODY OF THE EARTH

O Reader
They call these imaginations.
I will not disagree.
But if my imaginations
Broaden and lighten you
Then dream with me
And become what you see.

S.

Also by Satprem

Satprem

BY THE BODY
OF
THE EARTH

or
THE SANNYASI

a perpetual story

Translated from the French by
Luc Venet

INSTITUTE FOR EVOLUTIONARY RESEARCH
200 PARK AVENUE, NEW YORK, NY 10166

For information address:
U.S.A. and Europe:
    Institute for Evolutionary Research
    200 Park Avenue, Suite 303 East
    New York, NY 10166

India & Asia:
    Mira Aditi Centre
    62 Sriranga, 1st Cross
    4th stage, Kuvempunagar
    Mysore 570023, India

Library of Congress Cataloging-in-Publication Data

Satprem, 1923–
    [Par le corps de la terre. English]
    By the body of the earth, or, The sannyasi / Satprem ; translated from the French by Luc Venet.
        p.   cm.
    Translation of: Par le corps de la terre
    ISBN 0-938710-08-7 : $12.00
    I. Title. II. Title: By the body of the earth. III. Title: Sannyasi
PQ2679.A84P313   1991
843'.914--dc20   90-25241
                                              CIP

With grateful acknowledgment to Gloria and Anna.
Cover design: Tomb of Ramses VI at Thebes, Corridor G.
Manufactured in the United States of America.

Contents

to Sri Aurobindo
to the Mother

to Batcha
to India
    birthplace
    of my heart

A flame that cancels death
in mortal things
SRI AUROBINDO, Savitri

O Fire, thou art the son of heaven
by the body of the earth
Rig-Veda, III.2.1

FIRST CYCLE*

The Journey Outside the Self

* after many others.

SONG OF THE PASSERBY

O passerby
In the main street of this little planet
You race on and on
Toward a future that already was
O passerby who no longer remembers
You have been the actor in more than one act
Clad in brown or white
Clad in darkness or frippery
You have traveled more than one course
Toward the same unmoving point
And you are repeating the same gestures
Beneath monsoons and winters
Beneath devils that are more or less gods
And gods that are more or less white
You are repeating the same story
As if nothing had ever happened
O passerby who has yet to pass
Your story is perpetual
Upon my infallible road
On the one hand you toil unknowingly
And on the other you are king of ancient memory
Clad in flame and sweetness
The choice is yours
O passerby in the millennial main street
You go where I lead
Slave or king, sinner or sleepwalker

One does not change the road
One changes visions

There is no other passage in life
No other moment
But one single story from age to age

1
the street

*T*hey were walking toward a port amid the dust of the sweltering season. They were golden brown from basking in the sun so long, and their eyes were alive like the light at the bottom of a well. They walked in close procession, balancing their wares and some dreams, dressed in white like princes or naked like the bronze figures of their temples. They wended their way to the port in the fragrance of burning incense sticks and the stench of cow dung. It was this age or another, beneath the arched flight of great ernes, in the land where the sun burst open souls like tamarind husks.

The Eastern Traders
Shipping Company Limited

He was white. His name was Nil. His hands fingered his pockets, and his eyes darted left and right, aimlessly, like a blind man or a chimpanzee. She stood motionless, watching him, grave and beautiful in her white sari.

"So you are leaving?"

She raised a hand to her forehead as if to brush aside a lock of hair. Gold bangles glinted on her wrist.

"Yes, tomorrow morning. My things are already at the wharf."

He fingered his pockets again.

.*.
**

It so happened that, in the great avenue of Time, I merged with that man. Once again I assumed that role, oblivious of old gestures and past loves, of former words of good or evil— carried only by the same restless little flame, drawn by a thousand lost memories. Thirst, perpetual thirst. I am a thirst. It's all that has remained with me; it's my memory of fire.

Well, let's take stock. It's quite simple: At any place on the earth, at any point in the timeworn story, I can stop and say, "Not it. This isn't it." That's never it! I have yet to hit the mark; it's always an approximation, always wide of the mark. I live as if one day I am finally going to hit it, in the very center of the irrefutable catastrophe. Then, perhaps, I will be finished with roles. Somewhere out there a brother of light is waiting. I am moving toward him. Going home, to live in my real skin at last.

Then it will be absolutely IT. No more need to find my bearings; I'll be in the center everywhere I go.

.*.
**

Ninety-seven pounds to my name. I'll have three pounds and some change left. But what does it matter, since it's always the same anyway?

"Come. Let's go."

They melted into the crowd, swept up in a riot of cotton bales, pink pottery, basketsful of mangoes, ravenous goats, and green and pink lemonade stalls.

"But why are you rushing? Your ship doesn't leave until tomorrow. Where are you running to?"

I stopped short. For a second I looked deep into those eyes. I plunged a whole life into that second. I have seen many eyes, yet I have never found the gaze I was searching for—and I'm still searching. I've changed bodies, changed lives, only to find myself in this street with the feeling that I've been here many times before.

"Nil, please—"

Beads of sweat pearled her forehead. There was such a beauty in that almost immobile face, almost unstirred by emotion, as if it had to pass through centuries of softness in order to surface in two little pulsating bronzed veins. My eyes drifted to a pink gourd, a crow, the temple tower. Once again I was seized by that same absurd dizziness: to leave. Why leave? It would mean a world of things to organize, to set into motion, millions of pointless gestures to make, a layer of time as thick as seaweed to wade through. And why? It's as if one could only seize hold of something through pain; without drama there's nothing left to seize.

"Listen, Nil, you've thoroughly arranged your madness. Let me arrange a little happiness—one day of happiness. I am asking you for one single day. Then you can do as you wish."

What trap had she devised this time? They all set up traps to ensnare you; then they can eat you alive at their convenience. I don't want to be ensnared by anything or anyone. I'm free. I'm Nil. I am zero. Nobody's man.

Yet I'd like just to sit here and let everything slip through my fingers, like an absent-minded child who has ceased to will anything. Sometimes, inside, a door opens upon a strange softness free of the person, because one has become free of wills. I know that lightheadedness well, and I can sense the hour drawing near.

"All I ask is one day, just one day."

Mohini stood straight as a statue on the temple pavement among the pink pottery. Nearby, a child played with seashells. The scent of jasmine garlands in the offering trays wafted through the air. I can still see the scene as if it were today.

"Listen, I know an island—"

Suddenly they came upon us like flies, attracted by my white skin. That damned diseased skin! The ubiquitous white stigma, the mark of the foreigner. Will I ever be able to melt like air into the wind? Mohini opened her purse and started to distribute coins to the clamorous mob.

"Come on, Mohini. Let's get out of here. Let go of me!"

They were clutching at my legs. I turned abruptly, furious, with an urge to hit.

"O stranger—"

A man dressed in a flame-colored robe stood before me, eyeing me. For a second he was motionless, his begging bowl in his hand. I hated him on sight; there was such a smile in those eyes. Not just a smile, a huge glee, as if he were on the verge of exploding into laughter. But nothing exploded; it was as if held in check in the light of the eyes.

"O stranger, you've come back."

I was thunderstruck. Then, in a completely different voice, quiet, almost unconcerned, in a singsong rhythm, he said:

"Three times you've come; three times you've killed."

And he was gone before I could utter a word.

"Nil, Nil, please don't go!"

I dashed after him. I had to catch him and *know* at once, before it was too late. It was as if something in me had been stung to the quick, branded in red iron, jolted into hitting and hitting that man until he fell. And then I would spit on him.

"Nil!"

Mohini was calling me back. I rushed on like a madman, swerved into a narrow alley surrounding the temple, knocked down a child who began to scream his lungs out. No sign of him. Just a ring of hostile eyes staring silently at the brutal foreigner. And suddenly a god was there, surging forth from the wall, armed with a lance and mounted on a peacock.*

---

* *Kartik*, the demon-conqueror. He rides a peacock, *Mayour*, the symbol of victory over the forces of darkness.

I turned back, breathless, ashamed. The hot season was fraying my nerves. It was time to go. Pale as a corpse, Mohini was waiting among the pink pottery, staring ahead, her plait falling over her breast.

"Ah! Nil—"

She looked at me as if I were returning from a long journey, and she from another world. She spoke in a soft, almost inaudible voice.

"I thought you were already gone."

Her hand lightly touched my shoulder. Once again I was struck by that air of ancientness about her. She stood there in her white mantle, expressionless, without a quiver, like someone who knows and once again watches the unraveling of the same destiny.

"What did he say? What does he want?"

"A madman. If I catch him—Do you know him?"

"He's a sannyasi. I don't like his kind."

"Neither do I."

"Be careful, Nil, they know things that we don't. They're dangerous."

"What do you mean, dangerous?"

"They have renounced the earth. They are the thieves of heaven."

She said that with such intensity. I was nonplussed. She recovered herself immediately.

"They are not from here."

"Well, neither am I. In fact, I no longer know where I am from. Come, let's go. I've had enough of these daubed gargoyles!"

She snatched my arm and pinched me with all her might, like a little girl.

"Be quiet! You don't know what you're saying!"

Monkeys, and pistachio- and lead-colored gods peered down upon mortals from the high tower. Golden palms swayed gently in the air.

"Listen, I know an island. Please don't say no. I won't try to keep you. I am only asking for one day, a single day for my heart's peace. Then you'll be free to go."

A siren's scream rent the air.

The kettle on the tea stall blazed in the sun.

"All right, tomorrow morning at seven o'clock the *Laurelbank* weighs anchor for New Guinea, or the devil. Is that clear?"

"Everything is arranged; I have a boat waiting."

2
the vermilion island

"*L*ook, it's the smallest of the three. They call it the Vermilion Island."

I glanced behind me. My port had drowned, engulfed in shining mist. I could barely make out the black mass of a cargo hulk silhouetted against the glassy light.

"It isn't far, you know. You can be back in just forty-five minutes."

"No, not far. You mean that you brought me out here just to see this monkey roost?"

"No, to see just how far you can go."

With a toss of her head she shook back her plait.

"When the grace comes upon you, you will realize you haven't lived a single minute of your existence. You merely run in your head, with haphazard legs, and a heart as green as an unripe guava."

I wanted to take her in my arms. And I was furious.

"Look, Nil, look!"

Trills filled the air. Humming with parakeets, amid a riot of monkeys, a rocky promontory had emerged from the green waters. It was crowned by an ancient banyan tree whose roots seemed to encircle the whole island and hoist it above the water like a fabulous wreck. Slowly our boat changed tack, sheared off a rock and headed toward a cove. I stood gaping at the vision of thousands upon thousands of blazing coral trees in full red bloom sweeping down to the sea in thick clusters like a scarlet tidal wave.

She was watching me out of the corner of her eye. I was like a rock.

This was all very fine, but what exactly did she have in mind? The fishermen's village was deserted, my port had disappeared behind the promontory, and the only visible path from the beach led up the scarlet hill. I tried to repeat my formula—Laurelbank-seven-o'clock-Friday—in an attempt to ward off the spell. But everything had suddenly become hazy. The world had lost its geodesics, and I was about to founder in a sea of exotic honey.

With a kick, I sent a heap of mussels flying and started up the path without a word.

"It isn't far. The island is tiny."

There was such distress in her voice, as if she wanted to apologize, to tame me. But I was stuck on that "No!" deep inside me, my cry of freedom. I know she wanted to offer me the world in the hollow of her hand, a nice tidy little world where she would walk tiptoe not to ruffle me.

"I know another island, if you prefer."

"Already giving up, eh?"

"Oh! Nil—"

I am callous, I know, but the more I soften, the more I play tough. It's my last line of defense. If that crumbles, everything crumbles.

Yet, sooner or later, one will have to come to the *point*.

And perhaps there is just one point in life, and everything else is imitation, fake. Where is *the* Point? I have visited twenty odd countries, yet not a single one; I have traveled tens of thousands of miles and not moved an inch; I have lived millions of seconds and they are as unsubstantial as dust. Where is *the* thing, the real second in time? The Brazilian jungle is so well rendered in aniline dye by Thos. Cook & Son that one could confuse the rendition with the original. I know; I've just returned from there. And the Himalayas hang neatly on the twenty-ninth parallel, perfectly embossed and starched. Everything is, predictably, as in a geography book: in A-8 you will find peccaries and red monkeys. It's all mapped out and mathematical. Knowledge of the world has destroyed the world as surely as photography destroyed painting; we have the choice between reinventing the world or dying between the pages of an atlas.

But there is also that burning country deep in my heart, untouched and untouchable, my one and only treasure; everything else can be left behind, including Mohini. And yet, yet, I yearn to cry "Yes!"—yes to everything, to all things and all beings, to embrace this world and melt into it. No more resistance anywhere. And this is the mortal point of contradiction, the wrenching yes-no, the cause of a scorching friction. It is *the* Point, the *pure* Brazil. I can feel it. I am approaching the ultimate bastion.

A wrought-iron gate loomed before us, a Versailles-like gate in those crimson tropics. It hung, alone, between two crumbling pillars in the middle of a jungle of yucca trees. Mohini was silent as the dead. On a marble plate, the word *Salvaterra*.

"Here we are."

I took Mohini's icy hand and pushed open the gate. There was not a sound, not a breath. Another world opened before us. It was so utterly still one could feel the density of silence filled with scents. And everything was red—a riot of red flowers flashing on sparse-leafed branches as far as the eye could see. An immobile conflagration. Or perhaps a fabulous aviary of firebirds struck dumb.

"Your island is beautiful, Moni."

She smiled faintly and drew her sari over her breast.

A path, or what had been a path, opened before us, inscribing a wide arc across the hill. A chipmunk scuttled before us. Bits of white gravel could still be seen through the leaf mold.

"Moni, it feels like—"

She nestled against me. I fell silent. Everything was spellbound. I had the strange impression I had seen this before, lived this moment before. And it had nothing to do with the flowers or the place but with that cold hand in mine. Eyes half closed, I walked by her side as if feeling my way through the scent of crushed flowers. I walked toward an old memory, perhaps an old country, that would suddenly emerge around the bend. I always seem to recall a "country" I have to discover (which may explain my obsession to travel) and a "she" who helps me reach it. And each time I have fled, because it's always the same story—love, the trap. The trap and the key together. An old country where I would suddenly dissolve in an utter recognition of *that*.

"Listen, Moni, suppose we forgot everything, everything we've learned, everything they've stuffed into our heads—country, family, passports, religion—the false memory. What would be left? Can you imagine a pure memory, without any additions, a pure gold nugget?"

"But Nil, you've already burned all the bridges in a single glance, including this island and me. You're not here. You're never here, Nil! You are forever hopping on the next boat. Tell me, what do you think would happen if you burned your boat as well?"

I dropped her hand. Our communion had lasted three minutes.

She turned to face me.

"*I* love, and everything else is forgotten."

I love, I love. That's their big word—priests, women, simpletons—and then they end up with lots of little children on their hands, good war material. Anyway, love is past.

"Well, *I* don't love."

"You're a brute."

"Yes, a free one."

Her pallor was such a vivid contrast against that blaze. But I wasn't considering her. I was in the grip of my absurd rage, exactly as when facing that sannyasi—a dark surge from the underside, as if an old wound had reopened in me. Oh, there are wounded places in a man that seem to retain the memory of a thousand ruined lives, or perhaps the same recurring failure, and they are charged with awesome electricity; in one second all the fuses blow. Complete blackout. As if that were *the* memory.

"You're suffering, Nil."

"I am not suffering. I am free. And I hate sentimentality. It's like quicksand; it ends up dragging you to the bottom. I've emerged from the water; I was born under the sign of fire!"

She stopped and looked at me with that ineffable sweetness.

"When you've burned me, too, you will understand."

She said that quietly, without a trace of emotion, as if she saw things from another perspective.

My heart melted.

"Enough, Moni. Come, let's run! We'll start all over again. I open the gate, you enter—"

We ran like children up the path. A vast, sunlit terrace flowed outward onto the other side of the island. Footpaths could still be seen in the tall grass. Clumps of red hibiscus sloped gently down to the sea. A vine-covered house stood with its back against the hill. It looked like an old colonial residence, with stucco columns eaten away by the monsoon rains, a triangular frontispiece framed by two wings and a large veranda. The place seemed completely deserted. The only sound came from the parakeets squawking in the vines.

"Shall we explore, Moni?"

Her face glowed through her bronzed complexion. I had never seen her so beautiful.

"Not now. This evening. You'll see. It's a surprise."

I ran toward the west wing, setting off an eruption of green feathers and strident cries from everywhere. Then silence returned.

I looked around in amazement. There were red lacquered screens on the veranda, a flute player on a bronze pedestal, broken bits of porcelain, a gigantic empty cage destined for God knows what bird. The potted plants had surreptitiously left their pots and grown to the ceiling. Bits of plumage and bird droppings lay everywhere. There was even a peacock feather. I absent-mindedly tore off a leaf near the flute player. It smelled like wild mint. Mohini's low sweet voice came out from behind a pillar.

"In my country we call it *tulsi*. It's a plant that brings good fortune."

I walked to the high door, slid back the bamboo latch. A stream of sunlight burst in, touching a crystal chandelier and flooding the ceiling with splinters of light. Crystal ware glittered everywhere: in candelabras, in bracket-lamps on tarnished pier glass, in ornate lamp stands—a dazzling riot of Venetian glass suddenly seized with delight.

"Where are we? What is this place?"

Mohini did not answer. Then my eyes fell on an Indian sitar, then another, and another. Then on the most extraordinary collection of musical instruments I have ever seen in my life: sarods, veenas, ektaras strewn on the floor, hanging on walls, lying on chests or low divans; esraj, lyres, high crosses carved like ancient zithers or encrusted with ivory; bellies of every shape and size, made of amaranth wood or varnished colocynth, glowing softly. And even instruments, resembling lutes or mandoras, that I did not know.

"It was my mother's house. She was a great musician."

I looked past Mohini. I had a strange feeling of gently slipping into another dimension that was not the realm of dreams, but one where all appearances were imperceptibly and almost inadvertently altered: a subtle shift of lines, and objects took on a sudden depth; instead of lying flat against the walls, they assumed an extra intensity, almost a life of their own. Or perhaps it was just a slip of the eye that suddenly perceived another pattern of things within the pattern. And strangely, along with that deeper perception, the air began to acquire a different fragrance that had nothing to do with the sense of smell but rather with another country, quite familiar, but one to which I could not give a name. It was just at the edge of gentle memory, a dream just dreamed whose presence is still warm and vibrant, yet whose story line is gone, leaving only that fragrance of memory.

I picked up an ektara. It was tiny and single-stringed, like one of the instruments depicted on Egyptian frescoes. I touched the string. A slight quivering metallic sound echoed through the room, ringing the crystals one after another.

I don't know what I had touched, but the vibration extended far, far, as if a door suddenly opened deep within my memory, and I was about to disappear through that door.

"Come. Not now. This evening we'll have a celebration."

She took my arm. The ektara slipped through my fingers and broke on the floor with a poignant little sound. The door snapped shut.

Everything was as before; once again I had lost the thread.

"And I'll show you the Portuguese señor's treasure."

"A treasure?"

She drew me outside. The terrace was awash in sunlight.

"Yes. In the east wing. The treasure of the former Portuguese owner, a shipping magnate. He sold everything to my mother. My mother died here."

Suddenly I pulled myself together. It was stifling in here. I took Mohini by the arm and hastened down toward the sea. Brambles tore our clothes; a marble Venus was undressing under the hibiscus bushes. I had an urge to trample everything, kick Venus's buttocks, to commit some sort of incongruity to exorcise this island and me with it. Mohini screamed; in three steps I had crossed the beach and thrown her into the sea with all her clothes on. Then I dived in and swam toward the open sea. If I could, I would have swum all the way to the port, alone.

I turned back.

"What would His Excellency, your father, say if he saw you here?"

"I've forgotten everything."

"And what if I made you my mistress?"

She blushed profusely. Of course, here one did not throw girls into the sea or say such things to them. In fact, they were not "girls"; they always looked as if they had just come out of a temple, trailing three centuries of contemplation in their wake.

"Why did you bring me here? To lock me in your parrot cage?"

"Because you are leaving tomorrow, Nil; because I love you; because . . ."

I thought she was on the verge of tears. But I did not yet know what she was made of.

"Because you *cannot* go like this, Nil. Certain things are not fulfilled yet."

"What do you mean, fulfilled?"

She held herself absolutely straight in her wet sari, with such an expression of stillness about her that she seemed to merge with the womb of centuries.

"In your country things may happen by chance. Not in mine. Chance simply means one doesn't know the law of things. You do not know the law, Nil."

She gathered up a handful of sand and let it run through her fingers.

"In your country, the least atom doesn't revolve by chance. In mine, the least bird doesn't fly overhead by chance. But that law is of a subtler order."

"And so?"

She turned and looked me straight in the eye, detaching every syllable.

"So what is happening today began thousands and thousands of years ago, and will continue for thousands and thousands of years to come."

"You're crazy!"

"I am not crazy; I see. There are no gaps."

"Gaps?"

"You don't understand anything; there are no gaps in your so-called chance. There's one single continuum. If you put out a certain will, it will fulfill itself no matter what. Do you think it stops because you die or go away? It will catch up with you thousands and thousands of years later."

"Provided I come back."

"*It* is what makes you come back. Things must always fulfill their goal, Nil. Nothing can remain unfinished."

"The goal? The parrot cage with you?"

"Joy. Joy dispels all the clouds. If you have joy, being here or there makes no difference; you're free. And nothing is separate from you. You don't have joy, Nil. You have not reached the end of the story. You may well leave tomorrow, but—"

I bent over and kissed her on the mouth.

She abandoned herself to my embrace. In her wet, clinging sari she looked like an apsara stepping out of a Konarak bas-relief. The air was parching hot around us.

"There will be a storm tonight," she said.

What did I care? Salty droplets adorned her round golden face. Her throat smelled of sandalwood. I was drained, wiped-out, ready for defeat; love is always a defeat. She nestled closer.

Something in me was still repeating, "*Laurelbank, Laurelbank.*" What did I want to leave for? Didn't I have everything one could want of life? A beautiful and loving woman, and even wealth if I wished? What else could I want? She was twenty; I was barely twenty-nine. Which of my brothers would not have run halfway across the world to possess that? What more did I want? What more was I searching for? Was I not mad?

She seemed to have read my thoughts.

"And what exactly are you going to do there?"

"Where? In New Guinea?"

I desperately tried to clutch something convincing and irrefutable. But everything seemed to elude me.

"They say chromium and cobalt can be found there."

"Chromium? What's the use of chromium?"

I was beginning to wonder myself.

"Well, it's used in metallurgy, to make special alloys."

"Metallurgy?"

She opened her eyes wide, scanning the palm trees for that monster. That was too much.

"Look, I don't give a damn about chromium! Don't you get it?"

To tell the truth, I was the one who did not get it anymore. I would land there penniless, running from one consulate to another, from immigration authorities to mining offices to shelters for the homeless—those who make no difference to anybody—and I would always be too much, or not enough. And once I had found their deposits of chromium, or peanut butter, I would run away from their sickening success.

"But if you really want to go, why don't you go back to your own country? To the West?"

The West. Suddenly I was awake.

"I don't have a country."

"But I thought you had already prospected for gold in South America."

"Yes, and for mica on behalf of your father, for cocoa plantations in Brazil, for Greco-Buddhist ruins in Afghanistan, and for nonexistent treasures—the best kind, the ones that never disappoint you. Then Egypt, the Ivory Coast; I've scoured jungles and countries at a gallop. I've even had a taste of prison."

"Then why—"

"The trouble is, you always end up at the same point. Buddhistic heads or rivers with 'green rocks' are fine as long as you haven't found them. Once you find them, they're all the same: transparent and worthless, like the 'Special X' of your father's mines. It isn't a real find; it never touches anything in you."

Except once. I was in Egypt, and I had touched something (rather, it was he or she who had touched something in me)—a strange face and two eyes peering at me in a tiny dark temple on the banks of the Nile. There was just an interstice of light in the vault, and those two eyes staring at me—two eyelids opening out on centuries, extending far, far, far; and all the way at the other end, one is completely different. One has lived forever.

It had literally stripped me naked, pierced through me, and I stood there totally ludicrous, camera in hand, in my twentieth-century skin. Suddenly I felt deflated, then empty. There is no word for it, but for all my "civilization" I felt like a decrepit fake gnome, with false clothes, a false life, false science, and a little Kodak Instamatic to tickle the Sphinx.

"Nil, I don't know what you are looking for, but I can feel, because I love you. You're heading for despair. You'll end up all alone on top of your mines of chromium, which are as worthless as my mines of mica. You're running away from something."

"No, I am not."

"Death is upon you."

"This is blackmail."

"It's upon us all, Nil. Fate is upon us. What you are running away from today will come back upon you ten, twenty times, until you have the courage to face it and undo the knot. And each time it will be more difficult. All I know is that you will keep returning until things are fulfilled."

"Don't try to corner me!"

"I don't want anything for myself, you blind man! I am not trying to keep you! You don't see it, do you, Nil? You're like a wounded animal. Who hurt you? What has happened?"

"Nothing. That's just the point."

"Something happened. And I have something to do with it. I can feel it. I felt it from the first day. When you plucked that tulsi leaf at the door, I had the feeling of repeating words I had said once before. When you opened the gate, I felt we had made that gesture together before. It's as if everything were beginning anew. What exactly are you going to do there, Nil? What are you looking for?"

She squeezed my arm so hard it started to hurt. I felt I was being trapped, but I didn't know by what.

"Oh, Nil, life seems so natural that we don't pay attention to it; everything is so familiar. Yet there are sharp, unyielding little points that seem packed with the past. Everything we seek is here, Nil, at any instant, without addition or subtraction— it's HERE. Unknown to us, we are forever on the verge of a miracle that we can stumble on accidentally, as one stumbles on a rock on the roadside or picks a tulsi leaf. And if we can capture that, everything changes! Once, it happened to me. A sort of slight click takes place inside and every color changes. Life changes. The miracle is everywhere, Nil. It's right here at this very minute, if you want it."

"You're too beautiful, Moni."

"Oh, you're so vain! You only see my body."

"So what? I know all about your little miracle; each year there are sixty-three million little miracles that do not happen."

"Oh, you're impossible!"

She let go of my arm. The palm trees around us cast crab-like shadows on the sand.

What, indeed, was I looking for? Sometimes I feel one does not really "look for" anything; one is merely drawn ever faster toward a certain point, sucked in, as it were, like a straw in a vortex. We say we "look for" something because we feel the pull, but we have nothing to do with it; it's just the spinning, faster and faster. Once we reach the bottom, we know. It really seems as if the purpose of each life were to return to a certain ancient point—a memory, an event, an accident, a past failure—to something that holds both the disaster and the key to the new life. We must get to the bottom and wring the Sphinx's neck. That's what the whirlpool is all about, spinning faster and faster. In short, we walk backward toward the future. It's like that crab-like shadow on the sand: one does not leave the shadow; one reaches the point where it breaks down into its own light.

"Nil, for the last time, why are you going?"

"For God's sake, Moni, I don't know! Where is the secret, Moni? Who holds the secret to true life? In the ten months I've been here, I've seen nothing but temples and more temples. Your people are prisoners of their gods and of fate, while mine are prisoners of time and machinery, wasting their lives trying to make a living. No one truly lives, Moni. Where's life? It's betrayed on all sides, either by the gods or by machinery, or by an urge in the abdomen pulling us downward: family, commerce, sex. What I seek is a real life, you understand, a free life, ruled neither by a lower nor higher crab. Nobody has the secret! And the more I search, the more I find the opposite of what I am seeking. For ten years I've been dreaming of Greenland. And the more I dream of Greenland, the closer I find myself to the equator."

Thus spoke Nil on that tiny white beach, in this age or another, upon an island in the land of the sun. He looked small upon that beach, as if seen from on high, with his lovely dark-braided companion. He did not see, did not understand. He only listened to the sound of his own voice. But *I* saw him well, my brother under a shadow. I had borne his destiny more than once. I had merged with him here and there, following the long procession of his lives, like the figures on Thebes' walls beneath the great serpent of Destiny. And every time I had merged with his pain, his living contradiction, as if men took on a body just to resolve a particular impossibility.

> *O seeker*
> *In each thing, each being on this earth*
> *Lies a knot of contradiction*
> *An insurmountable point*
> *As hard and impenetrable as pain*
> *As tenuous as the last thread of life*
> *Miraculous*

> *O seeker*
> *There are a thousand faces to things*
> *A thousand contradictions*
> *Yet it's always the same*
> *There is but one pain in the world*
> *One single sorrow through many eyes*
> *One single place where everything meets*
> *Or breaks apart*
> *If you find the point*
> > *You live*
> > *Or die*

*

If she had not left me to prepare her so-called celebration, nothing might have happened. Sometimes fate seems to hang on a breath, an idle look, a chance step, a basil leaf plucked casually. And perhaps the most minuscule details—the gate one opens, the rock on the roadside one stumbles on—already contain everything, just as much as the most stupendous events, the latter being simply a magnification of the former. Each thing, each second is the microscopic and surreptitious rehearsal of a great, prodigious outburst that will leave us dumbfounded. But we do not see the little breath; we do not have the proper eyes.

And what haunts me is the infallibility of it all. Each thing moves with staggering precision, to the second. Even birds do not fly by chance! She may be crazy, but if I am here on this beach this evening, it is because every step I have taken in my life led me here, without any exception. Every delay, every detour was part of the way. Everything moves in a straight line by a million twists and turns. What step could be discarded in the story without discarding it all? Where is the minute when I could have *not* intersected this line or crossed that street without shattering the whole enormous play? One day the golden egg burst into a million worlds, and that tiny scar on my forehead was already there! Unless I am crazy? But if the other side of the world, too, is all programmed and mathematical, then where is my freedom? In A-8 of a far more terrible map, I've already lost the game.

> *O Child*
> *Everything is already played out*
> *And everything is free*
> *Depending on whether you look here*
> *Or there*

"Look, Nil! Look!"

From the vine-covered terrace Mohini was gesturing, pointing to the sky.

"The birds are coming, the birds are coming! The monsoon is here!"

In the northeast a black triangle was slowly drifting across the dazzling haziness of the sky. I shrugged and set off to explore the beach. Little red and white crabs scuttled in all directions. A flock of plovers rose from among the rocks. I would have liked to transfix them all, as well as each pebble and the palms' clawed shadows, and hold them under the fire of my gaze until the minuscule secret burst open. I always had the besieging impression of something essential I was unable to remember. What was it I had forgotten?

The devil with it. I resumed my walk.

The far end of the beach was blocked off by a huge mass of boulders, as if thrown up there by some gigantic explosion. I began to climb. The air was stagnant, stifling. The sun had begun to set. I could discern a second plateau beyond the first. I climbed higher. I was becoming very interested, as if my sole reason for coming to this island had been to scale these rocks; and Mohini with her gods, her fate, her birds, now seemed ludicrous, unreal, a sort of morbid fabrication. What did I care! I laughed. I climbed toward the third plateau. And that's where it happened. Something I have never been able to explain. Oh, there must be a very simple explanation, but I am suspicious of so-called simplicity. The simpler it is, the more miraculous it is; simplicity is the ultimate hiding place of the miracle. Unless it was the A-8 of the other dimension emanating into the A-8 of this one. A "coincidence"? It was like music. I could have sworn it was music: a voice, or perhaps a very soft instrument, like two droplets of sound. And very brief. Just a brief call. Two short little notes rising, rising. I stopped short, my heart pounding as if the call were for me. I turned around. The house was hidden from view behind the tree-covered hilltop; it couldn't have come from there. Yet it sounded like an ektara, the plucking of a string. But I had broken that ektara. And who could have played anyway? I climbed higher still. Nothing stirred. The air was as if solidified by heat. Suddenly strident cries burst forth. I looked up to stare at a huge banyan tree rustling with a tumult of frightened parakeets and chattering monkeys. Then silence again.

I was atop the promontory.

Below me lay the sea. A prodigious, gleaming, motionless expanse stretching as far as the eye could see, still as a sheet of molten mercury—a blinding immensity. Even the port had disappeared. There was not a shadow anywhere, not a soul. It looked like a lake at the beginning of the world, a white genesis on a day when eternity was smiling at itself. And they rose: two notes. Two pure little notes—oh, so, so pure—from behind the rocks. I circled the banyan tree. No one. Two notes of unbearable poignancy, whose pitch was at the point of cracking, but nothing cracked; they rose, rose. I was the one about to crack. Then came a third note. And it was as if there occurred an abrupt chasm in me, a memory lapse. Everything melted: the past, the present, memories, ideas, beauty, countries, faces, everything I had experienced, wanted—the thousands of threads that hold everything together. They didn't hold anything anymore. The fabric was giving way. I wasn't in this; I had never been in it. It was a mistake! As if life upon life had been lived for naught, completely beside the point, estranged from everything—from yourself, from other things and beings—and suddenly all that collapses and you are on another journey. Barely time to say, "Oh!" and there you are peering out through another window. Yet there is nothing grand or exalted to it; it's the opposite of exaltation: just a pure little note, and it was like the true note of the world. *The* note. As if there were only one. I felt like shouting, "Yes, yes, that's it! That's it!" Absolutely it. What I have been waiting for for millions of years! A sweetness of total recognition.

An invasion of softness.

It lasted only a few seconds.

I stood before a dazzling emptiness. Was it before me or in me? I looked at the sea, the returning catamarans, the crimson domes of coral trees, and I no longer understood. I understood nothing. Everything was false, empty, hollow, an exotic decor plastered over that luminous reality. What in God's name was I doing here? What was I waiting for? I must leave at once, get out of this place, start walking, pick up the thread again. But leave for where? Another country, my country, the true country I come from. Oh, I don't know anything anymore! My memory is clouded, and all my names are false. I am dressed in borrowed clothes. My life is a falsehood! Who will tell me my origins, my home, my name, my purpose? Have I not lived something else once, in truer times? Was I not absolutely different from this? Sometimes, I seem to remember another vaster country where I came from, as well as a certain music, and great snowfields beneath an unchanging sun. Where is my trail, my silver thread? Everything is blurred and I am lost. I have lost the password. All I know is that there is a burning in a man's heart. That's my latitude and longitude of fire, my constant bearings. There is an oppressive absence in a man's heart, a void yearning to be filled. A tiny wrenching note, and if one misses the note the world is false and everything is false.

"Oh, Nil, I was so frightened!"

She was dressed all in red, the mad girl! Blood-bright red.

"I looked for you everywhere. What were you doing? You look so strange!"

Strands of loose hair clung to her cheeks. She was breathless. Suddenly the world came hurtling down on me like a runaway truck: the parakeets, the monkeys, the stifling humidity, and this woman engulfing me in a scarlet haze.

"Come, Nil, the house is so beautiful! I have lit torches everywhere."

Everything became clouded, as if I had moved to the land of darkness. I had been dreaming.

"All the rooms are alight. The sitars, ektaras, sarods are sparkling. I'll play for you."

Had I dreamed or am I moving to another dream?

"Nil, Nil, where are you? What are you looking at? Don't you see the storm coming?"

We move from one dream to another, from one country to another—high, low, or delightfully and instantaneously light as a scent or a cry; red, blue, or endlessly gray with no one inside. We wander ceaselessly through world after world without a safe harbor.

I could not make anything out of my dreams. But was this one any more real because it was red and stirring my entrails?

"The storm is coming from the west, Nil. Don't you see it?"

An unmoving country, a home that endures.

"Come, Nil, let's get out of here. I don't like this place. It looks like a place to commit suicide."

I stroked her hair. The rock was searing hot.

"Come, I beg you. The house is resplendent."

The soft touch of her breast, her bronzed skin aglow in the sunset—yes, Moni, I like you brown-skinned and in red. Tonight we'll have a celebration.

Brown, yes; women are always a return to penumbra and oblivion.

"I have laid down the Kashmiri carpets. The floor is a forest of blue cedars."

I have lost myself before in your forest.

"Nil, my beloved, must you really go?"

"Enough, Moni, enough. I don't know anymore."

A gust of wind ruffled the sea, scattering dry leaves.

"At night when the wind blows, the house vibrates like an immense sitar."

"Yes, Moni—"

"When I was a little girl, I used to come to this very place. And I was scared."

"Of what?"

"I was afraid I would fall, but a white stranger came and saved me. Strange—and now you are here."

A flock of cranes flew by swiftly. The sea took on a leaden hue.

"It came to me in a dream when I was a little girl: I was standing here, exactly where you are, about to fall and—you know, Nil, I have a feeling the world is full of images that become real. They are here, alive, and sometimes we perceive them ahead of time. Then the accident happens."

"What are you talking about?!"

She pressed herself against me. The image of the sannyasi flashed before my eyes.

"I don't know, Nil. Sometimes I am afraid."

"You're crazy."

"No, Nil! I am not crazy. Fate is determined."

"Nonsense."

She raised her eyes toward me. That same almost unbearable softness was in them.

"But *look* around you, Nil! Open your eyes."

She stared at something behind me. I could feel something pressing on me, a sudden heaviness in the air. I had to get the hell out of here, and the sooner the better. But that gaze was tying me down. She took my arm.

"You don't see how full of images the world is?"

I don't know what she was staring at behind me, but the air was stifling. I was beginning to reel.

"Oh, Nil, if you wanted we could change fate. We could conjure up the lovely image that changes life. There are also lovely images in the world. We could cast out death, call forth the beautiful story and incarnate it in a body. Together we could create a life of beauty. Look carefully, Nil, look. A beautiful gaze is a creative gaze. And are you not Ni-Aksha, the blue-eyed one?"

"I am Nil-nothing-whatsoever and I hate hogwash. I am free, do you hear? And I spit on your fate!"

As I spoke, a blast of wind swept over the island, sending all the parakeets shrieking skyward. I could have sworn something happened at that minute. Something inside me stopped, looked out and photographed the place as if I were seeing it for the first time. I felt I should never have said those words.

She released my arm. She was still as a statue in her red sari.

"Let's go in."

I did not move.

"Let's go in. Night is falling. Don't you see the purple sky?"

A seething mass rumbled in the west. Short gusts of wind rippled the sea.

"Come, Nil, before it's too late."

Raindrops spattered on the ground. The hot earth exuded a smell of sweaty skin. She spoke quickly, as if she were suddenly afraid.

"I have laid out white clothes for you. Our house is radiant. There are torches everywhere."

"What is it, Moni? Are you afraid of rain?"

"Nil, don't leave me. Yes, I am afraid."

She had a strange, unfathomable expression on her face. But it was not fear. With a sudden clap of thunder, a squall burst upon us, sweeping away every single flower like a cloud of red birds.

"It will be too late, Nil."

I was like a rock. I could feel danger, but what danger? Where?

"Too late, Nil, too late."

And suddenly it dawned on me. My boat! My God, the *Laurelbank*!

I tore my hands away.

"Nil, I beg you—"

The horizon was a streak of purple, the sea frothed with foam. For a second I looked into those anguished eyes, at those trembling lips.

"Nil!"

Then I took off like a madman toward the landing.

My boat, my boat! I'll be cut off from the mainland, trapped like a rat. I scrambled down over the rocks, almost breaking my neck on a piece of crumbling schist. In half an hour it will be dark. Tomorrow the sea will be raging; it will be too late. I jumped down onto the sand, charged through the seaweed, tripped into a hole. My temples throbbing, my pulse pounding in my neck, on the verge of suffocation, I was gasping like a cornered animal. My freedom, my freedom! The wind was blowing furiously. I ran and ran.

I have been running for ten years. And I think I would still run halfway around the globe, or to the devil, if I had to. Each time I say "No!"; no to their little happiness, cheap little happiness, loving rattrap, flowery disintegration. I say no, and I will say no till hell freezes over if need be. No to your stringed music, your cozy joys, your islands of honey or down feathers, and your exquisite ways of asphyxiating. No to all that skill in dressing up the void and stuffing the mannequin with straw. I am just nothing, blank, the mannequin's skin who wants the real story and no nonsense. I want the true fullness. And *I am not revolting either*: I say no to your yeses and no to your nos. I have nothing to curse or to forget, for everything is the same: your freedoms are as heavily armored as your doors; your attachments are the two grasping arms of your destitution; your good is the back side of your evil, or its front side, and everything moves in pairs, as in a wedding, your black with your white, your joys with your sorrows, your god with his devils. Me, I am leaving the cavern, and you can count me out. I have nothing to hold on to—not a single day, not a single minute behind me! Nothing to safeguard; my luggage is empty. My life is make-believe and I am born only on paper. I am nothing, a complete nothingness that will not take your straw for an answer. I am leaving the mannequin. What will remain?

The house, "our" house, was glowing in the night. The rain-splattered veranda was streaming with light. I could feel blood on my forehead. No, there was no revolt in me. I called to "freedom," but I was simply crying out to THAT, as one gasps for air. Something else, something else, a complete elseness! Yet not lofty or removed. I ran through that red forest like a sleepwalker searching for his body. No, I have no home, no country, no wife, no name, no future, and I want no part in the wedding. I won't make little Nils who will make little Nils, who will make little Nils, and everything begins again and again. And nothing has begun! Not one second to take with me, not a single true minute. Where is the one meaningful drop in all this? It seems as if I have spent lifetimes watching endless empty Euphrates and Brahmaputra rivers flow by—for nothing.

I ran through the night as if they were all at my heels, those little Nils who made little Nils, who made little Nils, all crammed into one intolerable second, crying, "When do we begin?" The entire family madly scrambling through the night. I fled like a thief on that thick carpet of red flowers, to the sound of a music they couldn't hear, heady as wine: freedom, freedom, the *Laurelbank* and nothing else!

And I am still running.

On the beach three men were busy hauling a catamaran aground. The wind howled, sending thorns and foam flying everywhere. My mouth was full of sand. I went up to the eldest.

"Take me to the port."

"To the port! Did you say the port?"

He eyed me sharply, shouting against the wind. Then he turned his back. I shouted, too.

"I can pay!"

He threw his oar onto the sand. An empty basket rolled on the sand toward a cactus bush.

"Look, stupid! Here, look!"

I waved my wallet under his nose like a madman.

He stopped and looked at me, fingering a piece of rigging.

"Did you see the wind?"

"Listen, I'll make it worth your while. If we sail downwind, we'll be at the port in twenty minutes."

He looked at the sky behind me, then at the wallet. My heart lifted.

"I'm a sailor. I'll help you."

The other two men were fidgeting. He sniffed the wind.

"In ten minutes it'll be dark."

"So what? Let's head straight for the coast—we can't miss it."

I pulled out two bills—two lonely, soaked bills stuck together. It was ludicrous.

"Here."

He shrugged. My heart sank. My watch! I still had my watch. "How about this?"

I was frantic. I would have hit him if I could. He glanced at the watch, spit out a mouthful of sand, and continued hauling his boat. I was trapped like a rat.

My legs began to buckle as I realized the extent of the disaster: no money, no job, my ticket now useless and only half-refundable, six months' work to get another one. I was foaming at the mouth. All I could do now was to return to the house and play little family.

Abruptly I swung around, ready to strike. She was there. If a glare could kill, I would have killed her at that instant.

But I froze at the sight of her. She was standing on a slightly elevated sand platform, so perfectly still and quiet in the midst of that frenzy of wind and mangled flowers that she looked like a goddess adorned for a rite. Her hair loose, her eyes so large they seemed to take up her whole face, she looked at me without a plea, without a tear, without a reproach, as if already captured in eternity, alive only through that warm, sure softness peering at me, peering right into my soul as if it had always known me. We were not being separated. We could not be separated! We were together, always together, eternally together.

For an instant I loved her.

She approached without a word, drew off her gold bangles and placed them in the old man's hands. Then she looked at me again with that intolerable softness, saluted me with folded hands as one salutes the gods in a temple. And she was gone.

"Hurry, stranger. Night is upon us."

Thus they go
Lovers or enemies
Brothers and passersby
But who leaves, who stays?
Only the clothing changes
Or the hue of a sky over a white little beach
Only sorrow goes
And a child
On a pristine little beach
Gazes with wonder
At they who come and go
And no longer recognize each other.

3
the departure

*W*ater sang through all the cracks in the harbor. The air smelled of warm mangoes and the ebb tide. And my *Laurelbank* was safely moored to the wharf. I sang too! Every time I have sung. I was as light as the foam on nascent life. Mohini and her island had drowned in the Tartarus of a previous existence. And there's no turning back! These are truly life's best moments. I've spent my time spinning impossible lives for myself just for the joy of that single moment. It does not last. No sooner are we free from one life than we build ourselves new bonds, and everything begins again. The ideal would be to remain absolutely free: always on the verge of departure, forever in that minute of freedom in between two countries.

Suddenly I came to my senses. I was standing soaking wet under a lamppost. The lighthouse beacon swept through a chaos of streaming shadows, disappeared, reappeared, picked up the temple tower, disappeared, reappeared, picked up the temple tower. I looked at the glistening pavement, the hoardings, the deserted quays. The scene had suddenly shifted. I had gone through it all in the blink of an eye:

It was Port Moresby,
  which resembled Belem, which resembled Goa;
  I had found the gold mine, the chromium mine,
  the yellow island, the black island;
  I had married a Negress, and killed myself one evening.
  A lightning-fast life.
  Twelve thousand miles in the sweep of a beacon;
  I had gone full circle.
  It was the tenth time I stood under that lamppost;
  I was back where I started.
  I had never begun.

The puddles under the lamppost had gooseflesh prickles. With a kick I sent my shadow packing. A rat scuttled, splashing. That was it: one always returned to the tether, the omnipresent thinking tether. All I could do now was to get to the *Eastern Traders* and put another shirt on my back.

Perhaps a true departure would mean leaving the subject altogether?

The tea vendor's kettle sparkled on the street corner—exactly what I needed.

"O stranger, you've come back again."

I stopped in my tracks. Eyes glittering, he was squatting on a crate in front of the tea stall.

"Well, don't you recognize me?"

For a second I stood staring at that squatting shadow dressed in orange, at the oil lamp, the sacks, the copper pots, the tea stall resembling one of Brueghel's hovels, and I was seized by blind, murderous anger, like the first time. I pounced on him, clutching at his scarf, ready to strike.

He burst out laughing.

A triumphant, explosive laugh that rattled the crate and echoed down the street. I was flabbergasted. The tea vendor rushed forward and grabbed my shoulder. The sannyasi raised his hand.

"That's all right, Gopal. Bring him some tea."

He laughed again. The merchant had tucked up his lungi and braced his foot against a sack. The oil lamp cast fantastic shadows. And I kept clutching stupidly at that orange scarf, before a set of white teeth whose grin seemed about to swallow up the night.

"That's enough, Gopal. Do as I say."

Again the man sized me up in a glance. I was surely the devil. He jumped over his sacks and disappeared. I couldn't believe it. I turned and stared angrily at that boisterous owl-like figure.

"If you think that—"

My hand let go of his scarf.

"That's a nice fellow. Now sit down."

I wanted to scream, hit him, spit in his face; and then leave, stay, kick those copper vessels. Finally I regained my power of speech.

"You son of a—"

He placed a finger on his lips.

"Don't use words you might regret."

A spark of anger flashed in his eyes. But it was soon covered over, and all that was left was a kind of perplexing jubilation, like a giant looking down at the world from a mountaintop and literally exploding with laughter at what he sees.

"Will you tell me?"

"Tell you what, boy? That you're right on time? That you've run all over the place? That you're going to miss your boat if you continue this way?"

Again he dissolved with laughter, then mastered his mirth.

"Drink your tea."

I was totally mesmerized by that face. It was almost black, with piercing eyes and a hooked nose, like an erne in its tawny coat, and an intensity of life that could freeze in an instant into a mummy's mask. He pointed a lanky finger at me.

"What have you got there? Are you hurt? Eh, Gopal, bring some water."

My forehead smarted and my nose was streaked with blood. I must have been a pretty sight with my sopping clothes and torn shirt. For a second, Mohini's face floated before my eyes. "Will you explain what you said to me yesterday? Right here in this very street, you said: 'Three times you've come; three times you've killed.' "

"Did I?"

He looked at me with such innocent eyes.

"Then it must be true."

He calmly removed his scarf, dipped one end into his copper pot and leaned forward to sponge off my forehead. I jumped back, splashing scalding tea over my feet. I thought he would laugh again, but he wadded his scarf into a ball and tossed it in my face.

"All right, clean it yourself."

Then he turned to gaze into the night without saying another word. I was struck with stupor, numb, drained, a scarf and a bowl of tea in hand, staring at that wild-haired bum. My anger was gone; he had taken that, too. All that remained in me was a sort of absurd, sterile growl, as one feels before an old mortal enemy.

I made an effort to collect myself.

"Listen, will you tell me—"

Why did I keep insisting? I should have turned on my heels and left immediately. But the more I felt how foolish this was, the more insistent I became, as if I had an old account to settle with that man. Besides, his stony indifference was now beginning to infuriate me.

"Listen, you charlatan, impostor! How long have you been peddling this nonsense to people?"

He barely turned around and answered quietly, matter-of-factly:

"A man only seeks the contentment of his soul."

He paused to spit vigorously on the ground before him.

"And *you* are not content."

Then he bundled his rags, picked up his scarf, his staff, his sack, his begging bowl, and he set off down the street.

"All right, time to go."

And without knowing why, I found myself in the street next to that man, walking beside him. We went toward *Eastern Traders*, passing pottery stalls, a bareheaded beggar, the temple gates. What was I doing there? My eyes rested an instant on the pink pottery, the faded garlands hanging in the flower stall. He had said, "It's time to go" and off I went as if I had obeyed that command dozens of times before. A very strange sensation swept over me. I pulled up my shirt collar and walked on into the night.

"Eh, sannyasi—"

But he paid no heed. The clock on the *Eastern Traders* building read ten minutes to ten. I had the whole night before me; what did I risk? A tiny voice defiantly whispered in my ear, "And why not?" And the moment I heard that "Why not," I was surrendering. I still would have liked to know the reason for all this, but I no longer knew *what* I wanted to know! Giddily, I followed that tall, orange-clad shadow gliding barefoot through the muddy puddles and overripe mangoes and pretending I did not exist. What was there to know after all? I felt as light and soft as the fragrant night. I had let go of everything, abandoned myself to the current. Perhaps this was fate? The purpose of all our questions may not be so much to find an answer as to keep the wheels turning; while if we stop for a minute, with a real need to know what we are about, and simply stay there, floating, suspended, we realize we don't really need questions or answers so much as we need to feel a certain density about our life and ourselves, like a fish in water. Only when that density is lacking do we start asking questions. It's that simple. But neither the question nor the answer creates the density.

"Tell me, sannyasi, where are we going?"

He glanced over his shoulder as if to acknowledge my presence, and pressed onward without a word, his neck thrust forward like a whale parting warm water. A taxi splattered by, followed by a stream of rickshaws, cotton trucks, shadows toddling along under straw umbrellas. We arrived at the railway station.

He stopped under the clock and studied me for a moment with that air of glee, as if he were about to bite into an apple. Then he resumed his walk, passing the station and heading toward the warehouses. Even my curiosity had left me. I just wanted to be with this man, walk with him, be totally absurd with him, go to the devil with him if he wished, lose myself in such an inconceivable life that even I would not be able to make head or tail of it. And why not? My eyes fell on a billboard. *Nim*, said the slogan in white letters under the picture of a huge tube of toothpaste. For an instant everything froze. My eyes seemed to open beyond measure, taking everything in, capturing every detail with incredible precision, as if the slightest drop, the tiniest scratch, the tree by the railway track, were suddenly bursting with eternal life. And I passed to the other side. I was everywhere, not just through my eyes but *in* everything, in a million nooks and crannies and rustling little leaves: this droplet, that tree, this word, those shadows; all of them living, eternally living, immobilized—one second of respite in the enormous avalanche. Then the realization came in a white spark; yes, I was leaving. My gaze returned to the tall, stooped shadow striding through the night. Undeniably it was *him*; I had found *him* again. It's as if I had spent centuries wandering, spent entire lifetimes suspended in a nowhere, and now I had hit upon something, arrived somewhere, set out on the right track.

I seemed to hear the pealing of bells. The *Laurelbank* had sunk to the bottom of the sea, along with all my luggage. I had nothing left! Not even a toothbrush, a passport, or a name. I was unburdened of everything. I wanted to take the sannyasi by the shoulder, laugh with him and say . . . nothing. I kicked at a piece of scrap metal and ducked to follow him through a hole in the hoarding. We had emerged on the railway tracks.

The night was alive with crickets. The tracks disappeared into the darkness in a yellow stridulation, and I disappeared with them, as if I had let go of my body—a tiny half-burned cinder by the railway track; here I was high, very high and transparent all around, like a field of crystal astir with the quiver of a cicada. The sannyasi began running toward a train's red light. I followed him, jumping from tie to tie. The platform glistened; the night was as beautiful as a princess in a ruby gown. Ah! I know of a beauty that is not of the flesh and a music no sitar can render, and the signs of the night are my graceful treasures.

We settled ourselves in the last compartment. There were at least twenty people all over the place, amid a vociferous clutter smelling of perspiration and turmeric powder. The sannyasi squatted by the door, wedging his stick into the latch, and I sat beside him, my feet dangling outside. The train rumbled to a start. I had the best seat in the house.

"Well, my boy, what do you think?"

A wave of joy swept over me. I groped in my pockets, pulled out a leather wallet and found my ticket: "Port Moresby via Colombo and the Sunda Islands." You bet.

"Do you see this?"

He eyed me cheerfully. I took the ticket, tore it into a thousand pieces and flung them out the door. The sannyasi did not so much as blink an eye. Then I burst out laughing. A marvelous side-splitting, liberating bellow as if I were casting off thirty years of lies. To be sure, I had known prisons where the dead—and the living—were neatly trussed like chickens; I had floundered about in the jungle, sweated with fever and distress, dug in eagle droppings from the end of a rope in search of the Rajput treasure, and I had committed a few inordinate stunts best left unmentioned, but all that was still within the unreason of *their* reason, the tail end of the same cock-and-bull story. Now, however, I was out of the unreason, out of every conceivable reason and explanation, out of every negation and every opposite, out of the antipodes that keep one foot on the other side. There were no more "sides"! I was not even on the "other" side with the outlaws, the rebels—the law abiders in reverse. I was no longer "out" anywhere, because I was no longer *there*. I was in something else altogether, both regal and hilarious.

Now I understood the sannyasi's jubilation; I, too, was filled with jubilation.

"Where are we going?"

He looked at me with surprise.

"Nowhere, of course. This is it!"

I was nonplussed. Then it dawned on me: This is it! Yes, of course, this is it! We are right in it! There's nothing to search for. There will be nothing more in thirty years or three centuries from now if there is nothing *here and now*, at this very second, just as I swallow my spit and say, "damn." Where could that "otherness" possibly come from? This is it. We are in it, right smack in the goal. I am now exactly as I will be when they drive the first nail into my coffin. Actually, I'll be cremated; it's safer.

"Here, eat this."

He pulled out a cloth bundle and shoved a handful of grain into my hand.

"Come on, boy, don't be so serious; it's a beautiful night."

His eyes sparkled like sea foam. Leaning against the train door, his mahogany-colored body bare except for a few orange rags and the *rudraska* beads around his neck, he looked like a king.

As for me, I was back at my tether.

"Tell me, if we're in it, why did we bother to leave? We might just as well have stayed at the tea shop, no?"

He puffed out his cheeks and let out a groan.

"Well, why did you leave your mother's womb, boy? A man's got to be on the move."

"I've already moved a lot."

"Your head is what has done the moving. When your head quiets down, then you'll be still no matter where you are, and you'll run like a rabbit before God's wind."

"For starters, I don't believe in your God, and all your Oriental wisdom bores me to tears."

"And *I* don't believe in *cholum*; I crunch it."

He tossed a handful of grain into his mouth.

"And Oriental wisdom makes me laugh."

He let out another one of his roars, spluttering pieces of grain all over the place. He had cooled me off. I could not decide whether I loved or hated that man. I chewed a grain; it tasted like chalk.

"Look, son—"

For a moment he was almost grave.

"You want me to show you true life, but you will hate me and perhaps love me and then hate me again."

Great! Now he was reading my mind. I was really starting to have enough of this. Besides, there was something a bit inhuman about that laugh. He continued:

"Men do not like joy; they find it insulting. What they like is to be pitied. It's true, they *are* miserable, and pitiful. But it's no use shedding tears with them; they would simply drag you down into their hole until you are caught in the same mire; *then* they would recognize you. But you wouldn't be able to do anything to help them, because you would be *like* them."

He turned abruptly and gave me a hard look.

"First, you must get out yourself, you understand?"

"Get out, how?"

He remained silent a moment, fingering his beads.

"When I say 'get out,' I don't mean to run away somewhere; I mean to change your way of looking at things. When you stop hating and then loving me, you'll have begun to get out.

When you can keep your valuable papers in your pocket with the same joy with which you tore them up a moment ago, you'll be ready to laugh the good laugh."

"Then everything will be the same to me."

"No, *everything will be as it is.*"

"And what is it?"

"Look, boy, if it's philosophy you want, ask your Oriental sages. I have nothing to tell you; all I can do is show you."

Again he withdrew into his stony silence. I was beginning to realize this was not going to be an easy journey.

Night streamed by at ninety-five degrees Fahrenheit. I chewed another grain, then threw the rest out the door. I felt sobered, deflated, completely ridiculous, without a destination or a ticket, next to a man who didn't give a damn about anything or anybody. Indeed, we were in it—nowhere, stuck in this exotic rattler bumping its way to God knows where. I stared out at the night, drawn about us like a curtain, barely pierced by a glimmer, expecting God knows what. I am in expectation. Oh, I live in expectation of the marvelous adventure! I, the unbeliever, have a tremendous faith; I am forever ready to believe in the marvel! I seem to recall a once-lived marvel; I am just a man through forgetfulness, as it were. And sometimes, little golden glimmers come dancing through my night, tiny fireflies that are not from this world, and I rush forth. Yes, I run after them as if I had been waiting a thousand years in darkness and I were struck by a sudden recall: That's it, I've got it at last! I run toward the song of a golden cicada. All it takes is a faint glimmer in my night, a mere winking at the street corner, and off I go. I am the follower of a tiny glimmer, my bag packed in a jiffy and nothing holding me; I drop everything to follow the tune of that other song. What on earth am I doing here? Have I not known it all: their joys, their sorrows, their pity? I have played every role and I know all the repartees by heart; I need only look into their eyes to recognize the old story. I know them all as if I had sung at their weddings:

the rich, the poor, the men of God, or the devil. Where is the cry I have not uttered; the pain, the error I have not committed? I have chanted all their prayers and fornicated in their night. I am a man a million times over; I am through with the business of being a man! Yes, I believe in the marvel that is beyond their formula—and beyond their heavens. Could we be on the verge of an incredible new earth about to be born? I no longer know what I once knew, and I go on through the night like a blind pilgrim of a great gold-stirred memory.

> *O Pilgrim*
> *You are journeying in my sun*
> *In truth*
> *Everything is sun*
> *Only my image is inverted*
> *Every gesture from below*
> *Repeats a gesture from above*
> *And all reveals*
> *An eternal coincidence*

4
the infernal journey

I awoke to a procession of bare feet nimbly stepping around
me. I lay on a station platform, an orange scarf gathered
beneath my head. Piles of bags were scattered nearby. A
signboard swung above me. I leaped to my feet. He was there,
squatting on the ground, straight as an arrow, as if watching
over me. The sun was already high and beating on the corrugated metal roof. I was spattered with mud. Our train had gone.

In a daze, I looked at that throng, the crows hopping along
the quay, my soiled clothes. And suddenly, last night's dream
flashed back into my mind and heart with a swelling of joy—so
vivid, even more vivid than this crowd. It was intense, full, as
life never is—a thousand meanings packed into a whiff of
scent. I closed my eyes, letting the image become clearer, until
I could almost breathe it. Now I was fully awake, the fragrance
of the image opening like a flower. And each unfolding petal
reveals a new layer of significance, a further depth of the same
thing. Here, our odors are one-dimensional: they tell either of
jasmine or filth; they are artless. There, they encompass a
whole world. They are the smell of feelings—fear, hate, joy—
and they are stupendously precise, as if one had swallowed

the utter terror of the Inquisition or all the wild rhododendrons of the Himalayas in a single vibration. I have the constant sense that life here is but an abstract replica of a true image in the background; entering here feels like entering a caricature: it's hard, dry, deceptive, and horribly inadequate.

I was in a foreboding medieval fortress in the West, walking down a narrow alleyway paved with large flagstones. I can still see them: huge, polished, uneven, and I was dwarfed by the high walls that seemed to lean toward me with their small wrought-iron balconies. I walked, a tiny figure amid a foreign and shadowy crowd. Each member was curiously shrouded in silence, and that crowd had a particular odor—an odor of catacombs. I saw myself in their midst, very small, almost dark, as if I were looking at myself from over my shoulder. (At times I see myself from the outside and above, as if from the perspective of someone taller than myself, someone behind or over me, and I become a witness to myself. And the images I see in those instances remain indelible, fixed for eternity in their every detail by an eye that will not close. Perhaps it never closes, and it's I who from time to time join with that eye.) I was walking toward a gate; I knew there was a gate somewhere below. But as I advanced, I sensed I was not dressed in the proper way, I was not behaving in the proper way; I was different from them, perhaps from another place or another age, an intruder one stares at. Those stares grew more and more menacing and aggressive; and the more foreign I felt, the more hostile they seemed. Hostility oozed from everywhere, even from the walls, from the stones—a world of stone. I desperately groped for the right gesture, the right word. I walked bent over, crouching against the walls, filling myself with grayness, but to no avail. I was singled out by that silent mob. My uneasiness kept growing, becoming almost unbearable, stifling, as if my clothes, my face, my complexion were all horribly wrong. I did not know the password, did not know the proper gesture. Next, the police would come and I had no passport. I had nothing. I was trapped, a prisoner in that horrible stone fortress. Suddenly, from nowhere, a white horse appeared in the middle of the street—a superb, radiant, marvelous animal, so huge that it almost reached the top of the walls and towered over the mob, a formidable beast. Before I could understand what was happening, I was on its back, riding away at a fantastic, godlike gallop. Everything gave way before us: the crowd, the gates, the guards. Nothing could resist. There was vastness, freedom, open space—all the rhododendrons of the Himalayas in a single breath; my lungs were filled with them. I felt myself expanding, bursting forth, almost glowing; I was regaining my height and color. A liberation.

"Here, drink this."

I could still feel that white mane in my hands, the warm flanks against my thighs, the wind buffeting my face, the exhilaration in my veins. The sense of being carried away by a triumphant, irresistible power. We were entering a forest.

"Hey, boy!"

He held out a bowl of tea and some cholum. Iron carts rumbled by in the mugginess. Crows flapped about me. It felt like a furnace.

"What about our train?"

For a second he looked surprised, then pointed majestically at two trains steaming at the platform across from us.

I looked at the sun. East was that way, so these trains were heading west.

"But we've just come from there!"

He shrugged, picked up his staff.

"Come, it's time to go."

Thus began an infernal journey. We would head west, then east, and sometimes north, only to come back immediately to the south—and maybe we had not even left the vicinity of the port? I would look at my watch, but whether it was a quarter to six or seven o'clock made no difference: it was forever time to sweat and chew cholum. In utter disgust, I finally threw away my watch. He laughed as usual. I hated his guts. But what good did it do? I had embarked in this, so I might as well go to the end. Where else was there to go? I had exchanged my two remaining bills for a copper bowl and a bar of soap, and I was clothed like a tramp. Even if we returned to the port one day, what difference would it make? I did not have even enough money to get a shave, and my shoes, too, had been tossed off the train. I might go to a consulate for a compulsory repatriation. I know that refrain, as well as the red tape. And a repatriation where? Back to the Fortress and everything starts all over again?

"Will you tell me why I have come here?"

No reply.

"And not only once, but three times; that's what you said."

He did not budge.

Three times? It isn't three times I have come here, but thousands! To me, it felt like a flood of black lava as old as the Valley of the Kings. And I did not mean just a "here" made of corrugated metal sheets and railroad tracks, but one inside, far more stifling and intense, growing increasingly intense and acute like the odor of that silent crowd. Sometimes I was even afraid to extend my hand lest I encounter even more terrible walls. Perhaps that's what fate is; I could see it, almost touch it in that mugginess. No, fate is not a mystery; quite the contrary, it's a very well-known situation repeating itself. Slowly, expertly I was being pushed into a trap and I would be caught, without any chance of escape, by what?

"Whom did I kill?"

Silence. He kept fingering the beads of his necklace. Killing is just the final effect; deep within lies a point of utter culpability before which all the earth's crimes are nothing. This is *the* crime, naked, identical for all. Something lying in wait in our depths, like a beast caught in the glare of headlights. Something struggling to the death, unyielding, refusing, all coiled onto itself, harder than steel. It's there, deep within; I know. I have known it forever, and I am awaiting the moment as if every moment in my life were merely a dress rehearsal for *that* moment.

"What do you want me to tell you, son? Words are useless; what's important is to understand; and understanding doesn't mean to know about it, it means to *be in it*. When the time comes, you will understand. You people in the West have observed the whole world through your binoculars, and you've understood nothing."

He was infuriating. Sitting cross-legged, his back propped against a pillar, he looked perfectly at home. In fact, he was always at home, whether on train platforms, in freight cars or warehouses, in filth, among the whining of steam engines (he seemed to choose these places on purpose), and even with mosquito bites; and all those people hurrying along the quay were servants in his palace. A full-fledged pighead. And when he was not pigheaded, he was laughing his head off or lecturing goats. It was detestable. But, in fact, he was constantly and silently watching me. I had the feeling that, inch by inch, he was turning a screw in me, nearer and nearer to some invisible point.

"It's simple, son. Actually, everything is prodigiously simple. I'll tell you—"

He sniffed and pulled at his scarf.

"You see, once when I was young, I knew someone I liked very much. She went away; she was taken to the hospital. I was very sad. Then I thought how unnatural it was not to be able to see her simply because her body was no longer there with me. I wanted to be able to see her always. 'Suppose I thought of her very hard?' I asked myself. I thought of her very hard. I held her to my heart, and there she was. I could see her, know what she was doing. Later, I realized she was a silly little thing. And then you get tired of a face. So I started to think very hard about the river that I liked so much. There it was; I saw it, knew when the ferry would leave its shore, and even when it was about to rain. But then you get tired of a river, too. I thought very hard about tomorrow, because I always expected a miracle, and then I saw myself falling into the cistern while fetching water; the next day I almost drowned in it. I thought about all sorts of things and there they were; it was just a matter of thinking about them. You concentrate, you extend yourself outward, and then you see. But, after all, one day or another you will trip on the lip of a well, the neighbor's daughter will catch the measles, and the river is always there to look at. So I thought very hard about something that does not change, something that brings constant contentment."

His gaze rested on a flock of pigeons, then he closed his eyes. He was gone. That was it; there was nobody there. The abruptness with which he was able to tune out always amazed me. Or else he would suddenly open an eye to make the most unexpected gesture, or get up in the middle of the night and take a train, or beg for a bowl of tea when I was thirsty, or pull me by the sleeve when I thought dark thoughts. Then bing! Gone again! And all the mosquitoes in the station could not have moved him one inch.

"Something you can look at forever. Well, do you know what that is?"

He opened his eyes and sniffed again.

"In your country people don't know how to look. So they keep inventing new things to look with: things to look far away, to look up close, to look in the dark, to look sideways; but the eyes are never satisfied, nor are the heart and the ears. You are brilliant inventors, except your inventions are a sham. You haven't invented anything; you've only imitated. In the future you will be known as the great connivers. But you haven't begun to lay your hands on the Real Thing. The world is simple, child, as I told you, and there is but one thing to find. Then everything is invented, every day and every minute of the day. An inexhaustible invention of life. Then a man is content, always content."

He squeezed his nose between two fingers and blew resoundingly. I was overpowered.

"Sannyasi, you can see the future. Please tell me what it is I feel weighing on me, besieging me."

"But I don't see the future, you dimwit! I don't seek to see the future. I don't seek anything! Things come all by themselves, when it's necessary. It's a continual invention; it's empty, then it's filled with an image, at the spur of the moment."

"Then why do you say I have come here three times?"

"How do I know? I have no wisdom to offer you, except that which is put in my mouth."

"You are slippery as an eel, sannyasi, conveniently. But I do want to know, you understand. I want to touch. I want to see."

"You will see and touch. But you can't reasonably ask an ass to touch an eel. First, your ass has to learn how to swim, right? It's common sense. You all say: 'I want to see,' whereupon you cover your eyes with your hand for fear of being confronted with something other than your everyday sack of bran. And if it turns out to be other than your sack of bran, you don't even see it! You are right in the center of the miracle, o fools, and you don't see it!"

He took up his copper pot and thrust it into my hands.

"Here, as clear as this. In short, you would like something else while you remain as you are. Besides, men do not really seek 'something else'; they merely seek the same thing with a few improvements. They seek to become superior asses. But that will not give them the key to catching the eel; all they will achieve is an encyclopedia of the eel."

"So what should I do to be able to see?"

"It isn't a matter of doing, my boy, but of undoing."

"Undoing what?"

"Everything that stands in the way."

Suddenly he stretched out his arm and pointed at a pigeon near the coffee shop.

"Do you see what that pigeon is doing? It's pecking at lime. Why? Because it needs lime for the shell of its eggs. Does it like lime? No. Does it understand what it is doing? No. But it does it anyway. You don't like lime, you don't like cholum, you don't like the police, you don't like mosquitoes, or goats, and on and on. But you like freedom, music, birds, applesauce, and on and on. Hence, you don't understand and you don't do anything. You are full of your own music; you hear only your own music. Believe me, once you have emptied yourself of your music, you will begin to hear something else. You will peck straight at what is necessary, and the right thought will come to you at the right time. When I say, 'It's time to go,' it's time to go. I don't have to check the schedule: the train leaves. Did I not wait for you at the tea shop?"

This time I was spellbound. A door opened, letting a myriad little details burst forth from all sides: his unpredictable gestures, his almost unsettling, abrupt manners, without any logic; and those gestures were always right. Like the night I had lain on those raffia bags and he pulled me off brutally. He lifted the bags to reveal a nest of scorpions!

"You knew the scorpions were there?"

"Of course not, stupid! I don't know anything; I *do*. And it's not even that I do. *That* does. The 'I' has nothing to do with this; all the 'I' can do is copy, imitate, and make mistakes."

"But how—"

"Oh, how thick you are! There is but *one* life, child. Things are not separate: the bags, the scorpions, you, and I. It's all *one* life. The scorpions are not camouflaged! You're the one who wears a camouflage in your head!"

And what about his way of catching trains just as they were leaving, of begging from the right person (and never twice), of waking me up whenever I struggled with horrible serpents. I had the feeling that there lay a secret far more essential than seeing divine visions.

All the same, I hated him.

"It's all very fine to be on time, but what does it matter since we are going nowhere?"

He grew serious all at once. I even thought he might begin to shout.

"I am going somewhere, and this somewhere is everywhere. And it's essential to be exactly on time at every instant. For if I am not on time here and now, I will not be on time anywhere."

"But damn it, this is no life, to rove about from east to west and west to east like railway freaks, feeding on soot with cholum, and cholum with soot! Will you tell me what in God's name I am doing here? Life is supposed to serve a purpose, no? I don't know—"

"That's right, you don't know."

"And what about the world, and other people? What do you do for others, tell me? You laugh? Of what use are you? (I don't know what aroused the philanthropist in me; I suddenly sounded like a mouthpiece for the Salvation Army.) We are born to this world to *do* something, no? What does one do in your damn railway stations? Look at that leper, and your hospitals."

"They're full of ignorant people like you."

He stared at the leper.

"This one is dragging a whole cloud of black leeches in his wake. Look, child, there is only one illness in the world. I've told you, the world is simple. Men can build as many hospitals as they like, but as long as they do not cure themselves of that illness, nothing will be cured. You are searching for something else; well, you must first empty yourself of the old thing. And the hardest part to remove from yourself is not evil; it's what you think is *good*. There is nothing more sticky than that 'good.' It's the last thing to go—the ultimate wall, and the strongest one, because we simply don't see it. But if you don't rid yourself of both evil *and* good, you will never gain access to the vast truth. You will not see anything, hear anything, know anything, except your own noise, or your own virtues, which have never cured anything, let alone you. And now I've said enough."

It was the first time he had talked at such length, and it proved to be the last. Besides, I had no more questions to ask. I was in the grip of a struggle for my very life.

* *

Thus thought Nil.

He thought, but men think a lot of things. They think they are good, evil, merchants or kings, and wise. They don't know what they are; they are not yet born. He thought he was struggling for his life, but it was death that struggled in him; it was my life that was trying to penetrate him. Men are not born unless they die to death. Their life is merely a living death; they are merchants or kings in the process of dying. In truth, I was watching over him. Whether here or there, I had never ceased watching over the destiny of that traveler without a true name, for he has neither name nor sense as I draw near:

> *Peter or Paul and Paul or Peter*
> *They have tumbled into a body*
> *They move about like marionettes*
> *They do not know whence they have come*
> *Nor where they are going*
> *They are gray, they are in a hurry*

But I draw nearer and nearer, stealthily, as the centuries pass, as the carapace grows thinner and thinner. And one day I put my hand on his shoulder; I cast my shadow upon him, or so he thinks, for he discovers he is dead before he has even been born. He discovers me through that growing shadow:

> *They awaken clad in black*
> *And shod with lead*

And with a flame of pain that cries
           [their original name
They are black from head to toe
And discontent
They are going to die, maybe
They want to die and don't want to

And when my last shadow has covered his last cry, I merge into him and he merges into me, for we are forever one: I, his brother of light, his peaceful immensity watching the journey across eternal hills; he, my dogged discoverer, my pilgrim with a bull's eye lantern, my great bonfire on revealed heights. I, his deliverance; he, the deliverer of my abysses.

The sannyasi hardly talked to me anymore, even pretending not to notice me, as if I were a casual fellow traveler. Whenever I tried to draw his attention, he would turn his back on me and continue counting his beads. At times, I knew such spells of despair in those railway stations that I would have kissed his hands, or perhaps wept like a child, for a single word of affection. I would then grit my teeth and start counting the railroad cars. There was nothing, no one. I was not even at the end of the world, not even a negation, which still would have been positive in some sense. I was in nothingness, under a muggy and sticky sky, with goats trotting along the tracks, and that atrophied leper. The only difference between us was that he no longer hoped, while I still did. What was I hoping for? I have no idea. Perhaps he wanted me to stop hoping for anything at all? Or wanted to reduce me to the same sievelike state as my shirt?

I felt he was killing me bit by bit.

Days, then months went by. Or were they years? Time had lost all measure. I even had a vague feeling it was not moving forward but backward, in a very, very ancient history, an uttermost world, and each day I had to tear down *one* history in order to get one step farther.

And in the midst of that sweltering chaos, the same grating, stinging question kept recurring: What's the meaning? What *is* there? So I invented instant lives for myself: a man walking down the street with an attaché case. What's the meaning? An attaché case walking and walking; there's no one there, just a small attaché case walking. A man toiling in a lode of bauxite. What's the meaning? A small jackhammer banging and banging, and there's no one there. A man with a stethoscope, a man holding a rudder. All those men were crumbling one after another. The moment I took away their tools and their gestures, nothing remained but a beggar on a platform and an old familiar question burning underneath: What's the meaning? Where is *the* true minute, the one fragment of being without adornment or posture, without anyone around to fill the void? There is no fragment, nothing! Only screeching axles and roaming crows on the quay. Only the stark, burning question.

Yes, there is that fire underneath. That's all. Man is first and foremost a fire, like the primeval nebula.

"All right, let's go."

He would wake me up in the middle of the night to run after some improbable train, only to come back here tomorrow, eventually; and I did not know whether I was here or there, whether the chaos was inside or outside me. I collapsed with exhaustion in some corner, and everything collapsed around me: houses, castles, temples, places I did not even know, from another country, another age; each night everything collapsed around me. It was always the same kind of dream. I would explore a new region, as if forever searching for *the* place. The night before, for example, there was a huge pillar, and I stood there, very tiny, always tiny, in a gigantic stone hall with inscriptions on the walls, two great open wings painted blue like those of an Egyptian god; and suddenly everything collapsed in a thundering noise and ghastly chaos. The earth split open. And I was underneath. And just as I was about to wake up screaming, I saw myself tall, dressed in white and almost radiant, crawling from beneath the ruins. Each time the same vision, and that invulnerable being dressed in white and emerging from the wreckage. It seems almost as if he were emerging from a certain life, or a type of life, or maybe a type of experience symbolized by a castle, a fortress, or a temple. When I am there, everything is very familiar; I am "at home." The following night I visit another place, another life, and it begins all over again. But it's never *the* place, never home! I have no place, no refuge.

"Sannyasi, what does it all mean?"

"It means nothing. Things do not *mean*, my boy; they *are*. And you are, or you are not. If you are, you understand; if you are not, you mean nothing."

I hated his guts. Sometimes crazy ideas ran through my mind: push this man under a passing train and be done with it. Ah, to be done with it all! But I could not fathom the idea of pushing him in the back. I would rather grab him by the scruff of the neck and strangle him slowly, face to face.

Abruptly he turned toward me.

"Here, take this."

He handed me his knife.

"It may come in handy one day. Keep it."

And he went back to counting his beads.

I felt myself turning white as a sheet. I took the knife, turned it over in my hands. My eyes widened as everything became still around me: the crows, the leper, the sign over the water faucet: *For external use only*, the naked child splashing water over his head. I am quite sure I will take that sign with me into another life, as well as the patch of sulphur on the child's loins. Someday, in a railway station of the twenty-second millennium, I may awake again at the foot of a decrepit public fountain.

And that's when I began to think it was not he who had to disappear, but I. But disappear where? Into death? There is no such thing as death! It's a myth. And just then, on that platform, I had a sense of a prodigious conspiracy. Walls, walls everywhere: to the right, to the left, above, below, within, on this side, and on every possible side. Not one exit anywhere. A complete and flawless net. You tear up one mesh only to face another. There is no death; one simply moves to another room! Where is that incredible entity called a free man? I pulled out the knife, opened it. It was a Nepalese kris with a swastika on it. The sannyasi was counting his beads. Crouched in his orange robe, he too was a prisoner, as everyone else.

I felt overcome with dizziness, frozen in place. I did not know if I could turn my head to the right or to the left. This was it, the impossible point. I had reached it. You can't go backward or forward, or up or down, or even seize upon a reassuring thought. Every thought was a trap. Then it unfolded very fast, as in a drowning accident or an accelerated filmstrip: ten years of life packed in one second, ten little me's bursting to the surface like bubbles, each with his own little story—one image per life. And the image was always the same, regardless of the latitude and the attire: curled up in a hammock, shivering with fever (my first night in South America's jungle). No, not malaria, not tropical fever—*the* fever. Fever was always the last recourse, as it were, the ultimate way of taking the boat. But I had just come off the boat; I could not very well return to it! I had arrived from Europe, in my city shoes, to a jungle crawling with snakes. My legs were like two metal stumps, my hands were swollen with blisters, and the night was hissing in my ears like a furnace. This was impossible, impossible.

The next day I laughed and found my first speck of gold. I had become a prospector.

Another night, in the Brazilian *Sertao*, I was curled up on the floor of a shack, penniless, without even a map or an idea where to go or what to do, when a group of planters appeared from nowhere and put me in their truck among sacks of cocoa. And I rode through the night with a feeling of being taken to the firing squad. Then I laughed, and I planted cocoa. I had become a planter.

Each time, someone inside is on the verge of death; someone must be executed. And if he is not executed, it becomes truly impossible, and one dies for good. But those "someones" sprout up again and again like weeds, forcing one to reach a deeper level, making the battle ever more fierce and difficult; at each level, the puppet surges up again, ever more difficult to kill, clinging tighter. It is as if one were advancing step by step toward an ultimate stronghold, one last unyielding and diabolical puppet, a kind of deep-seated, irreducible *no*. This time, too, I was about to come down with fever, except that I was no longer a prospector, a planter, or a sailor. I was nothing, and this was the twenty-second coal car. I had already staked out a spot near the tool shed. I would go there, curl up in a ball and drift out in the dark.

"You little idiot!"

He hit me hard on the back. The knife slipped to the ground. I turned green, then white. Blood spurted from my left hand. There was not the slightest trace of laughter in his eyes.

"You're an idiot."

I was completely sobered up. I turned to him grimly.

"How do you know it isn't you I have come back to kill?"

He returned my gaze calmly, taking all his time. Then he went back to counting his beads.

My fever was gone.

"Sannyasi—"

He spat in front of him.

I stared at the blood dripping onto the cement, the knife on the ground. I did not know if I would weep like a woman or throw myself under a train.

"Sannyasi, I've had enough with your filth! Enough with your journey, enough—"

I stopped. I had no more words. I was like a dead man staring in front of him. He got up.

Five minutes later he was back with a barber.

"If you think this will help remove the filth, be my guest. In your country people like cleanliness, it seems."

The barber settled down in front of me. I sat still.

No, I was not dead, just wondering how *that* was still alive. If I closed my eyes for five minutes and held my breath, I would surely slip away. But that's just it: there is always an "I" slipping away like an eel, and as long as there remains a single "I," everything will have to be started over again! The only true dilemma in the world is this: *without* an "I," no life is possible (or is it?); *with* an "I," life is hell. This is the central contradiction, the underlying knot of everything. And the closer one gets to that center, the more burning and hellish it becomes.

The barber opened his bag. He had everything for shaving, cleaning ears, filing nails and powdering armpits. He filled his basin at the faucet, then squatted before me. I stared at him uncomprehendingly. I was there, yet completely removed. There was certainly something being shaved on that quay; there was also a plump nymph brandishing a can of *Dalda* oil on the toolshed wall, and dirty cotton swabs in the bag, a locomotive steaming on Track 9, passengers rushing about. It seemed as if the world had broken into little pieces, each one separating into its bit of existence, its little business tucked under the arm. They had plundered everything, and they had snatched me up in the process. All that was left was a plump, winking nymph and this fellow hacking away at my beard as if he were slashing through sugarcane, with a little water to lubricate it once in a while. My face smarted. The burning sensation was the only thing that held everything together. Were it not for the pain, perhaps the world would disappear like a flock of sea gulls leaving a bare rock under a searing sun? I was beginning to slip into something I felt around me, almost to see myself from the outside, but I was no longer the main object. It felt as if I could just as well be something else; it was simply a matter of where I looked: one can alight here, there, or somewhere else. One is the barber, the coolie, or the nymph. And I had the vague impression that this "one" could be all things at will. But that barber's dark face in front of me held me back. He had stolen my attention, like my own reflection in a mirror. Perhaps the other party, the man being shaved, had also stolen my attention for the last thirty years. Then it came back to me, the same exact scene, the same image, absolutely sharp and clear. Everything repeats itself; there are *moments* when life repeats itself. Maybe this is fate—these moments of repetition. I was entering a bathroom, flanked by two policemen, after three days of interrogation. I dipped my head into the washbasin, straightened up, and . . . there was *another* man in the mirror. A completely foreign face, and those eyes—especially the eyes—staring at me with a fixed, frantic intensity, as if I had suddenly passed into the mirror. "This is not me!" A kind of stupefaction, and then that denial. It was the eighteenth of November. I had just turned twenty. That's when everything began. That was the starting point, the first true minute of my existence, my first exit from the birth registry, as it were. We all wear a false head, but we are used to it, while here I had suddenly lost the habit. I would go about with a false head on my shoulders and everything was false: my name, my country, my papers. Ever since that day I have been searching everywhere for someone to replace the person I left behind in the mirror.

"That'll be thirty paisa."

But that burning sensation held everything together. When it stops burning, perhaps I, too, will take flight, leaving a little black barber and a billboard smile on a quay?

"Want to know something, boy?"

He bent over me, eyes aglitter; and "me" was no more than a hard little agglomeration set doggedly *against* him, against that barber, against something—everything.

"You are banging your head against a wall, a formidable wall . . ."

He exhaled loudly.

"No thicker than a sheet of rice paper!"

And he barked with laughter like a cavorting seal. I stared at him. There was not even any hate left in my heart; I was beyond it.

"If you stopped *thinking* about it for just one minute, son, it would be over. One single minute, and you tune out. The comedy is over! It's a screen, you see, a simple smoke screen. Ah, men are so crazy, son! They would be kings if only they stopped thinking."

"Sannyasi, I'm worn out."

"You're still wriggling quite a bit for someone who's worn out!"

"I'm at the end of my rope, sannyasi. Listen to me, I beg of you. My body is tired and my eyes are burning. Couldn't we go to the Himalayas, where everything is white?"

"Ah, the Himalayas!"

He threw back his head. I thought he was going to explode.

"When you come down from your Himalayas, my friend, it will be exactly the same, and you'll have to start all over again. Do you want to be a spiritual tourist, or what? You fool, don't you understand I'm offering you pure honey, eternal snow under all conditions?"

He extended a finger and pressed it firmly onto my solar plexus.

"The Himalayas are right *there*."

And it burned there, too.

"All right, let's go. It's time."

I plunged into a landscape of rails and sweltering platforms, interspersed with fabulous paddy fields aswarm with white birds. We headed toward the east, but north or south would have been the same; and I did not know if I was traveling outside, through a rocky desert strewn with mounds of huge boulders, or through the chaos of my own soul beneath the blaze of a white-hot fire. I went on and on, backward through time, more and more empty and old, burning like a carcass worn away by the sun. I traveled across a prehistory of the soul, far away, toward a primal wrinkle of pain under a great unmoving, ardent eye that felt nothing and wanted nothing. I descended through cataracts of rocks into yawning chasms, only to reemerge; I huddled in dark crevices, suffocating. I awaited God knows what breakdown, or wearing down, as if some iron-scaled monster would finally emerge from behind the hill and devour this whole nightmare, or else go belly up, sun-struck, and I with it.

One day, I reached the end of the journey. I did not have even the shadow of a refuge left; I was null and ravaged. In truth, we do need a carapace to shelter our smallness; and when the hurricane has blown our shelter away, we find ourselves null, unless we have the courage to take in everything. Perhaps fate will keep blowing away our shelters one after another, as well as our bodies and loves, until we are capable of loving everything and making our home in a body that does not die. That's what we are facing. Life hustles on; it races like mad in our little boxes of steel or silk plush, our homely nests. It presses on toward no station, or maybe toward the constellation Cygnus, at one hundred thousand miles per second, in a myth we call tomorrow. But tomorrow never happens; the train never arrives at Cygnus. It rushes on and on, pulling our boxloads of sorrow or silk, as well as our lofty thoughts, in its wake. It rushes on and on and nothing happens. No one for millions and millions of years to come, not a soul on the entire planet, not one living person! Or forever the same shadow recurring season after season, through autumns and winters, through Acropolises and Egyptian pyramids and dreary suburbs, through stone ages or concrete ages. Tomorrow is already here, and everything is beginning again. Yes, we are facing it. I have taken all the trains, and they turn in circles. Where, then, is my constellation Cygnus, my unmoving refuge?

O Traveler
Nothing happens
On this little planet
Except yourself
You are the sole event

So I closed my eyes; there was really nothing more to see. I settled my body down on a crate, crouching in the acrid smell of beedies,* alone and doubled over like a Peruvian mummy. Was I not dead anyway? What was it that kept beating in me? What? I stretched out my hands in that tomb of my body, groping for an answer, but I could not grasp anything except that burning question, that tiny wordless, senseless "what?"— a warm pressure against my walls. I had nothing, I was nothing, except a burning fire. And what else was there?

O brother, my twin in the depths of a tomb, what is it that makes a man live? What? One single question. I do not seek greatness or wealth, nothing stupendous, no apparitions or hallucinations or fabulous powers—just this: What is it that makes my heart beat? What is it that makes it possible for this to *be*? One little question no bigger than the glow of a firefly. I've asked so many questions in my life, and they are all the same. There is only one question in a man, a tiny cry inside that keeps asking "what?"—a pure "what"? It is all I have, all I can grasp in my night. It is my only possession, my only life, my blind, burning life, my life truer than life. Everything can be taken away, but that stays; everything can be added, but that is unmoved. Put it in a prison, a palace, a train, and it's all the same; bury it under gold, or mud, and it still shines,

* Small Indian cigars.

burning within. It is the cry of man—perhaps also the cry of the animal and the plant—a little flame within that burns everywhere, pervades everything, like a golden spark in the heart of things, a pure sound in the depths, filling everything, praying in everything, vibrating in the desert and in the stars, in sorrow and in joy. *That*, that everywhere, at the beginning and at the end, in the midst of everything: a unique life of a million fires.

I drew down the curtain of the world and cradled that fire like a bird in the hollow of my hands. And I didn't know what to do. Everything was so oppressive and dark in this body that perhaps it was nothing, and yet it was everything. Ah, what else is there! Outside, trains rumbled back and forth, people moved to and fro; it was like a living death. Inside, it was like a life yet to be born. And I stared at that nothing, that burning little nothing; it was imperceptible, but it was alive. It seemed to be located in the hollow of my chest. I clasped that bird-like warmth so tightly to my heart, perhaps it would live; I looked at it so intently, perhaps it would take wing and carry me away. And I spoke to my bird (or was it he who spoke?). It was a whisper, a prayer of no church, a lone voice that kept stammering, "I don't know, I don't know, but I feel; I don't see, I see nothing, but I feel, I feel, I feel." A tiny flame of something striving to live, with such a desperate need to live: "Oh, it *must* be, since I am so thirsty! It must, it *must*." It was almost painful in my chest. Where is it? Where is it? I've lived millions of years, knocked at all the doors. Where is vastness? Where is life, the great sun wherein I can plunge with wings outspread, and that would be IT at last? Ah, life is not alive! Life has yet to be. Indeed, what *is*? Days and weeks passing by, bodies walking by, bodies passing away, hearts feigning love, hour upon hour spent adorning, feeding, clothing one body. Where is the true minute, the boundless minute, simply for the joy of being? Where is life like the sweep of a sea gull above the waves? My whole heart was gathered in that pressure of flame, that wordless cry, and I pressed and pressed against those walls. I was like a compact mass, a suffocation, a coagulated lump of space, as if every wave in the sea and every cry of the sea gulls were concentrated there. And suddenly everything fell silent. There were no more prayers, no more words, no more feelings. A silence I had never known before. It was not an absence of noise, or even the fading of a spent prayer, or an appeasement of the heart. It was, curiously, a *substance* made of silence, a flow of solid silence, literally like a frost of silence descending upon me. Something that froze and wrapped everything in a soft, invisible snow: the thoughts, the heart, the stirrings of the body. It was both dense and transparent, crystalline like a frosty dawn at cockcrow. I was held there, within that mass of freshness, not certain what or who was held: *it* was held. It felt like a snowy diffusion through all the pores of my skin, a slow and gentle permeation, as if millions of little air bubbles were being instilled through all my body's cells, giving the body a sense of a subtle aeration, of dilation, of porousness. Then all that contained mass began to seep out through a thousand tiny holes in a sort of comfortable expansion, a releasing of countless little breaths in every direction. Meanwhile, what was I flowed out horizontally, the feeling of unfolding oneself, of spreading out in every direction—and "I" vanished. "I" had been the screen blocking the open space. The screen was gone and everything was flowing in—a sudden inhalation that continued flowing and flowing everywhere like the limpid coolness of the night's blue expanses. There were no more obstructions; I had poured forth through all the pores of my skin and lost myself in the sweet waters of the night. In them were a rumbling train, fleeting cities and villages, railway stations, voices hailing one another across quiet fields; but the sounds no longer came bumping against me—they rose from a great transparent night and vanished in the tall grass of my silence. Everything was still. So still there was not a breath of me or a trace of weight, not the least pebble of I anywhere. All went through me unhindered. I was far and I was near; I was in infinite points; I did not know where I began and where I ended. Crickets chirped inside me as in a great Asian rice field; and the train ran within, causing no movement whatever. Everything was bathed in a millennial quietude. The world moved in perfect immobility. Yet this was neither dissolution nor annihilation nor sleep. It was a living, teeming, alert immobility, as if innumerable eyes had opened at the ends of a million antennae, gazing steadily, free of judgment, feelings, or interpretation. *It* just gazed. At what? I don't know. The night had no boundary. A gaze embracing all, bearing all, self-contained, self-fulfilled; a bliss without object, content with being itself forever. And at times that perfect eye seemed to turn itself back on "me," immediately causing a slight local contraction, a minuscule discomfort; yet everything was so perfectly peaceful that discomfort was but an imperceptible wrinkle of being, a negligible image disappearing thousands of feet below—existent only within a boundless space, a blue depth encompassing that reflection of me.

It was still night—a nocturnal, almost vegetal bliss, like a fruit spread out in its own juice. Then something touched upon an invisible margin of uneasiness, creating a sense of limit, and I was instantly thrown back into the "I": the fire, the asphyxiation, the pain, the cry. The impossibility that pulls at us like doleful returning ghosts. Oh yes, we are returning, but it isn't from death! It was more stifling now than before. I had nabbed it; I could almost touch in my flesh that one misdeed, that seed of everything: of all evils, all sufferings, all revolts, all the aberrations that tear men apart—that one pain of being small, so very small and confined within a body. In vastness there cannot be even a ripple of suffering. That's what I had utterly caught hold of, or, rather, what had caught hold of me, clutching at my throat like a thief surprised in the night: the essential fault of not being in vastness. It was crushingly evident; it weighed on me like molten lead. For a second, I thought I would let go of everything, open my eyes and plunge back into my rocky desert and definitive smallness—tramp around with that sannyasi. That's when a cry rose in my being, so deep, so intense; I was before the wall of sorrows—the great ancient sorrow of being imprisoned without hope, as if I had been there thousands of times! Every route, every detour led there. There they were again, my brothers in misery, my fellow pilgrims of the night in expectation of God knows what, all gathered together within a cry. I had my back to the wall. This was the end of the road. I was before the Fact; there was nothing left to do! Then, simply, I had a second of abandon. I opened my hands and said yes. Yes, as one leaps into the fire. And I let myself disappear into it, body and soul and mind, without trying to retain anything from the past; there was nothing to retain, nothing of any value! I was only that fire. Nothing but pure fire.

And now that fire became like love. A pure love burning for nothing, for everything, just for the joy of burning. Everything was burned, consumed: past, present and future, evil, good, hope and despair. There was nothing to want, nothing to ask for, only to melt and disappear in that. There was nothing to need except to burn and burn and burn more and more. An abyss of sweetness. And it kept rising and rising, growing, filling my whole being with gold—an ardent pressure that vibrated and vibrated, overwhelming everything, invading everything, without my wishing or wanting anything. Oh, most of all I didn't want anything, not the shadow of a thing—just to burn and burn until nothing was left. Then I understood the marvel. It grew denser and soon felt like a tidal wave of power, an ascent of warm and solid force, stiffening my back, expanding my chest, tightening my throat. It was as if I were solidified. A pillar of fire. Then I heard the cracking of a vertebra in my neck.

And I went out.

Light, nothing but light! Space, the open air, lungsful of it. An immensity of light growing more transparent, more intense, azure blue, then silver blue, as it rose. No more me, no more I want, no more I yearn, no more I think or feel; it was all swept away, melted in its own soaring. And it kept rising and rising: a direct, imperturbable and effortless ascent in utter silence, a rocket of being within a white trail. It rose and rose all by itself, as if toward its own source, its matching density. It soared like an Arctic bird winging its way toward a great snowfield on high, with a sense of infinite liberation.

Then the ascent began to slow and I tilted into an horizontal plane, as if I had reached the end of my course, and everything became vast and wide and slow. This was another journey.

A vast blue expanse with a rhythm. A great eternal rhythm rising and falling like two wings over eternal hills, journeying on and on across steppes of soft light, across Labradors of plenitude; gliding endlessly through unperturbed ages, seas of calm vision, chance beatitudes like smiling gulfs. A slow, smooth flight through ermined centuries; a white, luminous migration amid a softness of eternity. And the one fabulous Harmony. A breath of harmony behind the chaos and the pain. A vast, serene respiration that makes the moons rise, as well as the breasts of men and the music of galaxies; that makes joy rise like a myriad golden bubbles, like a fizzing of recognition everywhere; that falls and falls interminably through rapids of mute meditation, chasms of sudden adoration, soft glades of love for no rhyme or reason, simply because it loves and loves uncontrollably. And the peace of being forever, the unshakable Strength, the powerful blue flow of silence through great canyons of eternity. I opened my wings, my heart, my body, the entire fortress. I was carried forever, within the great immobile Rhythm that carries the worlds. I looked, and it was full; it was *the* Fullness. A golden smile beneath the closed eyes of the world.

Then my body fell asleep.

I had a faint impression someone was calling me. I reassembled all the threads of my being, gathering them laboriously, pulling them in as if from a far-off land. A silvery flame passed through the silence, a quivering streak of color. I drew that light toward me and it produced a faint rhythm, like a fragment of some distant song, and simultaneously I saw the image of a brother. Which brother? I couldn't say. But he was evidently a brother. I drew the light closer, and that slight rhythm formed words:

> *O Brother*
> *What are you waiting for?*
> *It is time*
> *And life passes in vain*

Again and again: What are you waiting for? What are you waiting for? A poignant little voice at the edge of the world. I came down a few more steps toward my body, and the further down I came, the more clear and logical it became. The whole range of the descent appeared visibly. First, there was light— the immense Light—then the great Rhythm *created* by the light, then forms, sounds, increasingly sharp and clashing rhythms, increasingly somber hues. And I clearly saw those forms, words, and sounds as condensations of colored light. I had touched the wellspring of true language, perhaps of music. At that moment I understood the whole creative picture; I knew the source of that which sometimes came to me as distant music or, if I strained to hear, as words. In a flash of joy (because that light caused joy as well; it was the joy-light) I saw the whole of life as the art of condensing luminous vibrations that were the cause of events as well as the cause of music or architecture. And all the way down, suffering was simply the absence of light, absence of rhythm, absence of everything. The farther down I went, the harder, more opaque and compartmentalized it became. No more rhythm. Only

noise, chaos, fragmentation—a buzzing gray-black atomiza-
tion. The machine was back in full swing. And so was the
suffocation. Back to the cavern again. So I called the silence.
It descended upon me massively: a deep-blue invasion that
froze the swarm of thinking flies, a litmus dye that immediately
turned everything blue. Just a drop of *that*, and all became a
motionless azure. Peace again. Aquamarine freshness.
The powerful tranquility of the True.
I remained there between two worlds. The train seemed to
pass slowly over a bridge, with a very supple rhythm. Someone
shook me by the shoulder. I opened my eyes; we were entering
a station.

And entering the onslaught: the shouts, the rush, the crowd,
the grating rails, the grating lives. An enormous iron-clad
artifice in which one had to run from one compartment to
another before the automatic doors snap shut. And the next
compartment was exactly the same as the preceding one—a
supermechanism scientifically designed to measure the intelligence quotient of rats. But in this case intelligence didn't
mean vision; it just meant gnawing faster and faster. I watched
that bizarre display and took a step forward, only to realize I
felt so light, so unencumbered, as if I had long been weighed
down by endless baggage and suddenly, pfft, it was all gone!
No more baggage! My own inner density was no longer the
same. I jumped onto the platform in three skipping steps. I
heard a burst of laughter. He stood there watching me, staff in
hand, straight as an arrow. Suddenly a great joy came over me,
a crystalline, overpowering joy. I took his arm; my heart
swelled. I wanted to embrace him, tell him. . . . I gazed at that
tall orange-clad, triumphant Asian who dominated life with
his insolent smile and shouldered our windmills at one stroke,
then gazed at the crowd, and then at that other man over there,
on a platform, before a little dark barber, with his false head
screwed on his shoulders, and I too felt like bursting into
laughter at the world's agony, the world's farce, this whole

theatre of falsehood, with each being clinging to his sordid little business, his own little baggage, all curled up in a ball—the great misery of men locked in a box. And in an incredible, absolutely luminous and regal flash, I saw them all rushing from one room to another, from one corner to another, one idea or feeling to another, gnawing, gnawing. Not a single true appearance! A formidable fabrication. Not a single minute of being. There was not a single true minute in the world; the only true minute is when one opens the door and lets go of the corpse.

"Sannyasi—"

He turned his back to me.

Then he changed his mind, searched his belt, withdrew a handful of grain.

"Here, eat this."

"You know, I—"

"Yes, I know. But don't choke on it. You've barely taken half of the first step."

And that night, crouched in a warehouse reeking of fish paste, I heard divine music. They will say I am crazy or hallucinating, but I now know the world is deep and full of marvels, and behind our vain racket lies a vast kingdom of singing light. Like barbarians of old, we may be standing on the brink of incredibly crowded seas. Oh, I've heard sublime music in my life, and, for me, some of Beethoven's notes soared higher than many cathedrals, but that night it was as if I were hearing for the first time ever. In truth, until that day I had heard only muffled sounds, a *translation* of music. But this was no translation; it was no longer the expression of something else in the background that one perceives as divine; it was not even "hearing" music. I was not "listening" to music from the outside; I was *in* the music as one is in the ocean or under a waterfall. Music encompassed everything, gushing about me from everywhere. And blue—everything was blue, pure, cerulean blue, with each bit of space, each particle of blue, radiating its own music. It was a singing blue cataract, an immensity of singing light. And it was not disjointed, not cut in fragmentary notes forming a melody; it was a musical plenitude, one total Sound encompassing every possible sound and every chord in harmony! Such harmony that it struck everything it touched with absoluteness: one drop of that and everything became full, pure, beautiful, true—*it*, absolutely it, concrete divinity. A unique golden vibration reverberating through space, an immense eruption, a plenitude of pure music that filled the lungs as if one drank at the very infinity of the sky, as if music were nothing but space, nothing but the sound of infinity, and one flowed and flowed inexhaustibly in that singing blueness. And then joy. Or perhaps *primarily* joy. An abundance, an effusion of being that *created* the music—created all light and space, as well as the entire world of things—a unique substance of joy singing its own self, the grandiose outpouring of a single note produced by thousands upon thousands of violins rising to a crescendo, or by thousands upon thousands of voices swelling endlessly upon great azure wings, or by the lone pure call of a flute bursting forth from the eternal, lost in the eternal, leaving just that quivering little note upon the blue waters of the world.

That's how it was.

When I awoke the next morning, I was resting against a sack, my head in my hands, repeating in a daze: "It cannot be, it cannot be."

But it was.

I got up and wandered along the quays.

Then I looked around me. The sannyasi was gone.

ψ

SECOND CYCLE

The Journey
in the Great
Expanse

5
a white island

I had wandered in those train stations for so long that I did not dare leave them. It would have been like leaving a ship to set foot on an unknown land. From the sheltering shadow of a margosa tree, I was watching the little horsecarts jingle down the sandy road and disappear into a palm grove. I did not know where I was, but it felt delightful to be there without knowing, simply clinging to the thread of that little vibration within that filled me with wonder and a sense of absolute security. It had been there since yesterday, something vibrating softly within me, around me, like a current or gentle flow that linked me to that great expanse of blue silence, so slight I was afraid of losing it, almost afraid of moving; but all I had to do was to remain perfectly still for a moment and recall it, and there it was—it was always there! *That* was the real wonder—it did not go away, did not disappear like so many other homelands that vanish a day or a minute later. I had only to pull gently on the thread, draw a light breath within, and the vast blue country flowed limpidly.

I was at home everywhere.

It was just a matter of recalling it.

And I felt that no matter where I went or what I did, I would be carried along, as if enveloped in a great azure mantle—safe.

"Oh, there you are!"

A child with magnificent black eyes, about eleven years old, stood in front of me, eyeing me as avidly as if I were a sweetshop window. We smiled at each other. I felt comfortable; I did not sense any walls.

"Do you want me to guide you?"

I did not have a single paisa.

"Do you want to see your brother first or the temple?"

"My brother?"

He took my hand with authority, and we set out. The air smelled of salt, and life hopped along like a little chipmunk. All was simple, limpid. I had done so many strange things with that sannyasi that I no longer tried to understand anything; and, whenever I tried, everything vanished, scuttled back into the hole like a small forest animal. It seemed as if life were ruled by another law, a graceful law that vanished from sight the moment one stared at it. It was like a slight, almost amused breath that pushed one here or there, compelling this or that gesture, this step, that detour, the crossing of that path, without any reason whatever—and it was always the right thing to do. A minutely right law. And the minute one took notice of it, it slipped through one's fingers, as if thought drove it away automatically. And sometimes one stopped short in the middle of a railway station, or a gesture, struck with wonder, as if one had suddenly caught a multitude of little winks everywhere.

"You've come for the temple?"

"The temple? No."

He looked surprised.

"Everyone comes here for the temple. Your brother visits there, too. He is handsome, your brother!"

"Aah."

"He's a prince."

"What about you, little frog? Who are you?"
He drew himself up to his full height.
"I am Bala-Chandra, son of Bhaskar-Nath, the greatest sculptor in the country."
"Aah."
"My father's a hero," he added in a definitive tone of voice.
"And who are you?"
I was startled.
"You don't want to tell me your name?"
I had to pull at a shadow somewhere behind me. It felt as dark as a lie.
"My name is Nil."
"And what does it mean?"
"Well—"
What indeed? A name—one should have a name! A true name, something that tells what you are, as a bird tells what it is by its cry. And at that moment I realized the sannyasi had never asked my name.
"It means nothing."
"Oh, really? Nothing at all?"
He seemed very impressed.
"Mine means 'Little Moon.' They also call me Balu. Look!"
Open-mouthed, I gazed at an extraordinary landscape. I had often seen beauty in the forests of Brazil, in Rio, and on the banks of the Loire, but this was not just "beautiful"; it was like suddenly discovering "my" country as one discovers the face of a beloved.
Dunes, nothing but dunes of white sand as far as the eye could see, spread there like Arctic birds against a dazzling sky; and palms, great clusters of green and golden palms, their narrow black trunks half submerged in sand. I bent down, letting that sand run through my fingers. It was soft, cool, smooth, flowing; and the dunes flowed too, sweeping down toward the village like a giant white tide. And in the distance

stood the tall purple towers of the temple, looming over the
coconut grove and the white-terraced houses.

"It's really something, eh?"

Balu looked at me with perfect comprehension.

"It's over there at the end of the street. You can't get lost,
there are only two streets: the street of the railway station and
the street of the temple."

The silvery tinkle of horsecarts filled the air. The street was
almost all white, its rough flagstones layered with sand. It was
yesterday or today, a very long time ago; it was this life or
another; I was Nil, or who knows who. We made our way
through the pungent aroma of jasmine garlands and spices,
passing little street stalls, stray goats, and pink pottery. It was
in this country or another, beneath the arched flight of great
ernes, and I strolled along toward some unknown story or fate,
led by the warm hand of a child. Was it actually another fate
or still the same, centuries later? It was as if setting out on a
new life; everything felt light and vast, as soft as the dunes,
and I was within a great tranquil rhythm. Perhaps I was Nil,
but I did not really have a true name, or not yet. I had lost it
on the way. I had just returned from the long journey.

"You like pistachios?"

He pulled me by the arm. I reentered the small shadow.

"Oh! Where are we, Balu?"

"In the street, of course. Where do you think?"

He glanced at me suspiciously. Actually, it made no difference. It could have been the North or South, before or after
Christ. I felt carried along, guided, each footstep falling exactly
as it should, on this flagstone and not another. It was micro-
scopically precise, and all-embracing at the same time. At that
moment, I felt that in any other village or city in the world, and
maybe in any other time of history, I would have taken the
same exact footstep, made the same gesture, in the very same
way, at the same instant—only the name changes! As well as
small pink and green villages on parallels of latitude in India

ink. Life does not begin where we think. It extends in every direction. We are constantly walking in another geography. And from time to time the two coincide. Then there is perfect exactness: the inner gradation meets the outer, and each footstep is thousands of years old and we walk in a great rite. "Here we are."

A dilapidated house, the last on a little street lined with balconies. Beyond it lay nothing but a trail of ocher sand leading to a forest of thornbushes. Balu leaped up three steps. I found myself in the smoke-filled inner courtyard of a hostel bursting with pilgrims, piles of clothing, kitchen utensils, swarms of children and insatiable goats feasting on bits of laundry hanging between blackened pillars—an exotic *cour des miracles*, yet filled with the smell of incense. Balu rushed up to the second floor. It was deserted. We were in a long corridor lined on either side with tiny monklike cells and ending abruptly over the thornbushes like the rear carriage of a train. All the cells were empty. I walked down the corridor. In the last cell, feet straight up in the air, head on the floor, a white man was performing the *sirasana*, with an alarm clock near his head. Balu rushed forward.

"He's come! Your brother, Nil, is here!"

The stranger collapsed his body to the ground and looked up at me with astonishment. He had a strange red triangle between his eyebrows, straw-color hair, and the physique of a sailor. He looked Scandinavian. For a second he examined my rags, then put his hand on my shoulder and embraced me.

"Sit down, brother, and welcome."

The warmth of his tone left me dumbfounded. He pushed a mat toward me. Balu ogled him.

"Sit down. You have nothing to fear. My name is Bjorn. I'm glad you have come."

The cell was bare, except for a metal footlocker and some graffiti on the walls.

"He's called 'Nothing,' you know—Nothing-At-All!"

"You must be tired, hungry. Balu, go down to *Meenakshi's* and get some *dosais*, coffee, and pistachios for yourself."

The child was reluctant to leave Bjorn.

"Go on, run along!"

My mind was a blank. I seemed to have lost the power of speech.

"I'm so happy to see you, brother! God sent you."

"—"

"You don't have to say anything. You're my brother; Balu said so. Wait—"

He rummaged through his footlocker and pulled out a white *dhoti* and a fine linen scarf. I was struck dumb.

"Balu is never wrong. I can tell you're not a tourist, of course, so—It's rare to meet someone from the West here."

He seemed almost apologetic.

"Oh, I'm so lucky, brother! Listen, you'll find the well downstairs. And you need a towel and some soap."

He rummaged again through his footlocker.

"So you've fled Europe, eh? Oh, brother, men do not know how to love! It's so good to love. Go, but watch out for the monkeys. They steal everything. Yesterday they guzzled up my toothpaste."

He put his hand on my shoulder.

"I have been waiting for my brother for three years; can you imagine? Three whole years. And it's you who have come. Fate is strange indeed. I'll tell you all about it when you come back. We're going to discover lots of things together."

I mechanically set off for the well. I was in a daze, far, far removed from all that sentimental clatter, without any reaction whatever, as unresponsive as a stone. And all of Bjorn's vibrations pursued me, quivering and colliding in my head. I could almost measure their intensity and frequency. They were dark red, tightly knit, moving in small hasty waves, and extremely disturbing. I had the urge to take off right away—the sun and the blue expanse over my head. And no more words.

But then I felt bad. I emptied a bucket of water over my head and swept Bjorn away. And that's when I realized I had become another person. As transparent as crystal. Not cold, for it was very soft, but without personal reaction. There was an acute sense of perception, an extraordinarily precise vision of everything, but not a trace of feeling or reaction. An accurate and encompassing gaze. And I realized that I had lived for months— or was it years?—in a realm devoid of humans, while in the middle of crowds, bustling train stations, yet thousands of miles away from it all! It's as if I had to relearn life from another perspective. Once again I pulled on the thread of my little vibration. It was there, ever there, so soft and limpid, without any lapse, as fresh as a mountain spring. I was overwhelmed. An extraordinary feeling of gratitude swept over me, right there at the edge of that well, because *that* existed, because *that* was—that inexpressible sweetness, that secret sense of royalty, and free, so free, thousands of miles removed from the world's clamor and confusion, from separateness and confinement in one body. Oh, who will understand the marvel of that sense of royalty in the midst of everything? One is a prisoner in a skin, and all it takes is one second of recall to soar above it all, a laughing observer.

I doused myself with water, and all the waters in the world could not have felt as sweet as that freshness. As I gathered my rags, the sannyasi's knife clattered to the ground. For an instant I felt the urge to toss it into the well—I can still see myself with my arm in mid-air—but then, inexplicably, I tucked it into my belt and headed back to Bjorn.

He was seated cross-legged at the end of the corridor, wrapped in a white piece of cloth, like a prince. A curious prince for sure, with that red mark between his eyebrows—a bit theatrical.

Nevertheless, I liked him.

"You see, this is my lookout post."

The corridor opened out on an acacia grove. There were no dunes or palms, just the thornbushes leaning over the sand like Chinese umbrellas, the occasional pale green foliage of a large tamarind tree or the fretted shadow of a banyan, and in the distance, a solitary rock rising up at the edge of the sands like the colossus of Memnon.

"That's Kali's Rock."

"But where are we?"

"This is the north of the village."

"But in which country?"

"Didn't you see the signpost at the entrance to the bridge?"

"The bridge—"

"But where have you been? Didn't you cross a bridge to get to the island?—2,054 meters, 6,739 feet—it's written on the sign. Were you asleep, or what? A one-way bridge, before entering the White Island."

"An island—"

"Oh, boy!"

"Can one see the sea?"

"Okay, calm down. First, eat, then I'll show you around."

He spread several *dosais* on a banana leaf in front of us.

"My island is very beautiful, you'll see. Every morning when I arise, I come here and prostrate myself before the beauty of the world."

I looked at Bjorn with some surprise.

"Now then, who brought you here?"

"A sannyasi."

"Oh."

He frowned.

"I don't like sannyasis."

"Really? What have they done to you?"

"Nothing, precisely. They've abandoned everything. They don't possess the secret of the beautiful world."

I felt a bit miffed.

"What about you? Do you possess the secret, with your feet in the air?"

"Oh, that's nothing, just exercises to keep fit. But I tell you, there's something else! My island is a treasure island."

Bjorn clasped my arm. He seemed all excited.

"But first, tell me what you are looking for."

"Me? I'm not sure."

"Well, I'm looking for power. Oh, not for myself, you understand, but for my brothers—the power to effect a change, to change the world. In a sense, I feel bad; we've fled, we are deserters."

"Deserters?"

"I feel bad to be here while they are so miserable, living like madmen. But I am on the right track, no doubt about it. My island is a fabulous island."

He tossed back his scarf, his blue eyes bright as a child's.

"You see, brother, they eat, sleep—and they are miserable. They have central heating, libraries full of books—and they are miserable. They don't know about the Adventure. They don't know the secret of life."

Bjorn looked at me intently.

"What are you seeking?"

"But I don't know, Bjorn! It's simple. It's there. It flows."

"You've run away from them, haven't you? But I love them. Listen, brother, we are going to work together and find the secret. I am going to introduce you to Guruji."

He rested his gaze on Kali's Rock, and his words came out slowly, forcefully, as if he were seeing something.

"You've come here today, and that has a meaning, a reason, no? What is the meaning, the sense of this encounter, thousands of miles from our homelands, like two exiles?"

"But I am not an exile!"

"If you are not among them, breathing the air they breathe, then what does it mean? That's what I am asking. And that's what I have been asking for three years. And things are getting more and more stifling. Oh, Nil, it's as if we were approaching the end of a world, or the beginning of a new one. Never has the earth been so shackled, and never have they spoken more loudly about liberty. This is the age of gnomes, the reign of antilife, antiliberty, antifraternity; it is the time of Falsehood, *Kali-Yuga*, the Dark Age."

A crow began cawing down by the well. I felt myself drifting into another dimension. But Bjorn would not let go.

"And I have looked everywhere: in Europe, from Oslo to Paris, from Africa to the Himalayas and all the way to Tibet. I have been a nihilist, a Buddhist, expelled from the navy as a saboteur. It's as if every door had been closed behind us to force us to find the secret. What is remaining, tell me? Let's take stock. There are no more Americas to discover, no more adventure—it's all business; revolutions are staged, and the time of conquests is over. True, they may go to the moon, but they will take their Falsehood with them. They will take their own selves everywhere they go and will be miserable all the way to the seventh galaxy. So where is the door, the way out, our breathing space? Our countries send us to the barracks and our churches promise us heaven; as for the others, their mechanized future looks like an endless weekend at Disney World. They will not leave even a single pyramid standing; all they will leave behind is a pile of rust."

Bjorn rose to his feet. He was as if enveloped in a red haze.

"Let me show you something."

He bounded into his cell and came back waving a letter.

"It's from my brother Erik, dated a week ago. Listen, he was also searching and then he quit. We roamed the world together, and he ended up in the Sahara desert; that's all he could find. Now he's drilling for oil in Ouargla. I'll read it to you."

Ouargla, September
c/o S.A.M.E.G.A.
P.O. Box 77
(Oases District)

1 pipe, 2 pipes, 3 pipes, 4 pipes . . .
Whether there is oil or not,
it's all the same to me.
Yet this is out of place,
since I am "in the oil business."
I may yet get used to these pipes, gears and
pulleys, but at what price, for God's sake?
Your brother
Erik

Bjorn was silent for a while. I could read his brother's suffering on his face. It was closed, contracted, suddenly clouded—almost like a falsehood. Suffering is a falsehood.

"Nil, what can we *do* for our brothers? One must have the *power to do* something, you understand. Loving isn't enough."

He turned his stare toward me. I was totally overwhelmed by the avalanche, no longer capable of seeing anything clearly. He had completely disrupted the atmosphere.

"Can't you say something?"

Now he was angry. With Bjorn, everything could change into hatred at a moment's notice—the other side of the coin. Those dosais were like pieces of lead in my stomach. I felt slightly nauseous, and my body shuddered as if I had also swallowed Bjorn's anger and Erik's gloom. I was like a sieve through which everything entered.

"Yeah, I know, the sannyasis have found the trick: They renounce everything and scuttle into the higher realms. It's quite convenient."

"Listen, Bjorn, you don't know what you are talking about. Can one renounce a prison? All one can do is get out of it. And

I can assure you that the air is remarkably light and pure the minute one gets out of the box."

"That's my whole point. One gets out, and then one can no longer do anything to help life."

I closed my eyes. I felt as if I were being battered by that tide of little red waves.

"Nil, are you listening? Where are you? Have I tired you?"

He grasped my hands. There was the real Bjorn again, affectionate, fraternal.

The atmosphere began to loosen; one could breathe freely again. And suddenly I understood. How could humans possibly see anything in the chaos of their minds? They strive to know, to understand the cause, the course of events, the line of action, while every thought is like a pebble in a pond—making waves and blurring the vision.

"There is a secret, Nil."

Bjorn drew himself up and I was struck by his handsomeness. A tiny silvery flame began to flicker in the redness, which grew paler, almost pink, and Bjorn's voice was no longer just noise.

"You know, Nil, for the last three years I haven't stopped studying history, our history; and the more I study it, the more it seems completely different from the way it is usually looked upon, namely, as a succession of advances, of breakthroughs enhancing one another, with man becoming increasingly knowledgeable and intelligent, until he finally knows everything. But that's not how it is."

At that instant, a tiny spark glowed as bright as a diamond.

"It's more like a succession of things being exhausted, as if each age opened one door, explored one area, to end up in an impasse—a succession of dead-end achievements. Then everything collapses and we begin again along another line. There has been spiritual knowledge in India, occult knowledge in Egypt, Greek knowledge, scientific knowledge, but it would be a fallacy to think that our age is more knowledgeable than the others! It isn't closer to the goal; it has just perfected *one* line, one way of looking at things. Its sole merit is that we may now have exhausted all the doors and this is the last one on the list."

I looked at Bjorn framed against that breach of light, and he was as handsome as a Viking conqueror who had returned to embark on some new adventure. And I saw myself next to him, smaller, but of a different color, it seemed. I observed all that, heard Bjorn, but I was not entirely there. It's as if I were held somewhere else, far, far away, and I had to cross a vast expanse of softness to meet Bjorn, such a great bluish, enchanted range that I felt like drifting in it, eyes closed, and flowing with that noteless, voyaging music. And my body—I am not even sure I was inside my body; rather, the body was inside me, along with Bjorn. I only hearkened to the inflection of his voice, which rose in silvery whorls marked by an occasional spark of light. That little flame is what I followed, as if it alone gave meaning to the words, sustaining and encompassing them, and creating the right music—the words themselves were almost extraneous; I knew instantly what he had said.

"So this is the time for invention. The moment we touch that secret, all the lines will meet and we will be at the heart of *the* Matter."

He took me by the arm.

"You're gone again."

"No, I'm not!"

"We don't have the right to go, do you hear!? Our only excuse for being here in a body is to find that."

So again I settled for words. It was an instant lessening, a drop of intensity.

"Perhaps you're right, Bjorn, but when one is in a certain state, everything seems so simple."

"To you, perhaps."

"But it's a state of truth, one that sees the truth within!"

"What's the use of your state of truth if it can *do* nothing for the world?"

"Oh, Bjorn, you're so impatient."

"Do you see this triangle?"

He placed his finger between his eyebrows.

"That's the tantric triangle, the point turned downward, toward matter. No running away upstairs—a descent of Power into life and matter. We are here to discover something, you see, to invent—to invent something that neither science nor religion has found. We are before the final door, at zero hour. We are a new breed of adventurers!"

He fixed me with his blue gaze.

"We have sought new continents, oil wells, laws, machines and more machines; we've exhausted everything. We are sitting on a gold mine and we don't know it! Power is within, Nil; the adventure is within. Our machines are not a sign of our progress but of our impotence. We stand at the threshold of a world that will use inner vision as a source of creation; we are the pioneers of the power of the soul."

He hesitated an instant.

"Which is not without danger, however."

"Bjorn!"

A sound of running feet in the corridor.

"Guruji wants you."

He leaped to his feet. His eyes fell on me and I felt immediately uneasy: he looked like a haunted man.

"There's money in the red wallet inside the footlocker. If I'm delayed, go get something to eat at Meenakshi Lodge."

He wrapped his scarf about him. This was no longer Prince Bjorn, but someone else.

"I'll explain later. He's my Master, a man of great powers. He's the one who holds the key. We are going to find the secret together."

And he was gone.

***

I remained for a moment looking out at the acacia trees, the wind-swept sand, the mauve shadow around the well. The wave had subsided with Bjorn's departure; except for the lone cry of a crow, everything was as peaceful as at the beginning of the world, and even that cry was part of the silence. Humans are the ones who make noise, even when they are silent! Suddenly the exhaustion of having listened to Bjorn fell upon me: I felt wrinkles everywhere, thousands of tiny wrinkles pulling at my face, contracting my temples, and that minute and so artificial tremor fluttering in my head—the din of artificial things. A mask. I had entered a mask and all life was a mask, utterly lacking truth, even in suffering. In my half an hour with Bjorn, there had been *one* true second, when that tiny white spark had flared up. The rest? Noise, supposedly aimed at understanding one another. Yes, they talk of their suffering, their hopes, their revolts, but they are not even as real as an animal crying out in thirst or in pain; it's just noise tacked onto something that is beyond suffering, personal needs, and sorrows—a bedrock of tranquil reality, so tranquil and so close, like a well of tenderness for every misery in the world. One bends down a little, lays one's forehead there, and everything becomes refreshed, unwrinkled forever. Yet nobody wants it! How is that possible? I looked at Bjorn, Erik, and all my fellow human beings, those strange, artificial creatures who could no longer even claim the qualities of the animal, who built steel towers and steel wings but could not even fly; who could not hear and could not see anything, except with antennas and a helmet; who toiled and suffered in an attempt to duplicate the simple miracle of prehuman ages. They sang and sculpted and poeticized to express the misery of their lives, their powerlessness behind these false powers, or something behind that they so much yearned to grasp; and once they had grasped it, that was it. No more man, no more world—nothing! One soared to heaven and forgot everything. Was the purpose of becoming a man ultimately to forget about man and his artificialities and to return to the peace of unthinking things, to the tranquil vastness devoid of an "I" when the "I" is everywhere and nowhere?

a drop of blue water
a sea lost in its million crystal drops

O apprentice
Be patient
Nothing is lost
But your foolishness

I closed my eyes. Instantly everything dissolved, turned blue. Words, questions, sorrows were merely calcifications, wrinkles of an "I" trying to lock immensity into a cage, and suffering at his inability to do it. The "I" lets go, and everything is filled with infinity. Everything becomes smooth, meaningful, rippleless. Where is suffering, where is evil? Where is the question? There are no more ripples! Things *are*, and they are perfectly. And all is the *same*, only supple, vast, rhythmical—not harsh and broken up by an "I"-shutter that makes bumps and hollows and time divisions, and pain because everything is broken up. I sank there, melted into that smile. I don't know if it was due to Bjorn's shadow or to some hidden fragment of "I," but I seemed to feel a kind of limit within that immensity, a sudden sense of deficiency. It felt full, as full as a jar could be, but it was still a jar, something with an end point. And there, too, I touched upon an invisible margin of uneasiness.
Something remained to be torn down.

ψ

6
and a blue peacock

I opened my eyes.

Balu sat before me, as good as gold, his large black eyes fixing me.

"Where is he?"

"Who?"

"Bjorn, of course!"

I was startled by the passion in his voice.

"Bjorn? Well, he's with Guruji."

Balu puckered up his nose. He did not seem at all happy.

"What is it, Little Moon? What's wrong?"

He puckered up his nose again.

"I don't like it."

"Oh? And why don't you like it?"

"Because."

I could get nothing more out of him.

"Then come and show me the sea."

He took my hand.

The air reverberated with the silvery jingle of horse carts, the calls of the jasmine vendors, the distant music of bells and conches at the temple. Women were busy fetching water from the well; life flowed like a fountain. I walked down the main street barefoot and clad in white, light as air, and without memory.

"It's the full moon; the birds will soon be here."

"The birds?"

"Yes, many, over on the lagoon. Say, what are wild geese like?"

"Wild geese?"

"And snow, and herds of reindeer? Please tell me."

My eyes misted. The street was beginning to drift.

"Herds of reindeer?"

"And the lake, and the prince who turns into a swan, which becomes pink, and then he loses his color when the hunters shoot him?"

"Oh, that!"

The flagstones had become like a snowfield. We were in Lapland, standing at the edge of a frozen lake.

"You don't know how the prince turns into a swan?"

"Yes, it's because he falls in love with the swan queen."

"That's it, the swan queen."

His eyes widened.

"Yes, he loved her so much that he turned into a swan, and they flew and flew far away together."

"They went to Mount Kailas?"

"Yes, and the more he flew, the rosier he became."

"Oh! I understand!"

I do not know what he understood, but the world was like a smile.

"But then he lost his color. How come?"

"Well, it's because he looked behind him, and each time that made a little gray spot."

"No, that's not what Bjorn said."

"What did he say?"

I will never know what Bjorn said. Balu skipped sideways, looking up into the air.

"She's like Batcha."

"Batcha?"

"The swan queen."

"Ah! Why?"

But there was no answer. He kicked at a pebble, lost in his dreams. We were walking hand-in-hand toward a high tower in the distance. We had always known each other and everything flowed in a vast rhythm: the village and the jasmine, the echo of bronze gongs in columned halls, and the bird-thronged return of the new moon.

"Do you have brothers and sisters?"

"Oh, *lots!*"

His eyes brightened.

"How many?"

"*Lots*," he repeated with conviction. "But none like Batcha."

"Oh?"

"Yes, she's the queen."

He hesitated for a moment. Then he stopped abruptly, as if struck by something, staring at the tower of the temple.

"She's like Bjorn; they are going to die."

"What! What are you saying?"

His eyes widened. He dropped my hand and skipped off down the street.

"Balu, listen—"

He did not hear. He had already forgotten everything. No, that could not be. Bjorn would not die. It was ridiculous! I pulled myself together, chased away that lie! But it clung to me, touching a deep chord in me; something had been touched deep down, awakened. A pall fell over the entire street. And, suddenly, in that street that had been so clear and luminous I saw myself running and running, chased by a crowd, without any rhyme or reason. Just a vibration. A nasty little vibration that contained a world of anguish—whether a past or future world I do not know. The old Menace suddenly emerging like a reptile from its lair—Fate. The light, the immensity were gone; there was an instant sense of diminution, of a bleak pitfall, a universal decomposition: "I" as a disease. An abrupt fall, a clouding-over. I had no idea why. It was not the usual little "I" that I faced; it was a far more essential, deeper, more obdurate "I," that seemed directly linked to pain. An old memory resurging from the depths. This was it; I was face to face with *the* Fact. This was the last wall to tear down, or the first. Bjorn's words were coming back to me: "One must have the power to do something for our brothers, you understand." Indeed, what can one do? What is the lever of power? What can one do to heal this? Love?

At the same time, from far away, as if from the depths of a primal memory as ancient as that Menace weighing upon us, perhaps as ancient as our birth to this world, I seemed to recall a Joy—like the light of that shadow, wedded to it, one with it—a Joy endowed with *power*, a triumphant, mighty Joy sweeping everything away, dissolving everything, wiping out everything in a smile. Oh, not the joy above, which I possess and have possessed forever, as my inalienable right, but the joy *here*. That's what needs to be found! Up above, my joy looks at the worlds and smiles; it's my ineffable sweetness, my unvarying tenderness, like an immortal brother attending to this body, and all bodies, and smiling in a light of *absolute* comprehension. But here below, it does not hold. A mere breath cancels it, a single vibration ruins it. *Here* is where it needs to be found!

The sannyasi's image flashed before me. Despite his haughty laughter, he did not know joy either.

Then I wiped everything out of my mind.

"Hey, Balu, which way to the sea?"

He looked at me with complete surprise, then drew himself up proudly.

"Do you see the western tower? Well, you go past the eastern tower. You'll see, it's terrific."

I took his little brown hand in mine, and we merged into the crowd of pilgrims.

"And the tower is so high, baba! All the gods are there, and milk has been poured on their heads!"

That tower was truly incredible. It looked like a huge truncated pyramid, an Egyptian pylon gone amok. It was a deluge of idols and granite, an avalanche of gods and apsaras, of hermits and naked female dancers and emaciated pilgrims, all soaring skyward with the pigeons, ernes, and monkeys—grotesque, divine, in prayer, in pain, in laughter—exactly as the very multitude of the earth. And then the emptiness of the blue sky. The air smelled of jasmine, moist sand, the sweaty crowd. It was yesterday or today, amid the same interminable crowd, soon frozen in eternity, that haggled over baubles of mother-of-pearl or straw and perhaps blew into a conch.

Then the blue of the sky again. And everything begins all over: one pipe, two pipes, three pipes—

"This way."

We always begin again. What really changes under the sun? Where is the new, the truly different?

"Come, I'll show you."

He pulled me into a side alley. And there stood the full mass of the fortress, the enormous thousand-foot square of purple walls emerging from the sands.

"Fantastic, no? It's the biggest in the country. And so old!"

He searched for fitting words, shook his head, as if even the mention of a grandfather would not suffice.

"And it's sacred from top to bottom."

Then, emphatically:

"And I *love* Bjorn."

And that was that.

We walked down the little white street amid the ringing of conches and gongs. The air shimmered like mother-of-pearl. The little street stalls had given way to one-story houses in lime-coated granite. Children could be heard chanting in a school.

Here and there, a burst of green palms brightened the terraces.

Little by little I was overcome by a curious impression, almost an emotion. Was it the result of those high walls or the sand carpeting the street? Yet it was subtler than that, having to do with something in the air, a kind of familiar frequency, almost a scent, as in Thebes. So I closed my eyes. With that warm little hand still in mine, I searched, pushing against that wall of memory, groping my way through an obscure fragrance alive with presences; it was right there on the other side. I could feel it, bring back the smell of it. There was a very special quality to that emotion, one I had known several times before, in different circumstances and countries: all at once, without reason, something is aroused and begins to vibrate within, a quiver of recognition—before a human being, a wall, a sky, or anything at all—truly like having a secret at one's fingertips, something one is about to grasp, yet is beyond one's grasp; something intimate, more intimate than all the gazes and places in the world—a memory, a shock whose only reminder is the emotion, or fragrance, that came with it, like the face of a beloved whose features have faded, leaving that unique impression, or like the chant in the distance whose words were mingled, yet full of a peculiar presence. How strange that the more I seek the new, the more I am drawn into the past, as if an old enigma had to be resolved before gaining access to the new life.

"Appa! Appa!"

Balu dashed through a doorway, shouting at the top of his lungs.

"Appa, here's Bjorn's brother!"

We were in Bhaskar-Nath's house.

A tiny loggia at the entrance, its floor crowded with temple statues of every shape and size. Clutching my arm, Balu pulled me inside the house.

"This is Bjorn's brother, Nil. He's arrived."

There was a rustle of fleeing skirts. I stumbled down a dark hallway, tripped against an object that resounded like a music box, and finally emerged into a patio flooded with sunlight and carpeted with white sand: a large bright courtyard ringed by a pillared veranda and rooms with closed doors. A scent of sandalwood wafted through the house. As I turned around, I glimpsed a massive figure squatting, motionless, in a corner. It was Bhaskar-Nath, the sculptor, looking at me. Balu became completely silent.

I have never really been able to know who that man was, but his gaze captured me. Yet it was not something trying to take possession of me, imposing itself forcibly and piercingly and searching me. I did not feel any inquisitiveness; rather, it was like a living mass looking at me from everywhere at once or, rather, drawing me into another dimension, toward someone behind me. Never have I met a man of such density—a solid mass of power—yet at the same time gentle, with the body of a Roman gladiator and Balu's black eyes.

"Sit down."

As he slid a mat toward me, his youthful-looking wife entered the room and offered me areca nuts and a glass of water on a brass tray. She pulled a fold of her sari across her forehead, smiled at me with lowered eyes, then withdrew silently.

Silence pervaded the place, except for the distant chant of schoolchildren.

"You are exactly on time."

I was startled.

"That's how it should be—each thing at its appointed time."

He fell silent, fingering one of his rough models.

"It's the full moon. You are welcome."

And everything was wrapped in silence again.

"It's time." I had heard those words so often; and I was not sure what sort of "time," or "moon," this was, but it was so obviously true for me, at this moment, with the schoolchildren's chant and the scent in that house. I could *not* have been anywhere but here; this was *it*. I had roamed many countries, for many years—perhaps centuries, walked many steps and traveled many circuitous roads, and now I was here, right on time. It made perfect sense. And suddenly, in that tiny patio, at the end of those thousands of roads and steps, I think I saw through the web—the formidable web—the innumerable intersections of microscopic exactitudes that turned up here and not there, at this minute and no other. And this was more than exactitude by the clock; physical hours were merely a reflection, a mechanical and arbitrary translation to fill a time that does not exist. This was a kind of inner synchronicity that caused time to *become right*: the traveler was outwardly on time because he was inwardly on time, and the coincidence of the two made the meeting inevitable—a microscopic, unnoticed miracle. A prodigious web of unnoticed miracles. Sitting before that man, I suddenly perceived that each thing had its "time," or rather its soul-moment, as if another time constantly operated behind ours, and when one followed that time or rhythm or journey, everything unfolded harmoniously, smoothly, exactly as it was supposed to, with marvelous, faultless precision; while in the other time, everything grated and conflicted and jarred. It was like two superimposed worlds— one false, one true. A fabulous horizon was opening before me; life was becoming something infinitely fluid and plastic, almost a minute-by-minute creation. One only needed to be tuned in to the other journey.

Then everything vanished. I found myself watching the light play on a chisel.

"Who brought you here?"

"A sannyasi."

"Oh?"

He set down his sandalwood block abruptly. His torso had the same rich hue as his statues.

"Long ago," he said, "someone predicted that a sannyasi would bring misfortune to this house. I was seventeen. You were not even born, you see."

I was stunned.

"But—"

"Calm down, child, things happen as they must."

"But I'm not a sannyasi! I've just arrived. Your son is the one who brought me here."

"Really? Then why do you look so flustered?"

I was not flustered; I was in the grip of the same seething anger I had felt before the sannyasi. I could still hear his voice: "Three times you have come, three times . . ."

"Now listen—"

I stammered. I was like a child being robbed of his dream.

"Those people who make predictions should have their tongues cut off. What's the matter with all of you in this country! Balu told me—"

Bhaskar-Nath watched me impassively.

"Well, what's wrong in being forewarned?"

"I just don't believe in your fables. I, and nobody else, control my future. I'm a free man."

"You control it indeed."

He paused for a moment.

"But 'you' are something very old. Look, child, fate is not an enemy. There are no such things as 'enemies' in this world; everything is here to help us find the way. There are no 'misfortunes'; everything leads us exactly where we are supposed to go, by all the necessary detours. When one opens one's eyes, every moment is a marvel."

And a kind smile brightened his face.

"You are welcome here. This house is yours; all that knocks at my door is good. What are you looking for?"

"A little while ago, Balu told me that Bjorn was going to die."
Bhaskar-Nath nodded.
I was incensed.
"If Bjorn dies tomorrow, what do *I* do? Just twiddle my thumbs? It's decreed, and that's that."
"Look, stranger, do you think fate is some kind of medicine for weaklings?
Bhaskar-Nath drew himself up. He looked like a lion.
"In you exist both a possibility and a great weakness. The two together—almost *necessarily* together, I might say. The weakness is the breach through which the new possibility can steal in. This is what you have to understand. There are two things to understand, two poles of existence, a contradiction that is the key to everything; and if you don't understand that, your life is in vain."
His eyes held me with a tangible force.
"There is a world of eternal truth where everything already *is*, luminous, peaceful, beyond conflicts—free; and there is the world of apparently clashing forces, ours, where everything is *becoming* what it is. Two sides: one of light that sees, the other of force that acts. And we must hold these two sides in the same grip, like two horses pulling the same chariot. If you master one without the other, you get lost in the light that sees but cannot act, or you get lost in the force that acts but does not know. It is not a matter of choosing between one or the other—one must be both. Only then does one live in the powerful light—"
He smiled pensively.
"—the light of the next world."
Then, in the same breath, he added:
"You are on time. Your brother needs you. *He* was not led here by a sannyasi, but by a tantric—the opposite pole."
"Who, actually, is this Guruji?"
There was a sudden noise like a clap of thunder. I leaped up, just in time to see a magnificent blue peacock swoop down

before me in a whirl of feathers. I heard a ripple of laughter and turned around to glimpse a small round face peering down from the terrace above the patio.

"Batcha!"

She vanished in a peal of laughter.

"Batcha, will you please get this bird out of here? I've already told you—"

Bhaskar-Nath had raised his voice, but he did not mean a word of it. The peacock, right in front of me, straightened its neck and let out a resounding and triumphant cry as if to defy me. Then he proceeded to peck on the ground. I was completely bewildered. I looked at that peacock, at Bhaskar-Nath immediately behind, seated straight and motionless against the wall. In a flash I saw myself running behind that sannyasi through the streets of the port, and the warrior god suddenly springing from the wall and riding a peacock. It was all beginning again. Bhaskar-Nath was as still as a statue. The schoolchildren were chanting. I had the feeling of being thrust into a world teeming with signs, but without a key to decipher them.

"Shikhi! Shikhi!"

A small round face emerged from behind a door. She wore a long pomegranate-colored gypsy skirt and a red *tilak* on her forehead that glowed like a little flame against her fair skin.

"Batcha, the next time—"

The peacock raked the patio with a sweep of its tail and rushed into her skirts like a chicken.

They disappeared together.

It was a signal. Doors around the veranda swung open, a servant hurried by, the sculptor's wife began gathering sandalwood shavings from the floor. Through the back door could be seen the foliage of a margosa tree and girls winnowing rice.

"You see, son—"

From that moment on he would always call me "son," and I could have sworn that something had actually happened between that peacock, Batcha, Bhaskar-Nath, and myself. A peacock—why a peacock?

"—Once you begin to look at things with the true vision, there is not one thing in the world that is not pregnant with sense and does not carry its own message, not a single thing. It's as if everything were in league to force us to understand."

I did not know what there was to understand and I barely heard Bhaskar-Nath's words, but something was happening to me. Was it perhaps the presence of that man? The air seemed to shimmer. The objects, and even the walls, appeared to be suffused with light, as if on the verge of slipping into another dimension and opening, changing aspects; they were the same objects, the same person, yet so different, almost vitalized; I felt that one word could undo everything, tear open that veil of haziness. I stood at the edge of a dizzying frontier, and though I neither understood nor saw anything, I felt it was right *there*, just behind, barely removed. I picked up a bit of peacock feather from the ground and twisted it between my fingers. Its eye-shaped marking was shimmering, too, turning from blue to green to golden brown. Could it be that that peacock had a meaning for Bhaskar-Nath, for myself, and for Batcha—three distinct stories, or the same one? Just a bit of glistening feather. And the air seemed crisper, brighter, as if filled with another life substance; the chisels, the feather, the sand on the ground, Bhaskar-Nath's hands, everything seemed *connected* within another movement. Then my eyes turned to the feather markings again, and it's as if I caught a glimpse of the compact marvel. I had a sudden feeling that the world was full of superimposed depths, and the one fleeting little thing that happens to catch our attention may hold the entire story of the world, much as the momentary position of the stars holds the course of a whole destiny and encompasses in one second the story of a multitude. It was dazzling. Suddenly I could see and feel this world moving in a sort of prodigious ballet where each point was the center of everything and contained everything—a fantastic kaleidoscope ever spinning and shifting, ceaselessly rewriting the plot for a new ballet, a new story line, but the performers are always the same, and so is the story. And if that one spark of ruby or turquoise, or this one peacock feather on the terrace, happens to flicker, everything flickers. It dances and everything dances. The world is a miracle. It was dazzling, a wind of frosty powder on the blue crest of a mountain; and perhaps one same breath, at the same moment, had enraptured those Himalayas and my heart.

Bhaskar-Nath was putting his chisels away. The children were still chanting. I felt I had lived thirty years as a blind man in a flat, two-dimensional, precise, and meticulously mapped world, where each thing had one and only one meaning—a poor thing all by itself like an insect pinned in its box. That world was dead; it was precisely false. Infinite silver threads interconnected all things; one winged seed blew across the fields of stars; the world opened and everything opened, each petal covering another petal covering another petal—covering a single golden Sun.

I got up as if in a dream.

"Beware of Bjorn, son."

I looked at Bhaskar-Nath with his naked gladiator's torso, and I did not know what he meant. Beware of whom? There was but one light burning a million times, in death and in life, in my heart and in everything, and holding this entire world of men and things in the hollow of a single plumed seed.

He rose to his feet and went into a back room. He soon returned carrying a small sandalwood statue, which he placed in my hands.

It was a dancing flute player.

ॐ

7
the temple

*B*jorn had returned in the middle of the night. He seemed on edge, his voice hollow. The dawn was still only a green transparency alive with the cawing of the first crows. I could barely make him out in the shadows engulfing the well, but I felt his distress. There was a heaviness in the air that I could not penetrate. Only men can make themselves so impenetrable! They are the most opaque mineral in all creation. Yet, when they forget themselves, they shine like a diamond. What a strange thing. And it's only a veil. Think about it, and all turns black; stop thinking, and all brightens.

"Something's wrong?"

"I don't understand."

He flung a bucket of water over his head in a sort of rage.

"And it takes so damn long; it's like Erik with his pipes: one pipe, two pipes, three pipes. . . . It's been three years—three years, not three months, you understand—since he promised me the initiation, the supreme *mantra*, and then he calls me (without my asking anything, mind you), and he says, 'Today you will receive the initiation.' I run to him, overcome with joy. I sweep his house, empty buckets of water as if it were

Resurrection Day. He speaks about all sorts of things—hours go by—until he finally asks me what on earth I am doing there! As if he had completely forgotten everything. He must have played that trick on me ten times—yesterday, for instance. Or, out of the blue, when I am not thinking about anything or have abandoned all hope, he calls me, makes me sit down, and gives me a mantra—'the final mantra,' as he calls it. And it's truly like an initiation, oh, as if the entire body were suddenly unsealed. Just one syllable. The feeling of being lifted off the ground and spreading oneself out like powder—a deep-blue powder. It's extraordinary. Then the day after, in the middle of the conversation, he casually says, 'By the way, Gorom'— that's what he calls me—'repeat this one one hundred thousand times. Then we'll see if you are ready for the final mantra.'* So you see—"

I did not see, but I felt Bjorn's revolt. It was dark and painful.

"Forget it, Bjorn. Let's go to the sea."

It was almost cool in the deserted street. The sandstorm had not yet begun. The call of a ship's siren rent the morning air.

"Is there a port nearby?"

"Yes, on the mainland. On this side there are just coral divers."

Then, clenching his teeth, he added:

"When I think of others, of Erik, I should not complain. At least *we* know we are going somewhere, even if that somewhere lies at the end of one hundred thousand mantra-pipes; we know there's something at the other end. And I'll go to the end, regardless."

There was such a sense of desperation in this "to the end." The siren rent the air again.

"I remember, Erik used to say: 'The siren *is* the journey; afterward it's all the same.' And it's true, there is no journey—

---

* Mantra: sound-formula whose repetition is used to establish a contact with the invisible forces on any plane, from the plane of the gods down to the small entities used for magic purposes.

no journey at all; all we do is justify a siren's screech."

He kicked an empty gourd on the ground and sent it flying. In him, I thought I saw my own portrait from another existence. Oh, the beings we stumble upon are always like ghosts from a previous life or heralds of a life to come—one past, one future—and they cling to us, or we to them, through a strange kinship, as if to present us with that which we must get rid of, or conquer. And those are the only beings we ever encounter. The others vanish as if they did not exist; they bring no message to us.

"Do you regret anything?"

"Nothing. I'll go through to the end, no matter what. But it's so long. Christ! We must have the power, Nil, to be able to change the world. For thirty million years we've been making children—thirty million years to end up with a damn B.A.!"

"But what do you want to change? Unless you start changing something in yourself, you won't change anything in the world!"

"Fine. But I don't care about rationalization; I want to *do* something, you understand."

"Look, do you want to open hospitals, schools, cure the sick, share economic wealth among the poor, or what? And once your poor get rich, they will rob their fellow men exactly in the same way. Then they'll die, since everything dies, and they'll start all over again. As long as a single man remains mortal, nothing will be changed; it isn't the outside that must be cured, it's the inside. Or else nothing is accomplished. Do you want to perform miracles—soar in the air, pass through walls, appear amid a blaze of light in the middle of Oslo's main square? You will be regarded as a god, worshipped, hated. And babies will continue sprouting as before. This is the illusion, Bjorn: people want to have all the godly attributes without becoming godlike. So it cannot work. If they don't change inside, there cannot be any journey anywhere. Afterward will always be as before."

"But suppose you show them the power of the Spirit. Suppose—"

"You want to go into spiritual show biz?"

"Lord, how exasperating you are! All right then, let's head for the Himalayas and contemplate our navels. The trouble is, I'm not interested in my personal salvation or liberation; I'm only interested if it helps others."

"Listen, Bjorn, you want power. Fine. Let's suppose you possess total power, that you are all-powerful. How will you use that power? Do you have any idea what needs to be done? Do you know what is good and what is evil? What, indeed, is evil? That's still another question. Will you abolish illness, death, suffering? But what if suffering is the very means through which one passes to another state? Will you make your B.A. babies live to be ten thousand years old? They would only stockpile libraries, and savings and loans. I have yet to see an evil that does not have a complete meaning. Eradicate evil and you will eradicate the good with it. What do you know of what's good for the world? What vision do you have? If we had true vision, Bjorn, we would *automatically* have power. We lack power because we lack vision, because we would rush to eliminate what should not be eliminated."

"So I'll just pack my bags and go drive pipes into the ground with Erik. And the world can go to hell. Amen. Everything's for the best."

"Oh, Bjorn, why are you so violent? Look, there's nothing to eliminate, nothing to 'change,' as you say; it's something else. Sometimes, I have the feeling it's completely erroneous to seek something 'extraordinary.' The secret is not extraordinary. It's simply something *else*—perhaps no more than a change in the way we look at things. A gaze that changes everything!"

"I bet you'll end up turning to dust in one of your crystalline gazes! But I want to *do* something, even if I fumble; I want to live, I want to knead matter, I want— Actually, I am complaining, but I've found what I am looking for. I've found a lever. I know the secret—at least *a* secret—a rational secret, a rational miracle, something that men can grapple with and perfect. It's only a question of time and tenacity. A hundred thousand mantras are nothing! One just does it, and that's all."

The siren blasted a third time. We had arrived at the temple. An erne soared skyward. As for me, I could no longer relate to all their cockeyed stories. The bird swerved in flight and melted into the sky. Oh, every time, that tore something inside me, as if I were left behind. Deep within us lies a fragment of bird that remembers. And every time, I abruptly discover myself a man, as one discovers himself shrunken in a dream. God, this is not what I seek! Not intelligence, not virtue, not greatness, not powers, not superiority over this whole mediocrity—something else, something else, a complete "elseness." Another way of looking at things is what I seek. That's my story, my stubborn mantra!

There loomed the enormous teak doors, and the crush, the scramble, the torrent of colors. A turmoil of odors and beggars smelling of rancid oil, jasmine, and bats; a wild display of arborescent corals and shells; heaps of red and green powder lining the hall and rising alongside the pillars together with painted glassware, ribbons, straw baskets—everything whirling and shifting, exactly like the sculptured multitude above: mendicants and merchants, monsters and seers, pilgrims, monkeys and girls with braids, all swept along equally in a huge multicolored onslaught, where even ugliness became divine, even trinkets seemed suddenly endowed with an irresistible sacredness. I felt like merging in this, disappearing, losing myself in complete strangeness. I now know why these places seem so familiar to me: All my life I have yearned for a radical uprooting—or maybe a rerooting—as if only in the aftermath of some sort of inner convulsion would I be able to recover my true face and emerge at last from this leaden oblivion. Deep in us is buried the memory of some fabulous transmutation; our fairy tales remember better than we do!

And how I have searched. I have searched through bareness, negation, destruction; I have plundered like a vandal, defaced idols like the Thebes invaders, and there I was among that crowd of sculptured gods, devastated in reverse, satiated, bursting out in the great cosmic revelry. But something within me was saying no—an inner flame like a sword of light against that onslaught. I did not belong to that temple! I belonged to no temple, no place, no country. I belonged only to that light within. Or perhaps to a white minaret rising over the sands like a pure cry. But Bjorn was the one who was pulling me into the heart of this contradiction.

"Let's take the northern corridor."

He broke away from the crowd. I could breathe again.

"They all use the southern corridor. There are four of them, all enormous, circling the sanctuary. There is an exit on the eastern side, facing the sea."

We turned left into the northern corridor. And I was suddenly thrust into another world, into a huge, prodigious corridor, its sculptured pillars disappearing into the mists of time, almost as fantastic as the Luxor pillars, except this was a living Luxor, reverberating to the beating of gongs. I felt myself dissolving, and someone else emerging. Someone whose gaze embraced that entire corridor, as well as this tiny fragment of self walking around—a vast gaze suddenly opening up—and everything looked different. Eyes were different, perspectives were different; rhythm was different, yet had an amazing sense of intimacy, as if one had entered the very heart of things. That gaze encompasses everything, or, rather, everything is *within* that gaze: The world is no longer outside as something being "looked at"; it is experienced instantly. It is inside; the scene unfolds within. It is no longer a two-dimensional, isolated scene; it is a scene with inner depths, a succession of scenes one within another, or seen through one another, as it were: one merges with the archetype of the place, with its millennia, its history, its living depths. Simultaneously one is this microscopic character walking in the old scenery or, perhaps more appropriately, one is a series of characters rolled into one, a multiplicity of interwoven plots in one, as if one moved in several lives at once, several world strata. One gesture encompasses thousands of gestures, one footstep strides across several lives; one is but a living symbol; while behind or above, one is that embracing, eternal gaze, both the actor and the witness, the image and the one watching the image. One has picked up the thread of an old legend again, an innumerable life, both familiar and strange, as after returning from a long trip, and one walks on, a tiny image beneath an all-embracing and tranquil gaze.

I strolled there as if I had returned after centuries and nothing had changed. Perhaps I had lived somewhere else, in a dream, and now I could feel again the smooth coolness of the large flagstones under my feet. Bjorn and I walked side by side, barefoot and dressed in white, down the gigantic corridor that plunged toward a slit of sunlight one quarter of a mile away, amid a hundred pillars resembling a ship's framing ribs straddled by gaudy beasts. We walked over the large flagstones, soft and fresh as the centuries of the Nile, small luminous hierophants beneath the acquiescent gaze of dragons and mystic circles, painted red and ocher as in the corridors of Thebes. I had left my shadow at the door, along with the sounds of the world. I had left my name and my costumes, and I was going down the corridor with that one little flame of being in the hollows of my hands, that one soft freshness beneath my footsteps, eyes half closed, as if borne along by the silence. Once, perhaps, I had lived in daylight, and I had performed so many gestures elsewhere, in other places or countries, but everything had now melted into that white flame, everything had come together to follow the rhythm of that one walk. I held my breath like someone on the verge of hearing the word again and performing the gesture. I groped my way through a vast memory of gongs and cinnamon odors toward a slit of sunlight at the other end. A minute pilgrim going backward in time, I retraced the march of the ages, of forgotten existences, of vain and luminous lives beneath a great gaze, of stories upon stories in the midst of this ship, and I clasped that tiny flame to my heart, that one drop of light at the end of centuries and centuries. And my light almost sang. There was a sort of rhythm rising with each step, rising from the depths of time, from the depths of my lost sorrows, of my million footsteps across forgotten plains. It was as soft as those flagstones, endless and limpid as the smile of the dead, all the dead that I had been. And everything had melted in that music: all the faces and loves, the prayers and temples, the thousands of temples where I had hoped, prayed, worshipped, and all the gods once loved, the mysteries upon mysteries. A common thread of music linked all my footsteps, a high white singing tension whose existence was so swift that it appeared immobile, a unique eternal vibration. I walked beneath those sacred slabs like a luminous blind man, a tiny image borne along by a smile, and everything was lived instantly: sorrow upon sorrow, hopes and despairs. Ah, what was left? A single love had captured all my eyes, shrouding with light the endless quest, the myriad abysses, the deaths, the fruitless lives, and I walked as if toward a consecration, toward an ultimate triumph that rose forth with each footstep, that rose from the depths of my soul in a great white rhythm, as if the countless sorrows of my lives were released all at once, purified, freed, transformed into their content of light. Oh, what a pure song! What a triumphant light at the end! A million whiffs of tenderness born of a million sorrows that have known everything—wickedness, villainy, baseness, and wisdom—that have committed every evil and every good, loved, hated, and are simply sick of understanding everything! A unique look of love in the heart of every humiliation, a nameless something that has been there forever and recognizes everything—an overpowering recognition like a million cries of love arising from a million nights, a unique cry of fusion at the end as if one were a living holocaust of all the sorrows in the world, a concentration of the earth, a little image bearing a million men—ah, as if everything were finally going to burst open and I were going to place my forehead in the sun, open my hands and give forth that flame forever.

Bjorn pulled me by the arm.

We turned into an inner corridor, into a vast chant that resounded all around us like bronze, reverberating down a maze of corridors and sculptured pillars to return and strike the high vault, filling everything with a deep, flowing modulation, as powerful as the rumbling of the sea itself. We had reached the doors of the sanctuary.

Bjorn went down the steps.

I stood alone on the threshold, watching that small white silhouette wend through a thicket of pillars. He stopped beneath the high vault for a moment, as if lost. Then he went up the steps of the sanctum sanctorum, which rose like a granite island in the middle of the huge square. I was behind him, watching. And everything froze, became magnified; time expanded and my eyes widened immeasurably. The slightest detail became intensely alive with a sense of the absolute—everything had a meaning, a total plenitude, truly as if each thing contained its own unique eternity—then all grew still.

I had been there forever and I knew all the gestures. I was as old as the pillars and the flagstones, and I had so often watched that little golden flame draw its circle around sacred stones that perhaps I had become that stone myself, become that ancient, motionless gaze that sees everything, understands everything without passion or clamor, that embraces all beings in its silence and dissolves all sorrows in its vast, eternal sands. They cry out, lament, and pass on, while I am ever there! Beneath half-closed eyelids, my calm gaze has already contemplated the end of all these peoples, and the little gleam dancing in my eyes is the reflection of their own eternity.

I offer what they offer me, and my eternity is their very own; my joy is theirs for the taking, my peace flourishes on their lips; and if they are hard, am I not made of their stone? But will they see that light in their hearts? Will they see the god who stirs here because he has stirred there? Then a slight lessening of tension occurred. That gaze fell on Bjorn, on myself; or, rather, it focused or narrowed itself, with a feeling akin to changing altitudes or passing from open space to a particular point in space. And just at the transition, I grasped a fugitive secret, as if one could pass freely, deliberately, from one to the other, shift back and forth from the vast gaze to the narrow one and live in two worlds or two beings at once. And this was like the key to freedom. Just a small step backward and everything becomes vast, one, takes on breadth and depth—the sense of royalty outside things. Then a slight concentration and everything coagulates on this point or that, almost playfully; and if one gets caught in the play, then nothing exists but that sharp, isolated point of coagulation that no longer sees or understands anything except a thin crust of its own existence, a tiny scene from its immense history. I returned to the small image while retaining a vague, fleeting, yet intimate memory of all those depths, as if each odor, each gesture, each person were on the verge of revealing the key to an innumerable living legend. Then everything vanished. I stood watching Bjorn, my brother, perform the rite, and I was alone under the high portal as before a landscape of dream. Was it he or I who was roaming beneath ancient pylons? Had I not lived this whole story as well, in one place or another? All it would have taken was for me to insist a little, to step across that threshold. It was right there at the edge of my memory. Oh, I seem to recall an unforgettable life! I can almost conjure up the rapture of letting oneself flow in a world of marvelous abandon in which the small person is drowned in a powdering of gold, and one looks around from on high, with the gait of one marching to a triumphant sacrifice. One passes elsewhere; everything is past! Then, that marvelous cry of release as if one moved into another race. I know—I lived through that. I can almost recall a child, long ago, beneath other pillars. A golden disc had alighted in his heart and everything was set ablaze—the pillars and the stones were ablaze—as if the whole world were made of sun. It was so close, I could almost remember. All I would have needed to do is go down these steps again. But something said, "No, do not step forward," as though I *had* to forget. Oh, will I ever finish going back over the trail and counting my nuggets of gold, or darkness? Indeed, this could have been just another trap. Perhaps one had to overcome one's luminous past as well as one's past of darkness and go beyond them both.

> *O pilgrim*
> *You are the old-comer*
> *Of more than one shadow*
> *And a few victories*
> *You get down to the task*
> *Deliberately oblivious*
> *Until the day when*
> *In the great tranquil Memory*
> *You can embrace*
> *The snare of past victories*
> *And the dizziness of old humiliations*

Then I let myself go into that chant. And that's when I made my discovery.

It rose from everywhere at once, from a group of choristers squatting among the columns, and from another and another, each intoning their own recitation, and each wave mingling with another, amplifying and fusing with another, until the whole sanctuary was nothing but a vast sea of chant vibrating and reverberating against the walls like a high tide of bronze, rippling among a maze of grottoes and carved divinities, only to return and strike the vault again, while from the depths of the crypts, endlessly, rose the syllables *AUM namo namo namaha, AUM namo namo namaha.* And that *AUM* was a marvel of fathomless power, a timbre of golden bronze that seemed to well forth from the depths of time, alive with a million never-lost, never-stifled cries. It was not even a prayer, a call, a chant; it was an outpouring of being, the stark, grave, eternal voice of Man, like the voice of the sea or the wind—a sound that spoke of man the way the river speaks of water. Perhaps it was the very cry of the world being uttered through his lips, as when long ago, under the migration of the stars, he had stood erect to grasp his own mystery, when that first Word had risen, making him a man in the stony field of the world, capturing him as the first chisel stroke had captured the aurochs on the walls of a cave. *AUM namo namo namaha, AUM*— I let that Word rise in me, let that mystery flow forth from the depths of my night until it filled my entire temple of flesh. I was that man of old standing alone under the nameless vault. I was that conjunction of obscure forces. But something had to be articulated, something unique that I was, and though there was no word or language for it, it was there, like a child within the womb of my night—my secret of being, my own pure sound, my true name—that which I had to name in order to live, and if I did not find my name, I would be nonexistent, crushed beneath the stars, lost in the darkness along with the cry of the jackals. And I hearkened to that mystery, listening to that something in the depths, that sound of my forest, that whisper of my waters; and deeper still, farther inside, at my last breath, as it were, or perhaps at the beginning of myself, a tiny quiver, a warmth that gave rise to a cry. It was as if bursting with gold, and so quiet—the quiet of that which *is.* Just a tiny vibration, but so strong! It was certitude itself, the rock, the warmth, the fullness of my being. Like an adoration in the depths, for nothing, for everything, because *that* is and I am, *that* vibrates and I vibrate and everything vibrates—*that* and nothing but *that*, simple, the warmth of the world, the rock, the plenty of tenderness, naked love. That which I am, the cry that makes me be! And makes everything be! A tiny breath in the depths that holds everything in its warmth, that coagulates the worlds, the stars and the beasts, that coagulates body upon body in its chant—a unique cry of eternity within things, a single creative syllable—*AUM*. Ah, what did I need a temple for! There, no prayer is necessary; *it* prays and vibrates all by itself, singing forever and ever. There, neither fear nor hope nor expectation nor desire have their place; *it* is ever-present plenitude. There, no mystery or search remains; everything is understood, everything is *that* and speaks of *that*, everything is the unlit prison of that singing river!

I opened my eyes and looked around. And for the third time, something within me said no. It was as plain and evident as that Word vibrating within my flesh, as clear as the blue of the sky over our heads and over man's cages, whether Gothic or exotic. Oh, there is something that no temple or church can claim for itself; something that no being, no prophet, no god, no pope, whether from the East or the West, can secure; something no book, no myth can confine in its formula of stone or blood, in its letters of ink or light; something greater than all the saviors of the world, the intercessors and jailers of the True—a Truth vaster than all the heavens put together, too simple for their loftiness, too natural for their miracles; something that laughs in everything, sings in everything, plays at being priest or pagan, struggles in the night and in the day, and still smiles, despite all the struggles and sorrows of the day, despite the sacred and less sacred prisons. A minuscule golden vibration running everywhere, breathing everywhere, shining forth again and again in spite of all our light and our darkness, all our Bastilles of the spirit or the flesh. I just say no, no, NO! I don't belong to this temple! I don't belong to any temple, any formula, any prison of gods or men!

This time, I opened my eyes wide. I embraced that chant from under my stone porch, that music of man covered by stone, here or there, five thousand years ago or yesterday, in every language, in every heart, every black or white sorrow, under gods or devils—underneath, always underneath, and a prisoner. That chant in my heart was not praying or imploring; it was fearless, lawless, pounding and pounding those walls like a bird in its cage. And suddenly, with eyes wide open, I *saw* this startling mystery of *the mechanics of imprisonment in light*: They were chanting, as many others, elsewhere under other vaults, and I could see the tide of their chant strike against the walls, ricochet and fall back upon them like a shower of electrum streaked with great deep-blue pulsations that enfolded them, illuminating and bedecking them with gold, and filling the place with a compact mass of force, the colored translation of their own power of invocation as their chant reverberated—their own sumptuous reflection lit up their walls as it lit up the eyes of their gods. As for me, standing alone under my stone porch, I pounded and pounded against that vault, that prison of light, and *the more I pounded*, the more intense, powerful, and almost hard that blue pulsation became, as if I, too, like these men, had been caught in the luminous snare of my own incantation, locked in a gold-ringed sapphire like an insect in an amber bubble. Then I understood, saw, touched the secret of the Churches, that illumination in a box, that epitome of light in a cage, that salvation in a bubble. All at once I let go of everything. I opened my hands, dropped my chant, dropped my force, my poor light within a cage, and all my pompous reflections; I collapsed into an abyss of blankness—the sudden sense of sweetness of a lost child, wrested, swept away in a sort of triumphant cyclone, as one topples a wall in a single shoulder stroke, as one goes through death, and I broke through into an immensity of white light, oh, so white and so free!

The drums, conches and silver horn burst forth under the vault. Bjorn prostrated himself. The whole place was one powerful, sacred, deep-blue precipitate—yes, divine; one could plunge in this and lose oneself in a triumph of light. It was perfectly spellbinding and illuminating. It was the churches' powerful magic, the luminous concentration of thousands of years of prostration. The horns sounded a second time, followed by the high-pitched shenais, then a third time as I came out of the sanctuary. Their sound echoed in my heart like a great parting call, a casting off for the open seas, as if I had walked and walked, gone through lives, millennia, gestures, millions of gestures and sorrows in all ages and places; known hells, illuminations, pyre upon pyre within and without, endless revelations and salvations—all of which collapsed against the same wall. I had lived and toiled all that time just to reach this point, this blank moment, and everything was exorcized: the victories and the ensnarements, the illuminations and the devils. I stood naked and free for what had to be, like a pagan of God.

Before the gates, the great sun-flooded dunes rippled toward the sea, blazingly white and naked like my heart. This is where I felt like prostrating myself, without a vault overhead or walls in front of me.

Just then the little peacock-girl passed before me. She looked at me straight in the eye, without flinching. Then she disappeared among the dunes, holding her offering tray in her hands.

And that look swept over me like the first smile of a new world.

ψ

8
the man of secrets

The pilgrims were praying in the sun, waist-deep in water. The high dunes sloped down into the sea, as pure and soft as a white Arabia. I could have remained there forever, watching the suns rise and set, with no other desire than that smooth luminous whiteness flowing into an unrippled water, that simple, quiet annihilation. Beyond, the dunes curved inward, encircling a cove with a tiny, finely sanded beach, in sharp contrast with the green explosion of the contiguous palm grove, the sound of conch shells and bronze bells, the same endless chanting rising from the high towers. Two worlds. And a tiny white beach. My eyes went from the dunes to the palms, from the palms to the dunes to the pilgrims, and I too wanted to fold my hands, to pray, to adore—simply adore. Indeed, perhaps this was the oldest religion, the first stutter of beauty in man when something suddenly opens in him and he feels an urge to fold his hands, to pray, to chant, to clothe in words or colors that little stirring thing inside that yearns to give forth one drop of its eternity. I extended my hands, and everything was bright that morning because I loved. Sometimes the world is a glory revealing itself. I folded my hands as if to love were primarily to recognize, to recognize everything: a totality of love that does not want to leave anything out, because *everything* is moved by the same thing, the same tiny thing inside that recognizes itself everywhere; the world is a total oneness that sometimes marvels at itself. And in that perception, there was no longer any "I" and others—nothing is "other" anymore—just an all-encompassing love responding to itself everywhere, in every point, a swelling of being in which the heart seems to beat in everything. There is no more center; everything is the center! No more inside or outside; it's one and the same thing. No more eyes perceiving and discovering beauty and loving; everything loves, as if a myriad eyes opened, and one loved everywhere at once, like a vast snowfield of light where each crystal is a singing fragment of self. That sings, everything sings, everything is made of singing light; the world is an immense, ever-singing rhythm, and sometimes the heart notices it.

O Tara, O Mother

Alone on the tiny beach, a beggar stretched his hands skyward, as if begging to the sun.

O Tara
All is your will
You are the All-Will
You are the doer of the action, O Mother

He sang, and his words did not matter; they sounded in harmony with the truth. Every dune sang through that beggar.

You are the doer
O Mother
Yet they say I am the doer

And as he uttered the words *yet they say*, there was a kind of sadness in the air, a sudden little lapse, a second's hesitation as his voice broke. And all the pain of the world was in that second. Indeed, was it he or I who sang? I don't know, but there was that sudden little break, that lapse of an "I" within the totality, and at once a sharp pain like a suffocation; the "I" was pain, the intolerable pain of not being able to hold *that*. An immensity of music breaking open, something abruptly gaping, and an urge to throw oneself into it as if nothing and no one could fill that chasm.

O Tara, O Mother—

Have you heard that tiny note breaking inside, that sudden breach to infinity in a second? There is one second in a lifetime, one tiny second that counts.

"What's up, crystal-man?"

He placed his hand on my shoulder, and everything rushed back toward this body: an instantaneous shrinking, a second of suffocation; suffocation is our norm.

"I frightened you!"

In a flash, I seemed to glimpse a sort of total Person, who was us, Bjorn and I—an innumerable and immense Body, a single Body. And to assert a claim of individuality here, in this bit of a shell, seemed as absurd as pretending to be a ladybug on a white beach.

I regained my presence of mind, which was more like an absence.

"Has the sun gotten to you or what?"

He shook me. Sea water trickled from his flaxen locks. He looked like a Nordic god.

"Oh, brother, life is so beautiful! I could devour it!"

This was Prince Bjorn again, vital, voracious, childlike.

---

* Based on a Bengali song.

"Come, let's sit in the shade and I'll tell you the secret."

Everything darkened instantly. And Balu's words came back to me, so sharp and clear, with their little ring of truth: "He is going to die."

"Yes, the secret, *my* secret. Come."

And he drew me toward the dunes.

That notion of "secret" was so absurd here; it sounded so false. I watched Bjorn, Prince Bjorn, towel himself, along with that other one who seemed to be fastened onto him, the "man of secrets." Could this be the reason for Bjorn's impending death?

"When I was in Zinder with Erik—"

But I no longer heard him. My attention was fixed on that shadow following Bjorn. If I could find a clue, perhaps I could save him? What did "death" mean, anyway? It's constantly with us, following our every gesture, but at what moment does it *become* death? Yes, the moment . . . I concentrated on it as if I were on the verge of seizing that moment, that second when one swerves into death. Why does it happen? What was there in Bjorn that was calling for death? A man only dies because he calls for death. What is the false Bjorn?

Then came the revelation.

I stopped short in the sand as everything around me grew clear and precise: Bjorn's purple shadow, his tanned back glistening with droplets of sea water—every physical detail magnified, as if etched in light. Then that gaze embracing and piercing through everything—a whole world in the sweep of a microscopic, lucid second. There was nothing to understand, for everything was understood; it was a light alive with all explanations without the need for any explanation. Afterward, one had to pull and unroll a thread, but it was no longer quite the same; it was an approximation, a translation into a foreign language. A white little second that far, far below was capable of creating pictures or music, events, philosophy, but that was already dulled, half-dead. And I saw, first, a luminous and

white death, as it were, a death that was not the opposite of
life. We understand nothing of death because we always see
it as black, "against," the enemy, the negation, the defeat.
Defeat of *what*? On the other hand, I could see a black death,
that sort of antiself clinging to us, the false Bjorn—"death."
But that death clings to us to force us to become ourselves, our
true selves! It is the guardian of the true life. And every time
we stray on the wrong side, the death-self takes over, not to
"kill" us but to force us to regain the true position. Death is
the incapacity to regain the true position. This became transparent. Yet simultaneously, as I looked into that white second,
I saw that there was no death anywhere! Not a single atom of
death, no shadow, no negation, no antiself. All was pure light,
a quintessence of positiveness. Everything flows *toward* that,
for that, irresistibly, like the dunes, toward that total Self where
death is no more because we have become totally true. Suddenly all the whites and blacks in the world, all the for's and
against's, were disappearing in thin air. There was no death!
There was no "against," no anti-anything! All goes *there*, all
flows toward that, through every "for" and every "against."
There is nothing but light! There has never been anything but
light! We are constantly missing the point. We use words for
something that does not exist. Only *That* exists, only *That*
becomes, only *That* grows, only *That* moves toward the precipice of *That*. And even if we were for our "against" and against
our "for," we would still go there, exactly where we are
supposed to, in this language or another. In truth, the world
eludes us completely, except for a second, now and then. We
do not speak the right language.

"Let's sit here."

And I returned to that darkness we call daylight.

"I come here every morning."

A tiny building stood at the foot of the dunes. At first I did
not understand what it was. Then I realized it was a temple, a
miniature granite temple, scarcely taller than Bjorn, surrounded

by a tiny peristyle supported by four sculptured columns. The dunes soared behind like a great awning. The temple steps were half buried in sand. There was not a sound, not a breath in the air, except for the distant drone of the chanting and the frail voice of the beggar:

O Tara, O Mother—

As I ascended the steps, a strange impression swept over me, something obliterating my light, as if a new layer of being were surfacing. It welled up constantly that morning, as if worlds after worlds surged up, bursting forth like multicolored bubbles, each with its own particular rhythm. It was not a feeling of anguish, which would have had no basis since I was as tranquil as those dunes, but a sort of very deep heartbeat, as of a child coming upon an abandoned house or when in a dream we find ourselves in a strange, forgotten place that suddenly becomes intimately familiar: This is IT. I knew that kind of emotion well. It was always accompanied by a particular fragrance. Someday, I will have to understand.

I looked in through the tiny doorway. A ray of sunlight touched a bare rock standing on end. Fresh flowers lay beside a little bowl of red powder on the ground. The scent of burning incense filled the air. There was an atmosphere of Egypt in that tiny space, completely dark except for that stone. As I was about to leave, I spied Batcha in a corner, leaning against a wall, one cheek resting on her knees, peacefully asleep.

I drew back without a sound and joined Bjorn outside.

He was squatting silently on the northern side of the peristyle, looking out toward the palm grove. Barely thirty feet away, the sea looked like a deep-blue lake, the great dunes flowing into the turquoise deep. Not a bird in sight, not the slightest wave. Only the distant chanting, and that strange fragrance that had touched such a deep chord in me, and a faint solitary voice rising almost futilely amid the sands:

O Tara, O Mother
You are the guide
You are the tree within the seed
You are the mango and the shade of the mango tree
And the winding of the path beneath my footsteps
As you go, so go I

I listened in the silence. I was as smooth and barren as the sea, and I seemed to hear, from very, very far away, the murmur of another story—a story forever the same but hazier, associated with that fragrance and that chant. It was like an ancient memory, bound by sand and granite, on a day similar to this one, at the beginning of things, at the beginning of the story—a moment charged with power that returns, life after life, like wave after wave upon the same beach. Oh, we are returning from more than one island, and who knows which lost archipelagos we come from as we cross today's little beach? It was like a door opening deep inside me, induced by that fragrance of sand and a chant, something suddenly agape; and life was swept away as if one had lived constantly wide of the mark, pretending to act from a solid base, and one were suddenly face to face with reality. Nothing is perceptible, yet everything is charged with a presence. Bjorn, too, felt something, his gaze silently shifting from the dunes to the palm grove and back again.

"Nil, sometimes I have a feeling we don't know anything at all. We think we've grasped the secret, and we are just—futile."

He gestured toward the dunes.

"We have to keep fighting, though, otherwise we're finished. Dissolution sets in."

He clasped his arms around his legs, his jaw set. It reminded me of myself, squatting similarly in that train, traveling through my desert of rocks.

"What on earth are we doing here, Nil? Sometimes I don't know what it all means. It's as if I had made up a whole story and everything's wrong. Things were so simple when I was a child: there was the cry of wild geese on the lake, and I lay hidden in the rushes for hours, listening. The cry of the ganders was something I truly understood. The Maytime mists, the drifting sky, and that cry. As for the rest, I have sailed, traveled, changed colors and jobs. I have done Lord knows what, and it all seems unreal, like a fabrication. Nonexistent. But the cry of the wild geese, that exists."

He placed a finger on his cheek. He was such a delightful Bjorn!

"Well, perhaps your secret lies there?"

He looked at me uncomprehendingly. Then his face grew hard again with that look of fierce determination that made him seem so pathetic.

"Never mind. It's just a matter of hanging in there, that's all. Besides, I'm on the verge of finding. Even if it takes six more months, I'm getting closer. In fact—"

He brushed the sand from the steps.

"—in fact, it comes down to the same thing: what I am seeking now is what I was seeking then, except that this is an active dream, you understand, *a cry that has power*, not like the cry of those stupid geese. Listen—"

He was seized with enthusiasm again, caught up once more in his dreams.

"One day, I met Guruji on the lagoon when it was full of birds. 'I know how to call birds,' I said. 'I know the cry of the Arctic terns, the fulmars, the coots; I call them and they respond.' And what he replied was my first revelation: 'If you call the gods, they respond, too. When I call *Gorom*, you turn around and respond. *Everything* responds, provided you know how to call. You only have to know the name.' Everything answers, Nil, that's just it! Well, the mantra is the cry of things, their name. It's just as with the call of the geese: one must know how to call."

"So what do you want to call?"

"Everything! Listen, let me explain; it's fantastic."

"If it's fantastic, I am leery of it."

"Oh, come now. Everything has a cry, its true name: water, fire, human beings, the sap in palm trees, the stones. And that cry is the sound produced by the movement of the forces constituting the thing. We are a field of forces, a whole network of lines enclosing forces. They speak of 'atoms,' 'molecules,' and God knows what, but that's just a manner of speaking, a system of notation. There are many such systems—physical, chemical, religious, musical, poetical—each with its particular way of recording things. And basically, each tries to master and reproduce *one* attribute. But when scientists seek to reproduce that attribute, they need an enormous apparatus to do it. Musicians and priests, too, seek to reproduce. But if one knows the sound constituting the thing—whether stone, fire, god, or devil—one *produces* it automatically, you see. To name is to have power. The tantrics know the secret of sounds. They have the power."

"That's magic."

"But everything is magic! What is not magic? We are always manipulating forces unknowingly. The only problem is to be able to choose the right kind of magic, the most efficient one, the one that makes the most beautiful music in the world."

"And what exactly do you want to 'produce'?"

"I told you—everything! Complete mastery."

"But for what purpose?"

For a moment he was caught off guard, and his face clouded as if he were on the verge of anger. Then he regained his composure.

"I'll give you an example. I am the one who takes care of Guruji's house. In fact, I'm late; I'm going to be scolded. I do the cleaning, the shopping—"

"And you fork out your own money?"

Bjorn seemed startled.

"Yes, of course. I also bring in his wood. One day, as I came in, I suddenly remembered he had run out of matches. I ran to the bazaar, bought some matches, and came back to find Guruji in meditation by the light of his oil lamp. There was not a single match in the house!"

"So what! For six paisa, anyone can buy a box of matches at the bazaar. It's probably easier than learning the mantra of fire."

I thought he would explode.

"What exactly are you driving at, crystal-man? Are you trying to destroy me?"

There was panic in his eyes.

"I'm nearing the goal, I'm on the brink of victory, I—"

I knew then that I had put my finger on Bjorn's illness, the point that had to be demolished—the point of death. I have always wondered if I was wrong to want to demolish that. It was both his life and that which prevented him from living, as if the most secure point were also the deadliest. Sometimes I wonder if a man's summit is not his innermost abyss—like the two sides of the coin: the mortal illness together with the salvation. And perhaps it is not a "mortal illness," but a means to free oneself from an outdated summit.

"You don't understand."

Bjorn's need to convince me was so pathetic. Or was he trying to convince himself?

"To light that fire was nothing, just one of many possible masteries. You can combine mantras, mix sounds; you can cure or kill someone, induce illness, integrate, disintegrate, change the course of thoughts. You can call on the gods, fill life with superhuman energy. It's a chemistry of sounds, concrete poetry—you just call. People constantly call with their thoughts; they call for disease, death, catastrophe. They call for all kinds of ills while walking down the street. Let's call the lovely birds from the invisible world instead."

He looked golden in the sunlight. I could almost see his birds. But all this was unsubstantial, a froth of dreams. Behind, oh, behind I could feel and hear something else, noiseless, unassuming, which flowed and flowed so simply, so limpidly, like the true substance of the world: a greater visibility instead of a wondrous invisibility, something that infused the smallest grain of sand with truth.

Again his face clouded.

"The trouble is, it takes a lot of time. Five hours of *japa* every day—repeating the same mantra one hundred thousand times."

"But once you know the sound—"

"Of course I know it! But that's not enough. A mantra needs to be awakened, charged, like a battery that you charge through repetition until it suddenly awakens and you establish the connection. Then you are in control of the force. All you have to do is name it and it comes. But there is a great profusion of forces; there are many 'gods.' For the past three years I have been going from one mantra to another. Of course, he tells me that I, too, am getting 'charged' and that one day I'll reach a saturation point."

"You are completely off the track, Bjorn."

"And you're getting on my nerves."

"One sound is enough."

"*Which* sound?"

"Listen, Bjorn, you want to call the gods, but let me tell you something: we have been calling the gods for five thousand years and it hasn't changed a thing. You can have all the visions you want, make all the gods appear in front of people, but ultimately they won't be any more impressed than with their televisions or cinemas. Believe me, if the world had the power of vision, it wouldn't be any better for it; people would flip their psychic switch and treat themselves to an hour of invisible cinema, then they would swill down a bottle of beer and be just as bored as before. Because nothing changes unless something changes *inside*! Bjorn, the miracle of the world is not at all something fantastic; on the contrary, it's very simple—so simple that it escapes our notice. That's the secret. All the rest, as you say, is nonexistent; it's just noise, turmoil, a smoke screen. Your tantric, the priests, the churches are all in show business—the ham actors of the spirit."

Bjorn had turned white as a sheet.

"I've been working three years on this; I've staked everything on it."

I don't know what came over him, but he fixed his gaze on me, and it was as cold as a steel knife. Then, with his steel-blue eyes holding me like an insect under a microscope, he said slowly, emphasizing each word:

"What you need is a catastrophe."

And he paused.

There was a blank in me, a second's lapse.

Then a tiny wave broke on the beach with a purling of shells.

I was suddenly far away, completely outside of the story, poised on that beach as if I had awaken from a dream. There was that piercing look again, which captured every detail with dazzling intensity, that sort of otherworldly gaze. That look must have opened ten or a hundred times in me, and each time was the same: a second of eternity breaks through the window dressing, and the soul looks out. Everything is captured instantaneously, without the least feeling or emotion, as if viewed within a snowy silence; and, in that stillness, things are photographed for eternity. Thus are forged, every now and then, small indelible snapshots, tiny eruptions in white, or black, along an endless road leading God knows where, or why, beyond this life.

I think I will still hear that little wave centuries from now, even though I will not know its meaning; but it will stir within me like that odor of sand, that distant chanting, that turquoise sea, that shadow under the peristyle, and the white cascade of half-buried steps that no longer lead to a temple here on this beach, at this moment under the sun, but to a vast uninterrupted story in which I have wandered, prayed, suffered, listened to a similar little wave whispering across the sand in a purling of shells.

"And you *will* get your catastrophe."

He banged his fist onto the steps for emphasis.

Yes, I knew it; I was expecting that something, that "catastrophe," that age-old Threat. But what was it? I looked at the beach, the dunes, the pilgrims at their prayer. Everything seemed so simple, so luminous; how could there be a catastrophe in *that*? It did not exist; it could not be; it was impossible, an invention of those who *thought* themselves outside *that*. Suddenly I saw the illusion, the enormous illusion: it is as if there were two worlds divided by a gigantic chasm; yet it was the same world, a single world made of one substance—luminous, utterly luminous, without an iota of shadow, forever untouched by pain. There was *that*, only *that*, immortal, glorious. Then one wrong look and everything turns to the antithesis, the night, death, suffering, the utter contradiction of that, uncertainty bordering on terror, the Threat, the ground opening beneath one's feet. And the Threat was not the possibility of catastrophe or death, but the *fact* of being outside *that*, or, rather, of thinking oneself outside; everything was threatened because it was not *that*. One restores the look and everything disappears; it never existed! Yet, it's the same thing, one and the same world with the same events, the same "accidents,". On one side, the accident does not exist; on the other, everything becomes an accident, inexorably. Just one wrong look and everything is reversed: a sudden wriggling of snakes—Fate.

In the distance, the beggar kept chanting:

> *O Tara, O Mother*
> *You hide the lotus in the mud*
> *And the lightning in the clouds*
> *To some you give light*

You make others choose the precipice
O Tara, Tara
As you will me to move, so move I

I wondered whether that different look was not also capable of changing fate, of canceling catastrophe.

Then everything vanished and all that was left in front of me was Bjorn's contorted face, a small shadowy self staring at me.

"One day I will see the gods."

He got up. I clutched at his arm.

"Bjorn!"

I had to do something; he was going to his death. I could feel that death hovering over him!

"Bjorn—"

"What do you want?"

He avoided my eyes.

"There is only one thing that saves."

"One day I will receive the initiation."

He kept repeating the same thing, like a stubborn child, and I couldn't do anything for him. A feeling of anguish, then rage, came over me.

"He promised me that I will receive the initiation."

"He's deceiving you, leading you on."

"You're lying. You have no right to say that."

In a flash I saw myself pursuing the sannyasi through the streets of the port, consumed with anger, with an urge to strike him again and again until he fell to the ground, and then I would spit on him. It was as vivid as if it had happened yesterday. Now Bjorn was like myself, the recurrence of the same story. There is but one story, one single drama common to all men!

"Bjorn, there is only one catastrophe in the world. One is a slave, and one gains freedom—or one dies."

"But I *am* free!"

"Oh, Bjorn, perhaps it's because I have suffered my share at their hands, but all those teachers and their initiations make me sick. It's like a familiar nightmare, something that's forever branded, stamped in my flesh."

Suddenly, the whole story flashed back, along with the scene and the image. It rose from the great depth of my memory, carrying that weight of darkness and ominous threat with it. The more I see the light, the more areas of darkness I discover!

"I am talking about the very last image a man takes away with him as he passes into death."

Bjorn looked at me, bewildered.

"I've seen this several times in dreams—each time the same dream. But it was more than a dream; it was like a vivid memory of something that *must* have happened in one life or another. Each time, it centers on the same powerful man, eyes ablaze, head shaved, bare-chested, and all wrapped in blue light—my so-called master. I am standing in front of him, at his mercy, a tiny, powerless thing beneath his gaze. Oh, that gaze! And I spit my freedom in his face. A battle around a fire, without a word or a gesture. Then the curse he casts upon me. Finally, it's as if I were going to hang myself. That's the image I have, Bjorn—horrible. Oh, yes, they are strong and powerful and 'luminous'! I spit on them! They can all go to hell with their initiations!"

Bjorn was totally dumbfounded, and I was as surprised as he by that image welling up from some deep, forgotten recess within me, and surging forth with an overpowering accumulated pain and revolt. There was a sequel to this "dream," almost as dreadful as the beginning, that I never shared with Bjorn. I was wandering through a forest, searching for someone I didn't know—someone I *had* to find again, who was my salvation, my deliverance—an unknown "she" I was looking for and calling out to in terrible distress. But I couldn't find anyone; and I was going to hang myself.

"That's just a dream."

"You may be right. But if this is a dream, then nothing in life is more vivid. What do we know about the extension of things, Bjorn? We dream in both directions—in the past and in the future—and everything is linked. But if we can seize the image, we can defend ourselves, striking it again and again until it ceases to appear. I met you also in a dream, in a train, before meeting you here."

"That's nonsense; Guruji is not that way at all."

"Yes, he is; I can smell it around you. Mark my words, Bjorn, these are the charlatans of truth. Yes, they will dazzle you with fireworks, gods, devils, angels, supernatural powers. But I don't need the supernatural; I need a truer 'natural.' I don't need miracles; I need the Truth, the Truth pure and simple. A single password is needed: *That*. No teacher is necessary to help find that mantra. One day it wells forth of its own through the sheer persistence of your call; one day it is there like a reliable friend, like a country where you have settled for good, an air where you breathe freely. Bjorn, the sure sign of the supreme truth is that it is within everyone's reach; that which is highest has to be the nearest—"

At that point, I felt something descending massively upon me.

"—while all these shimmering and miraculous smaller truths need intermediaries to become accessible; and the smaller they are, the more miraculous they appear."

I could see Bjorn struggling with himself. I thought I had reached him.

"It's simple, so simple, Bjorn. It's right here. Only one password is necessary."

He took a step backward, as if in fear, his forehead brushing the top of the peristyle.

Pointing toward the dunes, he said:

"That is where your supreme mantra leads—dissolution."

He walked down a couple of steps.

"As for me, I am going this way—toward men."

He turned on his heel and set off toward the palm grove. Everything sank into silence again. A quivering, buzzing silence. I almost ran after him. But I stayed rooted to the spot, drained, my head battered by that chaos. Where was my beautiful truth now? A swarm of wasps seemed to be buzzing around me. All the light of truth had been swallowed up by those wasps, and for what! I had not helped Bjorn an iota. Nothing had happened between us except noise, babble, hot air. Each one draws the circle of his thoughts about himself and settles in the middle like a castaway in his island. I could see Bjorn sitting on his little island, and every person, myself included, each on our little island of truth—little true fabrications, little one-day commodities, little cozy molehills carved in something that was neither truth nor falsehood but an immensity of *That*. A totality of *That*. There is no falsehood anywhere, not the shadow of a lie! Falsehood is to see only one point of the whole. All I wanted was to nose-dive into that whole—my country, my boundless light, my freedom without a wrinkle. Yes, I can travel from island to island, play the savage for a while, and build castles in the sand, but my heart is not in it! No sooner have I traced a circle about me than I feel like jumping out of it, crying, "Yes-no! True-false!" Everything is true! So please leave me alone; let me drink in the air of the open sea. All I need is the open sea, to drink from the vast bowl of the sky. My days as a savage are over!

I swept everything away, cut the current.

And everywhere I was king.

ψ

9
Batcha

"You were very far away."

Sitting on the temple steps, her back against a column, she looked like a round-cheeked Mogul miniature.

"Oh, Batcha, there you are!"

She eyed me placidly, soberly, her head on her knees, her arms hugging her legs, a long pomegranate-colored skirt trailing about her feet. She was so fair and sedate, as fair as Balu was brown, a golden fairness, accentuated by the black plait falling across her breast; and that little red flame in the middle of her forehead added to her undefinable look. Yes, "Batcha is the queen."

"Did you sleep well?"

No answer.

"How is your peacock, Shikhi?"

No answer.

She continued to study me calmly, systematically, but without curiosity. I had the feeling she was taking stock of me the way she would have taken stock of a plant with an unknown scent. Presumably, I belonged to the cactus family.

"Hey, Batcha, what do I smell like? A crocodile or a cactus?"

A faint smile played on her face.

"You are too restless."

And that was it.

So I quieted down; almost playfully, I plunged into her eyes. I went very deep. It was the first time I went into someone without meeting any resistance; it felt so very comfortable, like going through a great velvet door and sinking deeper and deeper into something so sweet, so quiet, quiet as a lake, and— I started to cough. The spell was broken.

I could not match her repose. It was as if I were perturbed. An imperceptible smile creased the tip of her nose. I thought she was about to say something. Then she closed her eyes as if to take me along with her into her depths. She was as utterly still as a bird in a paddy field; not a ripple stirred in her. I was like a rumpus next to that softness.

Finally, I could not take it anymore.

"What is that red mark on your forehead? You are not a tantric, I hope."

Her eyes widened in mock alarm.

"Oh, baba, how can you say such a thing?"

"Is it an ornament, then?"

Now she was truly scandalized. She pointed her chin toward the little temple.

"It is the god's blessing."

"God? Which god?"

With a sigh, she laid her head back upon her knees. Obviously my questions were quite foolish.

"It depends on the day."

And she broke into a song:

> *I am the bird of the forest*
> *Talking with the spring*
> *hopping from leaf to leaf*
> *And laughing*
> *Neither fowlers*

> *Nor Prince Charmings can ensnare me*
> *Nor can sorrow*

"Oh, Batcha, you can sing!"

"Mâ taught me. She knows all the songs. She comes from very, very far, way up north, near Kailas. There is a lake there that is filled with blue lotuses. Tell me, how is it, farther north? Is there snow? Please tell me."

"Oh, I don't know."

"Yes, you do. Please tell me."

"I have forgotten."

"Forgotten? You are like Bholanath. Me, I often go to the country on the other side."

"What do you do there?"

"I walk around, go on adventures. It's so lovely! Yesterday, there was a red island full of birds, and suddenly a golden bird swooped down to me and I was so happy. I cried, 'Appa! Appa! Look!'"

Her eyes sparkled and her cheeks grew rosy like a peach.

"But this is a nice place, too."

She smiled so delightedly. I was mesmerized.

"And I love the gods."

"Oh? Why?"

"Because they love me."

An irrefutable logic.

"Do you ever see them?"

"Sometimes. When I am very quiet, I can hear them."

"Do they speak to you?"

She shook her head indulgently.

"Not in words, of course. It's like the sound of the wind across the dunes. It comes from very, very far away. And it changes. Sometimes it's gentle; sometimes it's harsh; sometimes it's like a bird fluttering by. It takes you along: you go here, you go there; you are driven and everything is arranged for you, including encounters."

A large thistle seed blew across the dunes, brushed against Batcha, slipped through my fingers, and disappeared from sight.

Batcha burst out laughing.

"You see!"

"What does that mean?"

"It means we're having fun."

"Who's we?"

"Oh, how complicated you are!"

She sighed.

"There are so many tales. Does the great Goddess play the veena in your country, too?"

"Goddess? There is no goddess in my country."

"No Goddess?!"

She could not have been more astonished.

"Then you know nothing."

She scrutinized me again.

"You have forgotten. You remind me of Bholanath."

I must have looked completely baffled.

"He's my favorite God, the supreme God. Oh, how sweet he is! He loves everything: gods, devils, the wicked, the good. He's a beggar."

"A beggar? The supreme god?"

"Yes, he begs. He forgets everything. He even forgets that he is very rich."

If I live forever, I think that little sentence will remain with me as one of those secrets whose key one can never quite grasp.

She rested her head on her knees again.

"Yet, you are not like in my dream."

"Your dream?"

"You were passing by and I saw you. You were quite handsome. But you weren't dressed as you are now; you were taller, too. Now you look a bit—"

She searched for words, wrinkling the tip of her nose.

"Never mind, you're nice all the same."

She flashed a broad smile, her face becoming round like a moon. I was totally disconcerted.

"Taller—taller than what? Do you mean I have shrunk? What an imagination you have, Batcha!"

"Imagination. What is that?"

"It means seeing things that don't exist."

"But if they don't exist, you cannot see them! How strange you are! How can you see something that doesn't exist? Balu told me you were called Nothing-at-all. Does *that* exist?"

She burst out laughing—a delighted peal of laughter rippling impertinently through the dunes.

"You are my dream down here, Mr. Nothing-at-all; you don't exist!"

Her cheeks puffed up with suppressed laughter; then she shook her head with an air of commiseration.

"You're so funny! And what about Appa—do you think he sculpts nothing?"

"Batcha, look—"

I was nonplussed. Suddenly I had the feeling of losing my footing, of being unsure which side I was on—this one or the other? Perhaps there was no frontier at all between the two? I looked at Batcha, at that shoreline, at life, with a sense of wonder. What if we were carving an image from elsewhere, like Bhaskar-Nath with his sculptures? What if we were all in the process of carving the image of a god, or a devil, that we were elsewhere? Then one's entire life is an image growing increasingly real, increasingly embodying its model. And sometimes we carve nothing; we are just a piece of wood.

"What a strange little girl you are, Batcha. Who are you?"

"I am Bhaskar-Nath's daughter."

She drew herself up to her full height, like Balu, except that she was taller than Balu.

"And what about you?"

"—"

"You see."

Unmistakably, I was an idiot.

"Well then, you don't understand."

That settled it. What astounded me was the authority radiating from that little woman, her presence. With Bjorn, or any other man, I could always escape, but not with her. She held me right there, compelling my attendance by her own keen presence. Woman is truly the presence of the world.

"Will you tell me your dream, Batcha?"

But she no longer felt like it. The moment had passed. She was looking out at the sea, the dunes. The sandstorm had been gathering; small deep-blue ripples shivered over the face of the sea. "You don't understand." That's also what Bjorn had said. What did I not understand? What was it that was closed inside? Yet everything was wide open! The minute I got out of that sense of "I," there was vastness, instant ease and absolute comprehension. Indeed, I was the last one to want to cling to that "I," the tether that pulls you back for grazing, thinking, talking.

"Here, watch."

She tossed a pebble onto the sand before the steps, sending a crab scuttling into its hole. Then I noticed there were hundreds and hundreds of little gray-white crabs everywhere. Seconds later the crab reemerged from its hole, waving its eye stalk about like a periscope to check the situation—"no more danger"—then it skittered across the sand. Batcha broke into peals of laughter.

"This world is so funny. Do you think the gods also send pebbles at us to see our reaction?"

This time it was my turn to laugh.

"Yes, they send impertinent little Batchas."

"They send dreams, birds. I always see birds."

"My specialty is snakes."

"Oh, no! The gods do not send snakes. That's more the work of demons. The gods send birds to eat the snakes. Shikhi kills cobras; he's the demons' foe."

Batcha remained pensive for a moment.

"Although the demons are the gods' brothers, too, so actually they are just playing together."

"Playing at eating one another?"

"Oh, they're just pretending to! There are always cobras and Shikhis, always gods and demons."

"In other words, we are the only ones who really get eaten."

She looked at me.

"Eaten?"

"Yes, we die."

"You mean when we are burned, over there?"

She pointed to the other side of the dunes.

"But that's not dying! We merely move to another place. How funny you are! Appa said so. Then we come back. And we can play, too. Tell me, were you dead before coming here?"

Suddenly Batcha's expression changed. For a second she looked at me with extraordinary intensity.

"Still, one is sad from not being together."

There was such distress in that little voice.

"We mustn't be apart! We must remain together, always together!"

She repeated those words several times with a kind of fierce intensity. Whom, exactly, was she talking to?

"It's like in my dream—"

All at once she turned to face me, holding me in the gaze of her large black eyes, and it was like a cry:

"O stranger, why do you bring me these nasty thoughts? I have not asked to know you! I don't want to be sad!"

I reached out to her, but she recoiled in anger.

"Don't touch me!"

Suddenly, through that outburst of anger, for a second, I entered her. And I felt close, so close to that child, with a strange feeling of intimacy, a desire to put my arm around her shoulders, stroke her hair, comfort her, truly as if I had caused her pain.

"What is it, Batcha? What's wrong?"

Her breast heaved in short gasps.

"Tell me what's wrong!"

"I don't know."

She looked up at me with a kind of incomprehension. Then she began to speak slowly, in a colorless, almost neutral voice.

"I saw you at the temple gate. As I looked at you, you seemed very tall. Then I came here and made a *puja.* I offered flowers to the gods. But all the while I was thinking of you; that was not right. Then I slept. And that's when I saw you."

She sniffed, making a comical little grimace that puffed out her cheeks.

"There was a kind of road, very, very wide, bathed in a lot of sunlight, like this beach, except it was made of water. It was water that looked like sand. I don't know quite how to explain it, but it sparkled a lot. You walked by without seeing me, as if crossing that wide, wide beach, as wide and sparkling as the sea. You were taller than you are now, but white, like the pilgrims from the north. You weren't dressed as you are now. You seemed to be dressed like a sannyasi, in orange. But it was you all right. I even called your name—I called you three times—oh, how I cried out your name! But you wouldn't answer, wouldn't hear me. On and on you walked, farther and farther away, growing smaller and smaller as you went, like an image vanishing from sight. All that sand kept sparkling, and I kept saying: 'It's going to be too late! It's going to be too late!' I called and called your name, fixing you so intently! I knew that if I lost sight of you for a minute, it would be over; you would vanish forever, and I would die. It was so strong."

Batcha pressed her hand to her breast.

"When you grew smaller, I felt such a pain here. That's what woke me up."

I looked at her, wide-eyed.

I could see it all so clearly, vividly, poignantly. It struck me to the depths with an intense light—the keen light of that which is true, as though the image of that scene were already within me, whereupon I felt a sudden shock of recognition: this is it. Yes, but "it" is what? I knew that kind of shock well: it was the contact with what is already there. One can only be touched by what is already there; the rest is simply nonexistent, the unsubstantial impression of passing things. I could see that sannyasi vividly, almost feel the weight of his presence upon my shoulders; then Batcha's gaze, her soft voice: "It's going to be too late, too late"—just a poignant little vibration. Oh, the foreboding sound of things about to take form. There are sounds that evoke a world, as a flash can evoke a whole picture, and perhaps it was the same thing in another language: the picture's music. There are sounds of darkness, violet sounds, poisonous yellow vibrations like a snake slithering under the leaves, and slight sounds that sing like a blue-tinted frost of victory. But this sound was dark-red and poignant: It's going to be too late, too late. It was somehow so familiar to me, something I had heard before. Suddenly, a hillside carpeted with scarlet flowers flashed before my eyes, as well as an island, a promontory. And then Mohini: "It's too late, Nil, too late."

I was staggered.

I could not believe it. All I could hear was that gentle voice, and the blinding immensity of the sea before me once again with the hulk of the *Laurelbank* looming in the distance. A whole world was reemerging from a former life: the bungalow, the sitars, the enormous bird cage, the tulsi plant with its aroma of wild mint, the monsoon, the shower of red blossoms swept by the wind. "It'll be too late, Nil, too late."

What on earth was the meaning of all this? What had Batcha seen? An image from the past? But I was not a sannyasi, not dressed in orange. Moreover, Batcha had nothing to do with

Mohini. An image from the future? But why Mohini, then? That story was over, dead and buried! I could still hear that same gentle voice: "Are you not Nil-Aksha, the blue-eyed one? What is happening today began thousands and thousands of years ago, and will continue for thousands and thousands of years to come."

I could feel Batcha's eyes upon me.

Suddenly I had an inspiration.

"Tell me, Batcha, you say you called me three times in your dream. What name did you use? *Whom* did you call?"

She frowned.

"I don't remember. But it was your name all right, your true name."

She looked at me mischievously.

"And it was *not* 'Nothing-at-all.'"

A charming smile lit up her face. Then, before I could understand what was happening, she grinned and stuck out her tongue at me.

"Batcha!"

She leaped to her feet, gathered up her skirts with both hands, and fled across the sands like a deer.

10
Kali's rock

I was about to leave the hostel when Balu rushed up to me. His hair was tousled, his forehead damp with perspiration. He was clutching a schoolbag.

"What's up, little frog? What's the matter?"

"Where is he?"

"Visiting the king cobra."

That was a stupid thing to say. Balu was really upset, jittery, pulling at my arm.

"But where is he? Where *is* he? Something has happened to Bjorn!"

"Now, now, calm down."

"Something has happened to Bjorn; I know it."

"Perhaps he's still with Guruji?"

"Not at this hour."

"Since he did not have lunch here, he must have been detained by his guruji."

"Oh, how I hate that man! Anyway, he's not the type that feeds anyone."

Balu spat on the ground.

"It's his fault. Everything is his fault. I hate him."

Balu was pale with anger. His eyes darting right and left, his nose in the air, sniffing, he seemed to follow the scent of a trail like a bloodhound. Suddenly, he grabbed my arm.

"This way!"

He started running toward the north, in the direction of Kali's Rock. I, too, was beginning to worry. I hurried behind him, scraping my feet on coral banks, stumbling in the sand. There was not a soul in sight. The trail twisted its way into a waving dreamscape of thornbushes and gnarled banyan trees. Balu plunged onward, clutching his schoolbag. What exactly was the bond between this child and Bjorn?

We paused, breathless, about two hundred feet from the peak. The air was stifling. The banyan trees writhed their branches skyward like tortured giants.

"This way. There are steps."

He pressed on through a jungle of acacia trees bristling with daggerlike thorns. The landscape was a chaos of scattered rocks and jagged branches outlined against the indigo sky like barbed lace. How truly beautiful this island was, how wild!

"Bjorn! Bjorn!"

The sheer western face of the Rock rose a hundred feet from the ground. The eastern face was a hulking stone mound. It looked like some gigantic Egyptian cat crouched on the ground.

"Bjorn!"

Balu's shrill voice resounded through the silence. A covey of myna birds took wing from between the rocks. A solitary erne circled overhead. There was not a sound, not a breath of air, just the scent of acacia and scorching rocks. I began to feel uneasy, but continued to climb in Balu's footsteps. Only an occasional birdcall or the clatter of cascading stones broke the silence. Suddenly I stopped dead in my tracks, overcome by a feeling of anguish. It had nothing to do with Bjorn; it was something else. It was that Rock, that smell overcoming me. I looked up, and I knew: the cry of parakeets, the promontory, the banyan tree—the red island. Then that Threat descending upon me. I looked ahead, searching for Balu, but he had disappeared on the other side of the Rock. I turned around. The island was floating in seething foam like a vestal virgin adrift on a raging sea. Then I heard Balu's cry.

"Bjorn!"

I stepped out onto the rocky ledge. There he was .

A sullen Bjorn, his jaw set, his lips compressed into a thin line. Balu rushed up to him and hugged his legs.

"Leave me alone! Go away! Just leave me alone."

He was braced against a recess in the rocks. There were bird droppings everywhere. It looked like a guano island in the sky.

"What's the matter, Bjorn? What's wrong? The boy was so worried about you!"

Balu rummaged feverishly through his schoolbag, throwing his note books into the air, and extracted a handful of peanuts.

"Here, eat. It's good for you!"

Bjorn closed his eyes and sank to the ground, his legs collapsing under him. Without a word, he stroked the child's hair, staring off toward the distant port. There was a port. One could distinguish a railway bridge, the froth beneath its arches, then the coast, the piers, and a small white lighthouse on the mainland.

A freighter at anchor was firing up its boilers.

"What's the matter, Bjorn?"

He turned to face me, a look of intense pain in his eyes. He had been crying.

"Erik has killed himself."

He shuddered and turned his face away. Balu ogled him like an idol; he had understood everything. I put my arm around Bjorn's shoulders, stroked his hair, took his sorrow into my heart. The three of us huddled together before that death as people huddle together before the storm, the wind, the night; and, if one dies, each other one understands his death.

"Erik, my brother, you understand."

Balu had laid his head on Bjorn's knees. An erne circled in the sky.

"Please, Bjorn, I love you, you know."

I looked at the child, the sea, Bjorn. I listened to that death. Oh, the minute we stop, it's there; it's always there, hovering like that erne, its breath as light as a wingbeat. I could see the face of my brother the gold-washer, who had died in the jungle, so serene in his hammock swaying in the wind while a small lizard rustled through the dry leaves underneath. The same silence. He was dead. The same blue sky overhead.

"You must be hungry, Bjorn. Please eat; it's good. And look at the nautilus shell I found!"

One day I confronted that sky and said no to death. We cannot understand anything about life until we understand our death! It was in their prisons, when everything was dying around me. I stared at that sky, while all those little bodies were being killed, and such a cry welled up in my heart: "No! I was not a thing one can kill. I could *not* be that. It was impossible, a falsehood. I was not mortal, not a body that dies!" That death was so outrageous. Suddenly I laughed. I soared, rocketed as if my cry had pierced a hole in this human carapace—and I emerged above. That was my first time. It was marvelous. There was that little detachable body held at the end of a string, a little puppet in striped sackcloth, and I was above. Oh, that cry of wonder when one breaks free, that sudden sense of royalty like a gallop against the wind on the blue steppes. I was free! What could possibly touch that? Nothing. No one. I was free and immortal! I laughed. I opened my great blue gaze, and I was king and free everywhere.

Bjorn turned toward me. I could still hear Batcha's little voice rising with the warm air, with the still face of my dead brother in the jungle, with Bjorn's sorrow, with this world of sorrow.

"Always together, always together."

"I'm leaving."

"What?"

He pointed to the distant ship at anchor.

"There's nothing for me to do here. What I was doing no longer has meaning."

"But where will you go? Back to *them*? That's madness!"

I was dumbfounded. It was a catastrophe, an unforeseen blow for me. With Bjorn gone, it would be the end of this island.

"You want to kill yourself, too?"

"But Erik is dead," Bjorn kept repeating.

"So what? It's just cowardice."

"Maybe, but he's dead."

Bjorn searched his waistband and pulled out a piece of crumpled paper, a newspaper clipping.

"My sister sent me this. He returned home from the Sahara just to kill himself, as if the desert weren't quiet enough. Listen:"

> 'Local police report a tragic death yesterday at approximately 9:30 A.M. in the Belle Vista section of Gjoevik. Alerted by nearby residents, squad members, accompanied by a doctor, discovered the body of a motorist lying in the front seat of his car. The vehicle was parked on Lillehammer Road, a few yards from the intersection of Route 23. The victim was forthwith pronounced dead. In a note addressed to the police, Erik Sorensen, 27, declared his intention to take his life, which he did by extending a piece of rubber hosing from the exhaust pipe through the back window of his car. He died of asphyxiation. The reasons for his desperate act are unknown.'

Bjorn's face was as hard as marble.

"That's his black humor, picking a place called 'Belle Vista.' And he came back from the Sahara for that."

"It's sickening."

"He was suffering."

"So what!"

"Their world is so ugly, Nil."

"Oh, but beauty is not in the world, Bjorn! Beauty is not pre-existent here; it is in our eyes of beauty. There is no such a place in the world as 'Belle Vista,' except as a spot to commit suicide."

"There was also a letter addressed to me:"

> Bjorn,
> I am killing myself tonight after a royal binge. My last words are for you. What lies beyond? Probably nothing very lasting, but if there is anything at all coherent and you decide to call it, I'll respond to your call. I don't suppose I will be malevolent on the other side, but one never knows!
> Beware of looking at yourself too closely; it can be rather ugly.
> > Your brother
> > Erik

"Ugly?"

A sort of rage swept over me. If I gave in to Bjorn's grief, he was finished. His end would be mine, as well as Balu's and Batcha's. Somehow, we all revolved around a common axis.

"And what does your brother think he is?"

"He had married a prostitute from Oran on a dare."

"So what? We all bear our share of ugliness and shame! Scratch a little below the surface and you'll see it. Ah, Bjorn, I've seen and gone through plenty, I assure you, and each time I was able to say: 'I am a part of this; this also is me; I too am capable of this; I am capable of everything!' Tell me one thing that is not human. Where is the pure, unsullied man? We are all in the same boat. There is but one Man in the world! I have gone through enough to cover four continents. I have worn down my hell through my footprints. Yet, when I reached the bottom of the hole, I saw a light shining there. So now, at last, I know. Now I see through the age-old stratagem: there is a dizziness in evil, but not the one we think. True misery lies not in being miserable but in believing in one's misery. Listen, Bjorn, every time I sank into darkness, I found that the most difficult task was not to recognize my own smallness, but to recognize what was great in me *in spite of everything*. That really takes courage. We are not very pretty, a mixture of scars and mud, and yet we grit our teeth and say, 'No! I am beauty, light, truth, purity, That which shines in the depths, That which is free, That and only That, and they will not get me!' Then, it's as if a flame of pain were suddenly kindled inside, flaring up with the intensity of love. After that, you can understand everything. Bjorn, evil is not evil; it's the secret door to love. As if the intensity of evil sparked a corresponding intensity of love."

"All I know is that he's dead."

"But *you* are alive!"

"Life for my own sake does not interest me."

"For God's sake, Bjorn, what do you think *others* are? How do you expect to save anybody if you are incapable of saving yourself? Oh, Bjorn, don't you see that we are like a battleground, and it's not a question of you, me, or 'others'? We are born to win a victory. We each have our own special victory to win, and every circumstance comes to help us toward that victory. In fact, it's like a tremendous conspiracy—a conspiracy of light—down to the least detail. As I look at that, sometimes I get dizzy. We seem to be born into life with just the necessary darkness to win our victory. So whenever I see a chasm opening before me, I say to myself: 'This is the moment.' Bjorn, we have understood nothing about evil if we haven't understood that it's the other hand of the same Angel of Victory. As Batcha said, the demons are the gods' brothers."

"I have spent three years searching."

"There's nothing wrong with searching. What else is there to do? Believe me, the real treasure is not in the finding but in the searching. Oh, sometimes I sense that that profound thirst, that need for something else—something else. That something inside us which yearns and seeks and aches with need may well be the true treasure. It burns; it *is*. It thirsts; it *is*. It needs; it *is*. It's the only thing that *is*. Everything else is meaningless. We are great not because of what we find but because of our need to find it."

"It's for him I was searching; it's because of him I sought power."

"But he told you himself that you need only call him and he'll respond. Do you at least know *how* to call him? You yourself said that we are a new breed of adventurers. Well, what do you think the adventure is all about? Finding magic potions? Putting one's feet in the air? Holding one's breath? The adventure is to be conscious of everything in every circumstance: in waking, sleep, and death, here, there, and in all possible ways, with the gods, in hell, and everywhere. Then nothing will separate us from our brothers anymore, not even death. We must find the place where we are always together."

"A fine speech for someone who was so eager to criticize Guruji."

"But there are not endless things to find! There is only *one*. When you touch that, you touch everything."

"Let's see *you* do it."

"We must know what we want, Bjorn. We must be coherent, as your brother says, not go after endless powers—just one. It is the key to everything! Without it, you simply fritter everything away: one day your bag bursts open and everything scatters. *That* is the coherence, the supreme coherence; with that, you hold *the* thread, all the threads, the password to everywhere."

"I don't know anymore, I just don't know."

Bjorn reached for the peanuts.

Balu's face loosened into a smile. His friend was eating; he was out of danger.

Quietly, he slipped another handful of nuts into Bjorn's hand, then looked up at me and gave me a grateful look. My hands were clammy, and I felt feverish as if I had swallowed Bjorn's suicide.

"Bjorn—"

The air on that rock was stifling, oppressive with the scent of acacia and hot sand rising in puffs. Balu dared not move. Bjorn gazed out at the port. I stared at that broad-shouldered Scandinavian with his red triangle between the eyebrows, and at the child who watched him adoringly.

"Bjorn—"

Balu clutched his friend's knee.

"You won't go back to him, will you?"

"What!"

Bjorn was purple with anger.

"What's wrong with all of you? What have you got against him?"

Balu made a funny little face. Then he snatched up his nautilus shell and smashed it against the rock.

"He doesn't love you."

"How do you know that?"

"Besides, he's a *vaishya.*"

There was such contempt in his voice that Bjorn was startled.

"But you are a king."

"A king?"

"And handsome as well."

Bjorn melted. He stroked the child's hair.

"What about you, Little Moon? What are you?"

"I watch over the king."

He looked up at Bjorn. I felt a current pass between them.

"I watch over you."

Clutching his schoolbag to his chest, Balu sat straight and pale as if he were challenging death. What linked this child to Bjorn—Bjorn, who had landed on this island after a trip of six thousand miles from the other side of the world? What was

---

* One of the merchant caste.

the connection among our three lives, the common thread? There was a time when I looked for miracles, yet now that I no longer do, I seem to see them everywhere. People speak of "chance," but what is it really? The smallest of those "chances" glistens like a star in the big forest of the world. Sometimes I feel that a casual gesture, a second of inattention, a hop to the right instead of the left, a bird feather, an idle breath, contains a dizzying world of premeditation. We do not see what connects these instants, the invisible thread running through the centuries to tie this second of wonderment, this critical juncture, this plumed thistle seed to another, unconcluded story, an old unkept promise, a forgotten hill, an ancient fountain where two beings once exchanged a fleeting smile. When did the story begin? To what signs, what bygone call, are we responding today? To be sure, we do not hold all the threads! We merely hold a few ephemeral, unnoticed moments here and there, shreds of a story as if a window suddenly opened onto a vast legend that disappears into intimate Scandinavias and lost islands, and that will outlive all our winters. Sometimes, I think there is more mystery in a trifle one bumps against by chance than in all the infinitudes of heaven, and that the key to the world is not in the infinitely great but in the twinkling of an eye one catches by accident. Balu, of course, lived those tiny miracles naturally, while I experienced them in bursts of wonderment, like the puffs of warm air redolent of sand and acacia rising from the rocks. Balu caught them instantaneously, as he had caught Bjorn's call during his class of mathematics, and off he went He had understood the whole situation. Our thoughts and words are thick disguises; we understand nothing. We clothe in noise a tiny sound that goes straight to the heart of things, traveling through ages and places in a second. Each sound from the heart goes straight to its goal, while outside we scream to the rafters.

Without a word Balu closed his schoolbag and rose to his feet. Hands joined, he saluted Bjorn with a little bow, then lowered his head before the idol in the grotto. And he was gone.

"What a funny little man!"

Bjorn gathered up the fragments of nautilus shell.

There was a statue in that grotto, a strange four-armed goddess who blessed you with one hand and cut your throat with the other. Stark-naked and jet-black, her neck adorned by a garland of skulls, she danced open-mouthed as if about to swallow the world. What message was she bringing us?

"I don't understand what all of you have against Guruji. It doesn't make any sense. Guruji tried to help Erik. He wanted to save him. He used his power to—"

"He was in contact with Erik?"

"Well, I gave him his photograph. He was working to make him come here."

"Oh!"

"What do you mean, oh?"

"He tried to make him come."

"But first, he wanted to separate him from that girl."

Suddenly I understood.

"That's it. But instead of making him come here, he killed him."

"What?"

"Listen, Bjorn. It's simple. He tried to make him come here by sending a force that would make him come, but you cannot apply a force without eliciting a corresponding resistance. You cannot apply a light without touching a corresponding darkness. The stronger your ray, the deeper the darkness. If the recipient is not ready, things simply break: he goes mad or he dies, like Erik. He dies because the amount of darkness is too great for the incoming light, you understand. I've seen it in myself, Bjorn. Every time I have progressed, reached a new height, the next day, or three days later, I have fallen into a corresponding hole, without fail. It isn't so much a 'fall' as it is the light forcing the darkness out of its hiding place, so to speak—a sort of law of the descending process. Why does this happen? I don't know. But one cannot descend farther than one's own capacity of light, otherwise things break. That's why Erik died. A kind of dark equivalence. It's mathematical: each step of progress is followed by a step downward. It's a funny thing, Bjorn, as if our capacity for heaven were tied to our capacity for hell."

"But—"

"Don't you see? Erik felt something pushing him out of his rut; but he went out through the wrong door. You can't push people faster than they can go. That's why the world is moving at such a snail's pace! If we wanted to, or could, make it divine at one stroke, it would simply explode. It needs to be purged in small doses. Our challenge is to accelerate the movement, to cram ten lives into one. It's like going through accelerated evolution, with all the risks it entails."

It was all becoming clear: Erik's suicide, the setbacks, Bjorn's storms, my own revolt against that sannyasi, that whole process of upward progression and sudden plummeting. But why? Why that law of descent?

Bjorn looked puzzled.

"Why, Bjorn? Why this automatic fall? Why can't we free ourselves simply? Evil? But I don't believe in evil. There's no evil; there's just something we do not understand."

Bjorn shrugged.

"That may be, but I am leaving all the same."

"Oh, Bjorn!"

There was nothing more to say.

The steamer, Bjorn's *Laurelbank*, sent smoke billowing across the harbor. The sun was setting. The idol looked almost alive, as if on the verge of cutting our throats, or maybe blessing us. I closed my eyes, turned off the current. One drop, one simple drop of *that* Harmony on the earth and all the jarring in the world would be cured forever.

"So then I am the one who killed Erik."

It was like banging my head against a wall. He stammered: "If it's true that Guruji pushed Erik, then I am guilty. I am responsible; I killed my brother."

"You?"

"Yes."

"Oh, Bjorn!"

"I gave Guruji his photograph."

"I? Which I? We are all 'I' and no one is guilty of anything!"

I seemed to see the idol's eyes widen.

"Where is 'I'? I don't know, Bjorn. There are passing currents—red, black, blue, or as light as snow—and one captures the currents, hardening them in a small human self, molding them into desolate and tragic destinies, but everything is so simple when one opens one's hands. In fact, there is nothing but light when one opens one's hands. I am not sure there is any shadow, Bjorn. All we have to do is open our hands and rise above our heads. Then everything changes and everything is the same, save the hardness. It's as if there were two worlds side by side. In one, all things flow so harmoniously, so simply, so naturally, free of our human cries and tears, which are like theatrical *additions* to the true world, fabrications of misery."

"Erik's death is not theatrics."

"Oh, that's the ultimate performance of the 'I'! He'd rather die by his own hand than retreat."

Bjorn leapt to his feet, his eyes ablaze with hatred. From that moment on, I struggled with him as though with my own death.

"Your path 'above the head' is without heart."

Clearly he wanted to kill me. It was the return of the old enemy, the shadow brother, whom one meets at the last door.

"You are not of our world. You don't belong here. I hate you!"

A wave of anguish swept over me—his, mine, it was all the same. Oh, I have had enough of this human sentimentality, this knot of helpless pity, this bondage of pain that believes in death, believes in smallness, believes in the inevitability of laws. *I* believe in joy! I believe we are great, strong, luminous, divine. I believe we *can*!

I got up and clutched Bjorn's shoulders as if I were grappling with my own death. The sun was setting and the sky was an orange blaze. Everything was suffused with orange light: the erne above the grotto, the sand, the sea, the guano-covered rock—an effulgence of light resembling a descent of the other world.

"You're suffering, Bjorn, but that's a falsehood. Suffering is a falsehood, death is a falsehood, pain and smallness are falsehoods. To the very end, even if I fall or perish, I will repeat like a mad king: 'We are the truth, we are the light, we are greatness and beauty, and singing joy, because we are divine.' An immortal Flame dwells within, a Fire born of supreme joy that laughs behind our suffering and our nights; a Fire of Truth that consumes our darkness and our shame, our sins and our virtues, that consumes all fates and all laws, because it is *the* Fate and *the* Law—a little flame within, capable of remaking the world. Someday that flame will seize men, and we shall fashion the earth like a fairy tale; someday the fire within will burn without, and this obscure matter will become the radiant image of the soul that inhabits it: malleable to its vision, alive to its joy, obedient to its command. Then each man will create his world according to the color of his soul; each will express what he is by the quality of his fire, visibly and materially, without subterfuge or artifice, without deceptive words, solely through the power of his fire; each will take his place within a higher luminous hierarchy, according to the beauty of the dream that inhabits him and his power to shape matter into the substance of that dream. Then the earth will emerge from falsehood and darkness. Life will free the Flame from its bodily or spiritual prison. A world of truth will be born. We shall be here below as we are above: free, vast, true, *that* and only *that*; and death will no longer be, because we shall be true in our body as in our soul."

Bjorn picked up a rock and threw it into space.
"All I know is that you'll end up in the pit alone."

11
the voyage of the Aalesund

*B*jorn was not out of danger; Erik's death had opened a door in his fortress and the enemy had gotten in. But I have often wondered who that enemy really was, and I seemed to glimpse the Friend smiling beneath his black hood; perhaps it is his way of breaking into our irreproachable prisons and drawing us outside despite ourselves, covered with mud and free of a timeworn virtue.

The just are impregnable. They are set in their light.

"Let's get away from here; I've had enough."

I looked at Bjorn incredulously.

"Yes, enough. Let's get out. Meenakshi's cook said the freighter in the harbor is Norwegian or Swedish, or something."

"But—"

"There is no but. If you let me down, I'll go alone."

He stood in the entrance of my monk's cell, hands on hips. His eyes were somber gray.

"Are you afraid?"

A dreadful feeling of anguish swept over me; my temples pounded. He continued to hammer out his words with a sort of rage.

"You have it easy here, haven't you, while I pay for everything. But enough is enough. We take the plunge. If you want to stay, you'll have to beg for your food."

I was stunned. Batcha's face came into my heart.

"What about Balu?"

He blinked.

"You don't expect me to stay for a child, do you?"

"—"

"He'll grow up; he'll forget. Do as you like, but I'm leaving."

Bjorn turned, and I followed him to his cell, where he started rummaging through his footlocker, tossing books and clothes in the air.

"Fair weather brothers, eh? How convenient. All the brothers are abandoning ship, it seems. I could drop dead for all you care; you've 'found the light.' "

"—"

"Furthermore, I've had it up to here with this state of permanent dreaming we live in. Will you tell me what on earth we are doing here?"

He picked up his *mala** and flung it against the wall.

"You don't give a damn, do you? You're laughing your head off."

"That's enough, Bjorn. I'll go with you."

I felt heartbroken.

Leaving. I was always ready to leave for any destination. In five minutes I would pack my bag; the more unexpected the better. But this time was different. Of course, one cannot "stay for a child"; one is levelheaded and "doing" something in life. What? I don't know. Perhaps begetting children to make up for the child one has betrayed.

---

* A string of beads used for repeating mantras.

"Six million mantras, can you imagine? Six million. Three years of work."

Bjorn kneeled before a heap of shirts and ties, among which lay a map of the Sahara and the sannyasi's knife he had taken from me.

"All this is useless. We don't need anything."

His voice softened. He paused and glanced at me like a lost child. Suddenly he appeared to be on the verge of tears.

"What's the use, Nil? I've lost everything, even my dream."

"Do you think we'll find it again wherever we are going?"

"We'll do something else, begin a new life."

"Something else? You think one *can* do something else? I think one always does the same thing under one name or another."

He gave an eerie little laugh.

"I know mantras to cure scorpion bites, mantras to neutralize poisons, to cure nervous spasms and hysteria, and make pregnant women give birth in less than thirty minutes! It's all here."

He waved an exercise book in front of me.

"If worse comes to worst, we could even open a maternity clinic or a hatha-yoga school!"

I wanted to clasp him and hold him to my heart, but I stood there, held back by a stupid sense of shyness.

"I don't even know how to live."

He stuffed his clothes back into the footlocker.

"We don't need anything—well, just a pair of trousers. We can hardly board ship disguised as Brahmans."

He tossed me a pair of blue jeans and a shirt, then gazed at the knife.

"Yes, this could be useful too."

Then he closed the trunk with a bang.

"Imagine, I haven't even seen the gods; I've seen nothing! I wanted to see the gods, you know, to see and love—yes, that's it, to love! You close your eyes and you *see*. There it is and you love forever. One day I saw Kali—oh, what a sight!—all black and so beautiful with her long hair. I thought: 'If only I could see her always, any time I wish, in any circumstance.' "

He stared into space for a moment.

"What a miserable lot we humans are: everyone looking out for himself and dying, while the gods remain silent. The one that loves us most is our own dream."

"—"

"I've lived in a dream for twenty-five years."

"Well, you simply need to pass into a larger dream, that's all. The only alternative is death."

"I've searched but found nothing."

"But it's right here! You are laboring to see something else, Bjorn, but it isn't a matter of seeing something else. It's a matter of seeing the same thing with different eyes! The truth is, we are mesmerized by the supernatural. Until we realize that what we must find is not elsewhere but *here*, we may achieve heavenly bliss, but we will continue to rot on the earth. I know, because I, too, have struggled with this, thinking the true world was elsewhere, a sort of private supercinema one attends crosslegged. But it isn't so! Everything is here, right here. I guess each of us has his own way of experiencing difficulty, but in the end there's only one: it's *the* difficulty. Your hang-up is with the gods, while for others it might be money, women, morality or immorality—their particular way of experiencing difficulty. People will get hung up on anything, even the spirit, even beauty, good or evil, as long as they have something to hang on to. That's the only real difficulty of the world: the 'I' hanging on and spoiling everything. There is not a single good that will not be corrupted by that 'I,' but just let go of it and everything becomes good. When you let go of it, the gods are no longer the reverse of the devils, or the devils the reverse of the gods; you are above the dualism. You are in *that*."

For a split second I wondered what it was that *I* hung on to.

"I'm just so tired of everything."

Bjorn got up, gathered his shirt and trousers, and stopped, a pair of shoes in his hands.

"We can't change our clothes here. The whole village would laugh at us. We'll get dressed on the beach."

He gave a low chuckle.

"We'll disguise ourselves as Europeans."

I went to my cell. It was bare except for a mat on the floor. I picked up my little flute player, who seemed to be smiling. Then I looked around. There was nothing else to take. I was as poor as Job. Yet so rich! I closed my eyes for an instant and everything dissolved—the confusion, our departure, Bjorn's anguish. Nothing remained except that little flame inside, so warm, so tranquil. Open the curtain and it's there, always there: the unfailing marvel. Outside was just noise, a false departure leading nowhere. We move about and make gestures, millions of gestures for nothing—a frightful nothingness rambling on in nothingness—while the only place to go is right here, peaceful, noiseless, smiling, waiting. Suddenly, all of life appeared so futile to me, a sort of jungle where one carves one's way trudgingly, making such tremendous and dramatic efforts, and then one pauses for a second, breathless; there *was* a flower beneath that bush! And everything is swept away in one stroke—the jungle, the sweat, the labor. Nothing remains but that flower. It was always there; it had never ceased to be there! It is for this that one has trudged and toiled. Oh, what an extraordinary shift of vision! Everything is understood, cleared up, fulfilled; one has rounded the foggy cape, like a child staring in amazement as the world changes colors.

But we don't want the smile. We want drama.

"Are you coming?"

He slammed the door.

We took a westward direction, crossing the entire island to the coral fishery. The freighter loomed before us in the harbor on the other side of the strait. Bjorn did not utter a word. He was like a suppressed storm. We changed our clothes on the beach. My trousers flapped about my ankles, so I turned them up.

"Please don't make such a face."

We set off for the mainland in a felucca with a triangular sail. I felt like an automaton.

Little gusts of wind blew over the sea.

"Look, she's Norwegian!"

It could have been Zulu or Peruvian for all I cared. We could have been headed for Tierra del Fuego or the for the devil; that didn't matter either.

Bjorn couldn't contain his excitement, hopping from one side of the boat to the other.

"Norwegian, can you imagine! Look at the blue cross! We are going to see the snow again, Nil, and the lavender rimming the fjords, and the ice. Enough of this furnace! You who used to dream of the poles—"

I didn't know what I dreamed of anymore, whether the cold or the hot, Norway or the equator. All I needed was a little inner degree. Everything else was like those trousers: a put-on; or like this ship: noise.

"The *Aalesund!*"

I dangled my hand in the water. The sea lapped gently against the sides of our boat. *Aalesund.* So what? I was on a different voyage and the world seemed to be draped in tenderness. Ever since leaving the island, I had the strange feeling of being carried by a force greater than my own, so soft, as if I were walking and moving beyond or outside myself and merely witnessing this small body, Bjorn, this ship, observing it all with that feeling of tenderness, from the perspective of someone who is already dead or far, far away, borne by something else or someone else. And the world recedes, dissolves, disappears into a mist of sweetness.

"Wait till you see how beautiful my country is, so wild, so rugged, with multitudes of white birds."

Bjorn's voice seemed to come from a distance, but it was a total Bjorn that I perceived, with all his depths and history, as if there were a fluctuating colored network around him with little sparks of light and darker streaks—yes, a darker streak. I heard a voice say: "My island is very beautiful, you'll see. Every morning when I arise, I come here and prostrate myself before the beauty of the world." That Bjorn was dressed in white. But his island had already lost its beauty, and tomorrow his beautiful northern country would turn gray and he would need to go somewhere else. I know the music, and I've worn down all the maps; the white birds are stuffed.

"Say, Nil, what country do you come from? You've never told me. You look like a dazed owl with a French accent."

"I come from a country that doesn't move."

His eyes widened and he stared at me for a second with the air of a stubborn child. I noticed that he had forgotten to remove his red triangle:

"What about your *tilak*?"

His face turned crimson. He rubbed his forehead with the back of his hand in a sort of rage. Now he was a very ordinary Bjorn.

"If Balu saw you now, he wouldn't recognize you."

I said that mechanically, as one points out a fact or a wrong color in a picture. In fact, the whole picture looked wrong: Bjorn angry, ashamed of himself, that enormous hulk painted with lead oxide, those feluccas awaiting their turn beneath the groaning cranes, the stench of phosphate in the air, the shouts of the *macuas**—everything seemed to glide before me like in a flat, artificial picture, a sort of two-dimensional imitation of the world. And that boundless tenderness behind, so quiet, watching the story unfold as if through an orange mist. And Bjorn ready to jump down my throat.

* Fishermen.

"You sure don't need the North Pole; you're already like an iceberg."

He turned his back on me.

I could feel his distress, too. I felt everything down to the most minute vibration, but it was as if held and transmuted by that gaze in the background, viewed through that sweetness of eternity which leans over the world and hears children crying. All is already golden on the hill and the ray shall soon touch this valley. Perhaps it was a time shift, a sort of acceleration of consciousness, which caused that orange transmutation?

"Hey, are you asleep, or what?"

I jumped like a puppet on a string. A man was standing at the bottom of the ladder. Five brief words and a piercing look that strips you bare. Bjorn climbed aboard first. A second man with a peaked cap. A look below the belt: click, clack. Three words like a growl and up you go. The air was filled with phosphate dust and swaying masts. Hurry up; you're in the way. A third man on the bridge. Same look again, and you don't even know *who* is looking. It seems like the visual appendage of a machine designed to slit your throat clean. Okay, checked, measured, shelved. Next.

"Don't say anything. I'll do the talking."

Of course I won't say anything! I went through the door, walking the chalk line.

A man sat before us, bare-chested, sweating. Same glance that strips you in a jiffy, and straight below the belt again; it must be the rallying point. I didn't understand anything, but it didn't matter. They were talking back and forth. That, too, was a kind of machinelike speech, like some wirework with angles and compartments; and soon one cube, two cubes, three cubes are placed on top of one another, a bit of wire netting, the right-hand drawer, that's it. He pulled out his pipe. Bjorn sat down and I sat down. He brushed back a lock of hair and

I did too, though I had no lock. No matter. Let nothing stick out, no matter what. I didn't move. I was in the dwarf-box. Neutralized, stupefied, rubber-stamped. A pause. Suddenly I realized I was behaving like a fool. A good and polite little boy, I sat next to Bjorn on a sofa covered in a floral print, studying with a sort of rapture, almost with compunction, an oil painting behind the man's head where a yellow Chinese junk sailed on an olive sea streaked with pink sky reflections. That Chinese junk will remain with me as one of the major discoveries of my life. At that moment, if he had asked me who I was, I would have trotted out my college degrees, my war medal, my uncle at the Navy ministry, and my birth certificate. I was in it up to my neck. A real electric shock. That's when I saw Bjorn, the man, and the junk suddenly become magnified like a close-up on a movie screen; there was a kind of shift of vision and I broke through it all. I no longer was in it; I was gone, disconnected! An intense flame seemed to leap within me instead, along with a cry. In a flash I saw all kinds of things, not the least of which was the difference, the prodigious difference. A moment before, I would have sworn by the reality of what I saw and felt; I was in the dwarf and it all seemed so *natural*, a kind of hypnosis, thousands of habits coming back with their curriculum vitae, including the grandfather's cancer which I would eventually get myself—a formidable habit. That's how it is, that's how it will be, and that's how it has always been. A habit of feeling, thinking, reacting, believing reminiscent of the stupefied shriveling one undergoes in a dream when one is trapped behind enemy lines and feels oneself growing smaller and grayer. One is trapped in the box, and asphyxiation is the order of the day. The world is a formidable habit watching its Chinese junk, and foundering on a make-believe olive sea. But with that cry bursting forth, everything melts away, even the cancer and the war medal; one leaves death row. Yes, there was a little fool outside, playing the approval game, but I was that warm flame within, that clear expanse, that rapture of a child stumbling upon his unbelievable kingdom, that secret lightness among the barbarians. My heart was overfilled with gratitude because there was *that*. The deliverance. Right there before that Chinese junk with its little man at the end of a scull, I was overcome by such emotion that I wanted to kneel, to prostrate myself and weep like a child because there was *that*, that marvel sweeping everything away in a flood of tenderness, toppling walls, breaking down doors in a great white wave of liberation. I don't know whether God exists, but *that* exists, *that* is true, *that* is large, the great freedom of the high seas, the open-sesame, the fabulous treasure amid a million inanities, that which brightens and changes everything before one's eyes, makes it come alive beneath one's fingers—the great awakening, eternal freedom, inalienable royalty. They could put me in irons or send me to hell; I was free in hell and free in their prisons. Death could die a thousand times; I was alive forever! Where were fear, anguish, the end? I could make my impregnable home anywhere; in the twinkling of an eye I was thousands of light-years away, amid the vast sweetness that spins the worlds and strives to smile through our myriad eyes. *And Everything is possible.* Everything becomes instantaneously possible. A minute earlier, events had taken place in an implacable order, according to an irrevocable law: cancer from father to son, the war medal forevermore, the cage without escape—a formidable cage whose boundaries are known and drawn once and for all, and there is no way out of this inflexible gravitation downward, this iron hierarchy, this communion through the lower abdomen. Then, poof, it's all gone; really gone. An illusion, a fantastic illusion! It's *all up to us*. It's as if we had traced little survey lines on a virgin world, settled within them, and "that's the law": a fantastic curriculum mortis, a huge intellectual cancer. My gaze fell on that man again, then on Bjorn, who sat with his hands folded between his knees. A loudspeaker was blaring out orders on deck. A wave of compassion came over me. I felt like involving myself in all this; I was almost happy to leave. Oh, I was happy in any case, outside it all, poised in a great white steppe, only involved as a little flame that loved for no reason, because it loves no matter what. But *they* do not know that they love! They do not know they are vast, light-years away, offered in their heart and soul. They do not know. So they are apprehensive. They think they are small and riddled with misery. They erect steel walls to protect themselves from their own vastness, and set up traps to retain a drop of *their* treasure. They are weak because they do not know; they are hard and mean because they have forgotten. If they knew, they would fling their doors wide open and draw unsparingly from the great treasure, drinking aplenty from the ocean of joy.

Someday their walls will crumble, leaving them amazed.

"Hey, Nil!"

He nudged at my ribs. I watched the man turn beet red before me, cough, then put down his pipe. I thought he would explode or throw me out. In a flash I understood. I lowered my eyes. And I made myself as small as I could, colorless, odorless. I crawled back into the hole. I know, they cannot bear that; to them, it's like an insult or a threat. One must keep the veil up. They cannot bear to be loved; they cannot bear joy. But were we so different? Had we not already left our island for this lead-oxide box? Indeed, we each have the measure of joy we can tolerate!

The man scribbled something on a slip of paper.

As I watched him bent over the table, it suddenly felt overwhelmingly evident that the world's divine totality was right there—total joy, total love, total everything—only waiting for us to be capable of containing more of it. Like an empty jug afloat on a sea of nectar, we pursue a miracle that is right here. Bjorn stood up and made a small bow; I stood up and made a small bow. He put the slip of paper in his pocket; I put my look in my pocket. And out we went.

"Now we must find the second mate."

Bjorn was white as chalk. I was miles away.

As we made our way toward the lower deck, a man called to us. He was the radio officer, a swarthy Mediterranean with a turned-up nose and a snoopy look. He directed a torrent of words at Bjorn, gesticulating wildly.

"—Chittagong, Rangoon, and back to Trondheim. You're in luck. Two deserters in Colombo. Ah, Colombo! What a spree! What a spree! There was this Singhalese girl—"

Clouds of white dust rose from the yawning holds. Men rushed about amid the roar of windlasses, diesel engines, commands shouted in English, Norwegian, German. Derricks swung overhead, trailing powder in their wake. I leaned over the side. Chittagong, Rangoon— In a few minutes I would be done for. It was like a dream. In fact, *everything* was a sort of dream: the little fellow attending to his winch, the radio officer, this ship, and even that world beyond—Rangoon, Trondheim, Oslo—which rushed on and on. There was not a single *real* minute in all this. It was "life," but what was it that lived? I don't know. They were all lived on, toiled on, acted on by life, by the mighty current passing through it all, and when the current stopped passing through the machine, it was all over and they were snuffed out. A fantastic unreality. Not a single thing existed for its own sake; all was like a movie projected onto a screen: flat little men, a flat ship, a flat world. And it kept unfolding, being unfolded, a huge projection in a void. The more I felt that unreality suffocating me, the higher I could feel the flame rise within me, scorching, living, intense, as if it grew in direct proportion to the void, as if fanned by that suffocation. And I saw that if I went down a few more steps, I would be face to face with an intolerable Fire.

I was like a living fire.

That's what lived. It was the only thing alive in all this, the only *substance*, the Life of life. Without it, there was nothing but air.

"I told you I don't know."

I turned around. Bjorn looked like a ghost.

"You're kidding me?"

"I don't know, I'm telling you!"

Bjorn now sounded upset. The little Italian threw up his hands.

"Do you mean to tell me that after three years here you don't even know where the girls are?"

Bjorn looked run-down, as if completely drained of his substance.

I took him by the arm.

"Come, Bjorn, let's find the second mate."

The Italian showed me the way to the mess hall.

"*È matto!*"*

Bjorn's arm was like ice.

We went down the iron ladder. Whistle blasts rent the air. A smell of saltpeter and hot engine oil rose from the deck. That smell triggered an uncontrollable feeling of panic in me, as if I were suddenly filled with lead. What was I doing here? What was this all about? A man bellowed in French, "*Ah, les vaches!*" I raised my head. The whole island lay before my eyes, milky-white, fringed with foam. Bjorn followed my gaze. It was an incredible island, with a blue peacock and a little girl dressed in a long pomegranate-colored skirt. I felt a wrenching pain in my chest. The whole sea shimmered with light. Bjorn clenched his teeth.

"Let's get going."

---

* He's cracked!

But I kept hearing Batcha's poignant little voice: "It was like a sparkling sea, and I called your name again and again. I felt such a pain here. That's what woke me up." Bjorn led the way to the middle deck. The stairs, the bridge glittered in the sun. What on earth was I doing here? Chittagong, Rangoon, and back. What did it all mean? I felt engulfed in an iron clamor, as if about to drown. A man hurried down the footbridge four steps at a time, cursing under his breath. Then, like a man about to drown, I saw the whole picture unfold before my eyes. Balu's small figure at the railway station: "Do you want me to guide you to your brother? He is handsome, your brother," The sannyasi had led me to Balu, and Mohini to the sannyasi. What succession, what fleeting whim had brought me to this point? And who had led me to Mohini? Was it caprice or some minutely precise design? What way were the cycles going? Batcha after Mohini? But was it really *after* or, rather, had there always been the same *she*, with everything revolving around a peacock's cry, from one life to another, from one island to another? One day I picked a destination at random on a map, and I left for French Guiana. But, incredibly, French Guiana led to Norway via Rangoon and Chittagong. All the maps are false! The sea routes run twenty thousand leagues under strange seas to emerge without any warning under the nose of some war god riding a blue peacock.

Aalesund 54,000 tons
Skipsverft
Bergen

Was the *Laurelbank* taking its revenge? Some acts do not reach completion until decades later, when they are long forgotten. Perhaps one day, in another life, I had embarked on a voyage that was concluding now on the *Aalesund*, with Bjorn. Perhaps Batcha was another voyage, Mohini yet another, the sannyasi yet another; or were they one and the same voyage extending through invisible latitudes? But where and when did it end? One touches one point after another—Mohini, Batcha, the white island, the red island—eventually to lose the trail while the point is out of sight, traveling some invisible course through eons of fire, nameless seas, forgotten ages, subsiding into blue Tartarus to reemerge here or there with a different skin color, a different face, different limbs, yet hauntingly the same. Or is it always one and the same story, the same limbs, like some huge shimmering radiolarian rolling through eternal gulf streams?

"Your sailboat is supposed to have capsized in the Palk Strait."

I must have looked puzzled.

"Don't worry. I know what I'm talking about. We'll grease the engines."

We arrived on the middle deck: the yellow light bulbs, the stench, the suffocation, the stifling fumes of tepid engine oil amid the whirr of blowers. What other voyage was this? Bjorn's heavy shoulders plunged ahead in this throbbing, clanking, humming sweatbox. Who exactly had led me here? What was the point, the real coordinates of this story? The question was so intense in my heart that I was getting dizzy. Bjorn's yellow fists kept forging ahead, tightly gripping the metal handrail. I was about to be swallowed up by that hold, while in a flash all those faces and places came whirling by—Batcha, Mohini, the red island, the white island, the *Laurelbank*, the *Aalesund*. I neither understood nor saw anything except those little multicolored incoherent bubbles appearing fleetingly, smiling, bursting, reappearing, smiling, bursting. What did it all mean?

I stopped to catch my breath, my true breath, a single inspiration of truth in that drowning! Abruptly, I saw a luminous hand pass in front of my eyes as if throwing or sowing something in a large sweeping movement. It was diaphanous and sleeved in billowy white muslin, and its movement seemed to bring together all those bubbles, those smiles, islands, and faces, weaving them together and filling the gaps, revealing blue valleys, then soaring to outline a luminous hill strewn with white birds—a whole picture. For a fraction of a second I clearly saw a picture in front of me, as clearly as one sees a Cézanne hung on a wall, except that it was made of light, bursting with sense, imparting a full and complete sense: the mountain, the blue valley with purple patches, and a stream of sunlight on the hillside with those white birds high above. I was *in* the valley. I saw myself in that picture, a little purple patch walking toward a hillside alive with birds. It was resplendent, all-encompassing, elucidating everything. I was no longer going down into a hold; I was heading for that hill filled with birds, carried by a stream of light. Then the picture expanded (or was it my gaze?) until it was no longer a composite of lines and colors; it had become *the* Picture, the essence, the total marvel of the world—a sort of total understanding bursting out in a white trail through that hand of an archangel. I saw myself as well as all those little purple points, those microscopic specks of life adrift in the valley that did not know, did not see anything except one spot after another: an orange flash, a portion of red island, a white-sand haven, a little girl passing by, and shadows upon shadows. But the archangel had already cast forth the tall hill, leaped over abysses and lives, strewn his white birds over the inexorable summit, while we journeyed through the centuries, blind travelers of a little shadow, of an orange or blue bubble, of a vice or a virtue, meandering across the vast nameless canvas, oblivious of the great vision, the golden path, believing our life stops at the ford, having forgotten that this purple shadow leads to a sun-swept hill and this abyss to a bird's velvet throat, ignoring the Hand that had strewn the wonder of a million lives across the whiteness of a divine dream.

Then everything vanished.

I was going down a narrow metal stairway. I was following Bjorn God knows where, and it was like a dream. But *where* was the dream? On which side? I was going down into that hold like a sleepwalker fraught with memories, a million men in one—and what remained? Little red, blue, or orange erratic bubbles, happy or painful islands, fleeting glimpses into intimate millennia, and that Pressure behind, that luminous sweep of the hand that draws us forth. It's all that remains: fleeting multicolored seconds, gestures exploding like thunder, encounters like the green buoy of a shipwreck on old submerged sea routes, flashes of memory like a sudden drowning in still waters, and faces upon faces surfacing with ambrosial smiles or a flavor of panic, as if they came from a familiar country— chances and chances by the thousands, all premeditated.

"That's on the starboard side."

Then the haunting memory of a treasure to reclaim, a true life, a different vision—something else, something else. A great Memory in the background, a mighty Pressure that draws us forth toward an already-lived future, toward a Goal whence we come, far, far beyond, beyond islands and abysses, beyond sorrows and time, on the wings of that golden bird, toward the fulfillment of the great picture, the all-embracing view. Then we begin a new canvas.

I entered that electric tunnel as one sets foot into an old life. The companionway disappeared in a haze of phosphate. Shoulders bent, Bjorn lurched along before me. The blowers stirred a mixture of oil and cooking odors. He stopped in front of a door, wiping his brow with the back of his hand. For an instant he stood still, and I could feel his emotions as if they were my own: the distress, the shame, the rage. Then he flung the door open.

About a dozen men in undershirts were seated at a huge, vinyl-covered table. The air was thick with stale tobacco smoke, the smell of cooking oil and beer, and unbelted laughter. I dove in there as if into a hellish life known a thousand times over, like something coming undone at the level of the lower abdomen and turning everything to rot; and then those dwarfs roaring with laughter. I was sinking, drowning under the wave. There was a bare counter to the right, cases of Brooke Bond Tea on the floor; the least object glared as if I had become lost in everything—the greasy shelves, the stuffed sea gull, the catacomb-like twilight—scattered into a myriad glances that captured and penetrated everything. Bjorn stood still on the threshold, hands in his pockets.

But it was no longer Bjorn standing there; it was Prince Bjorn, head high, eyes blazing, looking upon his destiny. I don't know what happened, whether it was his cry or mine:

"No!"

He turned around, looking past me.

"No," he repeated.

I will always remember that moment with the same interrogation. He made his choice; at that moment Bjorn's soul chose, although he might have been saved had he said yes and left on the *Aalesund*.

"I can't take this."

He let go of the door, dashed back through the tunnel like a madman, plunged ahead toward the gangway, shoving aside two men in his way, bumping into a grating, and knocking over a bucket of tar. We jumped into the nearest felucca.

Ψ

12
the silver birch

On our way back we took a shortcut through the dunes, Bjorn plodding along wearily, eyes cast down, shoulders bowed as if he were carrying a load. The sky was a blaze of blue. We walked in silence across the big white hills, going up and down with the swell, so smoothly that I did not know whether it was I going down or the wave falling, or if, far beyond these hills, a flock of eiders were about to soar into the crystal azure, leaving behind a dazzling snowfield. Bjorn did not see that great Norway with its downy fjords. He was still trudging through the tropics, laden with his cargo of heavy steel and obscure thoughts, and a small stubborn shadow that veiled the lovely snow. Don't you see, Bjorn? The world is as white and smooth as a child, as soft as a swan's neck, once you catch the great silent bird that glides across the expanses of the soul. Oh, Bjorn, the world can shift and shimmer like moiré silk. Which way have you pointed your skiff? I am going where you are going, but my eyes are bathed in enchanting snow and my footsteps are borne by an unmoving softness.

He paused at the top of the last dune. Half-buried palm trees, like cascades of rustling emerald, whispered about our heads, then swept down the dunes in a flight of black, dishevelled trunks toward the glistening lagoon.

A hundred yards from us, a house in ruins lay hidden among the palms at the foot of the dunes. It marked the end of the southern trail.

"It's Guruji's house."

But he was looking farther on toward the east, and I suddenly felt something strangely disturbing emanating from him, something I was to feel several times thereafter, always with the same uneasiness, like the sudden intrusion of a foreign, nonhuman element, a peculiar, catlike vibration. It was very strong. I followed his gaze to a solitary fire burning at the edge of the sands where the blue sea waters lost themselves in the sparkling lagoon.

"That's where they burn the dead."

He spoke with almost venomous delight. He had not forgiven me for leaving his boat.

"They are cremated and their ashes are thrown into the sea."

There was a noxious little vibration in his voice. No doubt he wanted to lash out at me, but I would not let myself be touched; I was as if held in that great white expanse. I felt like pressing myself to the sand and melting there, just a tiny grain of sand on the great dunes. It felt so sweet no longer to *be*. Oh, Bjorn, don't you see that the world is as soft as a flight of egrets, and as still as a well of eternity?

I closed my eyes. The same whiteness, and such quiet, reigned inside.

"A thorough job. No trace whatever."

"—"

"So you've won, haven't you? You're happy now. We are stuck on the island. That's what you wanted, isn't it?"

I could not utter a word.

"Say something!"

"Oh, Bjorn—"

"Tell me, what are you looking for?"

"I am not looking for anything!"

"Really? Then why did you keep nudging me aboard that ship, as if to prevent me from leaving?"

"You were the one who said no."

"Indeed? But *you* were always 'against': against Guruji, against the *Aalesund*, against Erik, against everything. Do you want me to drop dead, or what?"

"How unhappy you are, Bjorn."

What hatred in his eyes! But why? What was it that he hated so much in himself?

"Now I am trapped like a rat."

He sank to the ground, locking his arms around his knees. His face was like a mask—the mask that descends upon men when they pass to the side of the shadow, the grim god, the instantaneous possession like a creeping death. Yet that vast and supple cadence still ran in the background, that bedrock of sweetness in which everything coasted along in utter harmony, that perfect rhythm in which everything was engulfed in total love, without a cause or a reason—an absolute *yes* opening its great blazing eyes and gazing out. Each time, it caused a depth of emotions so intense within me that I didn't know whether it was joy or pain, such a burning life that it could have been death gazing out from the other side. It kept gazing out, saying yes to everything, to evil, good, suffering, non-suffering; understanding everything, purifying everything. Supremely right, supremely kind, it simply gazed out, sweeping everything away in its white Harmony like vast snowy wings for all the sorrows of the world.

"Don't you see it? Now I can neither leave nor stay!"

Indeed, this world is a curious fiction: look in one direction and everything seems black and insurmountable; look in the other direction and everything becomes wide open, possible, as you wish. The tragedy is to look in the wrong direction. There's really no tragedy! But Bjorn was stuck in the purple shadow of the picture and he could not see anything else.

"I can't go backward, Nil, and there is nothing ahead either!
It's closed in both directions."

"But there's Balu, there's—"

"Besides, I've had enough of this steaming heat—110 in the
shade; I'm fed up with it."

Yes, there is an insurmountable point, a point of suffocation.
One goes on and on, borne along by a force, then suddenly
everything shuts down; something refuses to go any farther—
a minute, irreducible blockade within. Ask me anything but
that. The instant cage. One has reached the foot of the public
fountain. I could still feel the sannyasi's slap on my back.

"I will never see Erik again. I will never see the lakes."

"Now, that's enough!"

Bjorn started.

"You're an idiot!"

He gave me a murderous look and I saw his hand move
toward his belt. I was completely indifferent, millions of miles
away. I did not care if he killed me.

He melted.

"Oh, Nil, Nil, I'm so lost. I don't understand anything anymore. To start that work all over again, that japa, those six
million mantras? I can't. It doesn't make sense anymore.
Nothing makes sense. Three years down the drain. It's impossible, impossible wherever I turn. This is the end of the road
for me."

Abruptly he turned toward the pyre.

"That's where I am going."

He remained transfixed.

I have often thought about that moment, and each time I hear
Balu's little voice: "He's going to die. He's going to die." As if
it had already been decided, consummated, and there was
nothing more to do because it was *already* done. I don't know
if it was done, but I know that, at that moment, I saw death
come into Bjorn, consciously, deliberately. He had acquiesced
and there it was. It was a fait accompli. A poisonous little

vibration like a minuscule steel snake. There is a moment, a black second, when one accepts, and he had chosen to die. A kind of illumination in reverse. Death outside joins with death inside. Afterward, there occurs the accident, but the choice has been made before.

We must either be reborn from head to toe or catch death. I turned toward a transfixed Bjorn. A palm leaf caressed his shoulders.

"You're a bastard."

It came out despite myself. He hardly moved, fixing me with his candid blue gaze.

"How strange it is, Nil."

His tone of voice had completely changed.

"It's strange how I've traveled all this course to arrive at this place. I've gone through Europe, Africa, the Orient, the Himalayas to end up here, before this pyre, at the foot of this tree."

He placed a finger on the sand.

"At this tiny point."

He drew a circle about himself.

"How strange it all is, Nil. There was a time when I imagined life to be vast, infinite, forever new; yet now I realize I was merely going round in a circle, which is closing in on me. This is it: I'm trapped inside."

Again he looked at me with that air of a bewildered child. The temple bells could be heard in the distance. Everything was so perfectly still and crystalline among those dunes. And then that completely changed, childlike voice:

"I remember, one day Erik and I were dreaming. It was long, long ago, and we were sitting by a lake underneath a silver birch. Life was so beautiful that one lifetime did not seem enough to live it. It was May, when the birds return from the south. Erik and I were pretending that a magician had appeared at the crossroads in front of the birch and he had granted us each one wish. Erik had asked for the power to travel at will, to know the world. My wish was to have four lives. I wanted to live to the fullest, experience all kinds of things. So that evening, under the silver birch at the crossroads, I divided myself into four and left on four different roads."

I could almost see Bjorn under the silver birch. Except that, now, it was a palm tree on the lagoon and the birds had not yet returned from the north.

"I left on four different roads, imagining that someday, years and years later, the four of us would meet again beneath the silver birch, and I wondered if we would still be similar enough to fit inside the same skin or if three of us would have to die in order for one to survive."

A gong reverberated across the lagoon. I could almost see those four little characters scrambling over the dunes toward the rendezvous, one through the southern trail that passed by the tantric's house, another through the western trail after leaving the *Aalesund*, another through the north. All those little me's we drag along, and then what? What difference does it make?

"That's nonsense, Bjorn. One arrives at the same point. All roads lead to the same point. There is but one character."

He placed his finger in front of him on the sand.

"Yes, the same point."

"What were your three 'brothers' doing exactly?"

"First, there was a sailor, then a revolutionary, then a seeker of the 'secret,' and the last one—the unknown one. I am not quite sure what the seeker of the secret was after, but there was a secret to be found. I remember something that was like the sign of, or the key to, the secret. It happened one day, or, rather, one night, in my room while I sat playing on the floor and suddenly realized that my body was lying asleep on the bed. I *saw* myself asleep in bed, while I went on playing with my toys on the floor. For a moment I kept looking at that body lying there, while I played on the floor. I was astounded. Then I became frightened and rushed back into my body. But I have never forgotten it. I haven't told anybody, but I remained greatly puzzled by it. Ever since that moment, I have wondered if the body was not merely a part of me, a sort of daylight dress. But who was 'me,' separate from the body? Me, somewhere else? Where else? It was extremely puzzling. Yet I most comfortably played, existed, without my body; it was only when I looked up that I saw the other . . . what other? Who was the other?"

"What about your sailor?"

"Oh, him; he died a while ago on the *Aalesund*. He was a consummate failure, an artist in his trade. For some reason, he had to founder at all costs; he could not find peace unless he foundered. The peace of damnation—nothing to save anymore."

He erased the circle on the sand with the back of his hand.

"It's as if I were dragging a terrible weight, Nil, some kind of horrible fault to amend."

"Why, of course! It's all the faulty selves, the little fakers we drag along with ourselves; that's what stifles us."

"I don't know. It's somehow linked to the cry of the wild geese on the lake, as if I had heard something unbearable in that call, something that ruined my taste for anything else."

"—"

"In any case, they've all perished along the way. Erik is dead, and we will never meet again under the silver birch."

"What about the other two?"

"Yes, there was the revolutionary—that's me: the one who wanted to save his brothers, change the world, find the secret!"

He turned his head toward the tantric's house.

"Poor secret. I'm afraid this one, too, is about to die. Perhaps he was the battleground for the other three. He's the one who loves. All he does, all he understands, is love. Nothing else matters. Sometimes, he sees himself greater than the gods because of his love."

Bjorn glanced at me. I felt like embracing him; I had never embraced Bjorn.

"Erik did not, could not, love. He only married his prostitute out of defiance; he called her his *fille de joie.*"

"Your brothers do have things in common. What about the fourth one?"

"No idea where he is or what he is doing."

"That's it, Bjorn! You've got it! Listen, suppose for a moment that you had been a mother-of-pearl merchant on this island or a swindler, a saint, a boatman, or God knows what, in four skins. I can assure you they would all have arrived at the same point! One day they would all have met the same fate or the same impossibility, the something inside that propels us to the heart of the matter. Then all the masks fall off and we are at the moment of truth. There is but one moment, one point, one 'character.' Once we have exhausted all the roles, we arrive at *the* person. We spend twenty or thirty years of our life believing we are something we are not—merchant, doctor, king, or rebel, when, in fact, we are something else altogether. That's what evolution is all about. Rebel indeed, because we are not what we are supposed to be. Do you remember the story of the prince who changed into a swan, sprouting little black feathers every time he looked backward?"

"There's no more backward for me. The *Aalesund* has left."

"So this is it. Your fourth is right here."

He swung around, glaring at me like a trapped animal.

"Or else *you* are the fourth, and one of us has to go."

"You're mad!"

"Then why do you shadow me? What is it you want? What exactly are you doing here? What do you keep telling me since the day we met? I'm wrong. Wrong to seek love, wrong to seek power, wrong to grieve for Erik, wrong to want to leave on the *Aalesund.* Wrong about everything. So what's left for me to do?"

"—"

"You've closed all the doors on me. I'm trapped. You've barred them all."

"You've lost your senses, Bjorn!"

"Now I've lost everything. Or else *you* have to go."

"It's a distortion!"

He shook back a lock of hair.

"You're above it all, aren't you? You watch the play from on high. Well, *I* don't feel like rising above it all and enjoying the show. I saw you on that ship, Mr. Crystal-man, looking down on those poor devils spitting out their lungs filled with phosphate!"

"But Bjorn—"

"There's no 'but'; I'm leaving."

"Then what? Do you think guzzling beer in the mess room will solve matters?"

"You're always right, Nil. *That's* your glass prison. Someday I'll break your glass."

He rose to his feet. There was nothing more to say.

Batcha's image suddenly plucked at my heart, flooding me with irrepressible emotion. He mustn't go. He mustn't. Bjorn mustn't die! I clasped him by the wrists with all my strength and turned him about to face me, riveting my eyes on him beneath that palm tree of the rendezvous.

"Bjorn, listen to me. You must listen to me."

He turned a murderous glare upon me. But I did not care.

"You can kill me if you wish, walk to your funeral pyre if you wish, but you must hear me out. It's our lives, and Balu's and Batcha's lives that are at stake."

The sannyasi's words flashed into my mind: "Three times you've come; three times you've killed." I felt it was not Bjorn or Balu or I who was in danger; it was Batcha. *She* was the pivot of destiny. So I went up against Bjorn's death as if it were Batcha I was trying to save.

"Look, Bjorn, one *cannot* truly live unless one has passed through death. The minute you set foot on the path of the true life, you face death, and you don't face it just once but many times, at different levels. Each time you open a new door, you encounter it; it is the gatekeeper: if you are not pure, you don't go through. Death is the defeat of impurity. We draw a circle, as you say, spending a lifetime to complete it and putting all our might, our ideas, our hopes, our conflicting little selves into it; it's our wave-band, as it were, our own vibratory environment, our particular tone of light, the station of our power, our psychological bubble. We go on building our circle, secreting our bubble. But as long as the circle is not filled, we cannot leave it; and once it *is* filled, its own force holds us and keeps us from leaving it. This is the gist of the story, the key to the mystery, as if the circle's gravitational pull also held the energy necessary to leave it. But, the point is, one *can* leave it. There comes a time, a point, when one can leave it. That's the instant of choice, and it feels like death. One either chooses or one dies. Going to the funeral pyre or the moon does not make any difference; one is already dead, walled up in one's circle, petrified in one's bubble. I know the point. I've gone through it three times in my life, each time with increasing opposition and difficulty, as if each time one had to overcome a greater power, break a tougher crust of self; one is one's own increasingly ruthless enemy. Yet, it's nothing but a lovely bubble, more or less clear, more or less powerful; it can be red or sapphire blue, gray or cerulean—of every color—depending on what you've put into it. But that bubble holds you. It's your own strength, and it's your own destruction. It's everything we've built in a lifetime, and everything that keeps us from moving to a vaster life. But there is a vanishing point, a way out; it's when everything is about to close in on you. Then you can go through in a flash, using all the power accumulated in the bubble. You pass to the other side or you die. Indeed, we die because of our incapacity to pass to the other side; if we could pass continually from one circle to another, we wouldn't die. Perhaps there comes a point when the circle, the bubble, ceases to exist, when one dies only if one wishes. That's what 'accelerated evolution' is all about. Instead of going through one circle in a lifetime, one goes through two, three; I've gone through three myself. Maybe I am in the process of completing my circle, too, trapped in a white bubble."

Bjorn seemed to hang on my every word. I felt he was about to let go. "So go ahead and climb on your pyre if you wish; it doesn't make any difference. I, too, will go there when my time comes; one gets one's hair cut, one's nails clipped, and is roasted at the end. But only the garment burns. That pyre is not the real one; it's just an imitation of the other, the real one, into which we must toss all our old skins one after another, all our victories and triumphs, all our beautiful experiences, all the lovely red or blue bubbles holding us; and the more beautiful they are, the more devouring. But beauty keeps increasing from one circle to the next, and so does strength and vision. Ultimately one loses nothing; one understands more and more. One must understand all. Perhaps this is the final destiny: to be all. That's why we die: the vase keeps breaking until it can contain everything. But when one comes to that point, Bjorn, one shouldn't miss it. There *is* a juncture, a turning point. However small one may be, however minute the circle, there is a moment when one sees and *can*. In every life there is a soul opening, a sudden breach into the next circle. Each time, it's like coming down with a mortal fever; one curls up in a ball and won't let go of the corpse. I know of only one way to get through, and it's not to tense up and strive and struggle, because, again, this is using the power of the bubble to fight the bubble; one must open one's hands and leap overboard, let go of everything, and surrender oneself: 'I don't know anything, don't see anything, don't want anything; I open my hands, invoking the archangel of the next circle.' Then, in a flash, one goes through. It's over. One laughs. There it is; that's all I know."

Bjorn was as still as a statue. I could feel his every pulsation beating inside me. He was on the verge of victory. The scales were about to tilt. Oh, there are lives that hang on one tiny second—it's really nothing, yet so incredibly hard! The whole energy of the bubble coagulated in a single point.

He regained his self-control.

"One does not escape destiny."

Silence fell over the dunes. The wind ruffled the palms. A bell could be heard in the distance. I was seized again by that odor of sand mixed with some unknown, poignant memories; ancient and familiar like those dunes, heavy with a scorching load like that sand-laden wind, they spoke of Ramnad or the Fayum. What do we really know? We believe, we think, we speak. Then a southerly wind comes, and our lives are swept away like a straw. The world is a fathomless stage, and we mean something else altogether.

"The gods are like stones, Nil. The Law is the Law."

> *O Child*
> *You know only*
> *My face of stone*
> *My inflexible law*
> *Because you know of me*
> *Only what you are*
> *You are the stone that will not yield*
> *The iron law*
> *And night and destiny are your offspring*
> *But I am still waiting*
> *Since stone became stone*
> *And the maiden smiled*
> *I wait behind your godly masks*
> *Your devilish masks*
> *In every second*
> *Every defeat*
> *In the night as well as in sunlight*
> *Everywhere*
> *Unchanging*

Without high or low
Without virtue, without fault

The little flute player flashed before my eyes, so charming, so playful, and suddenly all that tragedy of the world appeared to me so false, a fantastic fiction of morbidity superimposed onto such a charming, tranquil smile behind everything, in everything. A contrivance of our senses. It's ourselves who are creating and adding drama, imparting a false meaning to the whole story. We are acting in a fabulous play with caterpillar eyes! We don't have our true eyes yet; we understand nothing of the world!

"Destiny?"

"Yes, destiny. Don't you believe me?"

"Oh, Bjorn, destiny doesn't work that way! It isn't a blindly striking force; it's the path of our past closing in on itself, to open onto a larger destiny. The 'striking' is of our own making."

He made a derisive snort.

"Well, we'll see."

As he searched his pockets, my blood turned to ice.

"Let's flip a coin, shall we?"

He drew out a four-anna piece. He looked terrible.

"Tails you leave, heads—"

Another snort.

"How about it, friend? Shall we try to cheat the gods with a stroke of luck?"

As I looked on with horror, he threw the coin into the air, caught it, and covered it on the back of his hand.

"Bjorn, you're mad!"

"Really? Then why do you insist on staying here?"

"—"

"You see, you're afraid."

He was white as a sheet. His hand concealed the coin. It was absurd, a vicious lie.

"You're a coward!"

He flinched.

"You're running away, selling your soul to a filthy coin! Is that what your destiny is worth, a piddling little coin?"

He looked haggard. His eyes shifted to the pyre, then back to me again.

"What you don't know, Nil, is that when I arrived on this dune a moment ago I *saw* that pyre looming larger and larger, as if beckoning me."

"You're imagining things!"

"I could feel it reaching out to me. I am twenty-seven, Nil. I don't want to die!"

Suddenly I felt overwhelmed by Bjorn's panic.

"Come, let's get out of here. We'll go wherever you want. Let's go!"

Then, for the second time, I heard the sannyasi's voice: "Three times you've come; three times you've killed." We had to leave at once, break loose from this curse before it was too late.

A train whistled behind the dunes.

"Go where, Nil? The *Aalesund* has left. There is nowhere to go. That's what you don't see—that we are trapped on all sides. Go where? To the Sahara to drive tubes into the ground?"

I slipped my arm around his shoulders and gently stroked his golden hair. For a moment I thought he would burst into tears. But then, I don't know what descended upon him, he controlled himself, wresting himself free from my embrace, and dashed off across the dunes toward the tantric's house.

The coin lay glittering in the sand. It was tails.

ψ

13
three cowries for the gods and one for nothing

*T*he sea was all crinkling. It smiled through a thousand little dimples, sighing with ease, stretching itself, to ripple onto the sand in small contented, frothy bursts. I knew Batcha had seen me; she was taking her time which could not be measured any more than the pink cowries on the beach or the black and white zigzags of the wagtail. Now and then, she shook back her plait and remained squatting before some unexpected marvel. I could almost see her smile, feel that lightness which makes a delight of everything. In truth, the world is a fable designed to give millions of fingers and eyes, and surprises, to a marvel that hides from itself, and ceaselessly reinvents itself in the hollow of our hands. Sometimes I think we have invented death, and we could just as well reinvent immortality when we possess enough joy to find joy in everything. Is the world not to our liking? I breathe here or there, and the great gown becomes tinged in gold or amaranth.

"Here, it's all for you!"

She opened a fold of her skirt, releasing a shower of seashells on the small temple steps.

"All this for me?"

"Wait, I'll give a few to the god."

She carefully selected three cowries, which she went to place before the raised stone with a little bow. Then she smoothed out her pomegranate skirt and turned to face me. Standing on the threshold, her red tilak ablaze on her forehead, she looked like a goddess out of her sanctuary. She examined me calmly, with that expression of a queen; I entered there as into my home. Then she smiled, satisfied.

"Balu and I have had lots of adventures."

"Oh?"

"Yes, we went across the sea and came to a river bank with dunes, like here, except the sand was yellow. The river flowed, and there were white pigeons. We followed a trail that led to a very ancient house with pillars. And Balu found a gold coin—a gold coin this big—with writing on it. He said, 'That's Bjorn's treasure. Let's go find him.' I did not want to go because it meant going down into underground tunnels full of thorns, and there were cobras, too. So he pulled out his sword. 'I'll kill them all,' he said. He looked so tall and handsome with his red belt. We went in and everything shifted; Balu had disappeared and I was standing in a huge hall, very beautiful, like a temple, with blue designs on the walls. And you were all the way up there. But it was almost empty."

"Up there?"

"Yes, it was your house."

She paused, remembering something.

"Oh, and there was a man trying to bar my way."

"A man?"

"Yes, a sannyasi. He said, 'You don't exist.' So I laughed and he vanished!"

Batcha broke out into laughter, flashing sparkling teeth.

"Upstairs there was a large terrace, so pretty, flooded with a kind of moonlight. I felt so good. I could not see you, but you were there; I heard you. You were playing an ektara. It was so soft that it put me to sleep—the feeling of sinking into moon froth."

"My, oh my! But first of all, I do not play the ektara."

"Oh yes, you played."

Suddenly she became grave.

"Where were you yesterday afternoon?"

"—"

Sitting on the temple steps, she kept sorting out her shells.

"I could not find you."

"Why? Did you come looking for me at the hostel? I was out with Bjorn."

"Of course, not! Not with my feet. I came with—with—"

She searched for the proper words.

"I came *inside*. But there was no response."

"Oh?"

"A while ago, when I was collecting shells, you responded."

"I responded?"

She heaved a long sigh. What a numbskull I was.

"You said, 'I'm happy, oh, so happy!' "

"And what did *you* say?"

She pushed a shell with the tip of her finger, studying it a moment, her head tilted.

"Nothing. I feel at peace when you are there."

I felt a completely strange world opening before me; or, rather, I felt totally strange myself, confronting a well-known but long forgotten world that resurfaced unexpectedly from God knows where, as if, unknowingly, I had been living another life all this time, and there it was again. All my outward actions seemed out of step in comparison; it was as if I were in a dream in reverse, dressed in clothes that weren't mine, with a silly shirt and cockeyed shoes. I was waking up, and the sea was such delight with its sparkling little bubbles. Everything was so clear and limpid and easy; all one had to do was say, "I wish." It was so simple! I wish, and everything flows as I wish; one moves here, there, to many places in the twinkling of an eye; things appear, disappear, become tinted in blue or red. It all depended on a certain way of smiling, which made things flow this way or that, fashioned them, endowed them with color and unexpected depth, like a dream inadvertently come true. I looked at my two heavy, incongruous clogs resting there upon the sand, and I felt lost, as if I had lived all my life in the wrong scene. I looked at Batcha, listened to that soft little voice, followed that slight finger pushing a seashell, and I felt as if a curtain had been drawn open on another scene within the scene, revealing that the strangeness did not lie in some remote beyond but here, in *this* Nil disguised in twentieth-century clothes, whose brain knew how to solve all the problems of existence yet did not know how to join with Batcha at a distance, hear the unspoken language, feel without using his eyesight, or touch the invisible hands knocking on his door and lighting up their multicolored little lanterns in things. I had been taught everything except the essentials! My head had been crammed with rote! I had spent thirty years of my life as a cultured chimpanzee capable of adding, subtracting, smoking a cigar, and riding a bicycle.

"Tell me, Batcha, what exactly do you do to be with me when I am not there?"

"Nothing. I listen."

She laid her cheek on her knees, looking out to the sea. She was as still as a robin in a copse.

"I listen, and at times it seems as if I am resting my head on your shoulder. At other times, I can't; it's hard and complicated; or else you're all the way up there, and I no longer exist. Yesterday you were like a house made of steel."

"You listen *how*?"

"Just like that! I listen. I let things come in. It's like leaning over a river. And so I feel how you flow. Don't you feel Balu, Shikhi, Appa?"

She raised her head and glanced at me with surprise.

"But how do you live, then?"

"And how do they 'flow'?"

"Not like you, to be sure! They have another way. Each person has his own way. And then, it varies from day to day. Can't you hear it?"

I looked at her with bewilderment.

"But what do you feel, Batcha?"

"I feel music. It's like a movement of waves, waves that speak to you."

"And what about Shikhi?"

"Shikhi? You *do* ask such funny questions! Shikhi perches on the terrace and trumpets cries of triumph."

Head bowed upon my knees, I too tried to listen. Gropingly, I made my way into the great river that speaks. It was deep and soft as velvet and I let myself go. Then I thought of Bhaskar-Nath, or was he thinking of me? I repeated his name and remained very quiet, very still, attentive not to ripple my waters; I was like a lake, so clear that I did not know where "me" was anymore, so still that I felt like a block of crystal, yet weightless, light as a feather, ethereal. There was merely a whiff of self left, enabling me to find myself again, then disappearing in an instant by dissolving into an innumerable self that encompassed everything; I went from recalling myself to forgetting myself. Then everything became completely even, vast as a river flowing into itself, from which, progressively, an image was formed. Not even an image: a shower of waves making up the vibration of the image, just prior to the formation of the image—a kind of moving atmosphere of pale gold. Had I been blind, I would have said: Bhaskar-Nath. It instantly coagulated, becoming a powerful, golden mass—a golden fire—and I felt that I needed only draw nearer to merge with that current of fire. That current had a movement of its own, almost as if it spoke, but there were no words, just a vibration capable of forming words, or containing the force of words, their intimate meaning, just as it could form images or release streams of light, and all said the same thing; one leaned this way or that, and it formed either into an image or a sound. It was very clear, infinitely clearer than any spoken words, richer than any images, encompassing all possible nuances. It was indisputable and inimitable. When it said "joy," the entire essence of joy was there in all its power and quality, almost with its intensity of color. It was living sound, living light, a substance of joy. One could merge with that and bathe in it as in a torrent. Everything became concrete: joy was solid, a motionless torrent of fire. Our concrete world seemed like an imitation, a kind of shriveled lexicon opening unexpectedly and spilling syllables of ruby and sapphire on the ground. Then I felt another substance near Bhaskar-Nath, something soft and almost silken. It was Mâ. There, I felt, I was touching a mystery, perhaps the secret of that country; a slight little figure with no sharp edges, no hard spots, nothing to bump against, and very still—very intense—like a flame, and very secret, like a buried treasure no eyes could see, that would keep all its energy of light concentrated, unmixed, shrouded. Centuries might pass, but nothing would move that. Only the glimmer of a smile was visible, and a hand drawing a veil across her forehead. An extraordinarily powerful softness. She seemed to be offering me a tray of very beautiful fruits and saying: *khao, khao*, "eat." Those fruits filled me with a sweet energy like hibiscus juice. Suddenly I bumped against a dark whirlwind. It was Bjorn.

"*An'mona! An'mona!*"

Oh, the whole world is at our doorstep! We can go in every direction and be everywhere instantly! We know only a translation of the world in a barbaric tongue.

"*An'mona*—that's what you should be called—*An'mona*: 'He whose mind is elsewhere.' "

"Oh, Batcha, that's wonderful!"

She sighed.

"You have a good vision, but you don't see what's under your nose."

"I'm so happy, Batcha, so happy!"

She pushed her shells aside and gave me a look of commiseration.

"Tell me, Batcha, how does it work? Here we are on this beach and it seems as if I've known you for such a long, long time. It's so strange."

Now even words had gone. I was lost in an absurd delight, as if the little wave came sparkling against me, the sand rolling within me, the conch shells blowing in my breath. And all was clear, simple; life was like a great crystal scintillating with a myriad bonfires everywhere. I smiled. I was here, there, everywhere, feeling everything, living in everything, delightfully exploded into countless little lights of joy. I felt completely stupid, a gaping simpleton.

"Batcha, how, why?"

I did not even know what I wanted to say; everything was a kind of miracle. She rested her head on her knees and began to chant softly, releasing a flow of droplet-like words:

"Nothing-at-all, Mister Nothing-at-all, there are many beaches in the geography book, but here you are on this one, and I've picked these cowries for you."

She closed her eyes, an ineffable smile on her lips.

"There are days and days, many days in the calendar, and here we are today. You are here and I am here. What wind brought us here together? What wave brought you these cowries? There are many, many cowries in the sea, but these are for you, just for you, Nothing-at-all, Mister Nothing-at-all. It is today on many beaches of the geography book, but one and only one wave brings to each person a unique cowry. This one and none other."

I was astounded. She burst out laughing. I was abruptly thrown into panic, petrified with fear for no reason at all, as if . . . I don't know. Then I collected myself.

"This is silly talk, Batcha. There are lots of cowries. Whether it's this one or another, what difference does it make?"

She cocked her head and made a face at me.

"And there are lots of Nothings-at-all, too, so I wonder why this one has come here."

"Another would have come in my place."

"And where would *you* have gone? On a beach of the white countries? And whose place would you have taken?"

She raised her eyes to mine.

"That would upset everything, you see."

Her large black eyes penetrated me to the core. And in those eyes I followed, with a kind of stupefaction, the Nil who would take the place of someone else, who in turn would take the place of someone else, who in turn would take the— With amazing clarity, I watched her draw herself up, pick a rose-colored shell streaked with blue veins, and place it into my hand with a slight tap.

"Here, this one has been waiting for you for thousands of years."

And she burst out laughing.

I gazed wide-eyed at the shell in my hand, that "unique" shell. And I had an overwhelming feeling of being immersed in a fantastic world where the least grain of sand, the smallest pebble on the beach was imbued with absolute light, as if that absurd shell had *indeed* waited thousands of years to be placed into my hand by Batcha and by no one else, at that very moment and none other, at that precise place on earth and nowhere else. And where else could I have been? Taking whose place? There was a sudden sense of phantasmagoria, of a huge ballet of breathtaking precision, of an incredible, unique totality—a one and only earth-body—moving through time and space as a single entity, a fabulous clockwork in whose every point the whole world met, the symbol of everything else, the microscopic reduction of the entire universe, a gigantic puzzle, no piece of which could be moved or changed without producing terrible chaos. That is really how it was: each minute of the world with its myriad encounters and combinations, each point in space with its myriad objects and beings moving about was actually unique. Nothing could be different, otherwise *everything* would be different.

It was the second time I had felt this, and both times with Batcha.

"You look like an owl blinking in dawn's light."

I thought I would become crazy.

"And a blue-eyed owl on top of it!"

"Tell me something—"

I did not know what to say, but I saw. It was a *seeing* light I was immersed in, as if imparted with an incomprehensible comprehension. And then there was that dainty foot resting on the step, barely bronzed, beneath a long pomegranate skirt, and the sands, and our footprints stretching over the dunes— two lines, two sets of meandering tracks made of a thousand footprints, each exactly where it should be in order for the tracks to intersect here, now, on these temple steps.

"Well, speak up!"

I tried to speak, to formulate my question. But it was truly inexpressible. It was like a dense, scintillating cloud overflowing with *one* question, a pure question that might have taken a thousand and one forms; but it was *the* question. Now I understand; I know that what confounded me at that moment as an unfathomable mystery was that Freedom, that marvelous, unknown freedom, as if the world were created anew at each instant; and the more I glimpsed that freedom, the more I brought to light a kind of inexorable order in which one could not even take a wrong step. One takes the wrong turning, only to find out that the wrong path is part of the right one!

Both are *simultaneously* true.

"Batcha, why is it you whom I've met, and not another, here and nowhere else? What makes this be? Where does it *begin*? Why Bjorn, and not another? Balu, and not another? And what about this little beach; what has drawn me or pushed me here and not anywhere else? What force?"

Batcha looked at me intently, without a word, while I kept turning that unique, absurd seashell between my fingers. If it had waited thousands of years for me, it must have a message to convey to me! What message? A blue-veined rosy message unfurling ever-widening spirals, like a princess' steeple head-dress, to lose itself in a violet opening. And a knob—a tiny hard knob at the center from which the spirals unfurled. How vibrant and miraculous everything seemed that morning with Batcha. There are moments in life when everything loosens and opens up like a fairy tale; a thin veil shrouds a thousand worlds from us, or maybe just one, shimmering like a great tropical pearl. It's as if the least fragment of mother-of-pearl, the tiniest wagtail on the beach held the key to the entire mystery, and each thing contained everything, clear as day. I could behold that entire existence in the hollow of my hand, in that tiny symbol unfurling its spirals, its variegated circles—mauve, rose, blue—an incredible perpetual story, ever wider, ever more vivid, whorl after whorl, as if the same characters, the same circumstances, the same possibilities or impossibili-ties, almost the same scenes, kept recurring from one level to the next, but more precise each time, more intense, more charged with meaning and power; as if one returned again and again to the same places, the same soul-states, the same blue, rose and purple trail, but enlarged, magnified, set in a sharper light—each closer to the key that reveals all. Perhaps there is no key anywhere, only the light of an ever-growing revelation; no ultimate goal, but an eternal goal moving on an eternal spiral; and the spiral disappears into a white infinity above, or else plunges into that purple mouth, closing onto itself—or what? Perhaps each of those whorls stood for just one life, and at other points of the spiral, in other ages—at the homologous point below—I had contemplated a pink cowry on a small white beach and smiled at an eternal child.

At that moment, I seemed to see the great shell of the world winding its lovely spirals around vast rosy Indias and mother-of-pearl Egypts, repeating coil after coil the total story in each country and each being, in each age like a season, ever widening the same unique destiny, to soar above into a white infinity, or to plunge into that shadowy purple opening—or what?

"*An'mona! An'mona!*"

"Oh, Batcha—"

"Where were you, Mr. Nothing-at-all? You're always elsewhere. No wonder nothing at all happens; you wake up when it's too late."

Her face wrinkled into a frown.

"Look, Batcha—"

"I am not Batcha. Have you at least found what you were looking for?"

"Yes—No!"

"Then you've wasted your time. I've given my cowry to nothing at all."

"Are you angry with me?"

"I'm not angry. I think you're like my moon froth."

"Your what?"

"Can one talk with moon froth?"

She puffed out her cheeks.

"You remind me of Chavan."

"Who is Chavan? Another of your gods?"

"No, he's not a god. What do you have against my gods?"

"Why, nothing, Little One, I assure you!"

"They're very sweet."

"Yes, of course! So who is he?"

"He lived completely naked, eating nothing, just staring."

"At what?"

"I don't know. Just staring. He stared up above, the way you sometimes do. He stared so much that he finally became hard as a skeleton, completely immobilized, with just two shining eyes peering out. Then the white ants came and built their hill over him."

"Listen, Batcha, I really don't understand."

"You're as difficult as a math problem."

"Look, Batcha, you're very sweet and I do like you, but this has nothing to do with sentiments. Why is it *you* I have met and not someone else? You, Bhaskar-Nath's daughter?"

She raised limpid eyes to mine.

"Because it has always been me and we have always been together."

My eyes seemed to widen. Everything froze in place, magnified: the least ripple on the sand, the black and white wagtail, the sound of conch shells under the high tower, Batcha's pomegranate skirt—a suspension of time. A drop of pink eternity in the hollow of my hand. A sudden vista on the flight of centuries like a flurry of crimson birds caught in full light. My mouth was gaping.

"Look, Nil, look!"

She stretched her arms skyward.

"The birds from the north, the birds from the north! The birds are returning! The monsoon is coming!"

She leaped to her feet, clapping her hands.

"The birds are coming! The birds are coming!"

A huge black triangle swerved through the northern sky.

She bounded toward the palm grove like a scarlet arrow, arms wide open, running nimbly in the direction of the high tower. I extended my hand. She was gone.

All that remained was the south wind beating at the sanctuary door and the distant chanting that had been rolling for centuries, like the migration of birds, the spirals of seashells, and the voyages of the soul about an invisible globe.

ψ

14
the acacia forest

I took the northern trail by chance, though today I know there is no such a thing as "chance." I wandered toward Kali's Rock with an inexplicable sense of near happiness, a self-contained, self-sustaining kind of happiness that had grown within me, imperceptibly, like a very simple clarity—the clear foundation of existence. I felt light, tranquil, as if borne by the wind; but the least thought caused an instantaneous shadow, and anyone else's thoughts about me were immediately sensed as tiny ripples, whirlpools, or sometimes as an unexpected flood of tenderness, as if I had stepped into a cascade of honeysuckle. Now it was Bjorn who came whirling around me. In fact, I had gone out to escape him: "I'm doubling the dose." His voice droned in the torrid air: "Look, I've held it for forty minutes!" There he was feet in the air, head on the floor of his cell, or sitting cross-legged for hours at night, meditating—on what? "I'll go to the end"—of what? Perhaps to the end of exertion, to the other side of it; exertion was still a shadow upon that clarity. I wondered whether anything could be done for Bjorn. Sometimes I sense that human beings have something to exhaust, and once it's done, everything comes to them naturally.

I turned to the right without thinking, perhaps to find shade, and found myself in the acacia forest. I was trying to get rid of Bjorn's clinging presence by walking. The silvery jingle of horse carts could be heard in the distance, mingled with the shouts of pushcart drivers in the south. Then everything grew silent around me, and there remained only the ocher-tinged, almost scorching sand beneath my feet and the dales of thorn bushes punctuated by an occasional banyan tree. There was not a breath of air. A stillness and density of odors like a bath of wild honey; the silence itself seemed made of coagulated odors. The lacy shadow of the trees on the ground, the endless undulation of sand like a coral wave beneath large half-tilted parasols. I walked aimlessly. The sand felt so soft, and the sky was like an immense blue net in tatters. Here and there, small yellow clusters bloomed straight on the spiky branches. A bit lost, I plunged deeper and deeper into that fragrant wave of ocher as into a somewhat uneasy dream, drawn in spite of myself. A small lizard scurried into the thorny thicket. Suddenly it was no longer clear.

It was oppressive, threatening.

I wanted to turn back. But some unknown force held me in its grip, pushing me ahead. I swerved to the right, skirting the gigantic banyan standing alone in the midst of the acacias; that tree was so beautiful with its wild roots, like the rigging of a ship in distress. I took another step, and stopped dead. A shrill scream rent the air.

I never understood what happened. There was a half-naked girl on the ground, her breasts tanned, almost black, and Bjorn was next to her.

All I heard was her cry, and the ground opened beneath my feet. I should have turned back, run away, but I was paralyzed. She screamed again. Then she pushed Bjorn away, grabbed her bright yellow sari, and leaped to her feet. Bjorn turned to face me.

She fled through the acacia forest, clutching her sari about her. It was Nisha, Meenakshi's daughter.

Bjorn sat up, eying me coolly. I must have sunk to my knees, my legs buckling under me. He braced himself against the banyan tree, observing me in silence. He reeked of alcohol. Slowly he pulled out his knife and, holding it by the blade, thrust it at me.

The blade embedded itself in the sand a few inches from my leg. He burst out laughing.

An Homeric, ghastly, full-throated laugh which seemed to resound throughout the entire forest.

"What a spree!"

I was stunned. I kept staring at Bjorn, an unknown Bjorn, that tall, bare-chested, hirsute Northerner roaring with laughter. And that knife still planted in the sand before me.

"You were jolly well scared, admit it!"

Another explosion of laughter.

"You've just come for the conclusion of the wedding ceremony."

He reeled with laughter, as if he had never had so much fun.

"We'll have lots of black little babies, and I want you to be the godfather of the firstborn!"

He waggled a finger in the air.

"We must drink to that."

He reached behind him for the bottle of toddy.

"Here, drink."

I took the bottle. Everything was blurred. I was in a scarlet haze filled with the image of that half-naked girl. I had suddenly entered a world of rape and terror.

"Go ahead, drink! Drink, or I'll break your neck!"

I took a swallow. It smelled of grass. I was sinking into the nightmare. I was somebody else, returning from some lost life—a complete change of view, the trap opening from under me. It was right there.

"Not bad for a beginner. So sorry to ruin your saintliness, Nil!"

He snatched the bottle from my hands.

"What a spree! What a terrific spree! I'm making up for a twenty-year dry spell, and I have a hell of an appetite! By the way, what were you doing here? Spying on me, were you?"

"—"

"All right, never mind. Besides, I don't give a damn. I don't give a damn about anything. It's wonderful. You might call it a liberation—liberation in reverse. Let's drink to my liberation!"

He threw back his head and downed half of the bottle.

"One way or another, the whole point is not to give a damn, isn't it? And what do you think of Mrs. Sorensen, pal? Not bad, hey? Seventeen years old and a skin as fresh as a Muscat grape. I'm going to marry her, no kidding. Imagine, she loves me—someone actually loves me! 'You are my white rajah,' she says!"

He laughed again.

"My white rajah! We'll settle in a hut at the coral fishery. I'll make a canoe and some nets, and we'll go fishing. And I'll father lots of little black Bjorns!"

He sniffled with a sort of satisfaction.

"And from time to time, we'll make a little white one, who will seek his salvation in Christianity! Oh, Nil, what damn nonsense!"

Now he no longer laughed. He spoke with a kind of lopsided smirk, teeth clenched.

"And he'll marry a Norwegian girl who will give him fair little children, who will come here and sell their souls in the arms of a Negress. And we'll start all over again."

He grabbed the bottle by the neck. I thought he was going to drink more, but in one stroke he smashed it against the tree.

"It's too long, Nil. It's endless! Better go to the end right away. The end right away, you understand."

He wiped his lips with the back of his hand.

"*What* end? Do you know the answer to that one, Mr. Smart?"

Everything fell silent. The air was scorchingly hot. Something lay glinting in the sand in front of me. I bent down and picked up a broken fragment of a gold-colored bangle bracelet. It was made of glass.

"*What* end, hey? I'm already there; it's all over! I've already married her: I've got the hut, the canoe, and four little bastards running around on the beach."

He swung around with a kind of fury, as someone who has been double-crossed. I watched him clench his fist. Then he roared:

"And then WHAT?"

His voice reverberated through the silence. There was a smell of alcohol rising from the hot sand and a buzzing sound in my head. A ship's siren rent the air somewhere in the distance, to the west, as if from behind a veil.

"In four years, she'll have sagging breasts and the face of her mother."

He closed his eyes.

"I'm lost, Nil."

It was *I* who was lost, adrift in that scarlet haze, a golden bangle in my hand, and with that sound of the ship's siren.

"The whole story is over in a twinkling of an eye."

The siren shrieked again. I felt trapped in a horrible dream, incapable of moving, running away or even screaming—while the train enters the station and will run you over.

"Speak, for God's sake! Say something!"

That odor of black girl mixed with the scent of faded marigolds and coconut oil clung to me. Bjorn wriggled toward me on all fours. I knew he was coming to strangle me.

Suddenly I recovered my voice, screaming:

"Bhaskar-Nath!"

"What about Bhaskar-Nath?"

He cocked up his head, furious. I could feel his hot breath on my face.

"What about Bhaskar-Nath? Has this one got something against me, too?"

"We must go to see Bhaskar-Nath."

Bjorn sneered.

"To get his nuptial blessing or what?"

"We must go there, Bjorn. We must."

"Sorry, I'm going straight to my Negress."

He rose to his feet, then collapsed on the ground.

"Come with me, Bjorn."

"Guruji said I shouldn't."

He was clearly drunk, and I should have kept my mouth shut; but anger swept over me at the thought of Guruji. Oh, I could see so well through all those little sharks of the spirit!

"What has he ever done for you, your Guruji? How is he going to pull you out of this?"

Bjorn turned ashen. He sprang to his feet, brandishing his knife.

"No, Bjorn. No!"

I clutched his arm in an attempt to ward off this madness, this absurdity, this evil spell. I wanted to take him into my arms, raise him up, press him to my heart. Oh, Bjorn! He threw off my hand with a violent gesture, and in a flash the blade slashed my hand, severing the top of my forefinger. There was blood everywhere.

Bjorn looked at me, aghast.

There was not a sound in that forest.

"It's nothing, Bjorn."

He kept staring at me in horror, speechless. I took his scarf to bind up my hand.

"It's nothing, Bjorn. Really."

The knife dropped from his hand.

"Go away."

"Bjorn—"

"Go away, I'm telling you!"

My heart sank. I wanted to cry, to press him to my heart, to tell him—

"Bjorn, you're my brother."

"I am *not* your brother. Go away. All I can do is destroy. That's my sole power. Go!"

He jumped to his feet, stood squarely in front of me, hands on his hips. His eyes were terrible.

"Get the hell out of here!"

I got up, my throat like sandpaper. I tightened the scarf around my hand.

I looked at him one more time, then set off through the forest.

I wandered through that acacia forest aimlessly, temples throbbing, heart pounding. I was but a shadow held up by pain. It had nothing to do with Bjorn and his hatred—he needed to hate me as he needed to love—or with the smarting of my hand. It had to do with the abyss that had opened in the presence of that dark-skinned girl, and her scream, that frightened look on her face, her flight—a whole world reemerging from God knows where with an odor of panic. I was abruptly confronted with the *fact*—that was *it*. What? What fact? It was nameless, faceless; it was not even that dark sex, only that trapdoor opened under my feet and the swarming shadowy surge it released, and the flight, the scream, the great black sluice gates wide open, as if I had plunged there, sunk there time and time again, lost myself body and soul in a smell of sand and wasted flowers. What was it? I don't know. But that was "it." That's what I touched at that moment—the ancient curse we drag along through the ages, the shadowy memory, the knot of pain, the absolute obstacle. What kind of obstacle? An old nameless smarting breach, a "that" in reverse, a dark beginning of things. It was there, always there. I knew it. It had never ceased being there. Scratch a little and it's there. Scratch some more and it's still the same; beneath the great unmoving Light, the great Shadow has not budged. It's there every second of the day, untouched. Oh, where is the pure, unsullied man, that unique phenomenon? I have roamed three continents, consumed everything in order to consume that one shadow, and what? That was it, right there, the age-old Threat, the Shame, the weight one drags behind, the dark halo surrounding one and surrounding each thing—the least gesture, the least encounter, the most fleeting glance—as if at any instant, at the slightest snag, the tiniest scratch or misstep, everything would turn into a vertiginous opposite. It takes but a second—heart pounding, giddiness, a flash—and everything is reversed. One passes to the other side. One treads through the dark country. It's there at every second, beneath every smile, every scintilla of light. And the closer I came to touching that Light above, the darker it grew below, as if I became capable of a greater darkness. "I"—*whom*? "I"—*where*? It's the night without a face, the swarming multitude, the age-old story, an instant ruination of life. An obscure, multitudinous selfhood as weighty as the night of the dead and all the dead we carry within us, as old as the sorrow of men and the wrath of the gods. The great rout before the pack, the stoning at the city gates, pain, the great Pain in the depths like two eyes fixed on an immensity of sadness.

Ah, now I understand why we erect our antlike bulwarks and our vengeful little laws: breaking the wall above means breaking it below as well, and everything pours in—hell along with heaven! In the depths of the abyss as in heaven, there is no more "I"; there is an explosion of darkness below as there is an explosion of light above, and every suffering in the world rushes in along with every shame. And that's where I was. I was Bjorn. Was I not he? I was his darkness, his fall, his shame. Where, indeed, is the "other"? Where is that which is not myself? Where is the fault I am completely removed from, the heaven in a vacuum? And where are those world-liberated beings, those so-called saved souls, the cheats of liberation? If a single man is in bondage, the whole world is in chains! For there is but one Man.

I wandered through that acacia forest, walking blindly, endlessly, as I had once walked the creeks of French Guiana and the *minas* of Brazil, as I had paced their prisons—the old sustained pace of pain with a burning in the heart and unseeing eyes. One step, another step, and another, and it's all the same, all the desert. One is the night on two legs, the age-old pain, the pulsation of the blood; and even pain is dead, even the night. One no longer knows *who* is suffering or why; one is but a throbbing rhythm, a burning fire. One is the self of fire. Nothing but a fire. The burning is all one has. It has always burned. It's as old as suffering, or love, going back to the beginning of time, to the first step, to that unknown something that yearns and struggles. It has no name, no reason, no face, no destiny. It's lived so much that it has become everybody, gone through so much that it understands everything. There was almost singing in that forest, a singing fire, singing sorrow, or love, perhaps; all was fused in *that*. I am the self of fire, the ancient burning. Where is my sorrow, my downfall? I have no more night, no more suffering; I have only that burning. I have no more shame, no more past, no more yes or no, no more good or evil; it's all burned, all gone. I have that burning, just for itself, for everything, for whomever wants it. It burns, that's all. It's my hell, my heaven, my suffering or my joy, undifferentiated. It's my great fiery rhythm, my tiny burning point, my immensity of a unique flame. Where is my fail, my deliverance? There is only that fire burning everywhere. Where is the fault, the downfall? They are consumed. Where is death? It is consumed. In the end, there is only that fire burning, even above; everything is consumed. I have no more above or below, no more white or black; everything is one and the same. Where is my freedom, my bondage?

I raised my eyes and everything had changed.

Was it that ocher-hued sand, my fever, or the fire in my heart? Or perhaps it was the torrid haze shimmering through the tortured trees? The world seemed to be bathed in orange. It was not a "color," something tinting or shading the world; the very substance of the world was different. Or perhaps it was not "different," but just free from its false appearance of solidity, allowing true matter to shine through and radiate everywhere. The world was becoming what it really is. My eyes were seeing the real world. It was as warm and powerful as the fire in my heart, and extraordinarily dense—a radiation of warm and compact power—as if everything vibrated coherently, were made of the same substance as that flame in my heart, and suffused with inexpressible tenderness. I was with everything, in everything, burning everywhere, loving everywhere, recognizing all. Oh, it was a love that was not the opposite of hate or the opposite of anything, not the sentiment of anything; it just was, burning and burning. There was no object to it, no reason for it; it was not like something one admires and loves. Where, indeed, was the "I" who did the loving in this? One was a *single* burning substance in everything, a single living fire echoing and recognizing itself in everything, revealing unfathomable depths in each thing. I flowed into that, lost myself body and soul in an orange myriad vibrating with tenderness.

I emerged from the forest.

The siren blasted a third time. A little squirrel scampered across the path.

I felt as if I had returned from a long journey.

That's when the thought of Bhaskar-Nath came into my mind. Suddenly, I understood: *this* was the "powerful light," the power of the next world!

I looked at my hand. Bjorn, Nisha, the flight, the dark trapdoor opening beneath my feet—it was all like a dream. I had walked for a long time, for ages, for entire lifetimes, roamed continents: seedy bars here, seething creeks there, red forests, blue forests, occasional white havens, dunes of plenitude, as if I had touched heaven, and nothing; that heaven was but the other side of my shadowy flight, an escape into the light, eyes closed not to see. Now I was coming to port, to the end of the road. I set foot on that northern trail as if for the very first time in the world. The journey was over! No more haven, no more heaven, no more hell; they had vanished. The twin accomplices had all but drowned. There was nothing left but that burning fire.

Everything was pure. And everything was true.

"Nil! Nil!"

Balu came rushing upon me.

"Where is he?"

His eyes fell on the bloodstained scarf. He let go of my arm.

"Where is he?"

I pointed toward the forest. He gave me a horror-stricken look.

He ran off without a word.

"Bjorn! Bjorn!"

His cries resounded through the forest.

Suddenly, it became overwhelming. I saw Balu running, with Bjorn somewhere over there, and all that suffering, that misery of a world running and running, fleeing below, fleeing above, locking itself up in a white prison, a black prison, churches, legal codes, beheading the man on death row; and everything grows right back, over and over again. Then, yes, there in the depths of night, this firmament of orange fire that changes everything. Evil had never been evil; it was the secret door to deliverance. Good had never been good; it was the white prison for the blind. There, they were both annihilated and delivered from each other.

I turned to the left, unaware that I had just touched the Secret.

All I could feel was the pounding in my temples, the smarting of my hand, and Balu's little voice in the distance, calling out: "Bjorn! Bjorn!"

Giddily, I stumbled toward Bhaskar-Nath's house.

15
as you will

*O*nce again I walked past the high temple walls amid the drone of conch shells and gongs, hiding my bleeding hand. Everything was the same. Yet nothing would ever be the same. That absurd gash had set into motion a chain of invisible waves, as if that small external incision were the symbol of a deeper wound. Oh, everything is a symbol! I have yet to find that which means nothing, the wisp of straw blown by the wind, the fleeting slip-up that does not carry the obscure echo of a larger wave. Perhaps true vision is not so much in the ability to behold the seven wonders of the world as it is in the ability to decipher the eighth wonder of minute correlations. There had been one chance in a million for me to come across Bjorn in that forest, to take the northern trail, to turn to the right; and just as I was trying to avoid Bjorn's invisible presence, I had marched straight into the trap. This world is such a mystery. All our visions and rationalizations do not begin to fathom it. Along white or gray streets, our temple bells and our souls' anxious beating will keep reminding us that we are fragile beings whose strings are pulled by immense forces, while we walk here and there, swerving to the right down the path to perdition. But why is it so? Why? I would give anything to understand that chance second when we turn to the right rather than to the left.

I followed the high walls girdled with sand. Again I seemed to light upon the same little trail within, so slight, like a delicate thread, which linked this shadow of "me" beneath the temple towers to so many other me's who had raised the same question time and time again, beneath bells or gongs, sirens, or calls from a minaret. Each time, that little trail opened on a throng of undying selves, as it were, and perhaps this fellow walking here today swerved to the right to attend to an old detour of that fellow from yesterday. Life is ancient and repetitive, but we amble down the streets of the world as if we were born yesterday.

Once again I found myself in the narrow street with white-terraced houses and clumps of palms. Children were still chanting in the schoolyard. Here was the tiny loggia, the carved deities, the low-ceilinged corridor like an Egyptian hypogeum, the patio flooded with light, and that scent of sandalwood in the cool dimness of the house.

There was Mâ crushing rice in a mortar. She saw me, drew one end of her sari across her forehead, and smiled. I was in the bright country.

Bare-chested, a pair of steel-rimmed glasses on his nose, Bhaskar-Nath squatted in his corner, surrounded by chisels. He raised his head, and his eyes went straight to my hand. He did not utter a word.

"I cut myself."

He nodded and returned to his carving in silence.

"*Dao.*"

She took my hand and poured some fresh water over the wound. Her touch was soft, and she looked young enough to be Batcha's sister.

"*É ké?* Who is it?" I asked, pointing to the statue in his hand.

"Kali."

She raised her hand to her forehead and emptied the rest of the water jug over my hand. It smarted.

"Balu went out in a great hurry," she said.

She gave me a questioning look, then went out to refill her water jug. There was not a sound. Bhaskar-Nath remained obstinately silent, bent over his statuette with four arms and a sword, exactly as on the rock I had climbed with Balu.

"Bjorn is in danger."

No reply.

"I said—"

I stopped in mid-sentence, mesmerized by that statuette, as if *she* were somehow the reason for my coming here.

"Whom is she killing?"

Still no reply.

I began to feel uneasy, as if something heavy hung in the air, while my gaze kept returning to that idol. Suddenly, it seemed as if there were nothing for me to say or ask; everything was said in that statue brandishing its sword. All I had to do was look. Strangely, the more time passes, the more I sense that each object, each circumstance brings forth a special message, as if the very position of things and beings at a given moment exactly mirrored our own story, and their motion, appearance, or disappearance followed some invisible rhythm tied to our own, much as the motion of the moons and the tides echoes our downfalls and the return of the swallows on September shores. Everything moves together.

Bhaskar-Nath nodded his head. He looked at me and simply said:

"The time has come."

My heart skipped a beat. A sinking second. I wanted to cry, "No, no, not yet!" as if to stop time. Oh, I've always known that a time will come when everything will be crushed underfoot, shattered. In the depths, I almost wished it. All of life seemed like a fragile truce resting on a viper's nest.

"Your heart is crying, child."

"Oh, not yet!"

"Are you afraid?"

"I don't know. I don't understand. Enough tragedy, enough—"

Mâ had returned with a handful of marigold leaves that she crushed and applied to my finger. There was something oddly comforting about that pain. She offered me a copper tray full of fruit.

"*Khao, khao,* eat," she said softly. "It's good."

Exactly like the fruit I had seen in my dream with Batcha.

She smiled. For a second I had the impression she was feeding me through prison bars; I felt encircled by walls. A minute before, I had been in the bright country. Then everything shifted and I was back in the prison. But what exactly had shifted? It suddenly struck me that that's what fate is—a prison. And one goes from peace to agony as from one room to another.

"Why the fear, child? One *always* goes toward greater joy. This is the world's golden rule. There is never any return to darkness, only a progression toward more light. When you see, everything makes sense."

"I don't see."

"But the reason all this is happening is to *force* you to see! Look, look around you! Open your eyes instead of whining! Oh, child, child, what are you waiting for? Every minute of life holds out its hand to you."

"It's all that wretched tantric's fault."

"It's nobody's fault. Furthermore, you have no right to insult that man. Fault? What fault? If there were a single fault in the world, the world would crumble instantly. Only Joy is capable of creation!"

"Joy is fine when all's well and good."

"But your 'good' is infinitesimal! So from time to time it is shattered to enable you to continue toward a vaster good."

"Why do I keep thinking we should appeal to that tantric—*do* something?"

Bhaskar-Nath raised his eyes toward me.

"Do what? In truth, I don't know what can save Bjorn except himself, provided he is in danger of being 'lost.' You see, child, I cannot bring myself to see any 'loss' anywhere; even my shavings are used to make incense, and each cut of my chisel adds to the perfection of my work.

"He may die."

"So will you. So will Batcha. One dies only at the appointed time, not one moment before. Do understand, for Heaven's sake, that there is no injustice, no error, no accident! You will understand nothing of the world if you don't understand that obstacles, too, are part of the perfection. We totally lack appreciation for a Marvel that organizes each minute of the earth as a miracle. Oh, but when one perceives that, it is so compact, so overwhelmingly alive with miracles everywhere at the same time! One is overcome with joy, and one can never be the same again."

"But why can't we *do* something for Bjorn, then?"

Bhaskar-Nath did not reply, yet I could feel his concentration. I felt his patient, loving compassion turned toward me, toward Bjorn. Still, I had to act. I simply could not idly wait for Bjorn's death, and there was that sense of catastrophe hanging heavily in the air.

"If your 'Marvel' does everything, then what am I here for?"

"Yes, it does everything. And it is we who fail to understand that the Marvel is *always* marvelous, even when things are apparently wrong. Look, if you feel you must *do* something, then do it. Your actions, too, are part of the Marvel; so are your mistakes. But personally, I would like you to *see*."

Abruptly he reached for a chisel.

"Do you see this chisel?"

He took his statue in the other hand.

"Do you see Kali? She's the Mother of the Worlds."

He lifted the statue in the air. He looked like a god.

"Her right hand holds a sword that She uses to cut off the demon's head. She acts. She 'does something,' as you say. But there are not three different forces—one acting through the Mother, one through the demon, and one through my chisel. It's one and the same force. There is only one Force in the world, one single force moving everything. Everything is the Divine Force at work, in gods and in devils, in human beings, and in my chisel. Call it 'Divine' if you wish; the name doesn't matter; what matters is to feel it. My blade can either carve or kill, it's that simple. If it slashes your hand, you assume it's 'bad' because you do not see the god being carved in you. If Bjorn suffers, you blame that 'wretched tantric' because you fail to see his necessity for Bjorn. We only meet the obstacles necessary for our perfection. Perfection is what is at work in this world. Joy is what is at work in this world. There is but one Force in the world, a force of joy, and as long as we do not understand the utter SENSE of everything, we shall go to the hell of our own choice. We only see a fragment of the total story, a fraction of the course! Yet She is there. At every instant She is there, wanting joy for us, even as we cry out and lament."

"But—"

"There are no buts. All one has to do is take leave of the little self and enter the consciousness of the Whole. Then one is free and one understands. And one has joy."

I heard the rustling of a skirt.

She burst into the patio, hopping on one foot, her schoolbag in her hand. Then she stopped short. Bhaskar-Nath looked at her; she looked at me. Then she flushed as red as a poppy, and ran away into the courtyard.

He laid aside his statue, pensive. I heard laughter and the squeak of the well pulley.

"Master—"

"I am not a Master."

"It isn't only Bjorn; I too am in danger."

He started collecting his tools on the floor.

"What is it? What has happened? It seems as if something were after me."

No reply. He was like a wall.

Just then, Shikhi erupted in a strident screech from the terrace. Then everything fell silent again. Batcha's words came back to me like music from far away: "Shikhi perches on the terrace and trumpets cries of triumph."

Bhaskar-Nath gazed into the distance as if immersed in another world.

But I wanted to know, to understand that faceless enigma I felt weighing on me, which seemed to disappear and reappear at a mere sound, an odor, some insignificant incident—and yet it was full of significance. It was like the reawakening of an old association, the opening of a secret door that made everything feel different, endowed with a different sense, as if I suddenly entered the other story, the real story.

I closed my eyes. The music of conch shells echoed from the temple. A *kaddalai* vendor passed in the street. It was such a well-known, intimate world, more intimate than a place or a being, even Batcha, could ever be. It had something to do with the quality of the air—more abiding than a face, deeper than a country or a sky; or was it perhaps the quintessence of several places or beings—a very peculiar kind of vibration, or note, heard many times before and coming back from far, far away, as if stealing through corridors of opal, naves of silence, subterranean vaults where stalactites of forgotten memories hung amidst a plethora of suggestions and repressed emotions, sudden odors, nameless fears—such a familiar track that it seemed to follow ever the same old route. One did not see anything, yet everything was there. I was fastened on that minute trail, that thread of opal, yearning to know. Oh, but what in God's name was out there? What was it that came back from so far away? Holding my breath, I listened, listened, pulling upon the thread, pressing against that darkness as if the door would finally swing open and reveal the treasure. I was like a motionless well, a block of sapphire pressing, boring, sinking inch by inch into that yawning night, struggling to remember, clinging to an odor, a breath, a nameless vibration, the atmosphere of an ancient country, as if the recollection would suddenly dawn. WHAT IS IT? And there was no longer any Nil, gold-seeker, adventurer, or outlaw; I was no longer from here or there, from this island or that. I was an obscure line of beings gradually coming into sight, a confused genealogy going back over the trails of a hundred countries—deserts upon deserts; tropics; empty palaces; moonlit, dust-colored temples—pulling upon the thread of opal, the nameless thread, through corridor after corridor, through Sargassos of sudden odors, sands of despair, black Nubias. It was as elusive as a dream, but it was there—as present as remorse or a deceased beloved. Suddenly I had the feeling that there *were* no memories, nothing to recall; *I* was the memory, a formidable living memory, an aperture on a chasm comprising more than one world, an obscure body of a thousand bodies, a life crammed with a thousand lives. There was nothing to find; I was simply the ultimate residue, that opening onto something, that cluster of impelling tensions pushing in one direction. I was merely a direction, a certain chord. This was my history, my one vibration through the ages, places, and bodies—my note. But what was it?

I let go of everything. And everything sank back into the depths of the well. There remained only the surface Nil—that direction without a direction, that mystery to himself, that gold-seeker without gold—and I journeyed on through the great forest of the world, clasping shreds of memories to my heart: the color of a dress, the cry of a peacock, a glinting bangle, an improvised song, an odor of a thousand odors, and that something in the background hanging so heavily like a fatality. What, indeed, do we know as we skitter on the surface—passengers on a little island, a little margin of life, shipwrecked from how many worlds, travelers of how many islands—haunted, besieged by all we have done before, and all we have failed to do, trailing in our wake the dead who take forever to die and performers who haven't finished their performance? What force propels us to the right? What web ties all these lives together? What triumph was that peacock screeching, or what recurrence of things?

> *O Son, you forget*
> *You forget the sweetness*
> *That made you yearn to live*
> *And the Rose that will blossom*
> *You forget the golden island*
> *That gave birth to this voyage*
> *And the season of the obvious*
> *And the smile of coming together again*

Bhaskar-Nath shrugged.
"Maharaj,* tell me—"
He pushed his tools aside and looked me straight in the eye.
"No, I won't tell you."
I was startled. It was so unlike Bhaskar-Nath to speak harshly.
"I won't tell you. Because I'd no sooner tell you the past than you'd try to repeat the same old story again."
"So there *is* a past?"
"Of course, there is a past. And Wisdom wisely lays its seal of oblivion over it. Look at Bjorn rushing headlong toward his funeral pyre; it's so fascinating, so dramatic! Oh, there is a charlatan in every man."
"I have a feeling Bjorn's story is like the rehearsal of something that might happen to me."

---

* Term of respect.

"Yes, well, I won't let you run to your pyre. Or, if you do, it will be with your eyes wide open, in full awareness of the truth."

"What truth?"

He paused a moment.

"The truth is that men do not like joy. It's as simple as that."

"But there's a destiny, something propelling us, isn't there?"

"Yes, there is."

"Tell me what it is."

"If men knew ahead of time, they would never commit the errors necessary to achieve the perfection of the Goal."

I was left spellbound, as if on the verge of touching a momentous secret.

Bhaskar-Nath continued:

"Do you think your actions began just yesterday? Destiny is the past in reverse. We open up paths, then we automatically return to them. That's all."

"Meaning, we're heading for the pitfall, inescapably."

"We're heading for joy, inescapably; up to the last moment we choose suffering over joy, death and drama over joy."

"*We* choose?"

"Yes, always."

"Then there is no destiny."

"There is the destiny that *you* will. When a bull charges you, you can jump on him and be carried along, or you can dig in your heels and be trampled to death. It's as you will."

He paused, then repeated emphatically:

"*As you will.*"

"One can escape, then?"

"Not 'escape'—leap forward."

He stood before me, head shaved, chest bare, a mass of power.

"There is a moment, brief as lightning, poignant as death, a moment of utter clarity when the Force comes upon you—the force of the past, the past habits of suffering and dying and beginning again. If at that moment you muster the courage to grab that Force by the horns—that Force actually seeking your joy, coming to *compel* you to joy, sweeping upon you to shake off your chains—for Fate is really the other face of the Angel of Deliverance—if you have the courage to seize the Force and to say *yes* and to change your suffering into joy, then you live. It's the dawn of a new life. One dies by incapacity to take in joy. One dies in order to begin again in a greater joy."

He drew himself up, and it was as if Kali stood there in front of me.

"The secret does not lie in the past; it is ahead in the other man you must become through the very force seeking to destroy you."

He rammed his chisel into the ground in one blow.

"It's as you will. The same force can either kill you or save you."

16
even if I die

I believe I will never stop wondering about those microscopic points, those trivial little seconds when the entire equilibrium of things, and sometimes the entire course of life, is altered. The scales tilt ever so slightly to the left, and that's it; they will go on tilting more and more to the left. And if one watches the tilting, it takes place ten times faster, as if thoughts created the weight. That day I wondered what would happen if there were no thoughts. Perhaps *they* pick up drama the way a transistor radio picks up a frequency? But why that particular frequency and not another? Bjorn was sitting on a mat near the window at Meenakshi Lodge, about to take his first mouthful of rice, when he suddenly dropped his hand and said in a low, neutral voice, "Why eat?" From that moment on, he stopped eating. He only accepted the tea that Balu brought him morning and night, spending the entire day staring in silence at the ceiling of his room. He had become completely indifferent, would not answer when I spoke to him, and looked through Balu as if he were invisible.

"He doesn't love me; he loves only himself," Balu said.

And his eyes would fill with tears.

I recalled, again and again, that split second when Bjorn had gazed so fixedly at the funeral pyre on the beach: "That's where I am going." Before that second, the thought had never occurred to him. It had just come over him; he had caught something in the air, looked at the tableau, and that was it. That second had somehow crystallized—what? And what about that second when I had left Mohini on the promontory— what had *it* crystallized? Had the scales always tilted to the left, or were these "passing waves," imperceptible quivering breaths—now black as a snake's tongue or golden as a pollen mist, now sapphire blue, now white—glowing like diamonds or otherworldly fireflies? And they came, or did not come, according to a mysterious agreement with the color of our inner landscape. Everything happened as if we constantly attracted the circumstances and accidents—perhaps also the people— corresponding to our internal position, our soul's frequency, the darkness or beauty of our inner geography. Suddenly, I seemed to discern how I had traveled six thousand miles toward that invisible beacon, landing on a tiny white beach, drawn by a child with pink cowries. Bjorn, too, had traveled six thousand miles to this island, but it was death he had found.

"Really such a trifling little thing."

To whom was he speaking, stretched out on a bath towel, staring at the wall in front of him? Those were his first words in three days.

"A trifling little thing that gets burned to the music of clarinets."

"You're mad!"

He was contemplating the picture, and so was I. I was torn between anger and sorrow.

"No, Bjorn, not a trifling little thing, but a huge thing being burned. A huge corpse taking up all the space in your head."

He gave a start, closed his eyes. Then he turned his face toward the wall without a word. I was wrong, of course. Now he would continue to the bitter end to prove himself right, to justify that absurd instant when he had stopped eating. He didn't want to die in the least, but he would continue what he had begun. That was it in a nutshell. Had I pitied him, he still would have turned to the wall and continued fasting in order to bear out my pity. Either way, there had to be a corpse, the bigger the better, since the other one refused to die—that absurd little thing that believed itself to be Bjorn.

He turned toward me with a mixture of pain and hatred on his face.

"So what do you expect me to do, Nil? Even if I wanted to leave, I have no money, and there's Nisha. I'm trapped like a rat."

He pounded the ground with his fist.

"There's nothing left, Nil. I see nothing in front of me, no path to follow. Before, there was a path. Now it seems to have disappeared. Do you know where it has disappeared to, you who are so smart?"

I did not know what to say. I knelt beside him.

"Bjorn—"

As I looked at that Bjorn who yearned to die, I was overwhelmed by the helplessness, the ignorance of human pity, the all-consuming pity that can do nothing but witness. Oh, one day, in the depths of my being—I don't know where or when—I beheld for all time that procession of the dead beneath a scorching sky, and I swore it would never be again, ever.

Then I let go of everything. Immediately, I felt lifted above myself, looking down on that cell, on Bjorn, on those bodies, that island. I saw with almost frightening clarity the fantastic futility of those little fellows stirring about in a cell on the northern side of the village, on a speck of an island whirling some fifty thousand miles an hour around a sun, in the middle of a vast blue star-strewn ocean on the Bay of Bengal, somewhere between Mars and Venus, destruction and love, those twin sisters. Then one dies, but others will follow. Who will remember? What difference does it make? Our life is shorter than a stone's, or even a crow's. One day I saw this, oh, so clearly, on a railroad platform, and I left that pilgrim on the platform, in front of a crumbling water fountain. What difference does a pilgrim and his thoughts and feelings make? Who will remember? Nobody, not even himself. So I started to forget to look at the names of roads, islands, and railway stations; I even forgot the name of that pilgrim. Then I stopped looking at those roads extending no farther than a glance. I even stopped looking at that look extending no farther than itself; and when I had forgotten everything, the road shone everywhere before me, and my seconds lasted a bird's lifetime.

But misery still remains in the depths.

"Bjorn—"

No words would come out. I thought I could hear the sannyasi's voice: "A formidable wall—no thicker than a sheet of rice paper." But it was not amusing.

Days went by. I did not know what to do. He had grown alarmingly thin, and he was plagued with attacks of vomiting. The monsoon still did not come.

The monsoon would not come.

"What if I go mad?" he said one morning.

I did not reply. That too had entered, had been chosen and accepted. It was part of the scenario. I awaited the moment when he would start to do something crazy and continue to do it for no reason other than because he had started. Where is the madman who has not chosen—chosen in cold blood—his own madness? Oh, I know how it works! Is there a single illness or accident that we do not choose deliberately, because something passes in the air? But what was it *inside* that responded or started the drama, the tiny element that picked up the frequency—that frequency and not another? "We open up paths. . . ." Perhaps all that was needed was to cut the current and go above, into another chamber, another frequency? Indeed, we harbor death chambers, anguish chambers, garrets packed with desire, cellars alive with gruesome beasts—secret hypogeums, accursed sanctuaries that retain the full power of their spell like a dark womb of perdition. But there is the bright room, too. We need to change rooms, open the lovely path!

"Bjorn!"

He opened one eye.

"Listen, just stop thinking about it!"

He remained inert, his eyes obstinately fixed on the ceiling. There was a sudden clatter of footsteps in the hall.

Balu came rushing into the room, a thermos in his hands, very agitated.

"He's here—a man from your country. Don't listen, Bjorn. Don't listen to him! He wants to hurt you."

Bjorn rose to his feet. Balu knocked over the thermos, which shattered into pieces, releasing streamlets of tea on the floor.

"From my country?"

A man came in. Immaculate white slacks, open collar, the shirt drenched with perspiration.

"Whew, it's hot in here!"

Bjorn steadied himself against the wall, as white as a sheet.

"I see."

The man scanned the room with an expression of disgust on his face.

"A friend of yours wrote to me. Sorry, let me introduce myself: Hans Petersen, attaché at the Norwegian consulate. Someone by the name of Guruji."

Bjorn looked like a cornered animal. Balu stood next to him, fists clenched, ready to pounce on the man.

"He says you are in serious trouble—sick, penniless, a Norwegian citizen, and—"

I distinctly heard Bjorn swear between his clenched teeth:

"The bastard betrayed me."

"You must be repatriated. I have come to fetch you."

There was a deathly silence. I could see Bjorn's heart pounding against his ribs. His upper lip was covered with perspiration.

With a sudden movement he drew himself up, his hands on his hips.

"I'm staying right here."

The man gave him a startled look.

"Surely you don't mean to stay in this dump!"

He gave me a side look.

"In this country of savages? Look, I can endorse all your travel expenses back home, and you'll receive free medical attention from the consulate's doctor."

"I'm staying."

"It's my job to look after your welfare and if need be—"

"If need be, what?"

Bjorn braced himself against the wall, head high, face transfigured. This was Prince Bjorn.

"What do you hope to accomplish here anyway?"

"You wouldn't understand."

"What I understand is that you are a sick man who needs to be brought back to common sense, to his country."

"Common sense?"

I saw Bjorn's knuckles turn white.

"Well, I mean to a normal life, in a normal country."

"I don't want any part of your normal country."

"Look here—"

"And I don't want any part of your normal life. I don't want your common sense."

Balu moved closer to Bjorn, pressing himself against him, one hand on his friend's shoulder.

"I don't want your normal prison."

"Really? Listen, you must first get medical attention. Tell me, what is it you are looking for here?"

Bjorn closed his eyes for a moment and grasped Balu's hand. The man leaned forward.

"I don't know, but I know that I don't want any part of your world! I want another life, a truer life, a truer world. And even if I die, even if it's a dream, even if I'm mad, I believe in my dream over your civilized barbarism."

The attaché flushed crimson. I moved to stand by Bjorn's other side. Now he was glaring at the three of us.

"I have means of persuasion, you know. I can have you expelled and repatriated by force."

"Go away."

"But—"

"Get the hell out!"

The man adjusted his jacket over his chest and turned on his heel.

"I'll have to report this."

His leather heels stomped down the hall.

Bjorn collapsed to the floor, hammering the ground with his fist, muttering again and again:

"Even if I die, even if I die."

Yet, again, I thought Bjorn would be saved.

Everything seemed to organize itself miraculously. That morning, two pilgrims staying at Meenakshi's mentioned the existence of a "Japanese hospital" about fifty miles away on the mainland. I decided to take Bjorn there. It was simply a matter of breaking the vicious cycle, I thought. Furthermore, these Japanese were supposed to be experts in "natural cures," exactly what Bjorn needed. A train was leaving at nine-thirty the next morning.

But what about Batcha?

ψ

17
the pretty snake

I went toward her like a bird toward a spring. She was my refreshment, my grounding, the sweetness of being able to flow like music. When I was with her, I could be secure in the knowledge that the world had two feet and some seashells. Curiously, when I looked at her, the world moved differently— truly so—as if things arranged themselves, became harmonious, followed another rhythm, a different, utterly delightful and surprising law. When I was with Bjorn everything went wrong: I would trip on the stairs and nearly split my head open, I would drop my glass on the floor, let the water bucket fall to the bottom of the well. Accident followed accident in a kind of mathematically precise sequence, a black logic slanting life according to its pernicious theorem, like a medical chart traced by a doctor. At that moment, I wondered whether the chart followed the illness or the illness followed the chart. I had the sense of a totally arbitrary world, of a staggering mental formation that had scientifically falsified the world according to its theorem, and that things might in fact be *perfectly* different. It was enough to watch a bucket fall down a well, and to seize on an imperceptible gravitation not ruled by Newton's laws. Perhaps a psychic gravitation?

I turned into the street of the temple, and literally bumped into Nisha. She blushed under her glowing dark skin and gave me an equivocal look that swept into me like a burn. Then she hurried away. I could feel the blood drain from my face. It was the third time I had encountered her that day.

I felt a swarm of microscopic incidents come to light from all sides—the very things usually deemed "unimportant" that slip from one's sight like an eel beneath a rock. One glances at Nisha a moment too long and one catches Nisha's world, or Bjorn's, and, imperceptibly, things start tilting in another direction: one meets her three times in the street when one never saw her before; one bumps into all sorts of beings one never noticed before, but now they seem to cross the stage again and again, almost *creating* the circumstances needed to fashion another story or an accident. Imperceptibly, the setting has changed and one has set foot on a totally different stage, become subject to a different law and, as if in a film, everything must unfold exactly as the director has planned that particular scene.

It seemed as if everything had started gravitating in another direction.

"*O Moshai—*"

I turned around to see the two pilgrims who had spoken of the "Japanese hospital."

"At what time is the train for the mainland?"

I looked at them in amazement, then managed to utter:

"At nine-thirty."

They walked away without another word. I could have sworn they had shown up just to tell me, "Don't forget, your train leaves at nine-thirty."

This time I *had* to understand. What was it that kept impelling things in this particular direction? The power of thought? But thought was only the end product, the sign that something was *already* in motion. Something knocks on the windowpane and we lean forward, just to catch the accident. That was it: first, we lean forward, *then* we catch it. Thought is not what we think it is. It doesn't understand—nor is it designed for understanding! It merely provides a translation after the fact. The little light flickers—red, green, purple—but the current has *already* gone through it. We are just electrical terminals, frequency receivers. We are a certain way of tuning in, like Bjorn toward his ceiling. We pick up a fragment of music and call it "our" song, a shadow and it becomes "our" distress, a vibration and it's our desire, a speck of light and it's a gospel, while every light and every shadow is right there, every thought-free little note, just waiting to go through us to create a symphony or a disaster. We know nothing of the thought process that we still handle like primates; we are only versed in the *skill* of thought, a penthouse with varying degrees of brightness and salubrity. Yet there used to be another type of thought: a high motionless antenna piercing the azure crust, probing deep into the future and giving form to the great wandering vibrations of Tomorrow. There used to be another mode of reflection—active, creative, a power of foresight—similar to the kind Bjorn so effectively used to attract death; a pictorial, silent thought—magical—like a great blank canvas to capture life's divine vermilions, its golden flares, its archangelic smiles; a subtle canvas to make life resemble a picture. Ah, if only we could keep always before us an image of beauty, a pure diagram, a great picture capable of luring the world's harmony and beauty, a golden net to capture the great birds of joy—what a power that would be! And we would look at nothing but that, want nothing but that, and pierce the darkness of life with that incorruptible vision.

⁎

"Nothing-at-all, Mr. Nothing-at-all!"
She was stepping out of the water just as I approached.

She looked up and ran toward me with outstretched arms. I could almost hear her song in my heart, or was it my song? There are beings who are like a song; actually, we all are like a song waiting to burst forth—a song that does not know, does not dare; and when that music, that unobtrusive little tune starts flowing out, everything breaks down in a general debacle, and the world is washed away as if one had never lived.

That little peacock-girl sang, and the beach looked like a vast snowfield fringed with sapphire. The dunes flowed toward the sea as toward a blue swan princess: *Rani ami* . . .

> *I am the queen of the coral country*
> *I have three golden fish and a silver one*
> *I have all lifetimes!*
> *And my king*
> *Has caught a star*
> *Of rich purple*
> *He caught seven of them*
> *To make a garland around my neck*
> *And three bubbles from my laughter*
> *To crown his lovely diadem!*

Now she stood laughing on the steps of the little sanctuary, dripping with water, framed by the tiny columns. She looked like a little queen in a Kangra painting.

"I saw a sea snake," she declared triumphantly. "It was this big!"

"But that can be very harmful!"

"Oh, it was so pretty, green all over with yellow spots! We had a race."

"But do you realize these snakes are poisonous? It could have bitten you!"

"It was *pretty*, I am telling you!"

She crossed her arms over her breast as if she were cold, or perhaps a little bashful. Tiny translucent beads of water glistened on her cheeks and on the tip of her nose. The sea had turned her skirt the color of blackberries in May. The sight of her filled me with an inexplicable happiness; we laughed and laughed together, two children who had long played together, perhaps forever, on a tiny white beach that sometimes bordered this world.

"What about your monsoon? Sleeping?"

She looked skyward, grinning.

"Oh, it's just gathering water. Besides, the curlews have not yet arrived, Shikhi has not yet nested in the kitchen, and Bjorn's petrels have not yet settled on the lagoon."

"You know—"

"I know everything! It's in your left hand."

"My left hand?"

She opened her mouth and, grinning, blew the water off the tip of her nose.

"Yes, the conch you forgot to bring me."

"Oh!"

"You had promised."

Nothing-at-all
Who forgets all

"What happened to your tilak?"

She raised her hand toward her forehead.

"Oh, it must have been washed off by the sea."

She shook her skirt.

"It's all gone."

"Wait."

I hastened toward the sanctuary and took a pinch of red powder from the little bowl at the feet of the god; there were fresh flowers, and some incense still burning.

"Here."

And I placed a red mark on her forehead.

She looked at me with utter stupefaction. Then her arms dropped and she became ghastly pale. Tears began rolling down her cheeks.

"What's the matter, Batcha?"

There was such a look of distress on her face, while the tears kept streaming down. I was horrified.

"But what is it, Batcha? Please say something! What did I do wrong?"

She would not speak.

A mortal anguish took hold of me. Lord! I never meant to be disrespectful to her god! What had I done? What sacrilege had I committed?

"Please answer me, Batcha! What is it? Your god is very nice, Batcha. I like him, I swear. He's very nice."

She kept staring at me, transfixed, arms dangling, eyes searing, filled with light, as if mirroring the very depths of her soul. Oh, if only I had understood what I saw in her eyes at that moment!

Then with a shudder she gathered her skirt in her hands and fled across the sands.

I felt heartsick.

I remained there on those steps, watching her disappear. It's as if something had been torn, broken deep inside me. What had I done? What? There I was, alone; for the first time I felt *all alone*. I had never had a sense of being alone before. I always felt borne by something. Now, I was no longer borne; I was a separate concrete person—me. It was as if she had slammed the door in my face, stuck my passport in my hands: "Here, you're a foreigner," and now I found myself all alone, like an idiot, in a country where I had thought myself at home. What did I care for all their gods! I was not asking anything of them! All I wanted was to be happy!

I was dumbfounded—torn between pain and anger—like a child who has thrown himself into a friend's arms only to discover she was paying attention to someone else behind his back.

Heavy-hearted, I set off for the hostel to meet Bjorn, my brother. My brother? I stopped dead in my tracks. Weren't things beginning to go awry for me, too? Just as that thought crept in, there were two simultaneous sparks and I felt: "Here you are—this is it." Everything around me stopped: "Here I am. I've got it—I've got my second," that nasty little second when everything turns inside out. And just as I perceived it, almost exactly at the same moment, I heard a voice—toneless, impersonal, like a knife—saying sententiously, "Now that you've seen your second, it's done." And immediately I *knew*. In every direction lay an ambush and the least thought was a trap. I knew that it *was* done. Now I could scream my lungs out, protest, turn a deaf ear on it, blow on it, do as I liked. The thought was there, and the more I blew on it, the stronger, more resilient it would become, the more visible and almost compelled to exist. In a flash I had the feeling the circle was closing—an imperceptible feeling of dissolution, of encompassing decay. Anything I could do or say, look at it or not look at it, only added to the dissolution; I was strangling myself with my own two hands.

I started up the path again.

Quietly, matter-of-factly, something inside me said, "That's what fate is about." Everything was the same and everything was poisonous.

"Three rupees a conch! Three rupees for a pretty conch!"

Mechanically, I stopped in front of the coral shop. I could still hear Batcha's little voice: "It was *pretty*, I am telling you!"

"But do you realize it's poisonous?"

And that was that. I could scream, deny it, laugh in my own face if I wished; I had said it was poisonous, so poisonous it *was*!

I had performed foul magic and poisoned everything.

I suddenly realized that all this had happened *before* I had even become aware of it, even before the catastrophe had taken place. Indeed, five minutes earlier, when I did not even know what was going to happen, when I had not even touched that damn tilak, and I was there on the beach, laughing with her, I had already *sought* the poison, caught the poison, ruined everything. "But do you realize it's poisonous? It could have bitten you!" Everything was already there in those few simple words, that trivial gesture, that fleeting symbol, that little breath whose significance was an enigma, as if the sword were already preparing to strike—only waiting for us to find the snake pretty, or harmful.

Now I heard Bhaskar-Nath's voice thundering in my ears: "It is *as you will.*"

I stood there before the coral shop, clutching a conch.

In a brusque gesture, I raised that conch and dashed it to the ground.

18
the japanese hospital

*I*t was nine o'clock in the morning. Balu protested vehemently as I tried to convince him that the only way to save Bjorn was to separate him from that tantric.

"He mustn't leave here. He mustn't, he mustn't. Besides, he doesn't see that man anymore."

"Look, Balu, we'll soon be back. Don't you see how thin he is? If we wait any longer, he'll be too weak to be moved."

But he shook his head obstinately.

"He mustn't, he mustn't."

It was useless to argue with the child, so I ordered him to fetch a cart. He went out without a word, leaving me to persuade Bjorn to make the journey. To my surprise, he did not resist in the least, showing childlike docility and indifference. I packed his towels, his red wallet, enveloped him in his scarf and helped him to his feet. He could barely stand. I put his arm around my neck and we walked out into the corridor. For an instant, he turned around toward his "lookout post," contemplated the margosa tree over the well, the acacia forest, and Kali's Rock looming in the distance. I thought he was about to say something, but he braced his jaw.

"Let's go."

There are looks that tell all, even when we don't have a clue about anything. Inside, the course is already known while we are still calculating.

I felt wretched. At that moment, I should have stopped to heed the uneasiness I felt, the something that weighed on my heart like a ton of lead, but I, too, was continuing the gesture I had begun.

Balu was waiting downstairs beside the cart. With a gentle, protective gesture he grasped Bjorn's hand.

"Come, Bjorn, let me help you sit comfortably."

Bjorn seemed completely oblivious. He gazed at the street, the cart, the passersby, as if in a dream. I saw a small dimple twinkle fleetingly on his cheek. Balu propped him up against a sack of fodder in the back of the cart. Then he sat between Bjorn and me, legs dangling outside, and we set off at break-neck speed, the driver riding the shaft and shouting at the top of his voice as if he were a Roman charioteer. There was a jerk, and I was sent flying against the partition while Bjorn toppled over me. Balu was thrown off the cart and fell onto the pavement. It took another fifty yards or so before I could stop that damned driver. Then I rushed back to Balu, who rose to his feet, blood trickling down his forehead.

"It's nothing, really. It's nothing."

I took his arm.

"It's nothing, I'm telling you!"

He sharply shrugged off my hand.

I could almost hear my own voice back in that acacia forest: "It's nothing, Bjorn, really," while blood continued to spurt from my finger. Everything was being repeated.

I sponged Balu's face with a towel, my heart pounding like a drum. He was deathly pale. I should have stopped, turned back; and even if I could not understand Balu's reasons, I should have at least heeded the sign being thrust in my face. But I was locked within my implacable logic. "Signs" were only for dreamers. For the rest of my life I will know that there is no worse type, none more stubborn and noxious, than those who pretend to save others. All our good reasons are the first indisputable sign of unreason, for there are five billion reasons in this world and not one that applies to the other person.

At last we arrived at the station, where a second sign awaited me. But I was still oblivious, hearing nothing, seeing nothing except my own idea. I was even blinder than before because, deep down, I now blamed myself; and I was as foolish in my self-incrimination as I had been in my self-justification. In truth, we are complete fools in every way, as long as we have not broken loose from both our black and white logic.

> *O Tara, O Mother*
> *I am the chariot, You are the charioteer*

It was the beggar from the little beach. He came straight to me, hand outstretched.

> *You are the doer of the action, O Mother*
> *Yet they say I am the doer*
> *O Tara, Tara*
> *You are the All-Will*
> *And the winding of the path beneath my footsteps*
> *And the arrow of the enemy*
> *As you move, so move I*

I looked at him. For a second I felt that little music of truth, so simple. All I had to do was pause for a moment, tune in to the great current again, and I would have known at once. But I was so deaf! Sometimes I have the feeling that, deep down, everything is known forever and all our effort and striving and frenzied actions are only a resistance to that which flows effortlessly: fog over light. In truth, we neither seek nor act; we resist.

I helped Bjorn to his seat. Balu settled himself at Bjorn's feet, watching him intently. Blood continued to ooze from Balu's forehead as he sat straight as an arrow, head held high like a little warrior: "You're the king, and I am guarding you." How could I have possibly thought I was guarding him better with my good reasons?! I looked up to see Nisha peering through the train window, her face between her hands, a yellow marigold stuck in her hair. Somehow, she knew of our departure. They all knew! She ogled Bjorn, open-mouthed.

An acacia tree was in bloom near the track.

The train whistled.

Balu stood up, touched Bjorn's feet, then folded his hands before his forehead. Bjorn stirred and seemed to half awaken, looking at Balu with eyes brimming with light. I don't know what passed between the two of them at that moment, and I shall never know. Balu made a slight bow, his lips quivering imperceptibly; then, with teeth clenched, he walked away without a single glance in my direction. The train departed. I caught one last glimpse of Nisha with her face between her hands, then of Balu's small silhouette amid the crates of lemon, straight as an arrow, hands folded, saluting his king.

The train steamed away.

My heart sank.

Had I not been so blind at that moment, I would have noticed that everything around me was yellow: the acacia blossoms, the crated lemons on the platform, the flower in Nisha's hair—a yellow composition on a backdrop of sand and searing railroad tracks. I wonder if the color of my soul was not yellow, too.

For the second time, I sensed that the circle was closing. I felt it in a very simple way: all the little inner waves kept colliding, intermingling, bouncing back onto me, instead of vanishing into infinity. Everything seemed to have taken a false rhythm. That's what happens at the end of a cycle: things no longer get through; there is an obstruction somewhere.

We crossed the bridge. Our passage over the metal beams echoed the same cadence. Just as there is a color for each moment beneath the wandering stars, there is a music for each thing; and that slight little rhythm was so poignant, not unlike the first day with the sannyasi when I seemed to feel the presence of a brother beneath my closed eyelids.

> *O brother*
> *What are you waiting for?*

And it kept repeating: What are you waiting for? What are you waiting for?

> *It is time*
> *And life passes in vain*

That passage of time felt almost unbearable. My eyes went from Bjorn lying on the seat to the passing dunes. I had come full circle. We barely open our eyes and it's all over: we've already crossed the bridge and left the island. Life doesn't last a lifetime! What remains? Impressions, fugitive faces, the color of a sky, fragments of a song, gnawing remorses, and gestures, millions of gestures for nothing. But where is the hour that truly counts? The unalloyed other thing?

He was staring at me.

"Nil, where are you taking me?"

"To restore your health."

He put his head down with a heavy sigh.

"Have the petrels arrived yet?"

"I don't know, Bjorn. No, not yet. Soon."

"Soon—"

He relapsed into silence.

After the train, we had to take a car to drive another two hours under a broiling sun.

"It's just beyond the river," the driver kept reassuring us.

Beyond the river. Where on earth was that river? Bjorn was slumped in the back seat, knees pulled under his chin, eyes closed. I had to hold him to keep him from falling to the floor. We were driving through a landscape of rocks, enormous rocks, endless, polished like antediluvian skulls, interspersed with an occasional bright green paddy field dotted with little white grebes. Then the jungle—the dense, buzzing, tormented jungle—no higher than a man, strewn with rocky hills like a giant's heaps of marbles. Where could there be a Japanese hospital in the middle of this? I kept asking the driver every few minutes.

"Beyond."

I could not get anything more out of him. Beyond what?

It was two o'clock in the afternoon when we finally arrived.

A dozen normal-size trees, a village—perhaps a town suburb? Some dilapidated brick houses lining a dried-up river. A scattering of huts, a few street stalls, and a compound surrounded by high walls.

"Here we are. Shall I drive in?"

I looked up and froze, horror-struck.

On the arch above the gateway was a wooden sign lettered in tar: MENTAL HOSPITAL.

"What?!"

I glanced at Bjorn. His eyes were shut; he had seen nothing. Turn back? But that would mean another two hours' drive under that scorching sun just to reach the station. Bjorn half opened his eyes.

"For Heaven's sake, hurry! Get me inside."

He had seen nothing.

First, he must drink and rest. Oh, what a fool I was! What an utter fool! Tomorrow, at the crack of dawn, we would be on our way.

The driver parked the car under a tree. There was no hospital building! Just a bare tract of land covered in red laterite, and a solitary dilapidated bungalow with creepers clinging to rotten pillars. I got out and struck the gong. A drowsy, shuffling servant appeared to tell me that Dr. Ezaki never came downstairs before three o'clock. It was now two o'clock and one hundred and five degrees in the shade. The rocky laterite surface was as hot as a furnace; I could not even remove Bjorn from the car and seat him under a tree.

Dr. Ezaki arrived at three twenty-five. Settling himself comfortably in an armchair, he took the time to light a cigarette before introducing me to his assistant, Dr. Shimizu.

"I have brought you my brother, who is not mad."

"Yes."

"He is thirsty and needs some rest. We have just driven for two hours in this sun. To make matters worse, he hasn't eaten in three weeks."

Dr. Ezaki adjusted his spectacles, then launched into a tirade in an English as erratic as the surrounding rocks.

"You see, my dear sir, there is no such thing as illness. There is only an imbalance between different kinds of energy."

I felt dejected.

"We start from the premise that everything in Nature is made up of two principles: Yin and Yang, feminine and masculine."

I stared at that meticulous little fellow surrounded by chinaware, at the empty aquarium with its lone fragment of coral, and I felt like burying my head in my hands and doing like Bjorn: shutting my eyes and getting out of this.

"Thus, if you have an excess of Yin, for instance (which we can determine here), it is easily corrected by adding Yang elements to the diet. Eggplants, for example."

"Look, doctor, the man's dying of heat in the car! It's four o'clock. He needs a bed and some peace and quiet!"

The doctor gave a little jolt like a puppet, spoke a few words in Japanese to his assistant, then followed me outside.

Bjorn lay prostrate on the seat, drenched with sweat, his face covered with water blisters. A thread of blood hung from the corner of his mouth. My heart felt like lead. I wanted to cry in frustration. I tried to lift him, but he crumpled back onto the seat. Then Dr. Shimizu gathered him up and carried him behind the bungalow.

That's when I had my second shock of the day. There, in the middle of this barren, tortured landscape of laterite stood an enormous slab of concrete, about a hundred yards long and several feet high, and on it, a row of a dozen tiny cells, barricaded shut.

My mouth dropped open.

"You see, there are wild animals roaming at night, and there are floods."

Bjorn's head lolled against Dr. Shimizu's arm. A male nurse rushed up to us. I felt sick.

"You'll have as much space as you need. We have only three cases at the moment."

We entered cell number 4.

There was barely room for a bed, a chair, a water jug, and a copper bowl. They placed Bjorn on the bed.

"I'll send over some tea and biscuits, and I'll be back at five o'clock when the patient is rested."

Then they left.

I stayed there, squatting at the foot of Bjorn's bed, my head in my hands.

I called with all my might—what, whom, I don't know—my light, the truth, *that* which is real, *that* which is true, *that, that.* I called and called like a child in the night. Slowly, progressively, peace came over me and everything became extremely quiet and still. Then, I felt a great Force descend into me, into my head, my heart, my chest—a great flood of softness, so refreshing, so tranquil, yet so strong, as if I bathed in a pool of peace—such a concrete presence that it brought tears to my eyes. Yes, *that* is there, *that* is real, *that* is true; it's there, always there, and the world can crumble. Oh, he who has never felt the wonder of that flood can never understand my raving words!

I rose to my feet, stripped off Bjorn's clothes and emptied half a jugful of water over his body. Then I sponged his body which seemed to revive him. He opened his eyes.

"Don't worry, Bjorn, I'm here. I'm taking care of you, brother, don't worry. All will be well."

A faint smile flickered on his face.

Was it something in the tone of my voice that made him look at me so warmly, almost tenderly? I lifted a mug of water to his lips and he drank thirstily. Then he lay his head back on the pillow and closed his eyes.

How long did I sit there gazing at the rugged ground dominated by a large tamarind tree at the far end of the courtyard? I must have fallen asleep, for suddenly Batcha appeared before me. She was leaning over me. But it was more than Batcha; it was a luminous, almost radiant presence into which I sank as if I were melting. It was extraordinarily soft, a sort of dissolution into light; we were both lighter than air, as if made up of a luminous substance, a froth of light, but a living, conscious, prodigiously sensitive light whose every particle intermingled in a delight of ethereal fusion. There was a sense of absolute security, a security of unparalleled quality: one was forever, protected, wrapped in an indestructible body—yes, a body of light. And it was unmistakably Batcha. Although I could not really see her face or her body, it *was* her more clearly than if I were seeing her in the flesh. Indeed, her body was like a distortion of that light, a limited, starched representation, an almost arbitrary contour to give form to an earthly Batcha and force her into a mold. In truth, we have a dozen faces and manifold bodies, multifarious ways of being, and deep-seated stories from all ages that mingle in a vast inner efflorescence; but we see only one face, only one story. While now, I beheld a complete Batcha with all her faces and depths, almost all her various stories, brought together in a quintessence of soft light.

I had never seen anything like that before.

I felt rather nonplussed and, for a moment, I wondered if she was truly angry with me. Then everything vanished. A tea tray had appeared in front of me. I managed to remember that she appeared taller than I remembered her. Then I slid back into the uneasy grayness we call life.

"Would you like some tea?"

Bjorn opened his eyes with a start, looking around him with bewilderment. As he began to remember where he was, he gave me a look of distress.

"Let's go, Nil. Help me get out of this place. I hate being caged in!"

I carried him outside and settled him on the cement platform, propping him against the side of the cell with a pillow behind his back. He drank his glass of tea in one gulp.

"Give me more. I'm hungry."

My heart leaped. I handed him a biscuit—two, three. He was eating! I wanted to cry with joy, clap my hands. But I dared not say a word for fear of breaking the spell. He began to look around at the barricaded cells, the wall encircling the compound, the scraps of bandages hanging on thorn bushes. The smell of disinfectant drifted in from an isolated hut.

"What a bizarre place you've brought me to."

His voice was as soft as a child's.

It held no trace of the anger and reproach he had been expressing toward me for weeks.

His eyes returned to the tamarind tree.

"It's beautiful."

He gazed at the tree for a long while, a quiet smile on his lips. The tamarind was huge, almost bare of leaves, as if it had been struck by lightning, leaving only large burst pods amid a riot of tangled twigs silhouetted against the clear sky.

"It's so beautiful," repeated Bjorn. "It's just like the silver birch. I knew there would be a tree."

"We'll leave tomorrow morning. I promise, Bjorn. We'll leave this place and return to the island."

"Oh, that doesn't matter."

He nodded his head in silence, and I noticed there were tears running down his cheeks.

"Bjorn—"

He began speaking in the clear, high-pitched, fitful tones of a feverish child.

"It's strange, Nil, but I feel comfortable here! I am not even sure I want to go back. I just feel comfortable. Empty like this courtyard, but at ease, almost contented."

His eyes roamed over the rocky ground strewn with thorn bushes.

"The setting makes no difference, you know. Oh," he gave a choked laugh, "I've wanted so many things in my life, Nil, gone after so many things, and now I don't know what I want anymore; I think that I want nothing. There *is* nothing: no more Balu, no more Guruji, no more Erik. It's all empty. Yet, it's as if I had found everything. Everything. I am at peace. I seem to be exactly where I am supposed to be. For once in my life, I have the feeling of being where I am supposed to be. How strange."

He looked around with an expression of astonishment on his face, his eyes finally coming to rest on the tamarind tree. A child began to cry in the isolated hut.

"It's strange, Nil, but it's as if I had been waiting for this moment all my life. God, the trekking one has to go through! When it's all so very simple: there's no need of anything; we're right in it. A few rocks and a tree."

Again, he gave that brittle laugh.

"I wanted to be initiated. Initiated, can you imagine! Oh, Nil! I have the feeling of an enormous falsehood being cracked open. An enormous falsehood. Something that is constantly there with us, *over* our life, stuck over our life—a screen. Now the screen is gone, and there is nothing to find!"

He closed his eyes an instant, and I felt as if a wave of light were enveloping him.

Dr. Ezaki chose that moment to arrive with his little bundles of note cards and a stethoscope bobbing against his stomach. Bjorn sat smiling at the tamarind tree.

"Ah! There is our patient. We've eaten the biscuits like a good fellow. Let's see now—"

He rubbed his hands together. His assistant was at his heels, carrying a vial, a sphygmoscope, and some rubber tubing. Still smiling, Bjorn let them carry him back to the bed. I watched through the bars as he replied quietly and patiently to the doctor's questions and submitted to his prodding fingers. I didn't know whether to cry or sing. Bjorn, my brother, was saved! How simple it was! My eyes roved over the tamarind tree, the scraps of cotton hanging from the bushes, the walls. Then suddenly, I was transported to the *Appellplatz* of that camp—my striped clothes, my serial number, my head shaved like a criminal. A farce! A colossal farce everywhere, at every level, on every latitude, in every form. A masquerade. Evil and good were fabrications, hatred and illness were fabrications, folly and wisdom were fabrications; none of this was real! The only reality was something that smiled.

"How often were you eating wheat flakes?"

Now they were fastening a tourniquet around Bjorn's arm and thumping his ribs. Were they going to decide that he had galloping consumption or something? But Bjorn sat in the cage, smiling. He smiled and there was no more cage, not the least trace of consumption! But if he lost his smile, he would be in the grip of a formidable consumption and be doomed. That's how it worked, truly so. As for me, I was going to be killed by the first boot kick of an SS guard, but I didn't believe in the SS, oh no! All a farce, a gigantic farce, with not an ounce of truth on either side: neither with the victim nor with the executioner, the madman or the doctor. There was only that second, that pure second when the curtain is drawn back, and *that* shines forth. Then one smiles and one is invulnerable. The trouble is, we cling to that curtain! We enliven it with every conceivable color—yellow, red, blue, philanthropy, religion, love, hate, initiations, but it remains what it is, nothing but a curtain of falsehood. The moment we draw back the curtain, things become *true*. Everything becomes true. Everywhere, whether in a mental hospital or on the most beautiful beach in the world.

"Now I see what it is."

Dr. Ezaki left the cell. I rose to my feet mechanically.

"Tomorrow morning we will perform further tests, but I have reached a diagnosis."

I stared at him blankly. Perhaps he expected me to ask for his diagnosis.

"It's a Yang deficiency."

"I see."

Oh, yes, a Truth deficiency! That's really the only deficiency there is!

He gave me a look of disdain and strode away with his vial. I darted back into the cell and clasped Bjorn's shoulder.

"Tomorrow we're off, brother. We're beginning a new life!"

He smiled, then settled himself in his bed in order to get a better view of the tree.

"I heard them, you know."

"Heard what?"

"The birds."

"The birds?"

"Yes, it's all melted."

"Oh, Bjorn! You're not going to start again, are you?"

"Start what? You know, I watched them just now as they were examining me, and it was so strange, Nil. I don't see things the way I used to. Before, everything was sharp and angular, unyielding, opaque, conflicting; now, things seem to extend as if they had an unfathomable past, a boundless future, vast ranges of sweetness, as when towing a big fishing net in which all sorts of things get caught. It's like that. We tow a big net and we are tiny, so tiny, and things drift away, recede into the distance, and everything becomes very soft. Very soon there is nothing left but the cry of a bird from afar. Only that. The cry of a bird. No more Erik, no more Balu, no more anything. It all becomes vague, melted. Oh, but that cry! It sounds so sure, so true, so completely *there*—like the cry of the ganders on the lake, behind the mist. That call seems to come from so far, far away, and it sounds so *full!* It melts everything!"

He opened his hands on the bed.

"It's like the opening of a door—a door of snow. Tranquil, so tranquil. And one passes through it."

I stroked his forehead.

"Don't worry, Nil. You did the right thing and all is for the best. We'll leave tomorrow."

I left him resting and went to arrange our departure with the driver.

"Remember, not a word of this to the doctors."

Then I walked to the well behind the bungalow to bathe. My forehead was burning.

It was already sundown. Little chipmunks pursued one another among the rocks. Everything seemed so peaceful, like the end of a long journey. Yes, "all is for the best"; Bjorn was right. Indeed, all is always for the best! But we see only a portion of the story, a fragmented note, a segment of the film, so things are never for the best! Perhaps, after all, I had been right to bring Bjorn here? Perhaps I had only followed the little pulsation that impels things? Looking back, everything strikes me as a gigantic conspiracy, an organization so meticulous that it even uses our distractions, our good or ill will, as if it were all the same, all a material to attain the goal—ever nearer, ever the imperturbable golden meridian leading straight to the little door, without a second's waste, or an extra speck of dust, or any unnecessary suffering. Now I wonder, as I wondered that evening, if that little pulsation—the out-of-the-blue pilgrims with their Japanese hospital, the fortuitous encounters, the chance twists and turns—could not arise from a certain inner state, a certain clarity, an inner frequency that causes us to be in accord with one type of vibration rather than another, yellow or red rather than blue; thus, perhaps, the picture would be constantly shifting. The encounters, circumstances and accidents would be infinitely variable, yet it would be always the same picture, the same events, but in different colorations: Nisha instead of Batcha, the white island instead of the red island, and now this cement island in the middle of a rocky desert. Sometimes, in this life, I feel I am observing a caricature of something that might have been different yet is essentially the *same*—only disguised, with a grimace rather than a smile. Perhaps what we are witnessing is a fantastic magic-lantern show spinning the same timeless story, bringing forth a green castle here, a shower of stars there, a drama, or a song; and when the white door opens, it reveals the great eternal picture. Then, whether we are here or there, clothed in wisdom or in shame, in folly or righteousness, in yellow or red, we are in the vast smile forever, and the stars can crumble.

I was about to pour the last bucketful of water over my head, when I heard shouts coming from the village. I abruptly interrupted my gesture, and my heart froze. Surely it could not be Bjorn, since the cries were coming from the village! I flung on my clothes with trembling fingers, and rushed to the gate. A crowd had assembled at the end of the street. I hastened toward the knot of onlookers and, following their gaze, looked up. I was struck speechless. Bjorn was standing there on the terrace of the grain merchant, stark naked, menacing the crowd with bricks.

Then I saw Dr. Shimizu advancing stealthily behind him, arms outstretched. "Bjorn! Bjorn!" I yelled. But Shimizu leapt on him, clutching him in a stranglehold. Bjorn struggled frenziedly. Then he collapsed. A moment, later Shimizu carried Bjorn's inert body down to the street. Dr. Ezaki joined him and they returned Bjorn to his cell. He looked cadaverous.

"What happened, for God's sake? What happened?!"
Shimizu was dousing Bjorn's face with water.

"No idea."

Bjorn opened his eyes and looked about wildly, like a cornered animal. Then he caught sight of me. Oh, that look! Never in my life will I forget the accusation in his eyes, as if he were saying: "You! How could you?" Then he turned away and closed his eyes.

I would never see his eyes again.

Dr. Ezaki was calmly waiting outside the cell, smoking a cigarette, and looking so blasé about the whole thing that I wanted to strangle him.

"Good God, what happened?! Tell me!"

He exhaled a puff of smoke.

"I saw your brother going out into the street. He stopped a while before the gate, looking up at the signboard. Then I sent Shimizu out to help him since he could hardly stand on his feet. But when he saw Shimizu coming, he ran away. You saw the rest."

I sat at Bjorn's side far into the night, fanning his ashen face. The cell was buzzing with mosquitoes and the air was stifling. I kept up a continual flow of words, saying whatever came into my mind, for I knew he was not sleeping and could hear me. Yet, he never answered or stirred. Only the little dimple in his sunken cheek gave an occasional twitch as if to say: you've betrayed me, you've betrayed me. I watched that little dimple for hours. I held his hand, sponged his forehead—no sign of life except that little crease: you've betrayed me, you've betrayed me.

Finally I crept away to lie down, exhausted, in the adjoining cell. It was pitch black. Like it or not, tomorrow at dawn I would take him away from here. Oh, what a fool I had been! I sank into a heavy sleep.

When I awoke, the morning sun was gleaming upon the tamarind tree. I leaped to my feet and rushed to Bjorn's cell.

He lay doubled up on the ground, his head against the bars. The door was locked. I shouted my lungs out to call those damn doctors:

"Why on earth did you lock the door? Why?!"

"Wild animals, you see. There are wild animals roaming at night."

I took Bjorn in my arms. There was a large bruise on his shoulder. It looked as if he had hurled himself against the door.

He was dead.

19
the chandala and I

*W*e placed him on the funeral pyre, facing north, as if he were leaving for his homeland. There were only the chandala and I, and the sea nearby, rustling over the coral. Bjorn would never return to the island or see the lagoon again; this was as far as I could bring him. I had pleaded with the macua, begged him to take us across the water, but to no avail. The journey ended here on this beach, near a small white lighthouse marking off the island fairway. Close by, a freighter stood at anchor—perhaps the *Aalesund* or the *Laurelbank*?—exactly at the same place, amid the cries of the macuas. A rust-colored erne circled overhead. The chandala laid Bjorn on a bed of casuarina branches. Bjorn was wrapped in white and seemed to be sleeping. I stood at his side, but I can't say if it was really me standing there. I felt no sorrow, nothing. I was anesthetized. I kept staring at Bjorn, at this whole scene, as if it were a dream. A while ago, as he lay on the sand, I had knelt beside him and put a garland of jasmine flowers around his neck. For an agonizing second, I thought everything in me would burst. Then, all at once, I let go. I saw his body on the sand, saw my hand on his chest, that garland, the beach, the freighter, the lighthouse, the rust erne, and the two of us, so tiny and white against the sand. I was far away, on the other side of things. This was another world, another vision. It was no longer a question of Bjorn or me, of his death or any particular death; it was an eternal rite unfolding—something that had been seen, experienced countless times before, here or there, on one side or the other, by him or me—in white, always in white, with an erne circling overhead, a small lighthouse, and a ship at anchor as if we were about to leave, or had just returned. It was the same, infinitely the same—a sort of sacred catastrophe one met as one meets with a flood or a thunderbolt, or the ruins at Thebes. There was no longer any "me" to shed tears, no longer any death, any life, any particular person. There were untold numbers of me's entering or leaving a body in a grandiose rite, an endless return of things like the return of the birds or stars. It was as simple as the truth, as free of sadness as the truth, and as ancient as the birth of time.

Everything melted. My body remained below and I was pulled above, sucked upward, as it were, drawn into an expanse of light. My breath became still. I did not know whether I was on this side or the other, or whether it was he or I who was leaving. There was this sheet of soft, infinitely soft and radiant light into which one sank unfathomably, as into snow, and it was soundless, without limit—a high sea of downy snow, replete with vibrant, moving, sparkling light, like countless flakes of luminous tenderness slowly gyrating in an easeful immensity, a twirling of stars in an infinitude of silence and peace, and each flake was like a living being, each sparkle a pulsating millennium. There, one *was* forever; there, one could go on forever, free of weariness and lassitude and need, eyes fixed on an unchanging sight—an unfathomable delight of being free of any shadow.

The chandala drew me back abruptly. I heard the cries of the macuas. An onslaught of sounds and colors, and an assault of sharp, brutal light. I had a moment's suffocation, as if I were drowning. Where *was* death? On which side? I saw Bjorn on the pyre and the chandala handing me a firebrand. What did all this mean?

I took that fire.

Then, at his signal, I threw it upon the pyre.

Everything burst into flame at once: the twigs, the white scarf, the casuarina branches. A stain spread over the dhoti like a black flower. I glimpsed Bjorn's bare leg. The heat was overpowering. I jumped back, and everything came crashing upon me: Bjorn's death, the bare-chested chandala with his bamboo pole and water bucket, the pyre, the stretch of fractured madrepore in the midst of the sands, and the small lighthouse, the freighter, the cries of the macuas, the indigo sea lapping at the sand as if it were waiting to carry Bjorn off in a raft of fire. Death, death on every side, nothing but death, not the least living light! Then suffering, the feeling of being shattered—me. It was "I" who had brought Bjorn here, "I" who had dragged him to that hospital, "I" who had kept him from leaving on the *Aalesund*.

"I" was death.

You turn your eyes on yourself and death begins. You turn your eyes on yourself and encounter something so miserable, so pathetic, so riddled with falsehood. I had not had one correct thought since I had begun to look at myself and my destiny. I had done everything wrong, ruined everything. Death was not really the fact of dying; it was merely a corrupt look. You look at yourself and everything turns black. Even Nisha starts crossing your path, and devilish pilgrims appear on the scene from nowhere. You've entered the wretched story, merged with the caricature. Everything dies and keeps dying, but can die only because of the lack of underlying truth. Yet, it was still the same story being played out, but viewed from a wrong angle. Sometimes I feel that the entire world is simply viewed wrongly, and that the whole picture could reverse itself in a burst of dazzling light—and death would disappear like a shrouded dream—if only our gaze were true. Bjorn, my brother, I swear you will return; *we* will return and be reborn with sunlit eyes in a world that will match our vision of beauty.

I sat in the sand near the small lighthouse. The chandala was stirring the fire with his pole. I did not know what to do or where to go. I had lost my brother, and I felt thousands of miles away—from what I couldn't even say, since I had lost even my country. I was simply at the other end, while nearby lay that ship at anchor; there was always a ship ready to leave! I stood at zero point: nothing in front, nothing behind; and that point seemed to keep recurring in my life, as if I had to confront the same point again and again, always the same point, but each time more painfully and acutely. It's as if we spend our entire life revolving around a given point, and if we truly knew the point, we would solve the problem, break the back of destiny. As for me, I know the exact moment when I faced that point for the first time, *my* point. Perhaps it is the same one for all of us, just with different hues. It was at the tiny triangular window, framed by cypress boughs, of a small room overlooking the sea. I saw something—oh, nothing fantastic!—but something that appeared with great power, almost painfully, a sort of distillation of forces expressed in an image: a huge iridescent spider's web; and I was caught in its center, hanging by the threads. Shimmering multicolored threads, just there amid the cypress branches. And those threads represented all the things that were not me: my books, my father, my mother, my sailboat, geography, and laws. These had nothing to do with me, nothing whatsoever! "I" was that form in the center, held only by threads. But what if I cut those threads? What would be left? From that moment on, this question has haunted me. It's as if fate periodically confronted me with my question, in a very simple manner, by cutting all the threads. I felt that the answer began only when the very last thread had been cut. It was a life-death, all-or-nothing moment, a kind of excruciating vacuum from which, now and then, arose a very pure and very mysterious something akin to a new birth.

What I did not know, then, is that when one reaches that point, the release of energy is such that things are *forced* to change, and they change exactly according to how one sees them at that moment. Indeed, one had to look in the right way!

I looked at that fire.

I looked at the sweat-soaked chandala emptying buckets of water over his head, and at the rust erne circling overhead. I struggled against the wave of pain I felt descending over me, against my sorrow, against Bjorn surging from all sides with his flaxen locks and muffled voice: "Power. One must have the power to do something for one's brothers. What if I went mad? I'll father lots of little black Bjorns!" And the chandala kept poking the embers as if they were only wood burning. "You know, as when towing a big fishing net, and soon there is nothing left but the cry of a bird. We are a new breed of adventurers!" Then, that small heap of ashes. Bjorn was just a small heap of ashes. I struggled against my sorrow. I never wanted to love again. No more attachments, no more ties— free, free! It was like a seesaw: I was washed away by the wave, then I emerged from it; I went in, then came out of that self of sorrow. Whenever I came out, everything felt soft and eternal, just as it had been a while ago—a vast, vast expanse cloaked in softness, an infinite, attentive compassion gazing out, just gazing out. Then back to the "I" again. Suffocation, death, tragedy. Oh, not a great tragedy, but one exactly to my measure: that of a man faced with solitude and death—a small heap of ashes. Above, there was no tragedy of any kind, an impossibility of tragedy: *it could not be.* Two ways of looking, two rhythms. I went in, I came out, and suddenly something in me disconnected and passed above.

And I saw something. I bathed in something that filled me with wonder.

A tremendous inexpressible harmony. Each thing had its place, eternally, in an Architecture so fabulously precise—seen as light, nothing but light, a tableau of living light—that not a single atom could be removed, not one so-called shadow, not the minutest fragment of being, without upsetting the whole. Everything was there, forevermore, from the first moment the great nebula had exploded its flower of fire; through every point in the world, every particle of space, every heartbeat, ran the same thread of light; everything was held together without a gap or flaw or vagueness anywhere, indissolubly. It was a Totality of existence swept along in an immense white trajectory linking this short-lived point, this instant's foolishness, this poignant and solitary lack of meaning, to untold other points before, behind, and to other trajectories, countless trajectories whose goals lay not before, nor above nor beyond, for the goal was everywhere! Every instant was the goal, utterly, at every point of space and every second of time, with no lacuna in the future for hope, and no flaw in the past for regret. There was *that*, constantly and perfectly *that*, in every second—an infallible rite with millions of performers, a myriad timeless orbits running over and over through the same eternal coordinates, one and the same supreme movement connecting this pinpoint of pain, this splinter of self, this quivering of an age, to the crossing of a chipmunk or the passage of monsoons, to a child's song on a little white beach, to countless songs, to innumerable points of pain or joy mingling together and illuminating each other, and forming but one great luminous train, an immense snowy gown woven from a thousand threads, as if a unique Person were wandering through eternal azure fields.

It was the ceremony of the worlds—supreme, flawless—for no other reason than its own joy.

Below, far below, lay something that was "me," which stubbornly refused to deny tragedy, as if doing so would amount to betraying "life," real life. Something that *wanted* to suffer.

I paid the chandala, paid for the wood. The sun was setting. A wedge of birds was drifting through the southern sky. There were exactly three rupees left in Bjorn's red wallet. His journey had been counted carefully.

I was alone with nothing before me. I had come to the end of the road.

20
the return of things

I had been waiting for her since dawn, at our familiar meeting place near the little sanctuary. The sea was as still as a pool. The dunes hovered in the darkness. But my heart was restive. Plans filled my head; I wanted this, wanted that. I was no longer borne by the current; I felt I had to "do" something. Actually, it had begun the day I placed that tilak on her forehead, as if doing so had touched off a tiny spring that altered the entire course of things. I wonder if those trifles which seem to trigger consequences utterly disproportionate to their size are not traces from the past we stumble upon by accident, suddenly awakening an entire lost history, like the stray stone leading to the ruins of Tell el 'Amarna. But we do not believe in signs; we do not believe in the lost ruins of our secret Egypts; so we move here and there like bedazzled puppets. I, too, walked around in unknowingness. I wanted to "do" something, but what? I had also wanted to "do" something for Bjorn, "save" him in that Japanese hospital and "free" him from that tantric—each time to walk straight into the trap. Oh, what fools we are! What was I going to do now? Could I reasonably stay in this village begging from door to door?

Become a sculptor like Bhaskar-Nath, and marry a girl like Batcha, someday, and beget little white Nils who would start the story all over again? No, thanks!

And that "no" was as irreducible as stone. I could still see myself running through that forest of coral trees like a hunted animal, lashed by the rain, stung by the sand, as I fled across a carpet of red flowers. Freedom, freedom, the *Laurelbank* and nothing else! No matter what I planned or did, I always ended with that hard, unyielding knot that seemed to cry no *and* yes at the same time—freedom, freedom—as if the most perfect force and the most implacable enemy shared the same box. Until the end, I will never cease to ponder upon this absolute ambivalence: no sooner does one draw near the supreme password than the devil raises his head, as if one's most powerful ideal concealed one's most powerful enemy as well. This was the knot of difficulty: the intertwining of the two. Then, from time to time, everything loosens and one is borne by the current; all obstacles vanish; a different force comes into play that does not give rise to opposites. Then it all begins again at a higher level. It always manifests in the same way, regardless of the form, face, or being involved: a tiny induration recurring ever more powerfully and tenaciously from one cycle to another, as if it had inherited all the power of past truths. Perhaps it was the residue of the cycles—a kind of white dross, for it was not dark or black; on the contrary, it was a point of intense light, but hard—the supreme hardness of the good. Was destiny simply the moment when the dross dissolved? Amid that ascending green dawn, I remembered Batcha's story about her supreme god, forgetful of his wealth, who went begging from door to door, blessing both gods and devils.

She appeared to the music of conch shells and gongs. She looked so slender on that large expanse of sand, walking slowly in her long pomegranate skirt, her offering tray clasped between her arms with the gravity of a priestess. My heart leaped as I ran toward her; everything was swept away, as smooth as this beach. She turned her eyes toward me without saying a word. For a moment, I thought I was standing before Mohini clasping her offering tray, with that same motionless look among pink pottery. Then Batcha climbed the steps of the little sanctuary and disappeared inside. I wanted to follow her, to be with her, to burn incense with her, to do as she did, to enter her world. Everything was so limpid that morning, the faintest sound of the conches echoing against the dunes, the chanting flowing over the beach like a great bronze wave. I, too, wanted to offer flowers, to make a gesture, any gesture, to merge into the rite, to let myself be carried away in the great wave, to find the thread again—to adore, for no reason, just as one breathes.

I closed my eyes to join her, as she had taught me. All I had to do was turn toward her, silently, as one turns toward a river, and gently merge into her. I tried, and bumped against Bjorn, who was standing there with wild-looking eyes, pointing to something that terrified me. I pushed him aside, only to face Mohini. She was standing on a rock, motionless, vacant-eyed, staring into space. I pushed her aside, too. But I still could not find Batcha; those shadows were blurring everything. Now the sannyasi sprang up before me, staff in hand, arms flung wide to block my way. For an instant everything went blank—I could not recall anything. Each encounter had become like a wave engulfing me, a sticking, clinging world from which I had to extricate myself, as if each being represented a special prison, a more or less shadowy actinia trying to swallow me. I cut my way toward Batcha as through a jungle.

Then everything grew still. I began to descend, to sink into something very soft as if I were about to pass into another, deeper expanse. And this was very different from the grounds I knew, the vast bluish expanse where one meets the whole world. It was deeper, more intimate, of a different quality and color, as yet unfathomable. Nor was it "that" above, immense and white and luminous, where all is free, clear of questions and persons. It was something else, a different degree of "that," completely enclosed and warm. And it began to take on a slightly pink hue—oh, what exquisite sweetness!—and I could almost feel Batcha's fresh little hand leading me as I seemed gently to drift into a well of tenderness, just on the verge of— Abruptly, the sannyasi burst forth like a flame, grabbing my arm and pulling me upward.

I opened my eyes. The seashore was awash in light. A procession of inky clouds rolled through the southeastern sky.

Had I been able to find Batcha again at that moment, to follow the little path she was trying to show me, probably none of what took place later would have happened. I know that my words sound enigmatic, but I am walking one step at a time in the miraculous forest, and each step brings me closer to the secret—small touches of secret. That morning, I almost touched the secret: a law capable of completely changing the course of human lives if only we could grasp it. It took me twenty years, as well as a penal colony, the Amazonian jungle, and a few fits of despair, to grasp it. But I went so deeply into human misery that one day, as a grace, a pure grace, I was shown the light, and this is what I saw: every outer road seems to parallel an inner road, and the obstacles, the shadows, the accidents we have been unable to overcome on the inner road come back to haunt us on the outer road, which grows increasingly arduous and long and unmerciful as it swallows up a lifetime for the sake of a tiny experience that one day makes us exclaim, "Ah!" And that's it—a simple little "ah!" of surprise. For, in truth, we are the expression of a drama being played within, and a single victory along the invisible roads can save a lifetime, or several lifetimes.

Perhaps there is not just one degree of expression, along one tiny inner road, but several nested degrees, like a series of concentric circles, along increasingly longer and more difficult and darker roads as one moves away from the center. But each time we pass to a more interior circle, to a more accurate, truer expression, closer to the eternal, multi-degree drama, we gain the power not only to live better and see better but also to alter the law of the outer degrees and to refashion life according to the newly acquired vision—for to see more truly is to live more truly—until the day when we can reach the eternal center, illuminating Matter with a divine gaze and transfiguring the most external world into a true expression of the eternal Joy that conceived it.

It would take me years, and a great torment, to travel the tiny road I did not take that morning.

"Oh, Batcha, there you are!"

"*An'mona! An'mona!*"

She tapped her skirt, stretched both arms up in the air, gave a little pirouette and dropped to the ground in a peal of laughter. Then she delicately drew her skirt over her toes, and leaned back against a column of the peristyle.

"You are not angry with me?"

"Angry?"

She stared at me wide-eyed. She had such large eyes, that child, like those of the offering bearers of the Nile. She had the same aura of ancientness as those beings who live in their souls, and their smile.

"What do you think—that I could be angry with myself?"

She looked me straight in the eye and I blinked. Every time I have blinked, as if I were afraid.

"Bjorn is gone."

"Yes."

So she knew.

"Balu has been ill with a fever since yesterday. He moaned and cried all night in his sleep."

"What did he say?"

She hesitated a moment as her face grew serious.

"Oh, things. He was trying to open a door that had to be opened. He was searching for his sword to open a door. But then he could not find his sword, and he started to cry."

"Then?"

"That's all."

"Come on, tell me."

She shook her head and I knew there was no use insisting.

"I was just next door, Batcha, but I had no idea his door was locked. Oh, Batcha, do *you* know why he went away? He used to prostrate himself here before the sun: 'How beautiful life is!' I don't know, Batcha. I don't understand anything anymore."

She leaned toward me.

"What don't you understand?"

"Everything. What I have to do."

"But you are with me, so?"

She waved her hand toward the beach; one just had to play and everything would be taken care of.

"I really don't know, Batcha. Sometimes I think I understand. Everything seems vast and open. But then I open my eyes and I don't understand anything anymore; I collide with things, make mistakes. Where is the secret, Batcha? There is something I don't understand; I've found only half of the secret. I've fooled myself, Batcha; I'm still missing something!"

She eyed me intently and I am not sure what she understood, but Batcha always understood. She wasn't fooled.

"Have you eaten today?"

I was taken aback.

"Yes—no."

"You see? It's yes, then no. You have to know which it is. You're going to fall ill if you continue."

She changed the subject.

"Yesterday, the birds arrived on the lagoon. They fly straight to the lagoon from very, very far away to make their nest, and they never make a mistake."

"But I am not a bird!"

"Yet you came straight here from very, very far away. So?"

"But—"

"Birds don't say 'but.'"

"Then what should I do?"

She sighed.

"You *are* doing something! Why are you here, tell me?"

"I wonder."

She smiled softly, and a flash of tenderness stirred in her eyes.

"You see, you haven't yet arrived on the lagoon. Still, the waters of the lagoon are shining. Could it be that you came here to be born on the lagoon?"

"Oh, Batcha, this is just silly talk."

She pointed to the black clouds massing in the southeastern sky.

"What about the clouds? Do they talk silly, too? They release their drops of water and it rains."

She laid her cheek on her knees. Her plait swept the ground. She was so beautiful that morning!

> *I do not talk but*
> *I am the falling raindrop*
> *I am the flowing spring*
> *I gather cloud drops*
> *I move with the rhythm*
> *I listen to the sound within*

"Look, Batcha—"

> *And I sing while there is still time*

"That's all very well, but one can't stay like this, spending an entire lifetime on a beach gazing at the clouds! I'm no longer a child!"

"No? Who says one can't? How silly you are! Obviously, one does not stay 'like this' in one spot—one travels. Do you even *know* how to travel? I know some countries, you know some countries; we travel together."

She raised her head.

"Always together, always together. Here, there, and in every other world!"

She uttered those words with such force, with such a probing, challenging look in her eyes, like Bhaskar-Nath. Then she laughed.

"You are Mr. Nothing-at-all, so what can you do!"

Whereupon she began singing an enchanting song. I wish I could speak each word of that singing language, so simple and limpid it was, like an outpouring of transparent truths.

> *Over these dunes*
> *Over those dunes*
> *Our footsteps go side by side*
> *Our islands are itinerant*
> *And the wind*
> *Sweeps the vast sands of the world*
> *Scattering my song*
> *Scattering my images*
> *Yet I remain forever*
> *I leave, still I am*
> *With new eyes*
> *And new faces*
> *And I look*
> *Upon these islands*
> *Upon those islands*
> *At rose cowries on a little white beach*
> *At the lovely wave flowing from life to life*
> *At the beautiful unending story*

Everything felt so simple with Batcha, almost timeless. There was nothing further to do or find! It was all there, already found for us. We stood on the temple steps like two children, but we also walked over dazzling sands, on an undying island; thus it was—infinitely, without reason or cause, without possibility of accident, like a play. Perhaps all we had to do was to let the image from above flow into the image from below? Then every gesture would become right, and life would flow like a fountain.

"Batcha, sometimes I feel that life extends far, far back, to the sound of conch shells and gongs, like your song, and that we have always been and always will be; that life extends also far, far ahead, and we will always become more, in other bodies—increasingly beautiful and colorful and radiant bodies—and that life is slowly bringing forth our dreams like birds. But it's still very far ahead. Oh, Batcha, we're still in bitter straits!"

"Why bitter?"

"Still too many ugly things inside."

She shuddered.

"Oh, Nil! You ruin everything."

There was such pain in her voice. From that moment on, everything seemed, indeed, to go wrong, just as when I had put the tilak on her forehead.

"You're conjuring up ugly things."

"Absolutely not! They are already there. Just last night, I had one of those horrible dreams. I saw that man near a fire again. Then I was wandering through a forest, frantically looking for someone; I don't know who, except it was 'she.' This dream keeps recurring and recurring: someone I'm searching for as desperately as life itself. Perhaps it is a memory from the past?"

"As for me, I see lovely things. Perhaps a memory of the future!"

For a second her face expressed surprise.

"There was a road on the sea—a very, very long road, you know, as when the moon shines on the sea and there's a slightly pink reflection and a faint quiver like that of little fish. It was so nice and pleasant! And you were there, too, walking slowly behind me. Then we arrived in a country I did not know.

I don't quite remember everything, but at a certain point there were two roads—"

She paused reflectively.

"The road to the left went as far as the eye could see toward a mountain the color of *gerua*, you know, orange. The road, too, was orange. But I turned to the right and entered a huge green park filled with peacocks, scores of peacocks of every color—blue ones, white ones, a golden one; and I was showing them to you and telling you, 'Come, come! Look how beautiful they are! They're proclaiming victory!' But you weren't listening. You seemed to be preoccupied. Oh, yes, and there was a zebra, a lone zebra with black stripes, and also a huge rock plunging into the sea."

A shadow shrouded her face.

"Yes, and I also saw something ugly."

"What?"

"Nothing."

"Tell me!"

I was wasting my breath; nothing would change her mind.

"Look, Batcha, I must *do* something. I can't stay here forever listening to songs, can I?"

"You can't?"

She seemed perplexed.

"You're a grown-up. Perhaps you could be a schoolteacher?"

"What!"

Now she seemed all flustered, almost panic-stricken.

"You won't go away, will you?"

"Don't be silly."

"So what do you want to do, then?"

I had no answer.

"What's the matter, Nil? There is something like a dark cloud around you. What is it? What happened to you in that hospital? Did someone hurt you?"

"Of course not!"

"Then why do I seem to keep bumping into things? Only this morning I bumped myself. Look."

She raised her skirt, baring her ankle. She looked nervously about her. A sweltering haze hung over the beach. The air was oppressive with heat.

"Come, Nil, let's go home. The monsoon is coming."

"Home? I have no home."

She looked at me, nonplussed.

"But what's wrong with you, Nil? You're the son of the house. Appa said so!"

"Does the rain frighten you?"

She collected herself, her hands joined between her knees as if to calm herself down.

"I don't know, Nil. I love the rain, I dance in the rain, but today is different. Something is troubling me."

Then, in an anguished tone, she asked:

"Nil, you're not going away, are you?"

"I told you I am not going!"

"Then come. Let's go home."

The sea was as smooth as a sheet of mercury. There was not a bird in the sky.

"Let's go, I'm telling you. It's going to be too late."

I was paralyzed.

"Nil, you're different! There's something hard and closed in you, something enveloping you."

"Why? Because I don't want to be a schoolteacher?"

She turned white as if I had slapped her.

"Oh, Nil—"

Then she stopped fighting and abandoned herself, her hands splayed on her knees.

"You see," she said softly, pointing to the beach, "when I called you in my dream, there was this kind of light."

"What dream?"

"Right here, the first day you arrived, just after you came out of the temple. You were growing smaller and smaller, and the sand gleamed like water."

She looked so defenseless. I felt ashamed. But I could not understand why I was so irritated, as if everything inside me were raw.

A gust of wind swept over the beach. The sea was the shade of lead.

"What's wrong with me, Batcha? What have I done? Why is everything grating inside me?"

She looked at me in silence, her hands folded on her knees; and that look, so luminous, so clear, almost unbearably sweet, penetrated into my heart; but the deeper it went, the more the knot tightened inside me, as if in the depths lay a point of total refusal, something that said *no*. No to what? I don't know.

"Surely you don't expect me to settle down as a school-teacher, do you? And then make little children on the beach?"

"Oh, Nil!"

Tears began rolling down her cheeks. I did not know what I was saying; I was like a raging animal.

"You don't understand, Nil. There's something else."

She was stammering. She looked like a small wounded bird pinned down against that pillar.

"I want to be free, you understand."

"Free," she repeated mechanically.

There was such sadness in her eyes that I almost gave up and pressed her to my heart. I had an instant's hesitation. But then it was too late. I saw her eyes widen and the color drain from her face. She was staring in horror at something behind me. I whirled about.

"Come along, boy."

He stood silhouetted against the dunes, staff in hand, his robe an orange blaze. His teeth glistened as if he were about to burst into laughter again, his mahogany-colored skin aglow against the shimmering haze.

"Come, it's time to go."

With a toss of his head, he strode off toward the dunes. I rose to my feet like an automaton. For an instant my eyes lingered on the pale little face staring at me with bewilderment, the pain-filled eyes, the red tilak in the middle of the forehead. Everything seemed to come crashing down on me as I heard Bhaskar-Nath's voice thundering in my ears: "It is *as you will.*" But what could I possibly will?! There was nothing to will; it was all willed for me in advance. I was caught, overwhelmed by a calm, imperturbable force far greater than my own, sweeping away all things like a straw, shrugging off lives as if they were a mere overcoat. He had said, "It's time to go," and it was time to go.

I set off down the path, following him. Tiny crabs scuttled about underfoot. Suddenly, I cried out in pain. I turned around to catch two eyes boring into mine, searing with rage. Batcha gathered her skirt and fled down the dunes. She had pinched the skin of my arm to the quick, like a little girl.

Just then the monsoon swept upon us, torrential, roaring, like a bath of molten sulfur.

And everything disappeared behind a veil.

ψ

THIRD CYCLE

The Journey in the Gold of Night

21
the sannyasi

*W*e walked for days, for months, under the monsoon
rains and the sun, through tortured red plains and parched
rivers, countries of fervor and famine, paddy field upon paddy
field strewn with egrets and reverberating with the chirr of
insects; we crossed sulfurous torrents, chafing rivers, flooded
jungles alive with the chirp of blue herons; we slept in temples,
on roadsides, kept vigil on moon-laved banks where jackals
howled; we walked on and on until all the roads were one and
the same, and the days fused in a rhythm of dust. There was
no more cold or hunger, no more heat or fatigue, no more
haste, no more longing; only something that went on and on,
effortlessly, like the flight of rose starlings across the sunset,
or the prayers of the Brahmins, without high or low, endlessly.
We were going north, always north, barefoot and in rags, never
spending more than one night in the same place, never begging
more than once in the same village, and if the first door closed
on us, we took to the road again. It was the law, the simple
law. He never spoke, and I had nothing to say. Perhaps we had
been wandering for ages, coming from nowhere, for everywhere was the same. There was no goal before us, no memory

behind, no expectation, no regret, only that which went on and on, without reason or purpose. If I stopped for a moment and closed my eyes, he would pull at me sharply.

"Hey, boy, there's no time for meditation! Come on, let's go!"

Sometimes a shuddering wave of revolt swept over me.

"But what's the—"

Then he would pick up a handful of dust from the road and throw it in my face, shaking with laughter.

"Is it dust you are after, lad? Here, eat it!"

I did not know whether to laugh or cry. What did it matter anyway? Why worry over this small ambling thing? Was I not seeking something else, anyway? So why meditate, and on what? To inflate myself more than I already was? Or to stir up trouble? And everything would dissolve into such dizzying absurdity that even the "something else" was reduced to dust. There was only nothing walking in nothing, seeking nothing, with just enough life left to feel the dizziness of it all—a very perilous moment. But then this, too, would dissolve; it was merely a passing wave of "I." When everything became relaxed and peaceful in me, the sannyasi would unfailingly stop by the roadside and extract a handful of grain from his waistband.

"Here, son, eat. It's good for you."

He would look at me with such tenderness that tears would spring to my eyes. Then I would laugh and grab his staff.

"Hey, Sannyasi, time to go!"

We would both burst out laughing. The scales had tipped the other way. Everything was regal, light, oh, so light! There was no day or night, no tomorrow or yesterday, no time, not even anyone to manifest surprise; there was just something laughing, flowing, a marvelous nothingness, which was perhaps something, but without the least introspection. It flowed like a river, soared with the wind, was stupid like the sparrow, or perhaps wise like the crane on the paddy field. It instantly knew everything: the approaching rain, the goat's discourse, the passerby's question, the snake beneath the leaf; it was a little cascade cascading everywhere, so simple, catching its own reflection in everything. But one moment of self-absorption, one look too many, and everything became blurred and fuzzy. Everything was gone. Then the sannyasi would stop again in the middle of the road, put his hands on his hips and eye me while puffing up his cheeks.

"You're an imbecile!"

That was true.

Days and weeks passed, perhaps months or years. Then that lightness, too, passed, unless it was still there, underneath, rising in an occasional flash that shook the sannyasi and me with laughter. It was merely the great froth of life, a universal sparkling of a myriad bubbles in which one could delightfully lose oneself like a drop in the ocean, an ant in the forest, the sap in a plant. Yet something kept drawing me, calling me farther, higher. Unless it was simply the wearing away? I had walked so much along those roads, melted so much under that sun that sometimes I no longer knew whether it was this life or another, the Stone Age or the Bronze Age, years or only a moment ago. I walked even in my dreams, and when he pulled at me sharply, was I on this side of the world or the other? I was slowly sinking into a great country devoid of grief, of landscape, of season, of thought, of self. I followed the rhythm of my footsteps, which followed the rhythm of God knows what. They were no longer even *my* footsteps; it was a cadence flowing through me, or in spite of me. I trod the paths of the great country that stretches beyond all paths, when the body and the pain change into a rhythm of silence, when silence expands and becomes a swell, which becomes a song, which becomes peace, bearing a little shadow with a few rocks and some thorns. Where, indeed, is misery and the distress of being "me," when everything flows within the great river? Thorns exist only in men's hearts, but my heart had been so worn down along those roads that nothing remained of it; or perhaps it beat in everything, with the grass and the cicadas? Where was "me," that singular invention? All was vast, tranquil, and infinitely soft, as soft as the world before the advent of man, or after him; it was as smooth as a Gregorian chant and impelled by the great Law—a vast, flowing solemnity without a shadow or a wrinkle, immense and impassive, as if we spent our time muddling everything with our cries, our tears, and we had to stop being human in order to partake in the great sovereignty of the world and share the calm empire of the gods, or that of a little egret in a paddy field. Sometimes, I felt I would disappear completely. There would be a split second of suffocation and everything inside me would contract. A hard little knot knocking against itself—the pain of being "me," the lacerating thorns. In those moments, I felt as if Batcha were at the other end of the line, pulling, pulling: *An'mona! An'mona!* That's when I was confronted with a question, my recurring question, the only question that remained, as if "I" were simply a question, a one and only interrogation in a no man's land of immediate knowledge.

"Sannyasi, tell me—"

His eyes bored into mine. I struggled to keep my question from dissolving in the light of his gaze. Was I going to give up, shrug my shoulders and continue walking? But suddenly everything crystallized before me as at the moment of death. I saw the sannyasi's grimy scarf, the drops of perspiration trapped between the rudraksha beads of his necklace, the fig branch over the road, the dusty ocher path leading to the river. If I did not ask my question now, it would be too late; I would dissolve completely.

A kind of rage welled up in me.

"This time you're going to speak!"

I clutched at his scarf.

"Listen, Sannyasi, I don't care whether I live or die. I am not afraid of death. But I must know, you understand? I want to know why. Why all this? Why all these lives, this misery of being, this walking, this suffering, if the goal is only to be done

with it all? Why all these years, these millions of years to conquer life, if it is only to toss it away at the end? What of all this labor, the exertion of thought, the painstaking process of self-development, the travails of creation, if it is all finally to be annihilated? What is going on? What's the sense? Tell me!"
He stood as still as stone before me.
"Liberation? Beatitude?"
Then I really saw red. I was nothing but a ridiculous puppet by the roadside; yet, just then, it was as if millions of men were crying out in my body, a world of suffering sweeping over me. Oh, this was no metaphysics! It was pure physics.
"Then let me tell you something: You can keep your heaven! I spit in its face!"
I saw his cheeks beginning to puff up. Was he going to explode in laughter or anger? Right then and there, I launched into a burning prayer that sprang from the depths of my heart.
"If this earth has no meaning—a real, down-to-earth meaning—if it is merely a passageway to the Beyond, a means of escape, then what kind of heaven or beatitude can ever redeem all this suffering? If there is no heaven *for the earth*, no meaning *for the earth*, then this whole world is insane and I have no use for paradise. Let it remain above while I remain with the dead!"
He looked at me quietly, his eyes sparkling with amusement. My head was throbbing, and I thought I would collapse in the dust. If this was the end, so be it!
"You're not quite there yet," he said quietly.
With a shrug he continued on his way. In a desperate effort, I summoned up my remaining strength and caught his arm. If I did not finish it now, I was lost.
"But when I get there, there will be no one left!"
He turned to face me.
"Are you afraid?"
I can still see that river, that immense estuary churning sand beneath the setting sun, its sluggish waters thick with mud,

the ashes of the dead and the prayers of the living, and, in the distance, the golden haze of the sea. One could not tell if it was the tawny flow of the great river, the glistening sands, or perhaps the earth setting out on a golden journey—this earth. "What could I be afraid of? I have nothing more to lose." "Except yourself." Tufts of high grass dotted the riverbank. A jackal yelped in the distance. The river flowed by noiselessly, like lava. The sannyasi stood there motionless, leaning on his staff, his orange robe almost melting into the fiery sunset. "Except myself—" Who?

The jackal yelped once more, a long burst of hysterical laughter that traveled through the tall grass and seemed to echo from everywhere. Then silence. Which "self" was he talking about? Where? There was no longer any trace of "me" left in all this, no more life as such, no more person. What person was he referring to, exactly? There were grass, beasts, water; "I" came from far away, like that river, churning a worldful of mud and suffering and prayers, soon to be swept into the sea without further ado, dissolved into nothingness, while the jackal yelped, and will go on yelping. "I" had been rolling for centuries—nothing but a vast ancientness dragging along miseries, silt, and every possible shame in its heart, together with some rare wisps of joy so intermingled with pain that they scarcely made a difference. It rolled on and on, understanding all, bearing all; oh, what had not been churned in its waters? And there was this person standing on the bank, this tiny something looking out, waiting, as if it had been waiting for millions of years, through Ice Ages and passing peoples, while listening to the jackal's yelp, the wind in the grass, the cry of all those who had come and gone with all their sorrows and lost stories. I had stood there on the banks of the great river since the beginning of time; I was that uttermost gaze, that minuscule breath of all their breaths, that little sorrow of all their sorrows, that stark, ultimate question. Oh, I had known that gaze, that slight breath a thousand times, here and there, as life draws to a close, when everything is gathered together in a soul: the miseries, the days, the faces and gestures, the millions of vain gestures fused in an ultimate prayer, which is no longer even a prayer but just this uttermost cry: I am waiting, oh, waiting for the time of true life, living life, a world of truth; not this walled-in, dying caricature of life that knows nothing, can do nothing, does not remember where it comes from or where it is going—this total blindness in a body, devoid of sign or key except for some dreams and fables. Oh, to know, to *be* infinitely, live infinitely, perceive directly, find the thread again! To live in everything, love everything, spread oneself out in everything, feel and see everywhere, to one's heart's content, without separation or distance; to sing and smile in everything, in all that is and lives and throbs; to die and be reborn at will, to cling indestructibly to the thread and fill each minute with a totality of being as replete as all millennia combined. I am waiting, waiting for that hour of truth when our countless forgotten, wasted loves may love again, forever; when our countless gestures may touch the living glory they have fashioned in the night, when our betrayed lives may know the joy they have carved unwittingly and our lost breaths sing the great paean of the divine world. We will touch heaven with our hands, fashion the earth in the image of our souls and incarnate the light in a human body. Oh! I am waiting, waiting for the reign of Something Else, a being of truth upon the earth.

"All right, let's go."

"Listen—"

"What now?"

I looked at him calmly. I was in the true pulsation, secure in the quiet certitude of self-asserting truth.

"There's something else, Sannyasi, I swear it. Your dissolution isn't the end!"

He stopped dead in his track.

"What do you know, boy? You haven't even been born yet!"

He jabbed a finger into my chest just as he had that day on the train.

"If you're looking for a lion's answer, you have to become like a lion. If you're looking for human answers, then continue to whine, suffer, and die."

He turned his back on me. Then, with a sudden change of heart, he drew near.

"Men ask questions that are outside their condition, hence they don't get any answer. They only get ideas. One must change conditions, Mr. Foreigner. One must become like the lion!"

He strode off toward the river.

He hailed the ferryman.

A pink-tinged minaret, thronged with pigeons, rose in the distance. There was a forest of banyan trees on the opposite bank, and a village gleaming as if in a fairy tale. A muezzin's chant filled the air. As I stepped onto the other bank, I suddenly felt I was living a marvelous adventure. Oh, I might end up badly, or lose myself, find myself, be dissolved or not, but what did it matter? I was in *the* Adventure, the real thing, the living question one asks from life to life, like the life of life, the true "why" of all these millions of footsteps. I had picked up the thread; I was born to follow this one thread, this one burning question that was like the answer itself. What did it matter if I died a thousand deaths? I was before the only thing that matters, whether we are dead or alive—the kernel of the story, the moment that weaves all moments into one. In truth, we do not need answers so much as we need to live to the utmost the one question haunting us.

"Are you ready?" he asked without warning, in the middle of the bazaar, amid the fragrance of saffron and marigolds, while pigeons took to the air with a clapping of wings.

I looked at him, and everything seemed so simple, so natural, so perfectly well-timed. What did I need to be ready for? For me, everything was ready at each instant; even those pigeons took flight at the right time. It was, quite simply, miraculous. This moment in the middle of the bazaar was miraculous, astir with an inexplicable sense of eternity, as if it brought in its orb an infinitude of minutes that produced that clapping of wings around a minaret. The miracle of the world is not to see miracles! It is the sudden perception of what really *is*.

"For ANYTHING," I replied.

He smiled broadly, grabbed a bunch of bananas hanging from a fruit stall and thrust it into my arms.

"Here, eat!"

Then he purchased some rice and two lengths of white cloth, borrowed a copper bucket, and led me toward the riverbank at the edge of the banyan forest.

Two sannyasis sat there before a fire. They seemed to be expecting us. One was very old, with long plaited hair coiled on top of his head; the other, a young man, was meditating. The sannyasi filled his copper bucket in the river. The sand shone like water.

That evening, he took out a cake of orange clay, crushed it into powder on a rock and dyed the white cloth gerua.

"Tomorrow you will receive the initiation."

I awoke the next morning with the peculiar feeling of having gone through a memory-quake—one of those giant upheavals that sometimes occurs during our sleep, as if we were catapulted into another layer of being. I experienced a strange sensation of surprise. This banyan forest looked familiar, and I, too, was someone very familiar, but suddenly connected to another situation, almost another age. I relived something I had known before, but with my present body, which was a bit lost, yet went along like a child attending some mysterious rite.

"It's time."

Suddenly he loomed before me, wrapped in shadows. I lifted my head from the banyan root that had served as my pillow that night. It was not yet dawn. The great river flowed nearby. Cicadas whirred in the tall grass; the semidarkness was one immense cicada song. I gazed at the tall silhouette before me; it was like an old, very old situation being repeated. I picked up my scarf and headed toward the river with uncertainty, yet everything was certain and familiar. A man stood waiting for me.

"Sit down and take off your clothes."

I quietly obeyed. The cicadas fell silent for a moment, then resumed their immense high-pitched stridulation, as if in a primeval age. There we were, two small shadows amid the drone of the worlds, of a lesser existence than the cicadas, a lesser existence than the grass. We mustn't make any noise, or disturb anything.

I sat still.

He pulled out his instruments. He was the barber.

"Hold your head still."

I gazed over the great river in the dawning light. The air was crisp and smelled of vetiver. The sand felt as cool as the feet of a god inside a sanctuary. He sprinkled my head with water and began to shave my hair, snipping it off in tufts while he gripped my head at arm's length. Would he perhaps slit my throat at the end and offer me to the river, spic and span? Everything felt so sweet. There was nothing to want or not want, no fear, no expectation. I shared in the eternal reality. I felt carried by immense hands, along with the grass and the cicadas; I took part in a vast, soaring celebration. It was today or yesterday, and forever. This was a vast singing Sacrifice devoid of drama and fear, a simple act of love, because each one had to offer what he is, sing out his own song—for nothing, for everything, for the river and the dawning day, for the fading stars, for that great mysterious WHAT that throbs in the heart of each being. That's how it was. It was the Law, the true movement of the world—a great soaring rhythm of self-offering—and we were doing neither more nor less than the cicadas, but we had lost the thread, forgotten the rite and the music, which were there nonetheless, one and the same, and we were making the offering unknowingly. I recalled a day similar to this one when I had walked unknowingly to the sacrifice, and perhaps there had been many such sacrifices before; perhaps many barbarous offerings were necessary to recapture the song, but when *it* sings, there is no more need for sacrifice, nor perhaps to die, because that particular song is what makes us invulnerable. It was the winter season in barbarous lands, at a place called Buchenwald. We had walked through the portal into a white-tiled, neon-bright catacomb. They had stripped us and numbered us, probed our mouths, extracting gold. We were naked and ready, drawn up in tight ranks in the great white-tiled tunnel. Group by group, we entered the huge hall. There was not a whisper, not a cry, only the crackling of electric clippers hanging from the high vault, and men, perhaps, walking by twos under a dead-white light. They were scoured, shaved. They stared at the little clumps of hair strewn on the ground, the last remnants of their persons, piled there in blond or white heaps, in the staggering silence of a herd of shadows being led to the sacrifice. They had passed the second portal, entered the room with the chemical baths, the huge, white-tiled creosote pit. They had shed their impurities, abandoned their hopes, their despairs, their names, their years, their time. They walked two by two in silence, drained of hate, of fear, and even of surprise, under scorching or freezing sprays, beneath the stark white light of an unspeakably dreadful ceremony. They passed through gigantic, immaculate corridors without a word, without a cry, suddenly to be pitched, dazzle-eyed, into a courtyard white with snow, among other men, perhaps, their heads shorn, garbed in sackcloth, numbered, null and void like nothing in this world, indiscernibly living or dead.

Suddenly, in that fringe of the world, as everything was engulfed in stupefaction, something was kindled within me: a flame, a cry, an energy of pure life—absolute, equal only to the energy of impending death. And *that* was invulnerable. It was the very life of life; even death got its sustenance from it! A fire of being so irresistibly powerful that it made eternity burst forth like an archangel in the night, as if the very heart of death wore a face of eternal light.

And it sang.

I abandoned my head to his hands. Everything was being replayed according to another rite, or perhaps the same, always, but chosen. We pass again and again through the same place, amid a landscape of shadow or light, beauty or dread, through yeses or nos, beneath the high vault of banyan trees or the tunnel of the condemned. But once we have reached *the* point, it is the same, free of yes and no, free of dread. All becomes a cicada song. Tufts of hair were falling off; years and years were falling off. Oh, how wonderfully free that man was making me, so simply, shaving and scraping away the old grimace! That old, ferocious habit of resembling one's portrait, as if one's entire life were spent trying to match the wrong picture, when, in fact, it was matchless. Forever newborn, it simply gazed out, childlike, through another window—a great flowing river bordered by tall grass full of cicadas. Yet, at the same time, it was so ancient! When that window opens, it seems as if one had been gazing through it forever, pillowed on infinite tenderness; and this was the great river of all rivers, the moment of moments, the cicadas of a million lives.

The sun emerged all at once, pricking the forest with flame, scattering flecks of gold along the river. The barber prostrated himself in the sand. I got up and walked toward the river, naked and light, clear like a cicada's song. Tossing my clothes onto the riverbank, I walked on as if led by a vast hand. Everything felt so familiar that morning, like a dream coming to life, like a movie abruptly stopping on a particular image as we gasp and say: "Yes, this is it! I know this, I know this!"

That morning I knew everything.

The muezzin began chanting in his minaret.

I stood transfixed on the bank. Oh, there *is* an eternal image behind us, and sometimes it breaks through. There *is* a deep cry within, and sometimes it transports us. That cry suffused everything that morning, arising from very far away, very high above, vibrant, all-pervasive. There was a sudden chasm in me, as it were, a memory lapse, something that gaped: there was no more river, no more "me," no more body; only that unceasing, piercing cry above, something that kept calling and calling as if it had never ceased to call throughout the ages, in every place and time, every triumph and misery, every black or white skin. I had been that one cry forever, the something that sees and knows nothing but cries out, oh, cries out as if from the depths of time, like someone buried alive! And everything was swept away: my names, my forms, my life, all my lives and gestures, the millions of gestures, the faces, memories and hopes, everything I sought or wanted—what on earth could I want? I had been wanting *that* for millions of years! That, only *that*, to cry out for *that* as one drowns, as one loves, to my heart's content; a cry pervading everything, sweeping away everything—lives, deaths, the future, the past— making the soul burst into bloom, toppling walls, wiping out everything: no trace of anything left, not a single thing to want, not even a single truth to attain—just *that*, utterly. To cry out for *that* as one breathes, as one dies, or as one lives, just because it cries and cries by itself, because that is *it*, the one and only thing we are, that pure cry of being. An out-and-out white devastation.

I prostrated myself on the sand, and I no longer knew if it was east or west, north or south. Mecca was everywhere.

I stepped into the river. A bird flew up with a shrill cry. The air was like powdered gold. I felt there was something I must do, a gesture I must make. The sannyasi emerged from the banyan forest and stepped, flame-like, through the tall grass. I filled my cupped hands with water and extended them toward the sun. I wanted to sing, make an offering, participate in some way, offer something. I offered my water to the sun, stammered some confused words, though it was myself I really wanted to offer, to cast into the waters. But that self was so small, so paltry amid this great flowing torrent of adoration that vibrated and sang everywhere, with the waters and the grass, the sand and the spume; *that* dispensed itself with such abundance, soaring toward the sun, while this little body stood naked, so clumsy, so white! I cast myself into the river: "Take, take, take it all!" Oh, how beautiful the great river was, how harmonious, how loving! Thrice I immersed myself. Why thrice I do not know, but there was a number, a rite, an underlying order. I could feel, almost touch that rite as I groped my way through a great ceremony. Each droplet, each gesture had a meaning, a number, an aura of sacredness; it was sacred, the world was sacred, the river was sacred—for no particular reason. That's how the rhythm was; the rhythm was what made the sacredness, imparting sense and direction to things, automatically, like the infallible flight of a bird homing in from Siberia. I was deeply concentrated on that impalpable, vibrating Thing, so eager to make the right gesture, to merge with it.

Suddenly, I sensed that someone was behind me: a Presence. A great Presence.

A being, a light—something that knew and guided. I closed my eyes for a moment, and I felt I had to be clear, absolutely clear to allow it to flow through me, to let go completely, to be as blank and still as possible—offered. It began descending through me, impelling my body.

I stretched myself flat in the water, arms flung wide. This *was* the gesture, the only gesture: an instantaneous sense of sweetness. I was part of the rhythm. I had reached the goal. There was nothing to seek, nothing to attain—an instantaneous sense of royalty.

"Oh, boy—"

I climbed back onto the bank. I could still sense that presence behind me and everything felt very supple and easy—my body had become very supple; every step, every gesture had become invested with an infallible rhythm, a vibration that simultaneously saw and did. All I had to do was to be as limpid, exact, transparent as possible. There was this vast luminous movement, the luminous march of someone behind me, almost blending with me; and whenever the "coincidence" occurred, if only fleetingly, there was a perfection of truth: I was true and all was true. During that brief instant, I could see that *everything* was like that. The entire world was the projection of an immense luminous march, and that perfect "coincidence" was the sacred part, the truth of the world. Then, everything flowed in a marvel of spontaneity, with an inconceivable precision. *This* was the living truth.

He laid his hand on my shoulder.

"Son, you will now celebrate the last rites—"

I looked at him uncomprehendingly.

"—for your family."

My family? A sudden sense of abatement came over me.

"Afterward, it will be too late. This is your last chance. Do as I say."

I did as he said. I gathered some water in my hands. Tiny translucent fish were suckling the grass. He began to chant a verse in that bronze tongue which surges like the sea, and it immediately brought in another atmosphere, as if each word were imparted with meaning, a music that brought truth into being.

"You pour this water for the appeasement of your kin."

I poured the water. I let it trickle drop by drop into the great river. It flowed away with the river. I did not quite understand what was taking place, but it was in tune with the rhythm, consonant and in step.

"You no longer have a family."

He rose to his feet and tossed a few drops of water over his shoulder.

"Come."

I followed the sannyasi.

I cannot really describe what happened from that moment on. I was no longer myself, yet I was myself as I had never been before: an intensity of self, a luminous essence, something other than my thousands of everyday gestures, other than a certain habit of living this life, or even the memory of all that I had been and done—the veneer that makes up our face, or our grimace. It was not a state of destitution, a vacancy of self; yet, I walked naked through the tall grass, somewhat embarrassed by this pallid body of mine as if it were an ill-fitting garment. It was not the sense of expansion I had experienced before, when I had merged with the river, dissolved in the great rhythm. There was something supremely of "me" in all these gestures and memories, something that had a rhythm of its own, a vibration that held everything together, like a memory of all memories, a note of all notes—a something that had been involved in every adventure, every story, that had vibrated identically in all forms and faces, in all shades of good or evil. Yes, a unique music, *my* music, here or there, in black skin or white, in forgotten times or recorded times; the one and only Tale of the tale that weaves all tales, like a certain blue used by an eternal artist to compose either stormy skies or radiant and happy ones, but always in the same hue, *my* hue: a one-of-a-kind, eternal "me," oh, so utterly me! A concentration of me, as if twenty generations had joined to walk with me, feel with me, pray with me—such an intense epitome that it produced heat, a fusion of being so compact that light seemed to radiate around me.

Everything was suffused with that orange hue.

We entered the forest. The sannyasi walked before me, now and then his robe set aglow with a ray of sunlight. The sand underfoot was as soft as a gazelle. I could barely see my way. I went on from one golden shaft to the next amid awesome tawny pillars, intertwined in a riot of contortions, then soaring skyward to form into a vault from which a chance vine hung like a flaming stalactite. I advanced without knowing where I was going, a mist of sweetness over my eyes. I felt very small, very white, that great Presence at my back. My heart seemed to be ablaze, and everything mingled: the flaming banyans, the ocher sands, the great encompassing gaze resting upon me. An exquisitely gentle fire flowed from my heart toward all things, and I knew them all, attended to them all. I wanted to touch them, embrace them, take them in, like a man about to die who casts a last glance from on high at his body, at all bodies and all things, with an empathy of absolute understanding. I walked through that orange sweetness with the sense of recognition of an eternal lover. Perhaps I had been walking forever and this was a thousand years later. I was simply a little image, a symbol borne by an orange radiation. My every step seemed charged with infinite meaning, as if all footsteps and all roads led to that sandy path, culminating in that one step; as if all days were fused into this one, and all joys, all sufferings were dissolved, transmuted into that one golden, pink-tinged vibration enveloping me, filling me, so warm, so encompassing it seemed to caress everything, imbue everything, love everything; as if the thousands of beings I had been had gathered to be unraveled here and were looking out with me, burning with me, loving with me, bearing their oblation of pain and hope, opening their hands in this forest, offering up their good and their evil. To give and give—in the end there is nothing else to do but close one's eyes and abandon oneself. Oh, this is what I had been living for: that single moment when everything melts, everything falls away, that ultimate regality of self-offering, the end of all journeys; that orange denouement when one is bathed in a fire of tenderness, swept up in a song of love; that freedom of walking

without hope or expectation, like a dead man who has died so
many times he no longer has anything to fear or to lose, like
a living man who has lived so much he has no more desire of
his own. What else was there to want? What heaven? What
was there to fear? *That* already knew every heaven and hell;
it had gone everywhere, experienced riches and miseries. What
else was there to expect? There was that ultimate song, that
tenderness for itself, for everything, the deliverance of laying
one's forehead on the great sacrificial altar, of opening one's
hands, of giving forth one's note. There was only that little
image beneath an all-encompassing gaze. There was my brother
of light—my eternal brother—and I fusing with him at the end,
merging into his gaze, the little image into the large one, the
untold miseries into a great loving fire, the thousands of steps
into a great march of love, the thousands of days into a single
meaningful day. Everything was like an orange hymn.

They were chanting.

We stood before a large clearing on the edge of the sands.
The sea rumbled in the distance. Gnarled banyan roots twisted
about us like the rigging of a sailboat.

They gathered a pile of wood.

"This is it. Sit down."

He drew a circle about me. Their voices filled the clearing like
a bronze tide, mingling with the rumble of the sea.

"Do as I say."

He placed a bowl of ghee and some colored rice grains by my
side.

They lit a fire, as if for my funeral pyre.

I was alone.

Facing the rising sun.

Naked in the middle of the clearing.

They drew back from me, chanting.

"You now renounce the three worlds. Cast the three lives into
the fire."

I took three rice grains and some ghee and cast them into the flames.

"You renounce the world of the mind, the brilliant world, along with all its gods and forms. Cast it into the fire: *Aum Svaha.*"

I cast it into the flames.

"You renounce the vital world with all its lights and powers. Cast it into the fire: *Aum Svaha.*"

I cast it into the flames.

"You renounce the physical world, your flesh and its desires, your emotions and yearnings. Cast it into the fire: *Aum Svaha.*"

I cast it into the flames.

"You renounce all the worlds. You no longer have a home or ties or country. You are the son of the Fire."

I am the son of the Fire.

"You are That. In That you live, to That you return. Thus you are."

They chanted behind me, and I no longer knew who I was or for what and by what I existed. I knew only the fire that burned in my heart and burned before me in an incandescent mingling; I knew only that chant in the clearing, that fiery offering singing in my heart. I was that living fire. O Fire, great Fire, I know not what they say; I cannot understand their words, their world or their gestures; I know only that I am here, at the end of the world, at the end of all gestures, alone and naked before you. What more must I do? What is the truth, the simple truth? I ask for nothing but the truth, just the pure truth. What is the truth? It went on burning, wordlessly, as if the truth were simply to burn.

Then I cast everything into my fire: everything that questions, demands, hinders; everything that knows, doesn't know, shines, doesn't shine; everything that can be consumed and feeds the Fire of truth. O Fire, great Fire, I cast this life into your flames because it is not life, because it is small, limited, because it dies and what is true cannot die! O Fire, great Fire, I cast these thoughts into your fire, because they know nothing, can do nothing, because they turn in endless circles, without solutions, remedies or certitudes, because the truth knows, the truth can! O Fire, I cast these emotions, this confusion of feelings, this misery of the senses, this relentless yoke, this thirst, this perpetual thirst, into your fire. I cast my humanity into the fire, *Aum Svaha.* I am the son of another race! I spring from another birth. O Fire, great Fire, I have not come to this world to repeat the rituals of the dying! I am enamored of another life, the progeny of another Light. For where is life? What is there to renounce? Life is yet to be!

Then I placed the remaining grain of rice in the hollow of my hand and gazed into the flame one more time, summoning all my strength, my soul, in a supreme call to the truth, as if truth itself had to say the word or I would die at that instant. I call for the truth, the truth; and if there is no truth, may everything be consumed!

And something answered.

A rush of flame into my body, a crushing pressure; there was no fright, only the sense of being burned alive from within. No more nerves, no more cells, no more body—a dense, all-consuming fire. Then, from all sides (or within, I don't know), an onslaught of all those "me's," all gathered around, hovering and pressing against me, themselves like flame: the beings of my being, the lost, burned-out lives, the undying dead, the long, interminable scorching procession of which I was the final residue, the ultimate chant, the last living question. They were all there, gazing through my eyes, touching with my hands, vibrating within my body, all suspended in this extreme second. And they all held that grain of rice in their hands. I seemed to hear a distant chanting, something rising and rising, muffled and subdued like the hum of the sea, like the song of those sannyasis—a long invocation surging from the depths of lives, from the depths of the dead, each with his offering of fire. It was all the forms they had adored, sung, carved, or painted, all their hopes and despairs, their sacrifices and heartfelt loves, their defunct achievements and lofty summits. It was ever the same distress: pyre upon pyre, imperious idols—white and black gods, robes of every color and every misery; cries for relief, futile, irrelevant visions, realizations of dust, sparks of gold or snow, clear white moments that always end awry, pure salvations that saved nothing—a vast fiery procession mounting from the heart of night, from the depths of my lives, encompassing every face, every gaze, even the faces of the sannyasis, the grimaces of the tortured, the smiles of the blessed, all mingled together—one and the same immense supplication rising from the depths of time, from the depths of those thousands of men beating in my heart like the ape of yore in the primeval forest. This was the answer, like an orange flowering: *something else, something else—another man, another life upon earth!* It really sang that morning, caroling in my heart like a chime of the new world, the knell of the old: something else, something else, another being born of our fire, another earth born of our cry of truth, a still unknown something that will be born through the energy of our fire, just as Matter was born from fire, as Love and Beauty were born from fire, as man was born of a cry.

Then I opened my hand and cast the last grain of rice into the fire.

And something happened.

The touch of his hand on my shoulder startled me. I had completely forgotten about him and his initiation. I was in another world, thousands of miles away—perhaps in tomorrow's world. Oh, I had been that sannyasi before—once, twice, three times—and countless other things together with these men circling about me, and now I had returned to make *the* gesture, to consign the world to the flame once more, but as a supreme incendiary, an ultimate iconoclast, to consign that fire itself to the flame and break the back of the old story.

"You will now receive the initiation."

He sat down before me.

"Do as I say."

I did as he said.

He placed his right hand atop my head. I placed my right hand on his right knee. He bent toward my ear.

There was not a sound anywhere. The others had gone.

The sea rumbled in the distance.

He pronounced three syllables.

I repeated the three syllables.

And that was it.

He stood up. I stood up. He took up the orange cloth and placed it in my hands. Oh, now I understood why the cloth was of this color! Then he handed me a staff and a begging bowl. He took off his necklace of rudraksha beads and slipped it about my neck.

"Now you are a sannyasi."

He stood erect and still before me, his bare torso gleaming in the sun. He looked like a tawny erne.

"You are alone with the Truth."

Then, without warning, his face relaxed. He examined me with a sort of gleeful tenderness and burst into thunderous, triumphant, regal laughter, his head thrown back as if he were imbibing the wine of the gods. Then he turned his back on me.

I never saw him again.

As for me, I had burned his initiation along with the rest.

I was alone.

I was in a different state.

All that remained was a little heap of ashes in the middle of the clearing.

I was in another condition, perhaps that "something else" I had invoked. I felt utterly outside the scheme of things, subject to a different gravitation, yet I was not sure, for there was nothing special to see, nothing supernatural, no apparitions or revelations, no miracles. Yet, there *was* a sense of revelation: it was as if I could see something without seeing it, touch something without touching it, or rather be touched by it, like

a blind man or a baby born to a world so radically different
that there are no sense organs to express the sensation. Yet, it
was unmistakably there. It was not an illumination, a subli-
mation, or a glorified form of anything I might have known
before. It was something else. A complete otherness. I stood in
that clearing as an hominid might have stood under the first
wave of mental activity. But this was not thinking; it was a
different vibration of being; and it was right *here*—no need to
close one's eyes, to meditate, to soar to vertiginous heights or
go into ecstasy. It was *here*, with eyes wide open and both feet
planted on the ground: no need to expand oneself, to merge
with the cosmic flow or dissolve oneself; it was the opposite of
dissolution, more like a concentration, a formidable concentration of being, almost with its own weight, such a massive
density that I felt like a solid, radiant block—a compact mass
of vibration. But it had nothing to do with the vibration of
thought or feeling. It was a dense beam of vibrations, a single
vibratory mass, perhaps of thousands of vibrations, so swift
they became coagulated, fused into one, like energy about to
turn into matter; one more step, one slight increase of frequency, and all would be solidified. I was held there, immobilized like a bee caught in a honeycomb. It was a warm
energy—almost like a rush of fever, except that its warmth did
not resemble material warmth; it was more like intense love,
a paroxysm of love, or perhaps joy, a love-joy that had nothing
to do with human feeling or emotion: the *stuff* of love, a solid
flood of joy holding you under its beam. It was tranquil, so
tranquil, without the least excitation, commotion or even
quiver; or else a quiver of such high frequency that it, too, was
immobilized, sealed in eternity. And time was not the same; it
was like being on the edge of such an accelerated second that
it would turn into eternity, like experiencing time before it is
fixed and defined; and the same applied to matter: to live in
that matter meant living in eternity. It was a vast immobility
without a particular center; yet, it was right *here* in bright

daylight, a concrete eternity that could branch out anywhere in a flash, leaping over time—past, present, future. It could not perish, any more than energy could cease to energize. It was Energy itself, a supersun without a particular center that spun all the suns, atoms and bodies, the life of life—perhaps the life to be, the future life, unless it is already there, forever there, and for some mysterious reason one happens upon it. One crosses the threshold, as long ago inanimate matter crossed the threshold of Life to emerge into a swifter movement, as long ago the anthropoid crossed the threshold of the Mind and experienced a new type of acceleration, causing him to think and reflect. But it was inexpressible, unexplainable. I did not know how it worked—it just *was*. I cannot even say I saw something. There was nothing to see! It was yet to be for our eyes. Rather, one was seen by it. It was true Sacredness, the mighty Mystery, independent of any past, any memory, any initiation. It was the absolute Future, without a name, a label or a sign, without a quiver of being; it was simply there, a radiant, massive, imperious solidity: "I WILL." A motionless "I will" looking at the earth and waiting—perhaps waiting for our millions of cries to open the golden door and draw us across its threshold. A new Power upon the earth that had nothing to do with thought, matter, life, or even the soul. A motionless, ardent cataract of warm power charged with love.

I drew my scarf over my breast and set out straight before me.

22
what?

I never recaptured that great, warm Power that seemed capable of changing everything. It had come and gone—or disappeared underground, like a spring, to reappear somewhere else, in another time, another place. Oh, the interminable outer trudging we must go through to recapture *the* moment, the long drawn-out course necessary to plough through and clarify our matter to the end; each burst of light followed by a dark descent, as if one had to retrace the whole path, at every level, through every nook and cranny, every lost island—ever the repetition of the same circling round an invisible core, but each time more gripping, as it were, and with an ever greater acceleration. The same essential vibration recurring again and again, and organizing the least variation better to give out its one imperious note—my name, my true name.

I have done and tried everything. I have meditated, wandered, contemplated. But contemplation was of no help; eyes closed, you soared elsewhere, into immutable joy, oblivious to anything happening below. You went higher and higher, more and more divested and pure, into a dimension increasingly alien to the coarseness of the earth. But when I came out of it,

I was like an extremely sensitive radio antenna that the least false vibration would upset; I came down with fever merely by looking at people's eyes. I have walked and walked, disappeared in temples, lost myself in crowds, known the immense kindness of people. I have knocked at the doors of the poor, begged, sung *kirtana* in a clangor of cymbals and drums until I was ready to fall, but the one door would not open. I have heard black psalms, incantations that ended in a trance, drums and flutes that rent the night and revealed a still greater darkness, and the ceaseless chant of cicadas along river banks as if everything were about to burst with light, punctured at last, but nothing was punctured. I have worshipped, prayed to compassionate gods, fearsome gods, dread and naked Mothers daubed in vermilion. I would have prostrated myself before a pile of rocks, so great was my thirst to see the living god. But I found nothing greater than, one evening, an old woman laying her forehead on a bare stone while repeating His Name, until she collapsed with exhaustion. I have met sages, madmen, vagabonds who could read the future, but none knew the secret of the present. I have encountered hermits who knew the secret of the worlds beyond and the ineffable Plenitude, but none knew the plenitude of this world. I have seen small, dark beings capable of dispensing dazzling powers, powerful men who could fascinate with a single glance, but none was stronger than that little flame within. I have bathed in icy springs and rank rivers, meditated with the dead in cremation grounds, and done many strange things, but I have found nothing simpler than the cry of my heart. And in the end, at the bottom of it all, behind darkness and light, ice and fire, I kept encountering my thirst, my cry, my old question, now stripped of words, throbbing, pounding, more imperious than all the drums and more piercing than all the cymbals of their rituals—*WHAT?*

Time passed.

Would I, too, end up like Batcha's ascetic, shriveled and sere in his spiritual anthill, staring wide-eyed at—what?

Just as that thought occurred to me (or was it a coincidence? but everything is a coincidence, a miracle, and everything is decreed), my life took a new turn, as if a certain cry within, a tiny call, the opening of a little door, was enough to cause an instantaneous change of circumstances; one shifts to another wavelength and everything follows.

That day I met a *nanga-sannyasi.*

It was in the northern countries, where snow never ends. He appeared around a bend in the road, young and radiant, perhaps twenty years old. He was naked and covered with ashes in the manner of his sect, and he walked while sounding his *chimta.*[*]

"Yo! Sannyasi, *Siva! Siva!*"

"Yo! *Siva! Siva!*"

"Where are you heading?"

"Nowhere."

He laughed.

"I, everywhere."

We traveled together. He had the eyes of a child, spoke without rhyme or reason, sang *stotras,* or remained quiet for days on end, and his silence was as light as mountain air.

"I think the gods love us," he said one morning.

The mist still hung thick in the cypresses.

"Ah?"

"Yes, I feel them."

"How do you feel them?"

He scratched his head.

"Well, they love me, so I love."

"Oh, love, love—that's something I don't understand!"

"Then you don't understand yourself."

"Why is that?"

---

[*] Curved iron tongs used to stoke a fire.

"Because you are He-Who-Loves."

"How do you know?"

He leaned toward me, his cheeks dimpling.

"Because you do love!"

We crossed mountain chains and icy passes, dales dense with wild rhododendrons, sacred confluences seething with blue clay. He wore only a tiny loincloth tied with a string around his hips.

"Life is beautiful, companion! It is as bright as Siva's smile!"

After his morning bath, he would smear himself with ashes. My orange clothing seemed ostentatious in comparison, almost like a disguise. I felt like throwing away everything and going naked, too.

"Oh! brother, aren't you cold?"

He smiled triumphantly.

"Siva covers me with his love!"

We stood on the brink of a torrent, among pines, dolerites, and one enormous cedar with a violet trunk. The echo of gongs rose from the depths of the valley, while in the distance, above a thin, near-transparent veil of pearly mist, floated gold-tinged ice fields, made even more eternal as they were borne by the sound of that frail little gong: *tim-tim-tim, tim-tim-tim,* three times, always three times, an endless reverberation through the misty hollows.

I scooped up a handful of warm ashes and rubbed them over my entire body.

He looked at me, aghast, as if I were committing a profanation.

"But you're a sannyasi!"

"So?"

"This isn't your law."

He was confounded.

"My law?"

I felt like giving him a piece of my mind, but he looked so defenseless standing there, scratching his head; and my body remained as white as a leper's, despite the ashes. I plunged into the torrent and recovered my eternal wretched white man's skin. I must have been given the wrong skin at birth. "What a nuisance it is."

"Oh, you said it, brother!"

He stoked the fire he had laid among the stones. There was always a fire wherever he stopped. It was a rule of his sect. Whenever the fire died, he simply had to take up the road again.

"In other words," I said jestingly, "the body is the final obstacle, right?"

"That's right, brother. Once we are free, no more body!"

It was my turn to be stunned.

It was like a revelation in reverse. I stood there naked, perched on a stone by the torrent, surrounded by immutable ice and the feeble, futile echo of the gong rising from the heart of the valley. I was scandalized, overcome with horror. The final obstacle. Everything was becoming clear: the valley swathed in mist, that call, that cry of the dead, those toiling, ascending lives, that quest for the truth, that scorching ascent, and all that purified, sublimated existence straining toward the light.

"For *what*?"

I startled him, my voice booming like a thunderclap. He was squatting on the ground, hands on his knees, his chimta dangling.

"What's the matter with you?"

"So that's it, eh? Let's get out of here and be done with it. We're free, so off with the old rag! Just toss it into the fire!"

He was so appalled by my tone that his chimta knocked his rice bowl into the fire. As for me, it was like a thunderbolt crashing upon my head, a black apocalypse. An uncontrollable wave of revolt. I looked at the tree, at my orange scarf. I was going to hang myself; I had to hang myself *now*, spit on this whole thing and be done with it. I raised my fist. He threw himself upon me.

"No, brother, no! Don't do that! What is it? What's the matter?"

He looked at me in total bewilderment. Although he did not understand a thing, he could feel, as an animal feels. Gently he stroked my forehead.

"Now, now. Calm down, calm down."

My skin was clammy. In three seconds I had been drained of all my energy, as if I had regurgitated thirty years of meditation.

"Baba! You look like a *bhout!*" *

He drew me near. My eyes remained fixed on that tree. And suddenly I *knew* what had happened. It was so obvious! I could see that sannyasi hanging from the tree. It was I. I could even feel the leap into space. It had *already* happened; and I had come back to undo the knot. Everything revolved around that instant of revolt. At last I understood: I had come back to take the test again. Oh, now I know the signs! Through repetition, I now know what comes from the past, and it has *nothing* to do with romantic or fabulous memories! It is a certain intensity of vibration—moments pregnant with invisible significance, as it were, as if at that particular second, that particular place or incident were "charged" with a force of emotion or reaction utterly disproportionate to the fact itself. Then I know: *this* has happened before. The past was not a compilation of portentous happenings, with its string of lofty or petty beings, adventures, and extraordinary places. It was simply that intensity of soul that seemed to cling to a mere detail: a tree branch, reflected light on the sand, the sudden song of a child wandering through a wheat field—a "something" alive with an unexpected sense of eternity, imparting the simplest gesture with an everlasting substance.

"What a curious sannyasi you are!"

---

* Ghost, specter, or devil.

His gaze roamed over me, then moved on to the spilled bowl of rice in the fire, the smoldering wood.

"Bad thoughts always bring on confusion and difficulties."

"Oh, shush!"

He shrugged.

"All right, we just won't eat today, that's all."

"Eat? Why do you eat anyway? To feed this useless carcass?"

He recoiled. What an unexpected brand of sannyasi I was! Perhaps a venomous one.

"Do you mean to tell me that you want to feed your body?"

Suddenly Bjorn's words came back to me: "Why eat?" And that was like another door opening in the darkness and letting in a train of vibrations.

"Listen, brother, I don't have any wisdom."

He stood there, self-conscious before his fire, so touching in his eagerness to help. I softened a bit.

"What do you mean?"

"I don't have any wisdom, brother. I know only *one* word that my Master gave me. I am to travel the whole country on foot, and when that is done, I will meet my Master again and he will give me another word. After I have completed several rounds like that, he will give me Wisdom. So I know nothing, as you see, but I'm happy, for one day he will give me Wisdom."

My heart melted, and I clasped his shoulder.

"What is your word?"

He lowered his eyes and seemed to blush under his ashes.

"I am not supposed to tell anybody. It's just for me, you see; it's only good for me."

He raised innocent eyes to mine, as tawny as mountain honey.

"He said: 'Go forth and look at everything as if it were a secret.' That's it. So I look and look at the secret. I don't understand, but I go on looking because there's a secret.

Sometimes it's painful to look without understanding. But there's a secret, there's a secret; and I keep on looking."

He picked up his bowl, adjusted his loincloth and threw the remaining rice into the torrent.

"The fire is dead. We must go."

"Your fire mustn't let you sleep much."

"Oh, one day I will be so awake that I will no longer need to sleep. My fire will always burn. My Master never sleeps."

We set out down the path toward the plains. From that day on, I began to tumble down inside, as well.

Once again we were amid the odor of scorched earth, the mugginess of tormented plants, the cawing of crows, and the pungent aroma of sweat and saffron exuding from the motley crowds. Caked with dust, we abandoned ourselves to the fervid August skies. My companion gazed intently at everything along our path, searching out the secret, questioning without words; and the secret, I knew, was to rest one's eyes long enough on things, until the husk melts away, then one's gaze burst through everything.

"This is all very fine, but—"

Abruptly he turned and took my arm, perspiration streaking the ashes on his skin.

"Oh, brother, do you see those old vessels by the roadside, and the tender leaves peeping between the stones? Sometimes *everything* seems tender, even pebbles."

He sounded his chimta.

"I'm so very happy!"

And that was all. He just sounded his chimta as we went along.

"And after?"

"After what?"

There was such sweetness in his eyes. I shrugged and kicked at the pebbles. Then I saw myself kicking an old calabash on the deserted quays of that western port, with puddles shimmering in the lamplight, and the Laurelbank standing at anchor. It seemed so very long ago; yet, it was exactly the same gesture—ten years compressed into a second. Only my clothing had changed. What is it that does change? And Mohini, swallowed up in the red Tartarus. Freedom, freedom.

"Then *what*?"

He gave me a startled look. We were camped by the walls of a city near an old water tank with worn granite steps. The night air was filled with the croaking of frogs. Lotus blossoms glowed in the moonlight. He had lit his fire. I think I had a fever.

"What then, brother, tell me! I, too, have looked at the pebbles on the road, and I did find something, but what I'm asking is *after*. What happens after?"

"After?"

"Yes, after!"

"But then, what have you found? You said you found something."

"It was long ago in the West, in Brazil. There was a road near a river, the *Rio des Contas*—"

He peered up at me. He had bushy eyebrows and resembled my other brother, the gold seeker, over there in the forest: "We have to find it, Job. We absolutely have to find it." When we had unearthed our pile of gold, he had dropped dead on it.

"—the River of Pearls. I stood staring at those pebbles on the riverbank, and I was overcome by an unbearable sense of futility—all those minutes ticking away in nothing, with nothing happening, as if they did not exist and we were already dead. A corpse on two feet. In a flash, I saw all the roads I had traveled, all the countries, the streets, the ports, all those futile footsteps, all those thousands of nonexistent minutes. I wanted it all to *be*. I stared at those pebbles until I thought my eyes would burst, beholding every pebble on the road as if it were the Almighty, the unique event of my life. I wanted to retain something, not live another second without it. Oh, I swear, that is a stretch of road I will remember for all eternity! Then I set out to do this everywhere: in Africa, Asia, in trucks, ships, bars, ports, until it finally began to burn all by itself, like a flame—an automatic memory like a fire. This *is* the fire that never dies! It was my one and only possession. Everywhere I felt like a king with my fire; it kept burning, *existing*, and nothing else mattered to me! It was my wife, my country, my companion. I felt rich, fulfilled with my fire!"

He looked thunderstruck, his chimta dangling from his hand.

"And after?"

"That's just it. There is no 'after.' "

He gave me a puzzled and concerned look. I could feel my anger flaring up again. He dropped his chimta.

"The devil's behind your words."

"Well, good! The devil's better than nothing!"

"My Master says: 'There is a vast expanse, and we are free.' "

"But I *am* free! I know that vast expanse of yours. I go there as I please!"

He gaped at me, incredulous.

"Yes, there is a world above where one is free, and all questions vanish."

Silence.

"It's the *after* that bothers me. *After*."

He took one step behind his fire as if I had frightened him. To be sure, I lacked the ecstatic air and the white beard. Who knows, I may even have harbored a devil inside me. But free I was!

"You speak in anger. You do not have wisdom."

"That may be. But I need only to close my eyes for a second—three seconds—and I am gone; nothing matters anymore and I am immersed in perfect peace and infinite life. Then I open my eyes, and pfft! Everything is as before: the body ages, life decays, there is cold, fever, hunger, the beast—all the material for the pyre."

"My Master says: 'The aim is to save one's soul.' "

"But it's *already* saved, for Heaven's sake! It is free, eternally free; all we need to do is remember, and off we go into the light—in three seconds. But life is not saved, the body is not saved; *they* are in need of saving, because they are mortal! Heaven is eternal; it does not need me to exist! Or else life is a falsehood and we should all escape into beatitude."

"He says: 'We are the sons of heaven.' "

"Yes, by the body of the earth."

He straightened himself up as if I had hit him, swiftly crossed his legs, closed his eyes and went into meditation.

I was left with my burning anger, a devastating wave of destruction. I realized I was lost. If I moved, it would be the end; I would shake my fist at heaven and hang myself. I annihilated myself, became nonexistent, still as stone.

A snake slid into the water tank.

In that instant, trembling with anger, I saw something— "saw" as one penetrates into a painting. I saw that that force of being, that concentration of energy and light one accumulates day after day, year after year, like an infallible battery retaining everything—the least syllable, the slightest cry, the minutest aspiration—that subtle, power-filled fire that is like our color of being, our intensity of soul, could change into its exact counter intensity of darkness, atom for atom, flame for flame, and one could grow as dark as one was luminous, because it is the *same* thing in reverse: one touches the very shadow of one's light. At that moment, I understood Bjorn's death. That essentially creative Force can reverse itself with an equal intensity of destruction. It's either one or the other, for both are the same, viewed from opposite sides. When one leaves Truth, one immediately enters upon death. Once one has set out on the path, there is no turning back; the potential for catastrophe is as great as the energy of new creation, whether for the individual, for nations, or for the soul's destiny. Later, I saw also that the power of this reversal is not the Fall one may think, but the Light's dynamic explosion to clear out the path and propel us ahead. Where is the darkness?

He was smiling.

My anger was gone.

His body, tinged blue with ashes and moonlight, seemed to dance in the firelight. He looked like a Vedic god behind his fiery curtain. The frogs resumed their croaking in the water tank. A dog howled at the moon. Everything was so fragile, and everything was eternal.

I closed my eyes. I, too, could smile. One shuts the door below and takes wing through the fields of light. That evening, I found myself face to face with the great Contradiction.

Yes, one day the bodies open like flowers. One day, under the pressure of an inner fire, the shadowy shell bursts open, the great captive bird spreads its triumphant wings, and one glides endlessly, marvelously, through soft and luminous plains, through scattered constellations, high above bodies and the blue spell of the mind. With one's forehead upon great snows of silence, one soars through a pearly softness, drifts through light years, leaving the tomb behind, abandoning the travesty, returning home. Oh, the breath of those ranges of light—so pure, so simple! One breathes freely, flows unfettered, spreads oneself boundlessly, touches one's own infinity. It's the peace of being oneself at last, the vast, quiet refreshment of being in oneself—eternity in the wink of an eye! Transparency everywhere, like a sea of white lotus blossoms under an invisible sun.

And far, far below, a speck of being, a fire, a tiny flame aching to merge with that immensity of light. A blaze of being, a crying out, overflowing with gratitude because *that* exists— that wellspring, that inexpressible marvel—overflowing with thirst because *that* cannot be here as well, in a body. Oh, a truth that is not *all* cannot be the whole truth!

ψ

23
the little foxes

*T*he next day we arrived at a village amid the paddy fields.
The village lay like an island of lush mango trees under a sky
scattered with billowy clouds. Each house had its own mango
tree and high mud walls that cast cool shadows onto a single
dusty lane. The sun was high, the air smelled of moist earth
and new rice. A celebration was in progress. An arch made of
banana trees hung over the first door, and drumbeats filled the
air.

My companion struck his chimta.

"Shall we stop at this house?"

"There are too many people. Let's go farther."

He grew insistent.

"Farther on, the houses will be empty."

"Are you hungry?"

I was loath to enter that house. Why I felt that repugnance I
do not know, but I had learned to trust my instincts. I think
that events must have tiny tentacles that stretch out into the
invisible, and that's what we touch before they close in on us,
truly as if the plot unfolded on two levels: the paradigm above

or around, and its accomplishment here in the flesh. To this day I am not sure one can prevent that accomplishment.

"What are you afraid of?"

I shrugged, followed him across the threshold, and encountered Destiny. I have always wondered whether everything is not tightly interlinked, not only from last night's dream to today's accident, but right from our very first step in this world, much as the tree and all its leaves are contained in the verdant mango seed.

We were in a roomy courtyard. Women in colorful saris bustled to and fro; children ran about; knots of men squatted in the shade. No one seemed to pay attention to us. Half a dozen rooms gave out onto a pillared veranda, with garlands of jasmine hanging on the doors. The *mridangam* player was beating his drum.

"By the way, don't forget to cover your chest."

I blushed. *He* could go naked, but I had to cover myself. A group of children gathered around the nanga-sannyasi. I wandered off toward the rear of the courtyard to be alone. I think I could beg for ten years without ever getting used to stretching out my bowl. I stopped before the door of a little room at the far end of the veranda; and it was precisely because I was seeking a quiet spot to sit that I stumbled upon the very place I ought never to have gone to.

A basil plant grew outside the room. It was set in a carved-stone receptacle that seemed familiar, but that morning everything felt familiar, as if reminding me of or alerting me to something. The air seemed charged with signs and presences, or perhaps threats. Without thinking, I plucked a basil leaf and held it to my lips: a scent of wild mint, a train of indistinct vibrations, and at the other end of that scent, a small door seemed to open and I heard a distant little voice coming from behind a curtain of vines: "In my country we call it tulsi. It's a plant that brings good fortune." Mohini! A whole world conjured up by a scent of basil, as vivid as if it were in the adjoining room: a scattering of bird feathers, a tangle of climbing vines, the huge cage, the glinting crystal, the broken ektara; there was even a peacock feather on the ground. One opens the door by chance, to discover that nothing has changed. Within us lie scores of dungeons and many Atlantises that have never sunk.

I looked up.

And I froze.

A man stood in the little room, his back to me, just in front of the basil plant. There was a woman facing him. I could not distinguish her face, only her creamy-white forehead. A young peasant woman dressed in red, like a goddess. I watched, open-mouthed, as she carefully lifted her veil, exposing the dark sweep of her hair. Then the man raised his right hand to that snowy forehead above the dark curve of her brows. He was holding something between his fingers. My head reeled; none of this made any sense to me, yet I was as struck as if I were witnessing something I had known before, almost as if *I* had made that gesture.

I felt a violent tug at my arm.

Then the man slowly lowered his hand, revealing the red tilak staining that pale brow.

"What in heaven do you think you're doing!"

I was thunderstruck.

He pulled frantically at my arm. I could sense the eyes upon me, hear people whispering. I was in a daze, stunned like a man who awakens in a dead temple to see the gods move. He dragged me across the courtyard like a thief.

"Have you lost your senses?"

He was outraged. The door slammed behind us. We were in the street. There was a vault of mango trees, and that dazzling blue sky at the other end.

"Don't you know one isn't supposed to do that? What kind of sannyasi are you?"

He brandished his chimta. My head whirled.

"What were they doing?" I stammered, completely beside myself.

"Don't you know you're not supposed to watch that?"

"*What* were they doing?"

In a daze, I could only sputter my question again and again, Batcha's face suddenly looming in front of me, her pale brow, her eyes filled with tears, and that red tilak I had put on her forehead.

"What happened? What were they doing?"

"You didn't get it? It was his wife!"

"His wife?"

I felt dizzy.

"Don't you know it's sacred?"

He released my arm abruptly.

"What a strange sannyasi you are—and what strange words you speak!"

He spat on the ground.

"From now on, I think we'd better go our separate ways."

He adjusted his loincloth and gave me a final look.

"The night is upon you."

And he turned his back on me.

I watched, speechless, as his naked silhouette, erect and bathed in sunlight, descended the narrow street toward the clear blue sky beyond the mango trees.

He was gone.

I do not know how long I stood before that door, incapable of moving or thinking, while the mridangam player beat frenziedly on his drum. Finally, I left the village.

There were paddy fields as far as the eye could see, luminous stretches of emerald green, relieved by distant clumps of mango trees and a single downy cloud drifting across a cerulean sky.

My world had crashed about my ears.

I no longer understood anything, and my head was ringing like a hollow gourd. All I saw was Batcha, Batcha, Batcha. She was my lifeline, my luminous island. Why Batcha? I had no idea. I had not thought of her once in years, perhaps lifetimes; yet there she was, inexplicably, she and no one else, as if she had never left me. I had merely closed the door and now it swung open again. It was like a dam suddenly bursting, a green outbreak, and everything was wiped out, swept away: the light above, the peace, the white expanse. What did I care for all that?! What had I *done* all these years? What had happened to me? Where had I disappeared to? I stood across those paddy fields as if I had been struck on the head, gaping at the green deluge before me like Jonah in the jaws of the whale.

Everything around me came to a standstill.

A complete vacuum.

I saw all those paddy fields begin to widen and swell like the sea, almost one stalk after another, with microscopic unanimity, while the huge floating cloud of cotton overhead cast a verdant shadow. There was a blank second. Something was frozen, photographed, captured: that was *it*. And that "it" did not correspond to any thought, plan, or personal will; it was just *captured*, and it became true—a creative glimpse. The glimpse of the future: so shall it be. The entire world may cave in and men put up obstructions, but so shall it be, because it is decreed. I knew that second well—nothing in it, yet containing everything: as when I had said no aboard the *Aalesund*, or when I had decided to follow that sannyasi in the port. In truth, there is a field of creative energy above, a range of vision in which the future is like a sphere of light, and when one can manage to *see* from there, *think* from there, things become true, be it ten days or ten years later. All one has to do is capture the vibration, seize hold of it, then pull on the thread, unwinding it like a cocoon, and it becomes a creative thought, a bubble of luminous power moving irresistibly toward its goal. All my life, I have pulled on that thread: a flash going down the street, and I became a gold seeker; a flash in a creek in French Guiana, and I gave up my gold. I have fashioned new lives for myself in five minutes, scoured continents at a gallop—forward, always forward, pulling on that luminous substance as the magical stuff for molding life. When one life was over, there was another one and another one and another one—something else, ever something else—as if one had to carve one's way, pursue each spark, invent new lives for oneself, until indisputable Life emerges—*that*—then one can stop. But I have always begun again; and that instant was approaching again with dazzling clarity. I pulled on the thread, and I had to head south. I had to find Batcha. It was the only thing to do. I had to leave at once.

I got up, collected my staff and my begging bowl, adjusted my scarf.

The sweet scent of new rice went through me, along with the buzzing of insect wings, the croaking of frogs, and the muffled beating of the mridangam. I was returning to my body as if after a ten-year absence.

As I crossed the first paddy field, Batcha's dream flashed before me. Now I understood; it made sense: "I called you three times, three times. The light was like sparkling sand. On and on you went, growing smaller and smaller, about to vanish from sight, while I kept calling you and calling you. But you wouldn't answer, wouldn't hear me. And I felt such a pain, here, as if I were going to die." There she was, vibrant, smiling at the other end of the thread. She was pulling me. She had never ceased pulling me! She had brought me back to my body. Without her, I would have disappeared forever into the bowels of the white whale.

A wave of anguish came over me: What was she doing? Was she still alive? Now, fever descended upon me. Will I ever see the end of this?

That night I had a dream.

I have had many dreams in my life—weird, hellish, sometimes divine—but none that moved me like the poignantly simple dream I dreamed that night. Nor was it quite a dream, for I went into a world as real as China or Peru. Later, I wondered, in horror, whether what I saw was a glimpse into the past or a foreshadowing of the future. Indeed, everything is already pre-existent, and we merely draw reflections from elsewhere, struggling against shadows far older than we are, and trying to alter obscure decrees with a very inadequate light. Unless the shadows' purpose is to spur us on to a greater light?

I was in a "foreign" land, far off in the West. I absolutely had to find her again. It was a question of life or death, despite all the obstacles that barred the way: vast distances, guarded borders, ruthless officials who can annihilate you with one swing of their rubber stamp. Finally, I found myself aboard a giant train, split down its length by a bright corridor. I was dashing down that strip of light like a madman, as if the train were not advancing fast enough! I leaped over luggage, jostled passengers, skirted ropes, rushing on toward a beckoning light, which was She. When I reached the end, I suddenly emerged in a country unlike anything I knew. A world of silence. Everything was muffled, padded, without a sound. The air had a curious feel to it, with a pearl-gray hue as if a veil of gauze-like, transparent mist shrouded everything. Everything moved, or rather glided, behind that "veil," in utter silence. There were people, alone or occasionally in pairs, but never more than in twos, walking about in what appeared to be a garden or a park, its paths, lawns and shrubs suffused with pearl-gray, vaporous light; and the people seemed made of the same substance as that light, only slightly denser. They moved slowly, lithely, barely touching the ground, without any sound, as if engrossed in deep meditation, like a procession of monks. I would ask each one, "Where is she? Where is she?" acutely aware of my anguished tone. I was the only one making any sound, and I felt crude, uncouth. "Where is she?" Curiously, it did not seem I was looking for Batcha per se, but for "her," who was perhaps Batcha, too, though not necessarily with the face I knew—perhaps a "she" of many times before and many faces, but who was always the one and only *she*. They did not know anything, or did not answer, or else extended a hand in a gesture so vague it seemed to conjure up centuries. The more I asked, the more my anguish grew, becoming intolerable, like a death-stone in my heart. "Where is she? Where is she?" Mine was the only voice in that echoless world. There was not a sound in that park, nor even any flower. Then, for the last time, I approached one of the strollers, and the cry in my heart was of such intensity that he stopped in his tracks: "Where is she?" He slowly raised his arm, pointing to an area of the park that sloped down.

I went there and began descending through a succession of terraced gardens bathed in the same pearl-gray light. The garden at the very bottom was the one. I turned to the left and entered a little wood, a bower of curious gray-leaved trees and towering ferns. All was absolute silence, but a silence unlike anything we know as silence, completely devoid of vibrations, as if the world had stopped. And I *knew* she was there. I stopped in front of a tree where a mound of earth pushed up through a sprinkling of leaves and grasses. And inexplicably, I noticed little russet foxes emerging in droves from the grass and fleeing in all directions. *That's where she was.* Just a swarm of little russet foxes scurrying in all directions, without a sound, without a trace. Batcha no longer existed.

It was dreadful. More dreadful than seeing her dead before me.

I awoke with a start, my body covered in cold sweat.

24
Bhaskar-Nath

I reached the White Island the day of the new moon, as the sandstorm raged. I was weary and burning with fever. It was October, the epoch of Scorpio, the season of obscure reversals, of leaps into the dark, of breaches of light, and of sudden collapses. Not that I attach a special significance to the stars, but everything is significant to me, and the longer I travel, the more I see that everything moves together; each detail holds a clue to the whole, and at each instant I am hearkening, through this eruption of fever or that chance tripping, to the ebb and flow of a great tide that drives peoples and sets the worlds in motion. And woe upon us when we tune in only to factitious images and soulless rhythms. Yet I, too, had lost the rhythm. I was caught up in the mad bustle of men, staring at crates of lemons on the platform as if I might see Bjorn, just escaped from the Japanese hospital, spring up before me.

"Hey, Sannyasi, your staff!"

"Sannyasi, Sannyasi." Will they ever leave me alone? A pilgrim from the north stood before me, holding out my staff. In a sudden burst of anger, I yanked the stick out of his hands and broke it across my knee. He was dumbfounded. Then I thrust the fragments into his hands.

"Here, take it; I've finished my run."

And I left.

I walked through the warehouse where I had heard divine music, but there was no music in my heart—only a drumlike pounding in my temples, like Siva's angry dance. The same margosa tree stood outside the station, and I recognized the silvery jingle of the horse carts. But the child who had taken me to my brother was not there. I had no brother. He was dead, unless it was he who whispered in my ear: "Someday I'll return and break your glass." I was no longer borne by the smiling grace that arranged each step, each encounter. I was burning with fever, in the middle of a sandstorm, and in the gnawing misery of being just oneself.

"Hey, Sannyasi, take my cart! It's light!"

Sannyasi, Sannyasi. Every time, I lowered my head like an outcast, as if that orange symbol stigmatized and branded me, cut me off from others and from everything. The wind blew in from the south, rolling the dunes over the palm trees, throwing up showers of sand on the main street, along with spray-like volleys of thorns. My robe flapped about me, while people pointed their fingers, and women on their balconies whispered: *dorai, dorai*—the white man, the white man. I could see heads turning, a vague murmur mounting: *dorai, dorai*. I stumbled on, clutching my orange scarf to my breast like a thief: *dorai, dorai*—the white man, the reprobate, the accursed sannyasi, the man without a country, disguised in orange here, but actually clothed in black there; the endless masquerader who could not decide what skin to wear, including that of a naked sannyasi; the zero, the nothing-at-all who belonged neither here nor elsewhere, neither above nor below. Oh, who will tell me whence I come, my name, my country? Will not a great white horse come again to bear me off on his triumphant back and free me of this spiritual fortress as he had freed me of the white man's fortress?

"Balu!"

He gazed at me, open-mouthed, almost with panic, as if I were a ghost. Balu! Taller, thinner, standing there before the grain shop. I extended my hand like a beggar.

"Balu—"

He dropped his handful of grain and ran off as fast as his legs could carry him. Everyone was turning his back on me.

I took the road to the temple, my head pounding, white shivers rippling through my body, my mouth dry as dust. I stopped at Meenakshi's to ask for a glass of water. The mother appeared on the doorstep, hands on hips, dressed in a purple sari. She stared at me and her eyes seemed to say, "She's dead. Nisha threw herself down the well!" I turned back, wandering down the temple street amid jingling carts and blasts of whirling sand, heading toward a column that loomed in the distance like a deep-blue watchtower against the scudding sky. I felt so small and futile in that robe, alone, at the end of the road. There was nowhere to go from here, nowhere to escape. It was all over, settled. I had pursued all the roads, even the roads of freedom, even those from which one is not supposed to return. Nothing remained except a tiny door, over there, a snow-white child, while I went on and on, groping feverishly like a blind man, with this sole mantra ringing in my heart: Where is she? Where is she? Is she alive?

I climbed the three steps, my heart pounding as if it would burst. The loggia appeared before me—the divinities, the scent of sandalwood, the patio awash in light. I tripped against something that broke with a shrill little sound. I bent down to glimpse a child's ektara.

He was there, sitting alone in his corner, bare-chested, surrounded by his tools, his eyes fastened on me. I am not sure I even saluted him, but I sank into that look, immersed myself in that great calm force that washed away all my suffering, smoothed my brow, bathed my sorrows in soothing coolness, as if I had been walking and walking for centuries, running on for lifetimes, my body covered with scales. I wanted to throw myself at his feet. He stopped me with a gesture of his hand.

"Mani!"

A girl appeared carrying a water jug and a cloth. There was not a sound in the house.

"Tend to him. He's a sannyasi; this house is his."

Sannyasi, sannyasi. She walked up to me. I wanted to cry, "No, no, I'm *not* a sannyasi! Please stop this, leave me alone! I'm not a sannyasi; I'm absolutely nothing!" She poured water over my feet. Oh, I know he had done it on purpose, to make me understand I was a stranger, a sannyasi received in accordance with his station. I was filled with shame, lost like a child. I wanted to leave. Then the whole scene became crystallized before my eyes: the piece of orange cloth, the girl bent over my bare feet, her hair sweeping the ground. Everything sank into my eyes as into a well, the image becoming deeper and deeper, more intense, as if drifting into another world that revealed several layers upon one another. There was no more "me," but countless me's and countless times before, each gesture in the foreground repeating itself twice, thrice on other planes—or was it the other way round?—while I stood there, outside, about to begin again the old story, gesture for gesture. It was dizzying. Perhaps I was going mad from the fever?

"Sit down."

The girl placed a mat at my feet. A half-completed caroms game lay abandoned on the ground. They all had fled.

Mâ arrived.

My heart leaped. I wanted to clasp her hands, touch her feet. She stepped back, pulled a corner of her sari across her brow, handed me a tray and turned on her heel without a smile.

I felt sick.

"Maharaj—"

"You have returned," he said finally. "Of course, you had to return."

"Maharaj, where is she?"

He glanced up at me. Oh, I know I should never have asked that question!

"She lives," he said simply.

Blood rushed to my face. I closed my eyes.

"She will see you, if she wishes."

She lives, she lives! I felt burning hot, and chilled to the bone. I drained my water glass in a swallow. Then Bhaskar-Nath fastened his eyes on mine and, with the abruptness of a fighter, he said:

"Don't you see how you've shrunk?"

I felt as if I had been slapped. I could hear the sannyasi's voice at my back: "You little idiot!"

"Look, Sannyasi, it's all perfectly clear to me."

He clasped his hands on his knees, exactly like Batcha, looking straight ahead at the sandy patio. By now, I was completely sobered.

Then silence.

The odor of sandalwood swept through me, along with the chanting of schoolchildren and the music of conches, and it was all the same—today or yesterday or lifetimes ago—all was infinitely the same. What, indeed, changes? Beneath our rubble lies live Egypt, as well as every forgotten age, while a passing odor, a streak of sunlight on the sand suddenly strikes us with wonder, leaving us like eternal children in the onrush of the world.

"I could have closed my door on you."

I started. He clenched his fist.

"But one does not close the door on Destiny. One does not change destiny by closing the door. One changes destiny by being greater than destiny. If I were still capable of sorrow, I would speak to you with tears of blood in my eyes."

With a sweep of his hand, he pushed aside his tools. A sheet of paper lay before him, covered with accounts.

"You have arrived at the appointed time. You can't be blamed for following the law of your nature. But the moment has come when you *can* change that law, if you wish. For there comes a moment when one can do it."

"But why—"

"Be quiet and listen. I want you to see this clearly: only Truth can save you, for it alone has power. It's the *only* power. Batcha will die, perhaps, so try to understand. Destiny is not designed to crush or punish us, Sannyasi. It is designed to compel us to grow. You're a sannyasi, but your time as a sannyasi is over, and you don't know how to get out of it; you've never known how to get out of it. You've always repeated the same mistake. I want you to understand that one does not get out through cries, revolt, or fever, but by breaking through to another level of consciousness. Once you change your inner state of being, the outer will change and you will have conquered destiny."

He leaned toward me. I could see the veins throbbing in his neck.

"A difficulty that remains unmet returns to plague you again and again, each time stronger because of your failure to overcome it, until you have the courage to untie the age-old knot and exceed yourself. That's what Destiny is—the transition to that other state."

"But what wrong have I done? Tell me! I just wanted—I came to this island by chance, then I met Balu."

"By chance! Do you hear what you're saying? Do you really believe that the glass you bring to your mouth reaches your lips by chance? There is but one Body in the world! And if the tiny speck that is you has reached this island, it's because an arm mightier than yours, of which you are a part, has brought you here for a purpose."

"We are mere puppets!"

"Yes."

"Then what can *I* change?"

"Everything. You can change your state of being. You can choose to be a helpless puppet or the all-encompassing Body that knows what it is doing and why, and where it wants to go and how."

"What do I have to do?"

"It isn't a question of doing, but of being."

"I have striven to *be*. I've given up everything for that."

"That has been precisely your mistake."

"I found a Light above, and it was so marvelous! But the earth didn't exist anymore. The self is dissolved and life is no longer."

"That isn't so!"

Then he began hammering out his words, his whole being radiating strength.

"If you discard everything to reach the Light, you will know a glory of empty light. But if you include everything to reach the Light, you will know a glory of full light."

I could have sworn there was the same compact orange glow around him that I had seen in the banyan forest.

"Anything that touches that light becomes full, for that light is the fullness of everything, the luminous foundation of all that is. You can choose to doze off in it for eternity, dissolve yourself in it, go into it naked like a little saint. Indeed, you can choose anything you wish, for that light looks upon all things equally. It is the vast Gaze that makes what it looks upon *be*. If you look upon one tiny thing in that light, you become that one tiny thing; if you glimpse the slightest divinity, it becomes an absolute and luminous totality that leaves nothing else to be desired or seen. Anything touching *that* becomes *that*, absolutely and totally. It is paradise—the paradise of whatever one wishes."

His eyes bored into mine.

"And if you have given up everything to reach there, then indeed you will know a huge empty divinity and the earth will cease to exist. But I say—"

As he spoke, he slowly raised his folded hands before him as if he were saluting an invisible divinity.

"I say this is the advent of the builders of the spirit, the forthcoming reign of the divine workers who will remake the earth in the image of their vision of beauty. It is the age of concrete visionaries who will seize upon the eternal Gaze, not to doze off in inert beatitude, but to draw the Power from above into everything they do, every being they meet, every particle they touch, and make it yield its full measure of light; for indeed heaven is everywhere, in everything, every being, every earthly event, and it is up to us to bring about outside that which is already inside. But this is a far more exacting heaven, quite ill-advised for spiritual sleepers."

Bjorn's face flashed before me. I had the feeling I was exactly as he was before he died.

"Bjorn, too, sought Power, and he's dead. If I have taken the wrong path by going above, and he took the wrong path by going below, where then *is* the path?"

"You haven't taken the wrong path; neither has Bjorn. But you've covered only half of the path. Once you have found heaven above, you have found only half of heaven; the other half remains to be found here on earth. You have found Him, but not Her."

"Her?"

"Bjorn wasn't wrong in seeking below; he simply began where he should have ended. He worked below without the light from above, so everything foundered. Listen, child, Power is one. It's everywhere; there is but one Power in the world—in atoms, monkeys, and gods; but if you seize it from below, it is fraught with all the mud of the earth and it accomplishes monstrous miracles. You must first reach all the way above in order to bring it down all the way below. I, too, am a tantric, but I wear no red triangle, and I do not perform miracles; I unleash the quiet miracle lying at the heart of all things. I, too, am a sannyasi, but I have no orange robe; I have given up all things while running from none. I carve my heaven with my chisel, in all I do and see, every minute of the day, even in my accounts. Yet, I am neither a sannyasi nor a tantric, but something else. Listen, son, there *is* a secret."

Bhaskar-Nath was bent over, his eyes riveted on the ground as if to pierce it with light.

"You have returned here, and destiny weighs upon you. True, sometimes one stumbles along the way, as Bjorn did; there's bound to be a moment of stumbling. They call it a 'fall,' but then life in its entirety is a fall from a heaven, which we should never have left in the first place. Truth is greater than our morality, Sannyasi, greater than our virtues, and in error lies a heaven we had not foreseen. We fall and founder time and again in our life, every time stripped from our good, because, every time, that degree of heaven we have conquered must be brought down. If we did not fall, heaven would never touch the earth! It would remain above, completely separate and null. The higher you climb, the farther and more painful the fall; but that's where the secret lies. Listen closely. Each fall kindles your impeccable heaven with a heat of pain that has the power to transform the level of darkness it touches. And with fall after fall, some transformation takes place: first, in the world of thought, then in the world of the heart, the emotional life of every minute, the subterranean hideouts and obscure dungeons, then in the body—your body—illnesses and death. Death is the final enemy to conquer. The deeper you go, the more your sclerotic white heaven becomes alive with a fire of power and love, as if the very suffering of the night compelled it to grow beyond itself. Indeed, the heaven of the Spirit is but a wan copy of itself, as long as it has not plunged into the searing crucible of the earth. And when you reach the bottommost stages of the descent, your cast-down, fallen heaven will irradiate with a burning, dynamic, all-powerful, golden light, down to the remotest cell, the most obdurate matter, as if it were ready to burst beneath the pressure of that Night, *as if the true Sun were in the depths of the body.* The force of the fall is the very force of the Transmutation. When we have drawn our heaven all the way down into our bodies, it will touch the other half of its Truth, and the two will become one and matter will be changed."

He paused for an instant, and gazed about him as if he were perceiving something.

"Then we will no longer need to fall or die, for heaven will be everywhere, below as well as above. Each point will be the summit, each being will be his own heaven, each minute will be the total goal, and the pale beatitude of empty immensities will become the boundless felicity of earth's blessed myriads."

Bhaskar-Nath raised his eyes to mine. And I saw.

"Go now; it is time."

I rose to my feet like an automaton.

"Remember, it is as you will. One day you will know the delight of the two worlds, but first you must free yourself of *both*."

I started for the door, almost tripping again over the little ektara. Now and then, the air brought in the sound of conches and gongs. Then I was back in the street, dazzled, the south wind blasting about me.

"Nil!"

I whirled about to find Balu standing there, jaw set, teeth clenched. He pushed his fists deeper into his pockets, cocked up his head.

"She'll be waiting for you over there, tonight."

With his chin he motioned toward the beach. Then he turned his eyes back upon me and looked at me with such hatred that I was flabbergasted.

"Balu—"

He turned his back on me. I was alone.

ψ

25
too late

*I*f only I had been able to heed Bhaskar-Nath's words! But that sandstorm was battering me, my eyes were burning, and I could feel my fever rising. Only willpower kept me going. I walked into the temple, seeking shelter. I was not even hungry, just in search of solitude and quiet, but they were everywhere, gaping, turning about to stare: *dorai, dorai.* The conch vendors hailed me, the priests whispered, the flagstones were like ice underfoot. Someone pointed at me. I began to run down the northern corridor. Then I stopped short, breathless, before a huge stone horse rearing before me. Where on earth was I going? What was I doing here? All around me loomed gigantic pillars, rows of immobile carved gods, staring beneath the painted granite vault splashed with gaudy monsters, and echoing with the rumble of drums and gongs. I felt so totally foreign, so lost and burning with fever in that forest, at the end of the world and of all worlds, with my back to the wall, alone, on the brink of some unknown abyss. What was I doing here? Where was I? My legs leaden, my chest burning, I was suffocating, in a dream—worse than a dream. There was nowhere to go, no exit or return from here; this was the end of me, the ultimate resort, the spot from which there is no getting out. I dropped my copper bowl. It clattered against the flagstones like the voice of doom. I turned around and there they were, perhaps fifty, pressing toward me: *dorai, dorai.* I clambered over the buttresses and ran through a line of pillars.

I collapsed behind a bas-relief.

I closed my eyes, doubled over, shaking with fever, my head between my arms.

I sank into a heavy sleep.

What happened as I lay there, and how long I slumbered, I do not know. I was walking, knee-deep, across cherry-red, silken mountains rolling like a sea. I ascended and descended scarlet Arabias stretching as far as the eye could see, all alone, making desperate efforts to disentangle each step, trying to use a handgrip, but to no avail, for my hands sank and slid in that silken mire. Suddenly, without transition, I was standing at the edge of a forest beside a winding path, and I saw myself. I was dressed as a sannyasi, hanged in a tree. Unmistakably I. A group of men with lanterns were coming to cut me down. The image was eerily precise—my ashen face in the lamplight, that orange robe, those silent men—as if I were looking at myself from outside. As they lifted their lanterns to sever the cord, the image vanished, and I awoke with a cry. A dream? Maybe so, but the Himalayas are less real than that image!

I sprang to my feet. Rays of sunlight slanted over the daubed vaults. Batcha! I am going to miss Batcha! I ran like a madman down the corridor. Batcha! Batcha! Silver trumpets echoed through the halls, *yalis* opened their granite jaws, while I skimmed over chilly flagstones. I did not know where I was, here or there, in this forest or the other, searching for Batcha, Batcha—my salvation, my refuge, the light of my light. I ran like that hanged man bursting out of his corpse—dead or alive, I don't know. Never again! Oh, never again! It was a nightmare, a jumble of life and death, including concentration camps and initiation pyres, orange robes and striped overalls. Never again, never again.

I came out through the eastern tower. Palms crackled in the wind like sulfur flowers. Daylight filtered through a chalky veil. It was perhaps five o'clock. The beach was deserted, a powdery whiteness. I hurried on, eyes slitted against the buffeting wind, flayed by flying thistles. Then I saw her: a frail red silhouette beside the sanctuary, the southern dunes cascading behind her like an avalanche of foam.

She descended the steps.

She stood erect amid that immaculate quartz powder, a red figure in a brilliant, blood-red sari, lashed by the wind, her hair unbound. For a second I was terror-stricken: It was Mohini!

Mohini, just as I had left her on that storm-swept beach.

She stepped forward, holding her sari across her breast, a gold bangle glinting on her wrist—a very young, pale woman with a red tilak on her brow.

"Batcha, oh, Batcha!"

She looked up at me with eyes as deep and luminous as pools, then took my hand.

"Come."

She drew me under the peristyle. I sank to the ground, my back against the wall.

"Batcha!"

"Shhh!"

She placed a finger on my lips. She looked so pale, almost bloodless, as after a long illness. She settled down beside me, her hands folded on her knees, and studied me in silence. There was no need for words. It was like water finding water again. It was peace, the denouement. She smoothed away my pain, my fever, removed my cloak of thorns, bathed my smarting wounds, looking at me quietly, without reproach, as if from the depths of her soul, the depths of a peaceful garden where we were together, always together, free of passion and turmoil, pure as two children playing on the shores of a swan lake. I let myself go, melting there, casting off my shadows, my wrinkles, my sorrows. It was so simple there, without complication or duality—no man or woman, no sannyasi, no black or white, not giving and receiving. It was all one, all me, all her, like water in water, like the twin wings of a great bird gliding endlessly over an untroubled lake. On and on it went over seas of calm light, capes of plenitude, rose-tinged gulfs of oblivion, wing to wing, in the same, vast and soft movement. It glided through nights and days, through deaths upon deaths, free of suffering and shadow, forever flowing together—she or I, I or she—toward unfathomed depths, planes of crystalline tenderness, stations of motionless limpidity, and perhaps we would vanish over there, lost in rose-tinged diamond frost.

At that moment, I seemed to sense that the vast expanses above were here too, within the heart's intimate warmth.

"Batcha—"

A smile lingered on her face.

"Shhh! Not yet."

The south wind raged by, but we were so safe together in that invulnerable island, in the serene island of no country; it was our timeless island, our rock of eternity, beyond all lives, all deaths, after the white and red islands have sunk beneath the waves. I believe I smiled, too. All was so simple. All was exorcised. Then she spoke:

"How thin you are!"

"How pale you are!"

"I have waited and waited for you; oh, I have waited so long."

"What a fool I was!"

"Every day I called you and called you, but you would not answer. Oh, Nil, it was horrible, as if you no longer existed! Then, one day, about three weeks ago, suddenly you answered. You were there, warm, so warm, so vivid! Then I knew you were coming back. I began to live again."

Her lips trembled.

"And the birds returned."

"Oh, Batcha, I didn't know! I was crazy."

"You didn't know? You didn't know that I loved you?"

"You loved me?"

Now I understood. It was as if a veil were being rent, like a cry. She looked at me with such serene eyes. I was frigid.

"But, Batcha, you were only a child!"

"Can't a child love?"

She laid her head on her knees, looking out at the sea.

"When you were here, before, I felt such peace. That's how I knew I loved you. I felt at peace, at rest, like the birds that land to rest somewhere after a long flight. I was resting in you. I had found you again. You didn't feel anything?"

"But, Batcha, you never said a word!"

"Must one use words?"

She straightened herself up.

"Then you went away."

A little furrow creased her brow.

"You're very mean."

That same mischievous little smile crinkled her face.

"But I took my revenge! Remember how I pinched you, over there, on the dunes?"

My head whirled. A sudden rush of hope engulfed me. I was saved. A new life loomed before me.

Then the sudden trap, the impossibility: walls arising everywhere.

"What are we going to do, Batcha? I don't understand anything."

"You are here, Nil, so all is well."

"They'll separate us."

"Who?"

"The others—they hate us, you know. If only we were shipwrecked here, alone."

"But why? I like the world. I like Balu, I like Appa, and I like Nil, too."

That same mischievous gleam flickered in her eyes. She still had that round, childlike face, that air of living in the obvious.

"Poor Nil, you haven't changed! There's nothing without me and nothing with me. Have you at least found your freedom, Mr. Nothing-at-all?"

"Yes—No."

She burst out laughing.

"You see!"

"Oh, Batcha, let's forget everything! Everything! Let's begin again from scratch."

"Yes."

"It's just a mistake, a trap. Look, let's go away. Do you remember the queen of the coral country, the garland of laughter?"

"Well, Appa told me you would begin another life through me."

My heart jumped. She had suddenly grown serious. What a strange little girl she was!

"What else did he tell you?"

"Many things. He said, 'Another life is not the same life with improvements.' "

"Improvements?"

"It all depends on you."

"On me?"

"He said, 'Souls keep coming back and finding each other, each time to make further progress.' I, too, had progress to make. After you left, I kept seeing Kali's rock."

"Kali's rock?"

"Yes, and falling; oh, there was such an urge in me to jump!"

"To jump? But, Batcha, what am I supposed to do? What is it that depends on me?"

My eyes went from Batcha to the village with those dunes, those people—*dorai, dorai*. In a flash I knew it was futile; we were cornered, hounded, powerless before this conflicting world. Everything was already decided.

"I'm not so sure *anything at all* depends on me, Batcha."

She closed her eyes. How beautiful she was! The sound of conch shells came to us in waves over the dunes. Then she spoke, her words falling from her lips like droplets.

"When one is like this, deep within, one is at peace and nothing depends on oneself anymore. One is at peace and someone else does the action, and it's always right, always for the best. But when one forgets, then things become difficult."

She smoothed the hem of her sari over her toes.

"Perhaps one can accomplish the same action on one's own, but— It's the same action, but laborious."

She shook herself, as if to shrug off a shadow.

"He said, 'One must take the path where all thirsts are gone. Then Woman draws Man's dreams down into Matter and Man draws Woman's force up into the Light. And they walk together. If she does not rise, she destroys him; if he does not create, he loses her.' "

She looked at me with such tenderness that I wanted to take her into my arms. Blood rushed to my face. How stupid I had been!

That's when things began to turn awry.

My heart pounding, I took her hand, her soft, delicate, slightly trembling hand in mine—a simple little gesture; and no sooner had I touched that hand than I saw everything taking on a red hue.

"Listen, Batcha, it's all a mistake, a huge mistake. Let's begin again."

"Yes."

"I'll take you away with me; I'll marry you."

"But you've already married me!"

"Batcha, I'm lost without you, don't you understand? Let's get out of here!"

Her hand turned to ice in mine. Panic swept over me. Thousands of walls seemed to rise on all sides, holding me prisoner in this island just as I had glimpsed salvation. They were all at my heels, calling, *dorai, dorai*. It was a horrible waking dream in which you run and run and soon your legs give way, and there they are, behind, about to get you. Exactly like Bjorn!

"Batcha, please listen to me. We'll go far, far away from here. We'll begin a new life."

Then you fall to your knees and it's all over for you.

As she looked at me wide-eyed, I could feel that wave of anguish rising, tightening inside like a suffocation, and that panic was spreading to Batcha in turn, uncontrollably, like a forest fire. In the background a glacial, imperturbable voice was saying, "Ha! You *too* want to take, and you're trying to walk off with your booty."

That voice made me even more desperate to escape, as quickly as possible, before they stopped me.

Batcha's hand felt like marble in mine—like Mohini's when I had opened the gate to the park.

"You'll see; we'll be happy, very happy. Everything will work out; we'll settle down in a village in the north."

She kept shaking her head, unable to speak, her eyes brimming with tears.

"We'll have a hut on the riverbank, and we'll be free. There will be green paddy fields all around, and I'll earn my living by teaching in the village school."

"But Nil—"

She buried her face in her hands.

"Nil, Nil—"

She kept repeating my name like a prayer. She was on the verge of yielding, I could feel it, and that would be deliverance. I was caught up in a red haze.

"You'll see; we'll be together, always together."

All at once she drew herself to her feet, pressing both hands against the wall; she looked like a cornered little animal standing there before me.

"But that's not it, Nil, not it!"

There was such despair in her voice.

"That's not what 'another' life is!"

"Ah, forget that! They're lying, they—"

She laid her hand on my lips.

"Stop it, Nil, I beg you. Stop it. Let me go."

I barred the way. This was my last chance; if I let her leave, I was lost. It would be the end of me.

"If you love me—"

"But I do love you, Nil! Don't you understand? If I didn't love you, I would go with you!"

"Then come."

"It's your death, Nil, don't you see?"

"My death?"

"You will soon leave me. You've always left me. You always thirst after something."

Her lips trembled. She pressed her hands against my shoulders, trying to break free, pushing, pushing.

"Let me go, Nil, I beg you; let me go. Appa is calling me. I can feel him calling me. I must go."

At a loss for words, I backed away slowly toward the steps. I could only see that heart-rending white face against mine, that red tilak on her forehead, those two arms pressing and pressing against me! I descended a step. In a minute it would be all over; she would be gone. I let my arms fall.

"You're abandoning me."

"Never!"

It was like a cry. For the rest of my life I will see her standing at the top of those steps, resplendent in her red nuptial sari, her hair unbound, sand swirling like foam about her feet.

"Never! Even if I die, I am with you. I am melting into your heart."

I descended another step.

"For the last time, Batcha, I beg of you: if you have really married me—"

"It's too late, Nil! You're a sannyasi!"

Too late—

I clenched my fists.

I cannot rationally explain what happened at that point. Everything took on the sudden sharpness of those instants when several years or lifetimes are packed into a few minutes. The being snaps and one enters several levels of consciousness at once. One lives simultaneously on several planes, as it were, peers into several worlds, and what happens here is no longer distinct from what happens there. Perhaps it is madness, or the release of multiple memories. One is no longer *one* being but a whole world of departed beings suddenly reemerging with an intensity compounded by a pain and a revolt that had never been dissolved. I was a pillar of rage—oh, so miserable, a poor little puppet! I saw myself standing at the foot of those steps—saw myself utterly—small, livid, fists clenched before Batcha, lost forever, with my life in ruins. As I was about to shake my fist at heaven, I heard Bhaskar-Nath's voice—heard and saw at the same time, as if his voice had materialized into letters, forming a screen of purple light between Batcha and myself:

Djamon' Tomar Ichha

IT IS AS YOU WILL

It is as if thunder had detonated in my ears, splitting something open inside me. In a flash, I saw everything from above, as if from over my shoulder: an image superimposed over this one, more interior, deeper than this one, coming out to merge with this one as an almost perfect replica of what was happening outside: the figure of a sannyasi, similar to me but taller, shaking his fist at heaven, and a red-clad being resembling Batcha, standing at the top of the steps, then collapsing with a sudden cry. "No! Don't do it!" and her head smashing against the pillar. She was dead.

I turned to stone, a petrified mass of fire. If I moved, it would be all over; the image would turn into flesh and she *would* die.

I stood at the foot of the steps like a statue of rage, fists clenched against that orange robe, buffeted, battered by the swirling sands.

It was she who moved.

I closed my eyes for an instant, whispering, "*Mâ—*" Mother. She descended the steps. I did not move, did not make one gesture. I felt somewhere between prayer and death. She approached.

She came near me and removed her gold bangle, laying it at my feet, then she slowly raised her hands to her forehead and joined them together before me as before a god in the temple.

She was gone.

I watched her frail red silhouette grow smaller as she stumbled away across the sands. I stood there immobile, unblinking, until she disappeared behind the tower. It was the end. I closed my eyes, dead to this world.

I was dead.

That's when I felt a great, warm Power sweep through me, enveloping me with Love like a Mother, then from somewhere far, far beyond I heard a quiet, almost neutral voice saying: "A first time you have conquered."

What I had conquered I do not know. There was nothing to conquer anymore. I was like that hanged man stepping out of his corpse. I was dead and I lived.

I picked up my gold bangle and started up the path.

The sand stung my face, lashed my bare shoulders, filled my mouth. I walked on as if in a dream, sinking, engulfed in red. I was groping my way through a scarlet haze, and there was a body in my arms. Batcha, my beloved, was dead, but I would carry her with me. No one would ever find us again, I swear! I would hide her and keep her with me forever! Try as they might, she was mine, mine, my life, my love. She felt as soft and warm as a bird in my arms. I ran along the beach, holding her against my heart; I ran and ran through the village, still holding her. I had passed to the other side, but I did not care.

I was engulfed in the wonderful catastrophe, holding her forever. *Dorai, dorai*—murderer, murderer, perjurer! There were fifty of them, perhaps, a whole mob.

Suddenly I collapsed, the breath knocked from my body by a stone that struck my back.

There was no one in sight.

There was no one in my arms, no dead body!

I pulled myself to my knees, gasping for air, a sharp pain in my back.

A peacock shrieked.

It shrieked three times—a shriek of triumph—there on the terrace before me, in the setting sunlight.

My head whirled and everything blurred. I no longer knew if it was today or yesterday, in that side street in the port, that accursed street where I was running behind the sannyasi with an urge to strike him until he fell to the ground, and to spit on him. Then suddenly, that god surging forth from the wall, mounted on a peacock. Oh, now I understood the reason for my hate! But *I* was that sannyasi on the ground, and I had lost everything.

I rose to my feet.

Balu's shadow slipped down a side street. Balu! I let out a cry.

It was the end. I was going to hang myself.

26
the vision

*T*hat sannyasi was hastening to hang himself, for he thought
he had lost heaven and earth, the beloved, and the light that
makes one love. He no longer knew anything. Eyes burning,
he was hastening down that sand-blown, vanishing trail. It
was the northern trail and night was falling, while the scent of
acacias mingled with sea salt, gusts of thorns, and maledic-
tions. He was headed for Kali's Rock.

His head was ringing with voices from the past.

"Hurry, stranger. Night is upon us."

I had turned the boat into the wind. She was all dressed in
red. She had placed her gold bangles in the boatman's hand,
and I sailed away! I'm still running; I've never made it to the
port.

"I have laid out white clothes for you . . . the Kashmiri
carpets . . . the floor is a forest of blue cedars."

But there was Bjorn's forest instead: "I'll marry her. We'll
settle in a hut. I'll make a canoe and some nets, and I'll father
little black Bjorns!" I could still hear him cry behind my back:
"In four years, she'll have sagging breasts and the face of her
mother!"

"But that's not it, Nil, not it!"

That was not it; there was nothing, only the night and the buffeting wind at my back.

"Nothing-at-all, Mister Nothing-at-all, there are millions of beaches in the geography book . . . but one and only one wave . . . brings to each person . . . a unique cowry."

I had lost even the one shell she had given me. I had always lost it. "Here, this one has been waiting for you for thousands of years," and I had left. I am still running.

"You've always repeated the same mistake."

Mistake? What mistake? There is no such thing as a mistake. You said so yourself.

"A single day. I am asking you for one single day."

Yet, in the depths of my folly and distress, something kept repeating obstinately: "You were right to leave, and even if it were to be done again, I would do it a thousand times over."

"I want to be free, do you hear? Free!"

Well, you have your freedom, so what are you complaining about? You won't be part of the wedding ceremony, but what did you expect?

"Too late, Nil, too late."

This was more poignant than everything else. Although it had no reason or meaning, it stung in the depths like an ever-burning wound.

"Three times you've come; three times you've killed."

I certainly am on the promontory.

"Bjorn! Bjorn!"

It was Balu running with his schoolbag, while a covey of myna birds took wing from between the rocks. "Something has happened to Bjorn, something has happened."

"Erik is dead. He has killed himself."

One pipe, two pipes, three pipes. Erik is dead and Bjorn is dead; they're all dead. They wanted none of the pipes, none of the cheap little happiness. And what did *I* want?

"Something else, something else, another life on the earth!"

I had burned everything for that, laid everything to waste. Now I was on my way to hang myself for that same cheap little happiness. "We'll settle down in a village in the north, with green paddy fields all around. We'll have a hut, and we'll be free. And lots of little white Nils!" Was this really what I wanted to hang myself for? But could I deny Batcha, too? I was incapable of denying anything, even the sannyasi! On I went through that acacia forest, pressing ahead in a poignant contradiction that kept growing and growing, clutching at my throat.

"It's closed on all sides, Nil. I am trapped like a rat on this island!"

There was Bjorn, naked on the terrace of the grain merchant, clutching a brick.

"Shall we try to cheat the gods with a stroke of luck? Tails you leave, heads—"

I scrambled up to the promontory, brambles tearing at my hands. The island was wild with foam. There was Mohini leaning over my shoulder.

"A fine spot to commit suicide."

They were all there—Balu, Bjorn, Batcha, Erik, and that naked idol, mouth wide open, sword in hand. An erne rose skyward with an angry shriek. My back against the wall of the sanctuary, I now faced the void while the wind flapped my orange robe as if to tear it. *Dorai, dorai*—murderer, murderer, perjurer.

"You did want freedom, Sannyasi. Now you have it!"

Even Balu had placed the blame on me. They all had turned their backs.

"You now renounce the three worlds. Cast the three lives into the fire."

I cast a grain of colored rice into the flames.

"You no longer have a home or family ties or country. You are the son of the Fire."

"I am the son of Fire."

"Then what more do you want?"

"I found a vast light above; I've given up everything for that."

"That has been precisely your mistake."

That void at my feet, that yawning darkness, was simply the other side of their heaven. I could just as well have disappeared into an abyss of light with the halo of a saint over my head.

"Every day I called you and called you, but you would not answer. Oh, Nil, it was horrible, as if you no longer existed!"

That little voice was like a knife in my heart. I had lost her. I had lost everything. What else was I still searching for?

"I climbed back onto the bank. There was a vast luminous movement, the luminous march of someone behind me, almost blending with me; and whenever the coincidence occurred, fleetingly, there was perfection of truth. Then everything flowed in a marvel of spontaneity, with inconceivable precision. *This* was the living truth."

Oh, how could I repudiate that?

"An'mona! An'mona! Nothing-at-all, Mr. Nothing-at-all!"

"What a fool I was, Batcha!"

And Mohini, clutching my arm.

"Death is upon you, Nil!"

"This is blackmail."

"It's upon us all, Nil. Fate is upon us. What you are running away from today will come back upon you ten, twenty times, until things are fulfilled."

"Don't try to corner me!"

But it was I who was cornered now, with my back to the wall, like Bjorn. What on earth had I done to deserve this? What wrong had I done?

"*I* love and everything else is forgotten."

"Well, *I* don't love."

"You're a brute."

"Yes, a free one."

"You are running away, Nil."

She looked so white in that red forest.

"When you've burned me, too, you will understand."

She had said that quietly, without a trace of emotion. She looked so pale beneath that extravagant nuptial crimson. I did not understand. I simply could not understand. How could I possibly say "no" to freedom? On the other hand, could I say "no" to Batcha, to the earth? Either way, I was a deserter! Yet, saying "yes" to their cheap little happiness was the utter lie, the disgusting success. I had not come here to make little Nils, who would make little Nils, who would make little Nils! That's not it, Nil, not what a true life is!

I was a traitor to both sides, as if heaven and earth could not be true one without the other.

> *O Child*
> *Heaven needs earth to become true*
> *As earth needs heaven to be free*
> *For they will become true through one another:*
> *Heaven by earth's pain*
> *And earth by heaven's freedom*

I had not found the place or the key. I had only found Batcha, and lost her.

"Ha! You too want to take, and you're trying to walk off with your booty."

Yes, I know it's my mistake; the moment one speaks of love, everything goes wrong. But did I love her any less when I did not know that I loved her? And what could I have done? Things had gone wrong of themselves, in spite of me, the day I had put that tilak on her forehead; yet it was through that red tilak that I found her again in the paddy fields. Oh, everything is an impossible contradiction—we just do things and that's it; the die is cast once and for all. I kept turning and turning around that tiny, burning, elusive point: the crux of the story. There was always that yes-no, that flight followed by a return, that freedom versus love; yet, I felt that the "no" of my flight had *as much* meaning as my return itself, as if the mistake held the key to the total truth—its red mark that divides as well as brings together.

> *O child,*
> *I have told you there is no mistake, ever. The mistake*
> *is not to grasp the true meaning of one's actions.*
> *You think you left because of freedom and returned*
> *because of her; you think rebellion is what is making*
> *you raise your fist, and suicide the reason that made*
> *you climb up here. But you know nothing. In truth,*
> *men do as I will, unknowingly making the necessary*
> *gesture; yet, after all is done, they realize it was not*
> *for gold that they have run, not for a little happiness*
> *they have killed, that the dead girl was never*
> *dead—no one dies; for who kills but Myself? Their*
> *gestures fashion an end they had not foreseen, and*
> *for which they did all the running unwittingly.*
> *So keep going, but my drama does not have the sense*
> *you give to it; for when your eyes have opened, you*
> *will see that there never was any drama—all is the*
> *same and all is clear.*

My hands smarting, my body feeling like a rope in the wind, I summoned all my strength in a last effort. This was the end. "For the last time, if I must live, if this life has a meaning—"

> *O Child*
> *For each one, there is an impossibility*
> *A burning contradiction*
> *If you have found your impossibility*
> *You have found the supreme possibility*
> *For it is both the obstacle and the lever*

"I ask only that she be returned to me!"

There was no reply.

Then Balu's image flashed before me, hopping down the sidewalk that first day.

"Batcha is the queen."

"Oh? And why?"

"She's like Bjorn: they are going to die."

That's what he had said—"*They* are going to die"—not "*He* is going to die."

"It's too late, Nil."

I whirled around.

That black idol was standing there inside the cave, sword aloft, arms like a wheel. A rage swept over me and I grabbed her by the neck. I would jump *with her*—not die without settling an old score with her. I braced myself.

"You're snickering at me, stoneface. You play with us like puppets, don't you?"

I could have sworn that she smiled.

"You would be only too happy if I jumped!"

Silence. Even the wind seemed to grow still.

"Well, I am stronger than you! I have something you don't have; I have the mud of the earth, the night of the earth, the pain of the earth. I even love a dead girl whom I will never see again. Oh, Kali, you can bless, you can slay, you can crush me beneath your yoke, but I love. I love, and that's my sole possession, all I have left. I have no offerings, no drums, no trumpets, and no heaven to look forward to. But I love. I have no powers, no light, nothing of worth; I am the perjurer, the zero, the nothing-at-all. I have no country, no family, no home—they have turned their backs on me. But I offer my love for the asking, for nothing, for everything: for the wind, the night, the sorrow of the world, the sorrow for nothing, for all the passing shames, for the uncaring. I love and love; that's all I have. I am because I love! And even in the pit of hell I will go on loving."

Suddenly my anger died down with the wind. There was no more sorrow in my heart, no more night or day. Even death did not make sense anymore. There was only that little flame burning in my heart, that ultimate treasure.

I stood on that rock alone, staring out.

There was nothing and no one left. Even people did not matter, and memories were falling into dust. This was the great quiet shipwreck, and even the shipwreck was behind; there was no more ship, no more tears, no more sense of separation—everything was already separate. One was silent and free of sorrow—the gaze of the last survivor. One simply gazed out. Even death was no more—it stayed on the side of the living; it belongs *before* the shipwreck, for it is about loving this and not loving that, wanting this and not wanting that. There was no more abyss, no more anguish, no fall, no despair, not even a quiver of hope; only the vast smooth waters of the Beginning, only a vast tranquil lake filling up with its own eternity, while something gazed out—as if it had gazed forever, beyond lives and deaths, beyond the happy or unhappy islands, the resurrections, and the shipwrecks.

A solitary cricket chirped in the sanctuary. I raised my eyes.

A plane droned overhead. The sky was as clear as an aquamarine, and strewn with stars. Two little red and green lights drifted in the northeast, headed for Rangoon or Singapore. This was the twentieth century of the story.

"In my country, even birds do not fly overhead by chance."

Nor do planes. At the beginning of the story, some twenty years ago, I was on the same parallel, thousands of miles away in a South American jungle, with my brother the gold-seeker. We were lost in the vast clamoring night of the Oyapock, dwarfed and ludicrous under the high vault of balata trees, convinced we were searching for gold. Every night we would hear the Rio-bound plane flying high overhead; and we laughed, for we felt so much higher than that plane, two small insignificant fellows laboring all day through the marshes to extract some unlikely flakes of gold. But our dream was so much truer, our impossible advance through the *dai-dai* and among collapsed trees so much surer than their calculated route between two cities overflowing with gold. Tonight, high overhead, that plane was flashing a signal, while I stood alone and null on this rock, in orange tatters as unlikely as my gold-seeker's rags. I was still in search of the vein of gold—indubitable life—and it still eluded me. Even my dreams had betrayed me, and my own brothers would repudiate me if they saw me.

"Hey, Job, what are you looking for?"

"A pile of gold to ruin the world's gold!"

But it was I who was ruined. Where, then, lay the truth?

One day I had set out in search of a truer life, and I had plunged into the adventure for gold as I might have plunged after the lyre bird or the North Pole—anything as long as one breathed freely—but I had found borders, police, mapped forests, and discoverers who only discovered their own gnawing misery. I found that the adventure lay elsewhere, clear of any tropic, and that all the outer roads ended within. I had become a sannyasi as I might have become a whirling dervish, a Corybant, a naked, ash-smeared beggar or anything—as long as one breathed freely, and life was unfettered and true. I had found the great paths of radiant light above, heard unforgettable music, the Rhythm that imparts rhythm to all things, drunk in the great liberating current—but I had lost the earth. Every road led into its opposite, every adventure closed in on an anti-adventure, as if every yes changed to a no. Or was it merely the end of one trajectory, a transition toward a greater yes, a truer adventure? Perhaps there had never been any no, nothing to repudiate, nothing that repudiates: just an ever-wider Yes rising in a spire like a seashell's whorls.

The Rangoon plane had disappeared with its cargo of confident men. The night was limpid. Lights dotted the shore. A steamboat lay at anchor like a Christmas toy beneath the great tree of the night. Then a lighthouse—just where Bjorn had been cremated. He was dead. They were all dead: Erik, Bjorn, the sannyasi, the gold seeker. Erik, dead, my brother of a Sahara that did not stop at the thirty-third parallel; Bjorn, dead, who sought power for his brothers. The sannyasi, dead, who wanted freedom. I was the last survivor, the fourth one of the silver birch, the absurd nothing-at-all who was not from here, not from there, not from above or below. From where was I, then?

"Want to know something, Job? You and people like you are from nowhere."

From nowhere, or from a place yet to be born?

Bjorn cried out:

"Even if I die, even if it's a dream . . . I believe more in my dream than in your normal prison!"

I believe, yes, I believe; even if I die, I believe. We have no idea where we are, and we knock on doors like the blind. We are the sons of a new race, the adventurers of a truer life, and even if our rags betray us, they are truer than ourselves! We are the sons of a new world in the twilight of the intellect and the machine—the sannyasis of something still unknown. We grope in the dark, ignorant of the way, ignorant of our own words and meaning, yet knocking at the doors of the future, stammering the words of the next man, releasing the lights that will build tomorrow's world as surely as the ancient glimmers of the ape built today's world. We will force the earth to grow beyond its own matter and its heaven. I believe, yes, I believe utterly, like the primate in his cave, like the deluge. Even if I die, I still believe!

As I fell exhausted at the feet of the idol, I heard a quiet, neutral voice say, "A second time you have conquered." But I did not know what I had conquered. I was like a corpse on its bed of stone, and I had lost everything.

⁎⁎

That night, at the feet of the divinity who blesses with one hand and slits throats with the other, I had the most extraordinary vision of my life. A grace, a sheer grace was bestowed upon me when I had lost everything, and I would like to tell about it for all those who suffer the pain of separation and do not see or know. Now, however, I know. I know there is a place where the souls are forever together, and that the body's death is not death. I know there are other existences, and that this futile, miserable, confused life, like a tale without rhyme or reason, is but a link in an immense unending Movement, and that yesterday's actions explain today's actions. From one life to another, through all our suffering, questing, calling, we are *all* moving toward a total explanation, a moment of completion, an all-embracing consciousness in which nothing is separate, divided or mutilated, in which we can seize the thread of all our lives at once, as well as the joy that wove the rainbow, thread by thread. For, in truth, we are a growing light, a widening consciousness, a joy forged from body to body, and we advance from separation to oneness, from ignorance to all-knowing truth, from the body's oblivion to the memories of the soul. Pilgrims in a marvelous adventure, we progress toward the total story and the complete revelation, each life as a step in the ascension, each shadow a fold in the inevitable blossoming, each death a transition toward other, greater lives. The outcome is certain! If some call me mad, then I say that the Himalayas are a geographer's delusion, and that the beauty captured, the harmony released, the hints of azure touched upon by all those who have searched, sung, carved, or painted, are a marvelous madness, more real than all the reasoning in the world; and perhaps that madness and those hallucinations are preparing tomorrow's earth. The world is a vision becoming true. We are the builders of an eternal Image.

That night, I consciously went into death and returned with knowledge. Not only did I see death but I lived, or rather relived, a former death, bringing back with me an indelible memory of the continuity of existences. I wonder if the future we uncover step by step is not a former past: an eternal seed unfolding. Suddenly it seemed as if the pieces of a puzzle had come together to form a complete picture. Incoherent, diffused scenes glimpsed here or there, sometimes years apart, were coalesced into a single whole, giving me the key to the story. It seems to me that each of us must have his own key, only we do not know that there *is* a story, that every image counts and has a meaning; and because those images spring up in our lives like will-o'-the-wisps, years apart, we do not understand that they are part of a great continuous film, and we tend to push them into oblivion; yet *everything* has a meaning and signposts abound. All we have to know is that they *are* signposts and that there *is* a trail. I believe that what I saw that night was not only an image from the past but an image of the future—and perhaps an eternal Image.

The first "scene" was the least in focus, for it was not so much an actual image as it was a well-known *atmosphere*, a scent of remembrance that keeps floating in memory's penumbra with a poignant intensity. I had already known this scene several times, with variations.

I was wandering through a forest, and everything about that walk was charged with heart-rending intensity. I had lost my way—lost everything. I was looking for her, looking for her everywhere, calling and calling in vain, and I could feel the breath of Death upon me. She was my life—more than my life—but she did not answer; nothing answered. This familiar image usually followed another scene in which I stood before that man seated before a fire, wrapped in bluish light, who hurled his curse upon me as I spit my freedom in his face. But this time, after wandering in the forest, I found myself perched in a tree, clutching a branch with both hands—I can still see those two white hands—then plunging head first to my death. I was killing myself. Then my vision began to take on a remarkable precision, truly as if someone were filming the whole story. In fact, I think someone within us films everything.

I entered death.

I was suddenly engulfed in extraordinary darkness; what we call "night" is luminous compared to that blackness! An absolute quintessence of blackness lacking any vibration that enables one to say, "It's dark." It was not dark; it was *the* dark, without the least spark of blackness, as stifling as death. Indeed, it *was* death.

Then I sensed—though it was horribly concrete, I could not see anything, only feel and touch—I was overhanging an abyss, my feet on a tiny ledge, my back against a wall—an enormous, black, vertical wall like a cliff of basalt plunging into a chasm. I was in the middle of the chasm, desperately clinging to that wall, incapable of the least movement. Yet, I had to move and cross that gulf to reach the other side. My life and salvation lay on the other side. To fall would be worse than death; it would be death *within death*. But I could not move. I was paralyzed, stuck against that wall, my two hands clutching the stone. I was unable to see or do anything in that dreadful, massive, oppressive silence like a world of absolute, implacable negation in which one must not be and *cannot* be.

Suddenly, in that staggering darkness, I heard Batcha's voice, *her* voice. Oh Lord, I do not know if miracles exist, but that voice in the darkness was the ultimate miracle. Her clear, crystalline, miraculous voice saying, "PULL! PULL!"

As she spoke, I felt what seemed to be a rope touch my hands. I gripped the rope: "Pull! Pull!" There was such an extraordinary power of love in that childlike voice, as if her very soul were seizing mine and pulling it out of the night. "Pull! Pull!"—an indomitable force piercing that monstrous blackness like a sword of light. The voice of a child.

I pulled, clinging to the rope, advancing step by step through that darkness, tottering on the ledge. I was like a drowning man groping for air, while that warm voice kept calling from the other side, so *sure*, so quietly powerful, oh, so full of love: "Pull!"

Never at any moment of my life had I been more frightfully conscious and alive than in those few moments of "dream." If I dreamed, then death *is* a dream and life in its entirety is less real than death.

Then, without warning, I found myself on the other side of that abyss, standing before a kind of glowing, radiant shell resembling the hull of a ship. As I looked upon that shell, a strange phenomenon occurred: I saw my body—from the outside, as if I had left it—make a slow, leisurely somersault in the air as in a slow-motion film, and instantly I found myself inside the shell, completely dazzled.

Everything there, including the air and the shell itself, was bathed in an extraordinarily white and pure light, like a diamond, emanating from everywhere at once, without any one particular source. It was a living, vibrant light, a substance of light.

She was there.

She lay white and luminous on a bed slightly to my left. It was Batcha. But it was more than Batcha, infinitely more than Batcha, like the luminous essence of Batcha, her pure reality— *she*—as if the earthly Batcha were only the image of this one. And how beautiful she was! How radiant! It was unquestionably she, unlike any other. Eternally she, lying there in a deep sleep.

Another "bed"—everything was made of that same luminous, snow-like substance—stood to the right of hers. I knew it was mine—hers on the left and mine on the right. I began to examine the shell about us, so luminous and perfectly enclosed. The impression was of being at home, marvelously at home, enveloped and protected for eternity, embraced in absolute security. Nothing could touch us. This was our timeless abode, our place of convergence. We were forever together, in our eternal center.

I turned around and saw another being standing there, who, curiously, did not seem foreign, not "different" from the place itself. He seemed to be wrought of the same substance as the place. He was a guard or an assistant, all dressed in white, but not as luminous as Batcha. An orderly, perhaps, as he seemed to be watching over us.

Gently he helped me remove my clothes. I suddenly felt very weary and dirty, as one does after a long journey. I wanted to take a bath. I took a step to the right, looked down at my feet, and realized I was dead; my *body* was dead. The shock of that realization cut the connection. I remember an instant of embarrassment at the sight of that body and I thought: "In that case, there's no point—" And I woke up.

The idol gleamed in the darkness.

A solitary cricket chirped.

Head in hands, I leaned against the wall, in a state of bewilderment and wonder as on the day when I had heard celestial music in that railroad station.

Then I understood.

Everything was clear. I knew that darkness was forever banished from my heart. I knew that death was a myth, that beings meet again in death as in life, and that we journey together, always together, through lives and deaths, and beyond.

27
She

$\mathcal{D}$aylight broke.

In the sand-covered main street, pilgrims come and go while the great ernes glide above the high tower; women go to the well; and the call of the conch shells mingles with the sound of the sea, the low rumble of the monsoon, and the return of the moons. It was yesterday or today, centuries ago and forever. Children chanted in the schoolyard, horse carts jingled by, and I was leaving. I was leaving. I saw every little sign along the street: the tea vendor, the munching goat, the jasmine garlands, the pink pottery. I wanted to take them all away with me, every odor, every gesture, that old woman over there, this running child.

"Hey, Gopal, hurry up, it's late!"

It's late, and the moment is already gone. I wanted to store it all in my heart. Oh, how quickly life passes! Sometimes my eyes seemed to melt with that street. The passersby, the shops, the laughter by the fountain, the silvery tinkle of the horse carts—everything was cloaked in an infinite mist, an immense and quiet softness suffusing all things with eternity; and what actually passes? I was there, eternally there, coming and going.

"Hey, Gopal, hurry up." I was trailing a vast soft memory in my wake; my steps were a thousand years old.

"Who will buy my pretty conch? Three rupees, the pretty conch!"

Everything was so utterly the same beneath the blue sky. Yesterday or today, what has changed? I had left, returned, returned a thousand times, and in the end what was left? Abruptly, my vision narrowed and everything became hard, frantic. The dazzling present was back, precise, acute, engulfing me, clawing me on all sides, as if I would expire here, there, in these eyes, that smile, that old woman, that fleeting cry; everything had grown so intense and painful. I was leaving, I was leaving. I wanted to retain all in my eyes, down to the tiniest wisp of smile. We leave everything behind when we go! I felt so old, so futile. What was left of all those lives? "Hey, Gopal, hurry up, it's late." And what about Batcha? Batcha, less than five hundred yards from me, in a little whitewashed patio resounding with a peacock's cry. I was leaving, I was leaving.

I stopped near the fountain. A dragonfly perched on the stone. My throat felt like lead. I held out my cupped hands and a woman filled them with water and smiled.

Smiled at *me*.

For an instant I raised my eyes to hers, and such love flooded my heart! Love, or a cry of gratitude, an instantaneous flame, as if what one experienced in all eyes was always the same deep encounter. A microscopic instant that contained the luminous distillation of all those lives, the fleck of gold in the depths, what is left after a myriad gestures and days. Oh, I have not been prince or king, but I have been that little flame within; I seem to recognize it everywhere, on every face and in the slightest gestures, as if I had known it thousands of times before. We run and run, and it's right there; we run after a tiny drop of *that*, and there is the complete story, in one second.

"Are you going to the station, Sadhuji?"[*]

He was no more than twenty. A sannyasi.

"I don't know. Yes, no."

He stared at me. I wanted to weep like a child. "You see, Nil, you haven't changed. It's yes, and then no. You're going to fall ill if you continue!" I stopped short. We stood at the crossroads. The station lay to the west, while the dunes rolled away toward the south. I no longer knew what I wanted. I no longer knew anything.

"The train leaves in half an hour. We can travel together if you like."

He was light-eyed, dressed in a saffron-colored robe. I seemed to see him through a mist. Go where? To what new paddy field did he want to take me? There were no more paddy fields! I had lost Batcha.

We started off toward the station. Pilgrims hurried by, a water carrier passed. I could hear singing.

He stood alone near the station, stretching his hands toward the sun.

> *O Tara, O Mother*
> *You are the creatrix*
> *The All-Will*
> *You are the doer of the action, O Mother*
> *Yet they say I am the doer*
> *I am the wanderer of your journey*
> *You are the winding of the path beneath my footsteps*
> *You are the hand that strikes*
> *And the hand that heals*
> *As you go, so go I*

I no longer wanted to leave; I wanted to cry, "No! No!" I gazed at the dunes, gazed at that billowing sand.

"What about your staff?"

[*] Another form of address for a sannyasi.

"My staff—"

A little chipmunk crossed the path, scurrying, scurrying. I whirled about and ran toward the southern trail.

> *O Tara, Tara*
> *You hide the lotus in the mud*
> *And the lightning in the clouds*
> *To some you give light*
> *You make others choose the night*
> *O Tara, O Mother*
> *As you go, so go I*

The dunes stood poised like giant Arctic birds against the azure sky. I followed the southern trail through the palms. Crows cawed. The day was drawing to a close. A child walked by, balancing a copper pitcher on his head.

"Are you going to the tantric's house?"

His hair was tousled. He had large black eyes like Balu's. Everything seemed to be repeating. Except I no longer had any brother here. The story was finished, or was it trying to start again?

"The tantric's house—"

"It's just over there."

But something said, "No, not there. That's not what I am looking for!" I was like a leaf before the wind.

I turned to the right and climbed the dunes. The sand felt as soft as cashmere, with an occasional black trunk poking up and releasing a cascade of golden palms. This is where I had talked with Bjorn for the last time, where I had heard the tale of the silver birch. I continued climbing. Everything was quiet and soft in the dunes. Even our footsteps had vanished. Oh, what was left? I bent down, took a handful of sand and let it run through my fingers. Everything felt so peaceful here, as if none of our sorrows had ever been! I could feel, almost touch, that foundation of universal softness, that fresh and guileless peace that knows no sorrow, anguish, or death. Thought is what shrouded that patient softness with its drama; but draw the curtain and everything vanishes, including the sorrow and the world's false music. And everything sings.

> *Over these dunes*
> *Over those dunes*
> *Our footsteps go side by side*
> *Our islands are itinerant*
> *I leave, still I am*

The sky over the great dunes was so blue; a purple cloud drifted across banks of snow. She was there with me; we walked together, always together, and it was *really* that way. It's just that my eyes didn't see well enough, my blind body didn't believe. Oh, one day in a truer, clearer, less animal world, we will be able to see and live in all the worlds at once, without separations, distances, or the delusion of the flesh; everything will be instantaneously there. The body is but a shell! Thought blurs and splits into gray matter the vast unbroken rainbow of our lives.

Then everything contracted again, the look hardened, the vision clouded. Pain and anguish were back. There was the implacable present, the cawing of the crow, and the train whistling beyond the dune—*that* was death, the falsity of the world. Our concept of time is false. We know nothing of time. We have invented clocks that merely record our sorrows and our own ideas of the world. We have yet to know time's fullness. We are not yet truly men!

In twenty minutes the train would leave.

I emerged under the silver birch and looked out in amazement.

Hundreds and hundreds of black—or perhaps gray-blue—birds were circling over the lagoon. Then, as if obeying a signal, they veered together at the far end of the dunes, flinging up their immaculate, luminous throats in a flash of sunlight, suddenly transmuted into great polar sailboats; then swooping down over the smooth-flanked swell of the sands, thinning into single file, they passed before me and disappeared in the distance, their dark bodies set off against the glittering waters and foam-rimmed quicksand of the lagoon.

Almost before I could catch my breath, they were back, swerving again—black, white, black, white. As they swerved, I swerved with them, swept up in that snowlike soaring at the end of the dunes, that burst of light like the rending cry of my soul. Yes, that's it, an absolute rending without return or hesitation, a fusion of light, a "yes" forever, an explosion in the absolute; then the returning darkness gliding, plunging, vanishing into the distant foam. My eyes kept going and coming and each time there was as if a cry inside me; something in my soul broke at the end of the dunes, a tiny white burst: yes, yes, that's where I am going! That's where I am, where I am coming from, where I am returning! That's my home, my eternal country, my vast, white-winged truth, my timeless flight. That's where I abdicate, where I melt, where all is true, purely true, and flowing. That's the life truer than life. *That* alone exists and is real, my cry, my fullness of light, my fire forever, my great white blaze above the worlds. That is where I am going!

Then darkness again, and Batcha's little voice calling and calling: "*An'mona! An'mona!* Nothing-at-all, Mr. Nothing-at-all!" I felt so small and so poignant amid those sweeping dunes, such a lost and lonely little thing! No, I could not leave. I would throw myself at Bhaskar-Nath's feet and begin all over again. Forget everything. It will be an unforgettable party! I will be a shellfisher. I will be the keeper of your temple. I will sweep your sanctuary, your threshold, your—

And then, nothing.

I kept going and coming, and each time something broke in my soul, a tiny fiber causing a stab of pain. If I closed my eyes, it would be over. I would go. It would be the abolition, the demise in light, the great white peace, the ultimate vacuum, the dissolution in a crystalline smile.

And *then*?

Again the train whistled.

I closed my eyes and called the truth, the light, the god of the earth, something, anything—for an answer, a sign!

That's when I heard a tiny little gong in the distance, rising through the clear air. Everything seemed to have stopped. Silence had suddenly fallen over the sands. Even the crows were still in the palms. The sea rumbled in the distance. I turned about. Not a soul. Nothing but black palm trunks marching down to the tantric's house, and just that faint, quivering sound, mounting, mounting behind the dunes: *tim-tim-tim, tim-tim-tim*. Three times, always three clear little notes repeated endlessly: *tim-tim-tim, tim-tim-tim*, filling me with anguished foreboding. I stared, transfixed, at the spot where the trail rounded the dune before the tantric's house. *Tim-tim-tim, tim-tim-tim*. Three staccato sounds resounding through the dunes.

And I knew! Cold sweat pearled my forehead. No! That could not be!

They appeared at the bend in the trail. First, the little gong bearer, then a cluster of white-clad men, and there, above their heads, a slight red figure. She.

My heart turned over.

I stared and stared. I thought I would lose my mind. That white forehead, the jasmine garlands, the red sari—Batcha. They passed before me, then turned left at the foot of the dune. She was white, so white! And that flow of long black hair across her breast. They turned again, and now I could no longer see her face, just that frail red form floating above their heads, a little patch of color meandering among the dunes. I kept staring and staring, unable to believe my eyes, while the little gong resounded across the dunes. I kept staring at that little patch of red receding in the distance.

Who was staring? I do not know. There was no longer an individual. Only two wide eyes, fixed and stupefied, piercing through centuries of stone and malediction amid an Egypt turned to dust.

They laid her on the pyre.

The little gong stopped beating. The dunes lay mute in their eternal whiteness. Now she was all alone on her pyre, at the meeting point between the waters of the lagoon and the waters of the sea.

They chanted.

They circled the pyre seven times.

She lay cradled in sea foam, facing north.

Then they stepped aside. All but one.

The chanting ceased.

A flame leapt.

No more chanting.

Nothing.

I watched to the very end, motionless.

I do not know how long I stood there, staring. Then I heard the sudden caw of a crow, and a voice: "Now it's time." I took a step. My legs felt like rubber. I felt like an old puppet being rewound.

I walked down the dunes.

The voice said, "This way," and I set out across the sands. The sun was setting. I was walking through vast purple valleys, then climbing again. I was headed toward that pyre. I could hear the roar of the sea.

A group of men squatted near the pyre. There was a small fiery heap glowing in the sand. I stopped before it. And looked.

And looked.

Then I sank to my knees in the sand. I prostrated myself in the sand, grinding my forehead into the sand, sobbing, sobbing until I ran out of tears.

It was the end.

The sea roared on.
I pulled myself back to my knees.
A tiny red flame was still glowing. I whispered, "*Mâ*—"
Mother.
The wind was caressing my face.
There was a blank moment. I could not see, could not hear;
I was completely empty, dead—without sorrow, null. I was on
the other side.
Then that flame leapt inside me. I opened my eyes on a flame.
I *was* that flame—only that one ardent flame, without pain,
without sadness, without memory, consuming everything. It
consumed me, consumed sorrow, consumed today and yesterday, Batcha, the sannyasi, and all the faces, ages, places and
memories. There was no longer any pain in me, no longer any
"I." There was no longer anything but that pure ardent fire. It
was like love. A love-fire. And it kept mounting, mounting. It
was an intense blaze of joy. A love-joy, free of any sentiment,
free of anything, absolute; just a clear, all-consuming, imperious fire. I whispered, "*Mâ*" once more. And it seemed as if my
entire being shifted, expanded, as if engulfed in a vast orange
flame. There was no more Batcha, no more life, no more death,
no dunes, no sea—just an orange blaze. Then *it* came down.
A cataract of warm power.
It devoured everything, engulfed everything, immobilized
everything. I was in this like fire in fire, like a torrent in a
torrent, joy in joy, without any you or I, without difference,
without here or there, far or near, inside or out. There was only
that—a motionless cataract of ardent, golden Power. And
above or behind that cataract, something like an immense
white radiance, dazzling, shimmering, brimming with utter,
triumphant joy, looking upon all this with such delighted and
sparkling love, such immensity of luminous happiness—a rock
of quiet, steadfast eternity. Death no longer existed there,

death had never existed there, only that inexpressible Joy that loves, a radiant love-joy permeating everything, transforming everything, transforming the vision. This is what we are living for! That utter plenitude. A vermilion fiery flower sinking in its own fire with the delight of a perfect confluence, as if the body had finally touched the living truth: *that*! That! I am immersed in it. It's here, right *here*, the living heaven! A motionless cataract of vibrant joy sweeping away the shadows, irradiating the bodies, enkindling all things, as if death and suffering were an invention of our senses, the earth's stubborn hardness an invention of our senses, as were all the yesterdays in the world, and all the separations. There was only *that*, eternally present, constant, the true substance of the world! A dense, golden, immutable eternity, yet unimaginably vibrant, active, intense, like the golden powdering of an endless world creation. Her, only Her, a torrent of joy that creates and recreates everything at every second, as if anything touching *that* entered a completely new and boundless life; a shattering of all limits, possibilities and impossibilities. It was Power. It was the overturning of the senses, the collapse of all appearances, the dazzling golden gaze of the Future. All the world's myriad faces and beings were but a spark of that. Where is the other? Where is she not? Where is tomorrow, yesterday, night, day? There is only that, everywhere, loving all forever, and *being* all: Batcha, the sannyasi, Mohini, the flute player, all those men and the birds on the lagoon. What is missing? Where is the void, the absence, the gap, the not-there? Where is the side that is not here as well? Where is the beyond? All is there and all is mine forever—burn, my love, burn. I love you in all that is, in all that lives. You have merged in me and I in you, merged in everything, in all that loves, in all that calls. We have passed through death's gates, and we are born forever! We *are* forever! O Tara, O Mother, it is You who does, You who loves, You who guides, You who pulls us through the day and the night, through good and evil, through sorrow and joy, toward the Light that loves. O Tara, Tara, O Mother.

I got up and walked toward the sea.

It lay like a huge turquoise at the foot of the dunes. Leaving my clothes on the sand, I plunged into the water. Then I heard a quiet, neutral voice say, "A third time you have conquered." But who had conquered and who could conquer? The "I" was a screen, an obstruction, death in the darkness. It was the misery of being alone in a body.

The great birds were swerving over the lagoon: white, black, white. It is as you will. The sun was setting behind the dunes, streaking the birds' wings with gold. In truth, a great golden heaven dwells in the night of the world.

I stepped out of the sea and gathered up my rags.

"Leave that dress, child."

Bhaskar-Nath was coming toward me. He put his hand on my shoulder, then handed me a bundle of white clothes.

"Now you are free. You can wear the dress of the world."

.*.

Thus, one more time I opened my eyes upon the world of men. Batcha was in front of me, running toward me with her arms outstretched. She was dressed all in white.

"Look! The birds are coming, the birds are coming!"

We were wandering through the great dunes. It was at Fayum or Ramnad, in this age or another, under the arched flight of the great ernes. The sea sparkled. I was playing the ektara. We were on the happy island, the Island of Truth. We were journeying together toward an ever greater beauty.

> *Only the clothing changes*
> *Or the hue of a sky over a little white beach*
> *Only sorrow vanishes*
> *And a child*
> *On a pristine little beach*

Gazes with wonder
At they who come and go
And no longer recognize each other.

Pondicherry
15 September 1968